CUBEBALL

www.ingramcontent.com/pod-product-compliance
Lightning Source LLC
Chambersburg PA
CBHW070445030726
47503CB00004B/909

CUBEBALL

MICHAEL LEON

ISBN: 978-0-9944209-0-9
eISBN: 978-0-9944209-1-6

Typeset and cover design by BookPOD Pty Ltd

To my son, Hayden.

Return Home

THE VIEW FROM MARSFLIGHT-12 took Mickey's breath away. He positioned extra cushions behind his neck as he readied himself for the advancing celestial event. The star-flight from Mars was approaching Skydome after a six month voyage. As the vast void of space momentarily darkened from the solar eclipse, Earth's thin, blue atmosphere put on a radiant show. He had missed Earth's natural aquatic hues. He then reminisced for a moment, to his home of the last ten years, living on another planet. On Mars, a red glow lit up the morning skyline as it danced with the Martian dust filled atmosphere. It was this eternal dance between light and gravity and his innate ability to decipher their patterns that made him who he was today. Then, the Earth's moon completely covered the sun, bar the smallest of areas, creating what looked like a celestial diamond ring. Mickey decided to capture the occasion on his *cubebit*

"Com, fix me a real time video capture of the lunar eclipse." Com – the solar system computer command system- automatically captured the eclipse on Mickey's cubebit. A default view twenty centimetre holographic cube lit up above his hand-held cubebit, providing Mickey a high resolution view of the celestial event.

"Enhance view to double size, Com." The holograph doubled in size, giving him a more detailed view.

"Automatic ret filters too." Mickey's retina implants were set to filter light to an acceptable level as the sun's rays changed in intensity.

He delighted in the beauty of the eclipse. The diamond ring shape reminded Mickey of how he saw the balls on a cube. Mickey had an innate ability to read the roll of spherical objects in a cubeball cube. When he played well, every ball he intended to strike with the cue-ball, lit up in his mind, on the exact point where he intended to hit it. Then gravity would do its work. That's what he loved about cubeball - the perfection of gravity.

He also appreciated his upgraded cubebit. The Alpha-D9 provided a high digital resolution that could screen real-life holographic images from as small as a matchbox to as large as a room. He watched the moon move across the sun and wondered where he would be by the time of the next eclipse. Uncertainty was filling his life again.

"End video capture, Com. Return to default app and adjust rettes to full enhance."

The holograph halved in size. Two spheres, the sun and the moon, were replaced by man-made spheres of various colours. They floated in a cube sphere forming a pattern that would be recognized by a dozen generations. The cube was undoubtedly a snooker table – but in three dimensions not two.

"Return to last saved game – Banquo versus Flaveau."

The cubebit moved from a pre-game snooker cube. Mickey was challenging the digital version of the current champion of world cubeball, Jean Flaveau. The perfectly positioned red and coloured balls were now scattered.

Like real cubeball, the gamer version consisted of a *player, strategist* and *programmer.* They pitted their wits, skill and technological knowhow against each other. The gamer version used Com as the digital programmer and strategist. Mickey's programmer recommended three possible offensive and two defensive plays. This game had the highest possible setting – championship level. So each shot was difficult.

"I want to play offensive, Com. Stats, please?"

"Preferred option is number two, a 2051 play first made by Hollows in a state championship. Three walls at maximum speed, then strikes five reds. Number one red into top right pocket and two of other four reds strategically placed for winning break. Degree of difficulty is ninety percent. Achieved three times...."

"Thanks, Com. Enough information."

Mickey remembered the play well. He attempted it once under real cubeball match-play conditions and had failed. The cubebit holograph was alight with equations, angles and lines, recommending the exact way to direct his cue-ball, but Mickey ignored it and played on instinct. He held the base of the small digital cue with his thumb and forefinger and slowly drew it back over the digital left hand that steered the front of the cue. His direction was set by Com, but the degree of power and spin was his choice. Mickey struck the ball with full power and extreme spin. The ball violently careered across the three walls into the bunch of red balls. Each of the five reds fell perfectly into place. In ten minutes, Mickey had cleaned up the cube for another easy victory.

"Close game, Com," said Mickey. He removed the pillows, sat back in his pod seat and relaxed, satisfied with his game. That was how he used to play the real game, confident, brash and always expecting to win. But his memory of those successes became ever more distant. He had turned his back on the real game, choosing to find a home that was as far removed from its insidious tentacles as possible.

Mars had been his home for ten years. It was an isolated cold planet, but Mickey's knowledge of Mars never extended past the one small city of a million people who inhabited Earth's sister planet. Its inhabitants were a mix of trail blazers, the ambitious and those who had something to escape from. Mickey was part of the latter group. He'd tasted celebrity for a short time, but abandoned that for ten years of relative isolation. Mickey lived out his years on Mars a very private man, happy to see his status slowly fade like a Mars sunset. And he was happy to keep it that way, but for one inconvenient problem. His considerable wealth, gathered as he rode the world stage competing, had finally run out. Well, nearly.

He had gathered the last of his savings to return to Earth. It was a costly exercise, for a return ticket to terra firma was expensive. The star flight alone cost half of his remaining savings. An inter-planetary flight, even in economy was afforded only by the few. His 'economy sleep dock', whilst sparse and confined was at least serviced by free on-flight gaming. Not that confined spaces ever worried him. Most passengers regularly roamed the space craft to cope with the tedious flight. Mickey happily kept to himself. No small feat in a metre and a half square pod. But of course Mickey had some unusual gifts. For one, he had become a cubeball gamer under the pseudo name of Banquo, since leaving Earth. Most cubeball gamers had crazy pseudo names for the fun of it. But for Mickey it was essential. If they knew he used to be a championship cubeball player he would have no peace, for very few computer gamers could play the real game that they idolised.

A flight attendant interrupted his thoughts. She smiled generously as she offered Mickey a standard non-gravity refreshment.

"Your water, Mr. Allen." Mickey readily accepted it. He was thirsty and hungry.

"Thanks. I'm looking forward to drinking from a glass again."

"Yes, everyone says that after three months in space."

"How long till we dock?"

"Just forty eight hours till docking, Mr Allen. Would you like nuts with your drink?"

"No thanks. I'll be eating shortly. Do you have any suggestions?"

"I hear number five is a popular dish. The recipe has a Martian influence."

"Thanks. I'll try that one." The attendant reached across him and took his rubbish, before heading to the next passenger pod. Mickey smiled courteously. The thought of enjoying a Martian dish for his meal break, lifted his spirits.

As he looked out the virtual portal window at the blue planet below, he found it hard to believe he hadn't played the real cubeball in ten years. But he could never completely turn away from the sport that he'd loved and played since a young boy. The virtual gamer sport had become bigger than the real game anyway, with over three billion fans throughout the solar system. The dedication that gamers applied to their craft had surprised Mickey when he first took an interest in the hobby. There were no riches to be won that compared to the earnings of the real players. Wealth could only be won through gambling. So very few made a living from it. But there it was. There were billions of dedicated gamers, playing the online version with little concern for earning a living. Over time Mickey grew to appreciate the virtual game, for whilst it required different skill sets, the strategies remained the same. Mickey remembered every championship game played and every competing cubeball player who strutted the world stage, with the obsession of a storm-chaser.

Spending three months hooked up to the online world was nothing new to him. He spent most of his time competing against other gamers or studying the form of the real cubeball players. Mickey knew every fact about the players' lives and more importantly, he studied every game they played. For this was his life. The game was more than knocking balls into corner pockets. It was the meetings of minds. For Mickey, a game was always personal. It was a chance for him to show what he believed in.

He would have happily stayed in his pod for all of the three months, if they'd have fed him there. He was forced to the common area three times daily to eat and refresh. He generally chose the quietest periods of the meal break to avoid being recognised. Mickey checked his cubebit and decided it was time to eat. He headed for the common area's quietest table, but was stopped on the way.

"Hey, you're *the* Mickey Allen, right?" said the slightly nervous young man who appeared to be in his late teens. Given his youth, it was likely he knew Mickey from old tapes of his matches.

"That's right," said Mickey, shaking his hand more routinely than with any enthusiasm. He readied to move away toward a table.

"Would you mind, umm...may I join you?"

"Sure," said Mickey unconvincingly, as they both sat in a corner pod.

Every table was a pre-fabricated pod built for two people. Man made gravity was maintained in passenger areas, but levels were adjusted regularly throughout the flight, depending on conditions and time. Although the dining bay always functioned on near full gravity throughout meal breaks, all utensils were weight reinforced for safety reasons.

Mickey switched on the cubebit and selected his meal. Six holographs materialised in the cube shaped screen. Each was numbered meal packages for their selection. Mickey spoke to the screen.

"Number five". An audio voice responded immediately, repeating Mickey's order, before billing his account. Retina verification was automatic and a charge of 199 credits was deducted from his account.

Mickey's young companion ordered the same. Once both seemed satisfied with their order, Mickey closed the cubebit.

An uncomfortable silence ensued before Mickey's young fan nervously re-opened friendly banter.

"I'm always hungry. The meals are all so small and bland."

"Yeah, I have two meals sometimes. I'll be glad to reach the Skydome, although it can get busy and it's hard to find your way around."

Mickey had only been to the Earth orbiting satellite once before - on his transit journey from Earth to Mars, ten years earlier. He remembered that he spent most of the week studying cubebit maps trying to find his way around. His dining companion welcomed Mickey's admission with some relief.

"I'm Manny, by the way." Mickey merely smiled, showing no need to exchange pleasantries.

"I worked on Skydome most of last year. I spent most of my time working at the Pool Bar."

"That's new. It's a water pool?" Mickey enquired, showing his first sign of interest.

He had heard of the many expansions carried out in the last eight years, but not this feature. Two sky lifts operated now to cope with the exponential expansion of space travel. The Moon and Mars had developed rapidly, from the earlier years of the mining-led expansion. Even in the eight years Mickey had called Mars home, the growth had been remarkable. Mons City, Mars' only city, housed half a million permanents, but grew to a million during peak tourist periods.

"No it's not a water pool. It's a cubeball bar. It's fitted out with a dozen high tech cubes. It has even got a championship cube."

"Oh, yes of course."

"You should come and play. The championship cube is fitted out with the best graphics I've seen."

"Yeah maybe," said Mickey, with little enthusiasm. The last thing he wanted was to be surrounded by old fans, dredging up a past he wanted to forget.

"It'd be an honour if you'd play me. I mean, I'm not that bad. I played a bit of the local college circuit in my teens....and like, I'm well connected." Mickey knew Manny was offering more than an exhibition match.

"Yeah, like I said. Maybe, kid." He stood up quickly, cutting him short.

"It tears like no other supp you've ever tried before," said Manny. His eyes darted across the common room as he'd spoken louder than he should have. Mickey scanned the room too, before returning to his seat.

"You claim you know me, right?"

"Sure I do."

"Then you know I've seen just about every crystal since Adam. You should also know I don't suffer time wasters."

"Look I've been working the Skydome a year. No one holds that job unless they provide the best service."

Manny's eyes narrowed, allowing Mickey to see his new companion in a new light. He'd vowed to never tear planck again. But at least this kid could update him on the latest techs and supps. Mickey prided himself on keeping ahead of the game. He knew what was happening in the world of cubeball. But he had been ninety million kilometres removed from the big arena – Earth.

"First thing, I don't tear planck. I can beat anyone in the game clean....understand?"

"Sure, Mickey. I don't mean to offend. I just wanted to help."

"Second thing, I'm the best because I prepare better than anyone else. That's why I was the best. So should I want to be the best again, it would pay me to know what you know. What's your product?"

"Saturn Planck. Tears you clean into another universe. It makes red planck look like blurred vision."

Mickey had used red planck on a number of occasions. This was known as the A-list planck. All the top players had supplies. It was illegal but almost impossible to detect.

"Who's using it?"

"A few of the A-listers."

"Name them," demanded Mickey.

"I can't do that. You know that." Mickey knew what he said was true. If his new friend so much as hinted to anyone of illegal dealings, he'd wear a lawsuit that would leave him permanently in debt.

"How much then?"

"A lot."

Mickey moved to get up. He wasn't in any position to buy. But he could win the sort of credits Manny was implying.

"I could arrange a sample," said Manny, keen to hold Mickey's interest.

"You must be a wealthy man," said Mickey.

"Well, let's say one good turn deserves another."

Mickey knew where the conversation was leading. He feigned a wary glance to see Manny's reaction. On cue, Manny opened his Felini labelled jacket just enough for Mickey to see what he was carrying. Three tubes protruded from his inside pockets to reveal his contraband. Three clear, thin cylinders were marked with the Pi symbol. They were high quality narc tubes, specially developed to synthesise powerful narcs such as planck. These miniature laboratories carried nano-microtisation capability that could transform illegal planck into undetectable chemicals that would be used in industry-approved rettes or supps. Each tube had to be a million credits.

Manny mixed in circles Mickey was familiar with. He had torn illegal narcs on a handful of occasions. He knew it could help him win cubeball games. They were used by many professional cubeball players in the industry and seen as calculated risks worth taking. The technologies were digitally updated daily to ensure they remained untraceable. Authorities were constantly reviewing their surveillance procedures and they regularly caught desperate competitors. But those with enough credits could stay ahead of them.

Mickey brushed his well-worn jacket sleeve, before speaking. "You're talking to the wrong man. I don't carry that sought of credit."

Manny straightened his jacket. Confidence filled him now. He leaned forward. "Who talked about credits? A man with your skills could be supplied in different ways. Think of me as a sponsor." Mickey lay back in his seat, considering his response.

"A man like me could be easily busted too. I'm not ending my career for some shit head sponsor who can't walk the talk."

They finished their meals in silence. Manny finished first, seemingly in a hurry. He picked up a couple of serviettes, one for himself, another he passed to Mickey.

"Consider this a gift. This won't end your career. It'll kick-start it." said Manny, before he left.

Mickey returned to his compartment with a sachet of planck concealed in the serviette, Manny had passed him. He rested back in his seat. His mind remained on the conversation he had just had. Could this young overly confident man deliver what he promised? Mickey had heard many sponsors' pitches during his time in competition. He'd learned very few could back up their claims.

He locked the planck in his travel case, then he set his pod screen to 'Earth view'. Immediately, a magnified view of Earth and its moon lit up the surround screen. The Moon was slowly emerging from behind the blue planet, on its regular rhythmic dance. Celestial gravitation was on full show. The beauty and precision of gravity and the structures it created were a celestial work of art. Small wonder he loved the game of cubeball, the twenty-second century's adaption of the noble game of snooker. What he didn't love was how money drove the professional sport. More was gambled on this sport than any other. For Mickey, it would always be the precision of the game. It provided a certain aura that both relaxed and excited fans in equal measure. A sense of wonder and power also could be felt, particularly in a packed stadium. The best players in the world were locked in a technological battle in front of their adoring crowd.

Mickey thought back to his many games of the past. Cubeball was so much more than the traditional game on which it was based. The rules were much the same, but the green felt covered slate tables were replaced by a four metre cube shaped holograph. Each shot required a skilful eye. Traditional snooker hand/eye coordination was no longer enough. A professional player needed the support of advanced computer systems that made the vital calculations possible, as well as technological and chemically enhanced hand/eye coordination. The famous old art of snooker had changed considerably in the last hundred years.

Mickey had talked enough for one evening. He wasn't even in the mood to engage Com with voice commands. Instead he switched his cubebit setting to 'eye com'. One simple face gesture lit the cubebit, filling the small cube shaped holograph with new 'texts'. One stood out. Riley had responded to his text from Mars. It had only taken her a week, he thought; not bad for her. But the news was bad. His little sister wouldn't lend him the credits he requested.

"Bitch," he thought, as he slammed his fist hard down on his armrest. Hell, his sister was wealthier than he ever was, a thousand times over. She had no right to begrudge him a small request for help after all he had done for her. He immediately deleted her text, not even considering a response. It could wait till they met.

He glanced at the next text. *MyBank sent a follow-up low credits reminder.* Mickey passed only a casual gaze before filing it. Then he moved to the next text. Another follow-up from a gaming fan - 'Alpha'. *Who is this guy?* Mickey wondered. He was either a persistent gamer or a nutter. It was his fifth text this week. For a change, Mickey took the time to study his message. He wanted to *challenge Banquo to a cubeball gamer match.* Mickey immediately shook his head in the negative for he had over a hundred challenges sitting in his text cube. He was one of the top rated gamers who were regularly challenged by 'wannabe' gamers hoping to pull their rankings higher. It always gave him a kick that none of these challengers knew he was once a real cubeball champion. The skills he showed in a gamer match-play paled in comparison to his real match-play skills.

He nearly deleted Alpha's text, but the final paragraph of his long-winded challenge caught Mickey's eye. He wanted to base the challenge on a championship match played a decade earlier. That match-play was a memorable contest between the best cubeball player there ever was and a young up and comer, brash, raw, but blessed with natural talent. That gifted player was Mickey Allen.

Mickey saved it to a priority text before scanning the remaining messages. He skimmed and deleted most of them. The usual scams, porn or money making offers. Only one other caught his attention long enough not to be deleted. A health check text offering discounted supps and techs. Compared to most cubeball players and gamers, Mickey was pretty clean. He had some minor retina plants and did inhale rettes and swallow supps. But he mostly smoked to relax, rather than tear. He accepted the health check and asked Com to set up the full retina check.

"Laser line activating," said Com. Mickey held his head still as a smokey-green line ran over both eyes. A minute elapsed.

"Retina upgrade recommended for left eye, seven grams of rettes and five grams of supps being activated. Supply will be available at Skydome on your arrival in two days. Your health check is complete.

Thirty thousand credits deducted. Next health check recommended in ninety days. Shall I engage?"

"Just hold and remind," said Mickey, cutting in quickly. That was nearly the last of his credits. Another health check engagement would leave him with no credits and no way of getting to Earth. As it was, he was just shy of the Skydome lift fee. With luck Riley would come good with a little persuasion.

"Anything further, Mickey?" said Com, in its low monotone voice. Usually, Com relaxed Mickey, but not even its programmed tone could lower his stress.

"Just move pod screen to island mode, Com and check me in the morning."

The pod view of Earth and its moon were replaced by an island setting. Mickey lay back in his pod berth and allowed the tranquil setting to take his mind away from his problems. He pulled out a rette and inhaled deeply. Mickey immediately relaxed. His retina implants reacted too. The island scene took on a very real mood. He felt as if he'd been on that tropical island for a full summer, quickly soothing his volatile mood.

As he absorbed the virtual scene, Mickey wondered how he would get to Earth if Riley would not help him. He hadn't asked her for help in a long time. Not since he moved to Mars. Before then, he'd pushed his sister more than he should have. The slow waves lapped on to the fine island sand. He started to feel the soft rhythm of the warm water stroke his feet as he took three more drags of his rette. He studied the rolling waves in detail. They rolled like a cubeball perfectly cued. This was a place and a feeling that Mickey knew better than most. He wore implants, but deep down he believed he could see better without the techs.

He stood alone in that regard. All the cubeball professional players were armed to the hilt with the best techs money could buy. Standard fare required that they have super retina plants, synched to shades that were wired to their team's super coms. They could almost see an atom with those techs. But what they gained in definition, they lost in instinct. They had to invest a small fortune in cue techs just to match their super enhanced eye sight. And it snowballed. Most of the emerging players had to enhance their hand-eye coordination with rettes and supps. Their team budget would be drained by the supply of chemical enhancers that they needed to stay ahead of the game, let alone the techs. And then there was planck.

Mickey used it sparingly, and only for special encounters. Compared to his competitors, Mickey was relatively drug free. Sure he used techs and supps, but he still relied more on the skills he was born with. Reflex and instinct let him reach a high better than any supp or tech could deliver. In that place, Mickey could not be beaten. But even techs and supps were addictive. Every professional player paid a price to be the best. Mickey too lived with the extreme highs and lows of living a substance enhanced lifestyle.

He was about to close his eyes when he spotted a perfect miniature wave curl from ten metres out. The roll was sublime and took him back to that one perfect night when he won his first championship. Funny how so much could be won and lost on the same night. The night he thought he'd never play again. He'd forgotten how he felt when the spheres rolled that special way. It was like they responded to his thoughts and rolled only to his commands. He studied the wave and felt them follow his thoughts. Then they broke perfectly on the shore. It reminded him what he could do. That was a place no one else visited. Mickey stood alone.

It was then that Mickey hatched a plan in his mind. He sat forward in his pod, and touched his mouth with his finger, as if to stifle the words that pressed to release. He had a brainwave. It was as if a subliminal message floated above the small smooth wave and caressed his resolve. Mickey would play again, at the Skydome. He would accept his new friends offer and tear. If it was as good as Manny had said, he would win enough credits to return to Earth, without his sister's help.

2

ⅿⅠꓢⅮⅇⅯⅇⱯⅢⅢⱯ

MANNY ESCORTED MICKEY THROUGH to Skydome's pool hall. The entry was overseen by two security officers. One held his gaze on Mickey.

"I know you from somewhere? Have you been to Skydome before?"

"Just arrived," replied Mickey, looking more interested in entering the pool-hall then conversing with the officer. Manny interrupted, showing agitation in his voice.

"He's keen to see the new cubeball cubes, Officer Martin."

"Back working here, Manny?"

"No. I'm transiting back to Earth. I've been off-planet almost a year now."

"Lucky. Got yourself some credits?" The officer eye-balled Manny, seemingly waiting for a response. Manny smiled wryly.

"Enough credits to enjoy tonight, Officer Martin. It would be nice to continue chatting, but my friend and I would really like to enjoy the view." The guard didn't grace Manny with a response. He simply waved them through. Manny responded immediately and ushered Mickey into the crowded room.

The orderliness of the entry was replaced by the noisy cess-pit of human traffic that filled the Skydome pool room. The expansive deck was long and narrow. On one curved wall lay the bar. Alcohol, rettes and supps formed the backdrop to the elongated carbon re-enforced plastic bar. A dozen bartenders served the hoard of gamers. Hands extended in all directions. They held their holographic credit cubes high like candles as they waited to be served. Jazz fusion pumped in all directions, swaying the music holographs like rainbow waves across the ceiling. But even the loudness of the music could not overpower the voices of the seething mass of 'transit voyagers', seeking a break from their inter-planetary journeys.

The other long wall afforded the very best view of Earth. The planet's crystal blue offered an alternate experience to those who could afford the seats. Transparent light walls protected those rich enough to reserve seats, from the pool room din.

Mickey cast his eyes toward the home planet where he was born. Then his gaze turned toward the long arena that lay between the bar and Mother Earth. Manny had been true to his word. The cubeball tables lay in a row like a neatly laid out deck of cards. In the middle sat the ace of diamonds, a championship cubeball table lit up the arena. The cube shaped holograph was fitted with full graphics and the space was surrounded by seating to hold a few hundred fans and wannabe players. The air was thick with the smoke from rettes as it floated toward the music vids.

Manny looked across the venue before spotting someone who sat alone in one of the Earth-view pods. He took Mickey there and pointed to Mickey to sit down. He shook the guys hand, exchanging a small parcel concealed in his palm. The guy left, not even exchanging a glance Mickey's way. Manny sat down, glancing toward Mickey before he surveyed the pool hall. Mickey looked in the same direction, toward the championship cube. It must have been the latest version, as the holographic images were of the highest quality.

"Not bad is it?" Manny said. Mickey nodded his approval.

"You want to play on it?"

"Looks like a long wait," replied Mickey.

Two competing combatants had attracted a crowd of interested onlookers. Mickey briefly studied the game. He soon bored of it and turned his gaze to the view of Earth as both players were rank amateurs. He wondered how life on Earth was now. He knew it was more crowded. Over a billion more people inhabited Terra Firma, since he left ten years ago. Countries were increasingly cramming more of its population into vertical cities. Less space was being kept for natural beauty as more purpose-built holograph halls took the place of forests and parks. Citizens were flocking to virtual worlds for their relaxation. Cubeball players, fans and gamers were a case in point. Large spaces were created for the maniacal followers, both under and above the ground. Whole cities were created to house addicts hard wired to the technological dream world.

"This is for you," said Manny, interrupting Mickey's thoughts. It looked like a normal rette. But Mickey could tell Manny had plancked it.

"Thanks." He went to put it in his coat pocket, but Manny held out a lighter and lit it.

"You're playing in ten minutes, so smoke this now." Mickey glanced toward the championship cube.

"Looks too busy to me."

"It's organised. You're playing one of the Skydome pros. So planck up now if you need the help."

Mickey thought not to accept, but he didn't know how good his opponent would be. It had also been a long time since he played.

"Thanks, light it."

Mickey took heavy drags on his rette. The lights around the pool bar appeared to brighten. The view on Earth also illuminated with brilliant sea aqua and sandy yellows. After four deep drags of his rette, Mickey could see the light shine on every individual dust particle that swirled around the room. Intricate patterns swirled as the partying crowd mingled around him. Mickey cast his gaze toward the playing arena. His sight lasered in on the large cube like a telescopic sight. He reached that point that every cubeball player seeks – he had teared through normal vision and opened up sight that allowed more frequencies of light to enter his eyes. He looked to Manny. He didn't have to say a word. Manny knew he was ready.

"Through here. The cube's ready," said Manny, as he guided Mickey past the interested onlookers. Mickey was about to play his first game of cubeball in ten years.

Game commence flashed before Mickey, signalling the beginning of another encounter, one of many in his life. Digital holographs flickered on, hovering around the cube playing surface. The game would soon start. The cube was transformed by the intricate technology turning the pool room's game centre into the equivalent of a NASA flight deck. Each grid of the cube's 3D holographic surface transformed into colours of the rainbow as the computer programmes sprung to life. The luminescent cue-balls flickered in response to its commands. The dazzling light show drew in the crowd.

Mickey surveyed the familiar grids, four playing rectangles on the cube-shaped competition table. Online holographic images dotted the cube arena, providing an endless stream of information for both contestants. Mickey was about to commence the game when a roar reverberated around the pool room. A large, life-size holograph cube was streaming a live coverage of another cubeball game being played on Earth.

Jean Flaveau, the current world cubeball champion was being introduced to an adoring public. It seemed only yesterday that Mickey had matched wits and skills against him. A decade ago Mickey was a young gifted star with a sublime talent destined to become a world champion. No one could read the game like him. He was blessed with the eye of an eagle and a natural ability to make impossible shots possible. Ten years on, Mickey wondered if he'd lost his special gift. Manny's planck had fully kicked in. He moved his arms in front of the playing arena. He could feel the air as he gripped it with both hands and drew it apart as if it were transparent curtains that allowed him to see the playing arena with crystal clarity. That was 'tearing'. His reflexes were heightened and his sight was telescopic.

Something in the light had returned, like a long lost lover whose familiarity had re-cast their spell on him. The planck allowed Mickey to enhance his unique skill. At his peak, Mickey could see the light in its minutest detail and the shadow it cast on the cue-balls. Those shadows revealed lines, spin, curve and pace. Now Mickey could see with perfect clarity, as if a special screen opened before his eyes showing him the way to direct the balls. Like the 3D computer holographs that illuminated the playing surface, Mickey's own personal holograph, his mind's eye was a place that could not be measured by technology. In that place, he controlled the twenty one red and coloured balls like no other. In that place, he was king.

"Tonight's British Championships final has drawn a record viewing audience of over one billion fans. There's been a record three billion dollars gambled on the series to date. So the big question is can Flaveau go on to win his fifth world title in three months time?" asked the commentator, excitedly reviewing Flaveau's live telecast match. Mickey's mind cast back to when he played Flaveau. He was interrupted.

"You're not a bad player. Let's make it interesting and up the stakes from 500 credits to say 5,000 credits?" asked Mickey's brash younger opponent. Mickey knew from their practice warm-up that his challenger had limited skill and less hope. *This would be an easy win*, he thought. Whether it would be as easy to claim the winnings from this giant of a man was another thing altogether. Mickey was beyond caring. The planck made him feel invincible and dangerously conceited.

His opponent was no better than a club player, typical of that generation, decked out in 'PE glasses' which allowed him to play with an accuracy that belied his experience. Mickey had played his kind before, knowledgeable about the latest new technological programs but limited skills to match. He hyperactively slipped his cue from hand to hand as if handling a deadly snake. That was a sure sign he was using narcs. But even with drug and technology assistance there was little chance Mickey would lose. Not fairly anyway.

"Good luck my friend," said Mickey.

He sat precariously on a high stool at the far side of the cubeball cube, surveying his predicament. His first problem was that he didn't have 5,000 credits to pay his opponent if, by chance, he lost. But that wouldn't happen. His second problem was more worrying. His opponent wasn't alone. No one was with him in the cubeball playing area, however Mickey was sure he had half a dozen mates somewhere in the crowded bar area.

He couldn't see them, but every now and then his opponent stole a glance out to the busy thoroughfare. A large crowd had assembled to see the live telecast of the British Cubeball championship on Skydome's state of the art holographic cube. It would be a night of rich pickings for the educated gamblers and heavy losses for the less informed.

"You break, pal," said his opponent, impatient to win his money and more. Mickey downed his now warm beer and in sportsman-like fashion offered his opponent the break, to which he obliged. His opponent, whose name he had forgotten, struck the cue-ball with all of his strength, which was considerable.

Amazingly, not one ball fell into a pocket. Mickey laughed to himself. It was just his first beer but he was intoxicated already. The planck was reacting to alcohol badly. But he wasn't worried. He knew that even drunk he could sink every ball without too much effort. The balls were spread delectably close to most of the pockets and were screaming to be potted, and quickly.

The question was, how easily should he win? Pot all twenty one balls effortlessly and reveal the mismatch or string it out and make a game of it? Either way he would win the game, but the latter strategy offered him an opportunity to win the ensuing, inevitable argument. Yes this giant of a man would undoubtedly call on his friends to pass judgement on the fairness of the bet. And if that didn't work, no doubt his fists would resolve any differences of opinion.

The strategy of fear and intimidation was nothing new to Mickey, having spent the majority of his cubeball career dealing with power and the abuse of it. His prior manager Johnnie Draxma was a prime example. Johnnie wasn't dissimilar to the lout he was facing tonight. He was just more subtle in his dealings.

"Your shot, buddy," said his opponent with the belligerent smile of a man who thought he had played a great shot. He was actually proud that he had spread eagled the balls to every cushion. Mickey just smiled.

"Nice shot," Mickey lied, as he approached the table and surveyed the carnage. He took longer than usual to focus for his head was beginning to spin. But then his will to win took over as he surveyed his line of attack. *Three breaks may get me out of this pub safely*, he thought to himself, before setting up the first of his breaks. Common sense nearly prevailed, before something snapped in Mickey's head. Maybe it was a moment of madness, or fate, or the familiar sound of the 'championship's theme music' streaming throughout the pool room? But whatever the catalyst, for the first time in eight years Mickey knew what he had to do.

Fuck it, one break tonight, he said to himself as he cannoned all twenty one balls effortlessly into the pockets. By his twenty-first shot, a large crowd had gathered to witness his unfolding exhibition match, including two large guys who looked as unhappy as their friend Mickey had beaten. All three approached him, their intent clearly not to congratulate him on his easy victory.

Mickey looked around for Manny, but he had disappeared into the crowd. He thought to run but his three assailants had surrounded him. Mickey held his cue like a weapon, ready to defend himself.

"Listen, gentlemen. Keep your credits. I don't want them. So there is nothing to fight for. We've just had ourselves a friendly game and nothing was lost." His opponent continued to advance.

"You don't seem to understand. This is more than a game for me and my friends. This is our livelihood. We don't take kindly to assholes who cheat. Give me all your credits now or we take what's left of you to the authorities. No one plays that well without narcs."

All three held their ground, waiting for the first excuse to unleash hostilities. Mickey knew then he wouldn't talk his way out of the situation. He also knew he wouldn't part with the last of his credits without a fight.

"The only guys who should be handed to the authorities are deluded thugs who falsely believe they have any talent for the world's greatest game. Your only claim to fame is for bribery and racketeering."

Mickey swung his cue with all his strength. His enhanced retinas allowed him to pinpoint his target with deadly accuracy. He smashed his opponent just above the ear. The large thug stood for the briefest of moments before he lost consciousness and fell where he stood. Blood flowed from his ear and mouth. His body was motionless. Mickey feared he had killed him with the blow. He wanted to help, but the other two assailants set out to revenge their friend. Mickey felt a force crash down from behind him. First a blow around his head and back forced him to the ground, beside his unconscious opponent. He tried to get up but more heavy blows to his body filled him with stabbing pain. He lay on the floor, defenceless to their relentless retaliation, until mercifully he lost consciousness.

Mickey only remembered snippets of the crimson splattered evening of red cue-balls and blood, most of it his. Mickey lost the fight and his winnings. Then the night really turned ugly.

"Let go of me, asshole," he said, mistakenly believing he was being held by one of the thugs that came for him.

"Settle down sir, we don't want to hurt you," said one of the two large security officers escorting him from the pool room. Mickey was still drugged enough to believe he could escape his predicament, as he attempted to break free from the 'strong arms of the law'.

"Fuck off, the pair of you," he said lashing out uncontrollably, taking one officer by surprise as his right elbow winded him. But the second officer retaliated swiftly and decisively as Mickey felt something solid hit the left side of his face. He fell heavily to the ground, dazed.

Yes the night was pretty well fucked, he thought, lying in a pool of his own blood and the weight of two large offices with their knees planted squarely against his spine, screaming orders he didn't understand.

For one crazy moment, Mickey thought he was back in his old home, his father screaming at him as he stood between him and his sister. He was about to shout out to his father that Riley deserved the rebuke, not him. Then his eyes began to focus. Two security officers were pushing him into their security van, a modified 'paddy wagon'. He landed on the cold, carbon-plastic floor of the security van. Then he heard doors slammed shut and locked behind him.

Cold steel cuffs cut into his wrists. His head and bruised body ached. The security van suddenly jolted forward. His will to fight had drained from him. He slumped back against the wagon's steel cage and stared forlornly at his bloody cuffed hands. Emotions welled up in him as his hands began to shake uncontrollably. It surprised him, for a good cubeball player's hands never shook. In disgust, he clasped them together tight praying for the shaking to stop. *Steady hands*, he thought before crying uncontrollably not believing his situation. He was 35-years-old. He should be in his prime, playing the circuit as the world's best cubeball player. Why had it come to this?

The van slowly moved through the Skydome's corridors, leaving Mickey to ponder his situation. Dimmed ceiling lights flashed past him as he held his steely gaze upwards. The planck was wearing off now. Pain was surging through his body. He was probably lucky to be alive. He focused on the lights. Mickey always found refuge in its glow. He counted the number of lights as the van continued its journey along the many winding corridors. All he faced now was a long ride to the sky elevator and his return to an Earth jail somewhere. It was not the return he had imagined. So he was left to contemplate memories of his past as he tried to make some sense of his downfall.

The security van stopped abruptly at its final destination jolting Mickey from his thoughts. He had sobered sufficiently to accept his fate.

"Please step down, sir," said the officer, who Mickey had struck and winded earlier.

This time the cop had a baton in hand ready for anything. He studied Mickey closely, like a cubeball opponent who had suffered losses in early games – cautious from earlier wounds of defeat but ready to strike back. Life was like that, every defeat against an opponent revealed a little more of the victor; drawing a competitor's respect and deadly focus to win next time. Yes, he wouldn't be struck again and Mickey knew that.

"Yes officer, sorry for what I did...the drink...sorry," he said, the defeated one now.

Mickey had resigned himself to some 'jail time' as the two security officers held him firmly and led him away. He felt a mix of dread, but inexplicably excitement too as he faced an uncertain future. There was one thing he knew for sure. He was returning to Earth that night as they bundled him into the security room located in 'Earth Lift Two'.

A Skydome Doctor was administering a drug to Mickey as he spoke.

"You've sustained many bruises and lacerations. This will control your pain until you are taken to a hospital." Mickey knew the syringe delivered more than pain relief. It was also administered to ensure he would not cause any more trouble that night. He knew the drug would take effect quickly. He needed to know something before he left the Skydome.

"How was the other guy? He was unconscious and bleeding. Is he okay?"

"He refused assistance. He and his friends are being interviewed by authorities. It seems they won't be pressing charges, or you'd not be heading to Earth. You're a lucky man, Mr. Allen."

Mickey was relieved. The authorities would have tested him for drugs if they'd have pressed charges. Something wasn't right about what had happened. He had badly injured his opponent and yet no charges would be laid? Mickey feared he had inadvertently strayed into a planned trap.

Everyone paid their dues for wrongdoings in the sport of cubeball. Experience told him that the time would come when he would have to pay for his evenings' indiscretions. The question was to whom would he have to pay?

Mercifully, his fears and pains disappeared as he drifted into a deep sleep. The two day journey to Earth was usually a difficult one for passengers. Many suffered motion sickness. But Mickey would be saved from that as the drugs would keep him safely immobilised until he reached his next port of call on Earth, the exact destination unknown.

3

Early Match Play

MICKEY HAD PLAYED CUBEBALL for as long as he could remember, ever since he was old enough to walk and peer over the family pool table. His parents purchased a small cottage on Chicago's outskirts long before he was born. His father was apparently more industrious back then and he had built a small add-on sunroom at the back of the cottage.

Mickey disappeared most nights to the ramshackle back room to hone his skills at cubeball and to escape the interminable tropical heat that radiated through their stifling, oven-like brick home. Mercifully, the sun room was surrounded by large slat windows that allowed some ventilation.

It was there he fell in love with cubeball. He dined with his family every evening in front of their 'vid cube'. The dining table had been long abandoned by families. The vid cube had taken pride of place in every fashionable home. But Mickey's mind never strayed too far from his evening match play practice. He was a typical ten-year-old who bored easily and fidgeted constantly. Growing pains, his mother called it. Every night he would re-enact the games his cubeball idols had just played.

The pool table was as ramshackle as the sunroom. They hadn't the money to afford a cubeball cube. Mickey had to practice on an antique pool table, with its green faded felt, torn by constant use or misuse.

This was how they used to play in the twentieth century, before the technological additions of the cubeball revolution. Mickey drew the lines that dissected the pool table into four equal rectangles by chalk, pretending they were the same as the 'live lines' that flashed on the modern cubeball cubes.

He often pestered his father to play a real game which he imagined as a championship play-off. His father was good enough to beat Mickey in his early formative years. However, unlike Mickey, his father never practiced. So by the time Mickey turned ten he regularly lost to his young son. Mickey was a persistent little bugger, as his father used to say.

As Mickey's skills grew, he turned to playing alone. His parents were not competitive enough to make the games challenging. Riley was improving quickly, but she was only eight-years-old. In a few years she would challenge him more. He didn't mind playing alone though. He increasingly relied on his imagination to re-enact many drama-filled tournaments where he played in front of large, adoring crowds who admired his skills. And Mickey knew all the top players.

Every night the commentators built the tension of the game and educated cubeball fans about the facts and figures of the game. Cubeball was more than a game now. It was a global event. It had become the highest ranking television show in the world as the constant advertising reinforced to its maniacal fans. Two billion viewers worldwide and jackpots that made one lucky viewer a millionaire every day!

This was the other world of cubeball, a world that the young Mickey didn't understand - not yet. In fact, the cubeball phenomenon screened every night, consisted more of 'strategy wrap-ups' and discussions on gaming odds than on actual match-play. Like most fans, his family enjoyed that side of cubeball, preferring the analysis to the actual playing.

His wide eyed gaze remained firmly on the skill of the players. To him the strategist and programmers were irrelevant. They never played a shot. They seemed to be viewers like his family, no more than hangers-on who thought of the money rather than the skill of the game.

It was not until a few years later that his sister took an interest in playing the game. Riley was twelve and Mickey was fourteen. She was beginning to lose her gangly frame and mature into a young lady. She had grown quicker than Mickey and was nearly as tall as him. She was stronger too and with that strength her confidence built. This annoyed Mickey, for Riley could be brash with him. Where Mickey had inherited the skill genes from his parents, Riley was gifted with intelligence, a gift she was not reluctant to demonstrate during their many cubeball encounters at home.

"Riley, the play you're referring to is the Beeson defence of 2039, not 2041," exclaimed Mickey.

Riley ignored her elder brother as she lined up the red ball. She stroked the cue-ball firmly so that it glanced the red ball and ricocheted across two cushions, before resting safely behind the brown ball.

"There, the 2041 defence. Played to perfection. Look it up?" Riley retaliated.

"Beeson then called a power-play and cut quadrant two. Your play, I believe?"

Mickey didn't look Riley in the eye. He held an expressionless steely gaze on the table. It was hard enough to make a shot at a red. But now, he was unable to hit any red ball in the second quarter of the table that Riley had nominated. The power-play call meant she would receive double points for her next frame. He played his cue shot harder than he should have, missing all the reds and leaving an open frame for Riley. She beamed a smile.

"Not quite how it was done in '41," she said. Her eyes were wide with the expectation of victory, as she cleaned up the table. She had never looked as happy in her life as she turned to her brother ready to claim her first victory against him. Mickey did not look up however. His eyes remained on the table as he spoke.

"Your third shot in the break was illegal," he said ungraciously.

"Bullshit, Mickey! You know I played that winning frame to perfection."

"Sorry. Rules are rules," lied Mickey, before he placed his cue on the table. "If you studied actual game-play more than strategy, you'd actually start winning."

Tears formed around Riley's eyes. "You're such an arse at times. I beat you, fair and square." Riley threw her cue onto the table and stormed out of the sunroom, directly to her mother in the next room. Mickey listened to her tearful complaints. He felt a jerk as Riley had played well. Yet pride had stopped him from congratulating her.

"Mickey, apologise to your sister," said his mother.

"Just as soon as she apologises for being a smart-arse every time she opens her mouth," said Mickey, before storming out of the house. From the back gate, he heard his mother call out to his father. Mickey knew he was in trouble now, so he ran from the back gate into the small farm reserve that adjoined their property. Mickey knew he'd return to a lecture about the finer points of the game. Even worse, he'd have to endure Riley's taunts. This is what frustrated him about his family. He believed one day that he could play the game like no other. Yet all in his family failed to see it, especially his little sister. No one saw what he saw in the game. He felt an outcast in the very game that he loved to play. They genuinely loved to talk about the game, rather than play it. If Riley could see that, he may have encouraged her more. But she spent most of her time challenging Mickey's knowledge of the sport rather than his skill.

Mickey lived in a worry-free world of cubeball, imagining his future as the next 'Hurricane' or 'Rocket'. They were his heroes, not the strategists. Life in that world was intoxicating except for one nagging, worrisome feeling that relentlessly grew in his mind over the next few years. He couldn't place it at first. Something was nagging at him which slowly made him doubt his glorious future as a cubeball player. Slowly, insidiously his doubts grew until Mickey felt he hated his life. But how could this be? He lived in a world of cubeball, which he loved more than life itself. No, it had to be something in his life.

Mickey hated school.

School was a bit of a blur really. He hadn't given it any serious thought except that he was told he had to attend to get on in life. But his problems continued to nag him, so he thought about school more. A lot more. He hated his teachers who knew nothing of his world. He also had no real friends to turn to. Mickey was the type of boy who kept few friends. He was self-contained in the bubble of his life as a cubeball match player and he was happy to keep it that way - until he met Johnnie. Nothing was ever the same after that.

Johnnie was his only friend in a world that he cared little about. It didn't start out that way though. Johnnie had a reputation as too cocky and self assured for his age. He constantly big noted himself in front of his wide circle of friends. Mickey had never had a life like that. Frankly, to be surrounded by so many people frightened him. Feeling fear was one of Mickey's early memories of Johnnie when they first met at the local pool hall.

Mickey had just turned fifteen and he wanted to spend his birthday present of fifty credits to play on real cubeball cubes. To his shock, fifty credits weren't enough to play a game. He was so disappointed for he had out-grown his antique pool table at home and was tired of competing with himself and occasionally his sister. Mickey wanted to show his considerable skills to others.

"I know you, don't I?" said Johnnie with a half intimidating look on his face.

Mickey merely nodded hoping to quickly pass Johnnie's glare, but also keen to view one of the six cubeball cubes for hire. This was the first time Mickey had seen the technological marvels close up. Johnnie sensed Mickey's excitement and baited him.

"Think you can beat me?" he said, pointing to a vacant cube and carrying an overly cocky smirk. Mickey believed he could beat him alright. He wanted to annihilate him and permanently wipe the smirk from his face. But he had one problem.

"I haven't got enough money. I just came to watch."

This seemed to make Johnnie happy. He proudly reached into his pockets to reveal more money than Mickey had ever seen in his life. Yes, Johnnie loved to show his wealth and power. Whether it was fighting or money, it didn't matter. It was just the way he was.

"You ever played before?" said Johnnie contemptuously, expecting an easy victory.

Mickey wanted to tell him just how good he was, but something stopped him. He wasn't sure why. The cube playing arena was different, but the principles were the same. But then he had never played anyone else except his father and Riley, who he knew he could beat easily.

Maybe Johnnie was a good player? *Surely not*, Mickey thought. He was about to find out.

"A little bit," he replied cautiously.

I'll break then," said Johnnie, taking control of the situation.

"Nice shot," said Mickey, lying to his opponent. It looked the shot of an amateur and Mickey could hardly contain his delight as he imagined the humiliation he was about to inflict on his unsuspecting opponent.

Oh yes, Johnnie the tough guy, the rich kid. *The little shit would eat humble pie today*, thought Mickey as he lined up his cue to shoot. But then his hands came perilously close to shaking, such was his glee for what was about to unfold.

Calm yourself, he thought.

Rocket, Mickey's cubeball hero, never allowed his opponent to see his emotions, not while in combat anyway. He'd be cool, decisive, and deadly. That was what Mickey wanted as he stood up for a moment to take stock of how to pot all twenty-one balls. At least that's what he wanted Johnnie to think as he positioned his cue. In truth, he wanted to laugh. *Calm down*, he said to himself again and settled back to take his shot.

Of course he'd played this set of shots many times. Mickey knew the patterns of this game. It was second nature. First – red into top pocket – off cushion on to yellow and drop it in bottom pocket – easy. The first eight shots were all easy, which would give him twenty four points, a handy lead.

"Do you know the rules, champ?" interrupted Johnnie in his usual mocking tone.

Do I know the fucking rules! Mickey thought, trying to contain his anger. He really wanted to sink all the balls now and silence his smart-arse opponent.

"Yep," he responded, trying to focus now. But Mickey's mind was crammed with emotions he had never before felt at the cubeball cube. Mickey normally could concentrate his mind on angles, speed and momentum of the balls so that he could play the perfect game. This match was different. His focus had turned to winning rather than playing his natural game. This was a place he had never visited before.

Mickey had never wanted to win a game so bad.

Just pot the first one, he thought, desperately trying to block his cascading emotions. So Mickey set his shot, as he had done a thousand times and unleashed his skill before his unsuspecting opponent.

"Not bad," said Johnnie, surveying the remaining thirteen balls on the table. His smirk had noticeably faded as he focused on his reply break.

Not bad! Mickey thought. It was terrible. He had only managed to sink the first eight balls, and he was lucky to get away with that. His ninth shot disturbed him. Not because he missed, but because he knew that shot was usually his safest. Long shot across the cube - struck perfectly but missed! He had not missed that shot for a long time. He had been cheated. It had to be the cube. Its roll was different. Of course everything was different. No felt. No cue with chalk. Fuck, even the light was different and the light was the most important element. One he had never considered before, but one that changed the way he thought about the game forever.

Also to his surprise, Johnnie was a better player than Mickey first thought. Under pressure he developed a quiet determination and calm that enabled him to play at another level. But it was a level he knew Johnnie could never maintain. Mickey could see that he hadn't practiced enough to be a consistently skilled player. Mickey learned he could read a player that day. Not so much their match play. It was as if Johnnie was revealing his whole life there in front of him.

Yes, Johnnie knew how to win alright, and in that instant, their battle unfolded. Johnnie played six amazing shots that gave him a lead of six points, before he missed the most difficult of shots – but only just.

"Your shot," said Johnnie, no smirks now. He knew his opponent, too. Johnnie was in a dog fight, one he didn't intend on losing. He sat at the other end of the cube and studied the balls before he turned his gaze to Mickey.

Mickey had never felt anything like this moment. Try as he might, he could not keep the same intensity as he could in his imaginary games at home in the old sunroom. He was in a different world, more a battle than a match. He had to play different.

One red ball left. Of the remaining colours, the pink was easy, but the black ball was badly placed. It would come down to the black ball for victory. Foreign thoughts invaded Mickey's mind. Doubt. Momentum was not with him on this day. That sweet feeling that the final two balls would role perfectly into place eluded him. But he was adjusting to the three dimensional arena quickly.

The pockets were beginning to loom large in his sight.

The pink ball was automatic. Mickey didn't have to think too hard about this shot. But his mind remained on the black ball, the final ball - the winning ball. His nerves were tingling now, but he wouldn't show it. Mickey watched the pink ball sweetly glide into the pocket as he swaggered to the end of the table where he lined up the final shot. He stood at the opposite end of the cube to Johnnie now. Mickey never looked directly at him, but using his peripheral vision, he could study his opponent's every move and reaction.

It was all good. He had never seen his cocky opponent so quiet - not a word. He sat with his legs crossed seemingly relaxed but his eyes gave him away. They were glued to the cube now, analysing every possible angle, every way in that he could win this game.

So, it was down to Mickey to win or lose the game.

The black ball was badly placed. They both knew that. Usually, Mickey would have played the shot cautiously, jamming the black into a corner and floating the cue-ball back to the opposite wall - keeping the pressure on his opponent and waiting for a mistake that would undoubtedly come. But Mickey's desire to win with a dangerous but memorable shot proved irresistible. He had to make a three wall shot with extreme spin. He had a one in three chance of success, according to the com stats read – a world class shot. The thought that it would require the very best of skills sealed his decision

So on that day Mickey sealed his fate. That shot would cast a spell on Mickey's life for a long time to come. He lined up, steady but firm, angle of ball pinpointed – no mistake. It looked perfect, except for the light, the inexplicable fucking light and the peculiar shadows it cast in the cube. So small, its subtlety couldn't be measured, but it loomed large in Mickey's head.

"Go for it," Mickey whispered to himself just before he let loose with his pretentious, fateful, final shot.

4

Tɪᴍᴇ Oᴜᴛ

"Jᴇꜱᴜꜱ Cʜʀɪꜱᴛ!" ꜱᴀɪᴅ Mɪᴄᴋᴇʏ, as he studied the insignia above the stained glass window. He knew immediately where the Skydome officers had taken him – the Centre for Holistic and Environmental Change or CHERCH as it had been commonly called.

His body ached, but the sight of the stained glass windows motivated him into action. He lay in a dormitory filled with the lost and homeless. He counted seven other occupants in the room. They all slept restlessly. Mickey had lost all his possessions from the fight two nights before, so he could not tell the time. He guessed it was early though. The twilight cast enough of the sun's rays to distinguish the colours of the large windows that dominated the old church's clay slate walls that bordered the dormitory.

He was in one of the many dormitories surrounding the old church. Most of the old churches had been taken over decades earlier. It was simple economics - supply and demand. No one much cared for the old buildings any more. Most of them lay derelict after the demise of the old religion. So business-savvy entrepreneurs bought them to develop a new franchise. They started out as drug rehabilitation centres, but within a decade the abandoned churches had become home to many groups, ranging from charity to holistic lifestyle organisations.

Surrounding homes or businesses were resumed to cater for the increasing number of 'participants' as they called them. That was merely code for the desperate. Most of them were addicts in one form or another. Cubeball fans made up a good proportion of them, too. Gamers in particular fell victim to the addictive nature of supps and rettes. So the CHERCH targeted them. Within a decade, every church and its surrounding homes became the ghetto of choice for those who struggled in the technological world.

Mickey did not agree with their charter. He loved the technological world. He was once one of the grand players. He strutted the cubeball stage armed with technological weaponry to win the world championship. His name was on many of the supps and rettes products for which he earned considerable royalties. His face endorsed the natural drugs that CHERCH wanted removed. He had to leave this place.

Before he could make it to the door, two large male nurses came into the room. Their timing was too good to be a coincidence. The dormitory had to be monitored. Mickey's body and head ached too much to put up any resistance.

"Good morning, gentlemen. I was about to leave. Could you point me toward the exits?"

They both smiled as if Mickey had made a joke. "Sorry we can't do that Mr. Allen. We've been waiting for you to wake. The doctor is ready to see you now. Please come with us."

They stood over him, in no mood to argue. Mickey could do nothing else but accompany them. They already knew his name. What else did they know? He'd heard about these places. The rumour was that many patients had been brought to these quasi hospitals in the name of health, only never to leave them. He was on dangerous ground and he knew arguing would make it worse. Mickey's new life on Earth had started.

Mickey was escorted into the doctor's office. His head was throbbing. Both hands were lacerated and his right wrist so swollen it resembled an over-ripe mango. The doctor sat at his desk. He was a smallish man, probably in his mid-fifties. He bore the customary beard of an educated man.

"How are you feeling today Mr. Allen?" he said, pointing to Mickey to sit down.

"I've had better days," he joked, waiting for a response and receiving none. "Sore, sorry and hung over to be honest Doc, but I'm keen to get home." The doctor smiled as he surveyed one of the many papers on his desk.

"Dr. Henry's report gave you an all clear. You were lucky."

What doctor's report? Mickey thought. He hadn't recalled seeing a doctor since the brawl. There were the two solidly built security officers and nurses. Then he wondered *what type of doctor's report?* After all he was in a CHERCH, which worried him further.

"What do you mean lucky?" He asked somewhat defensively. The doctor continued to study the papers in front of him.

"Well for starters, your facial bruises could have been closer to your eye. If that had happened you may have lost the sight of an eye."

Mickey nodded his head in agreement as he touched the swelling around his eye. His cheek had swollen enough to partially close his eye.

"That's good news, doc," he replied with some relief. Losing the sight of an eye would mean he could never play cubeball at a professional level. He'd be no better than a rank amateur as his skill to read the angles and subtleties of the game would be lost forever.

"Then of course your wrist, lucky again – no breakages or you would have had six months of rehabilitation ahead of you. So all up, you have around a month of recovery," said the doctor, putting the papers down.

Mickey sat back in the leather chair. A relieved half smile of a lucky man filled his face. This wasn't the first time he had been in a scuffle - cubeball made for sore losers. He was about to thank the doctor when he remembered where he had been taken. CHERCH flashed in his mind, like a search light beacon. His first instinct was to leave immediately, but he kept calm, choosing to find out more about his situation.

"So why am I being treated in a CHERCH?"

The doctor didn't need to study the notes any more as he looked Mickey square in the eyes.

"Yes, well there's this ongoing problem you seem to be having with drugs." An uneasy silence ensued.

Mickey knew Riley had to be involved somehow. *Bloody little Riley* he thought angrily.

"I take it that Riley has arranged this?"

The doctor picked up his papers again.

"Yes, according to these files, you instructed the police to call your sister to make arrangements for your release. Is that right?"

Mickey couldn't remember much from the night, but he guessed he would have provided his sister's phone number. It was the only one he could ever remember, given she was his only family now. It had always fallen to Riley to bail him out when he was living on Earth. She'd threatened to leave him in jail next time. So this had to be her way of providing him a final warning.

"Yes, I would have provided her number," said Mickey. The doctor put down the papers again.

"Mr. Allen, your sister alluded to the fact that you've had a drug problem for some time. She requested you be sent here, as we have one of the finest drug rehabilitation clinics in the country."

"I don't have a fucking drug problem. I don't take illegal drugs. I only use supps, rettes and alcohol. All legal!" Mickey yelled defiantly and then some more. "I'm being held here against my wishes, I want to phone a lawyer now!"

The doctor appeared genuinely surprised by Mickey's outburst.

"Mr. Allen, I assure you that you can leave at any time, but could you at least hear me out?" he asked, calmly.

"On police advice, your sister agreed that you be sent to our hospital. We have medical doctors and nurses that can tend to your physical injuries, which is our main priority for you. But given your recent history of alcohol-related violence, the police recommended that you be sent here, where you can also have access to our drug rehabilitation clinic. Your sister only agreed when she knew it was voluntary."

Mickey calmed, "I could leave now?"

"Any time you wish."

Mickey was tempted to leave immediately, but his eye and wrist worried him. At the very least, he could wait until the injuries had healed, but if he copped any psychological shit he would just go. He re-checked the arrangements.

"So I don't have to attend your clinic?"

"Purely voluntary."

"There are no papers to sign?"

"No. Your sister signed the paperwork regarding payment. There are no other contracts to attend to."

Mickey relaxed back into his chair. A wry smile drifted briefly across his lips before he responded. "I'll stay for a week, but only if you personally update me on my condition daily?"

"I can promise you that, Mr. Allen, as long as you make me a promise too?"

Mickey opened his palms, signalling the doctor to tell him what was expected."

"Don't make any trouble while you're here. Is that a fair request?"

"You've got yourself a deal, Doc," he said, extending his hand and sealing their agreement with a handshake. "And call me Mickey. I don't like stuffy formalities."

"Sure. And you can call me Harry if you're a good patient or Dr. Vance if you're not." Mickey smiled broadly, accepting all conditions placed on him, before being escorted to his first home on Earth. "I'll see you tomorrow, Harry."

The next week was an uneventful one. Mickey had remained on a first name basis with Harry. He'd reluctantly settled into the 'outer wing', containing alcoholics and 'light' drug dependants. Mickey tried to keep to himself, as was his way, but word soon spread that Mickey Allen was amongst them. The older patients remembered him. Mickey was just thirty-five years of age but in this ward he was considered old. Even more chilling, Mickey learned that those in their thirties were considered elders, for usually by forty, addicts were more often than not dead from their addiction.

Surprisingly to Mickey, he'd settled into the 'outer wing' quite well, a little too well. The day was nicely balanced with the mornings and evenings taken up talking to his new fans about his halcyon days as a cubeball star. But midday was Mickey's time; he was alone in the ward as all the others attended the clinic sessions. Dave, his new and best mate in the ward, often stirred him to join them.

"What are ya, big Sheila too proud to join his mates?" joked Dave, in his Australian accent.

But Mickey would have none of it. He accepted his use of planck on the Skydome was one of the reasons he was here, but he was certain he had no substance addiction.

No, his problem was something else entirely.

Mickey's recovery was slower than he hoped though. The bruising had mostly disappeared and the lacerations were not as prominent. But his wrist was still giving him trouble. The swelling of his wrist remained, causing him discomfort. Dr. Vance had recommended he walk a lot more now that his facial bruises had healed. His bedside friend Dave, overheard the doctor's advice and chided him all day to get off his bed and join him at their daily rehabilitation session.

"Why not come with us today?" Dave would repeatedly ask. But Mickey always declined, for he was certain he had no drug addictions. But that said, Mickey did want a change of scenery. He had read every paper and magazine in the ward three times over. As he sat in the quiet of the empty ward, he realised he hadn't ventured beyond its white walls. It was time for him to explore. He hadn't ventured far when one of the nurses stopped him.

"I'm afraid you can't go there, Mr. Allen. It's a restricted area." She pointed at a map of the hospital and grounds on the wall.

"But you can go here. This outdoor area is reserved for 'low level' patients."

"The low level loonies like me," joked Mickey.

"No. But you will find some of the patients acting strangely. They're harmless though, I assure you," she said, before directing him to the outdoor reserve.

Mickey walked outdoors for the first time since his arrival. It was a cool, almost brisk mid-morning and the freshness of the air further lifted his good mood. The grounds were lush green and spacious compared to the sterile white cramped wards. He regretted not having explored the hospital earlier.

Benches and tables dotted the grassy landscape. Most were positioned near or under large fig trees that looked as old as the church. They complimented the grandeur of the church's clay brick steeples. There were a handful of patients in the enclosure, some sitting on benches and some choosing to slowly walk around the grounds.

He consciously breathed in fresh air for the first time since returning to Earth. Mickey chose a vacant bench in the centre of the reserve to relax in its natural surroundings. He listened to the natural sounds of the cardinals singing above him.

"Nice isn't it?" A voice from behind interrupted his thoughts. Mickey started to answer, but the stranger interrupted him.

"Could you move? That's my bench."

He thought to ignore the stranger, but he had a distant, self obsessed look that unsettled Mickey. *Just my luck*, he thought. He decides to go for a walk and a half-crazed patient escaped into this compound to threaten him.

"No problem," lied Mickey, choosing to sit on the other side of the table putting some distance between he and the stranger. Mickey said no more, returning his gaze to the large fig tree above him. He relaxed as best he dared, whilst darting the occasional nervous glance towards the stranger.

Some minutes passed before the stranger made any movement. His gaze was fixed on a small box he'd placed on the table, but his small, frail body constantly rocked back and forth on the bench seat. Mickey wondered whether he made him nervous. He was about to ask, when the stranger suddenly opened the lid of his small cardboard box. He removed two sheets of paper from the box and placed them neatly on the table in front of him. *Was he an artist?* Mickey wondered. Two pieces of paper had nondescript lines drawn on them, too erratic to be artful. The stranger sweated profusely now accentuating his nervous manner. Mickey made movements to leave, but the stranger spoke.

"I'm Ludwig." His gaze remained fixed on his papers.

"Hi, I'm Mickey." An uneasy silence ensued.

Ludwig took two blank pages from his box, two pencils and two sharpeners. He prepared to draw. Mickey witnessed Ludwig's obsession with precision and procedure. Sharpening a pencil is normally a trivial procedure that few people gave too much thought. But Ludwig was different. He spent an eternity preparing his drawing task.

The sharpeners were first. He positioned both on a carefully chosen spot on the table. Once satisfied with its alignment, he did something quite strange. He removed a small tape dispenser from his tin box and proceeded to secure the sharpeners to the table with the precision of an engineer and the assuredness of someone who had done this many times.

Mickey observed his laborious preparations, before he lost his patience.

"Can I help you with that?"

Ludwig ignored his offer. He methodically finished his task, almost smiling before he turned to the next task of lining up the pencils to the sharpeners and actually sharpening both pencils. A good ten minutes had elapsed before he appeared satisfied with his drawing utensils. He readied to use it. But then he stopped momentarily, almost as an afterthought, Ludwig revisited the conversation he commenced earlier.

"Pleased to meet you, Mr. Allen." Then he commenced drawing.

Ludwig slowly drew random lines on a blank white A4 sheet. But he wasn't a man in a hurry. He studied the sharpened end of his pencil as if he could only use one particular angle of the lead nib. Once satisfied he positioned the pencil on the paper and commenced to draw his first line. He repeated this process, always sharpening the pencil before drawing the line. Mickey watched for some time, fascinated by Ludwig's powers of concentration, but then boredom overtook him.

"What are you drawing?" No answer.

Ludwig was totally consumed now as he methodically drew lines on a page. Mickey gave up waiting and rose to explore the rest of the reserve. There were only three other patients outside with Mickey and Ludwig. All of them kept to themselves. Two sat at their own bench. The other walked the grounds lost in his thoughts. So Mickey slowly strolled around the perimeter of the reserve for a time, until he tired. His head and right arm ached now. The pain killers were wearing off. He considered returning to his bed but chose to sit down at a vacant bench at the end of the reserve. The beauty and serenity relaxed him as his thoughts turned back to green parks where he and his first love had walked together years earlier. A delightful time in his life that was all too brief. Mickey's reminiscing abruptly ended as he heard his name being called out from a distance.

"Mr. Allen, Mr. Allen," Ludwig shouted enthusiastically from his bench, signalling for Mickey to join him. He excitedly waved one of his drawings in the air as Mickey cautiously approached.

"This drawing is for you. It's perfect," said Ludwig, before proudly placing it on the table.

Mickey feigned a smile of appreciation as he studied the drawing. It looked no different from the others that lay on the table.

"It's unique."

"It's perfect," corrected Ludwig.

At that, he returned to his sharpener, pencil and paper and lost himself in his world of drawing lines on a page. Mickey thanked this strange man who spoke little, before taking the opportunity to head to the safety of indoors. He returned to his ward and showed the duty nurse Ludwig's gift.

"That's a first," she said.

"What do you mean?"

"I was watching you and Ludwig. That's the first time in a year that he's sat with anyone in the park area, apart from the doctor."

Mickey laughed and nodded. "Oh yes, apparently I was sitting at his bench."

"His bench? He's never sat at that bench. That's the first time that he didn't sit at his favourite bench which is over in the far corner of the reserve. Ludwig rarely speaks to people, not directly anyway."

Mickey didn't know whether to feel complimented or scared.

"He drew this picture. He said it was perfect," said Mickey, showing it to the nurse in the hope she knew what he was drawing.

The nurse merely smiled and shook her head again in surprise.

"Well, I think you've won a new friend. Ludwig has been drawing like that for years. This drawing is the same as all his others, the same style, just pencil lines and no pattern. But in all these years he's never given a drawing to anyone. You're the first."

Mickey smiled again and returned to his bed after asking the nurse for some pain killers. His head throbbed now. He taped Ludwig's drawing on the wall beside his bed before lying down. With luck one of the patients may explain the meaning of the drawing. If nothing else, it filled the sterile space.

The job done, he finally lay back on his bed to rest. Two pillows propped up his head allowing a clear view of the ward and Ludwig's masterpiece. *Scribbling by a lunatic*, he said to himself. However the more he looked at it, the more he sensed there was a familiar pattern in the chaos. A full hour had passed before he realised its meaning. By then he could not take his eyes from the drawing. He was so engrossed he hadn't noticed Dave's return from the rehabilitation clinic.

"What's caught your eye, champ?" said Dave, as he eyed the scribbled lines hanging on Mickey's wall.

"A fucking perfect masterpiece, that's what!" said Mickey shaking his head in awe, as if he were looking at a painting of the Mona Lisa.

Dave looked again at the drawing before shaking his head in disagreement and delivering his verdict. "Yeah and I'm Albert Einstein." He abruptly ended the conversation, choosing to put on his earphones and lie down to listen to music.

Mickey was left alone to ponder Ludwig, this strange little man who seemed to possess a special gift. It made him think of his earlier years and the special gift he had been born with and the curse it had put on those special friends who had come into his life. He had to find him, and tell him that he understood what Ludwig was drawing. He had to tell everyone that these weren't indecipherable scribbling made by a mentally ill patient. On the contrary, Ludwig was a genius.

5

TEEN DREAMS

AT AGE SEVENTEEN, MICKEY'S life was busy, but he didn't mind. The Chicago early morning was chilly. He quickly removed his gloves, so that he could open the security door to Chris's Billiards pool hall.

"Six-eight-two-five-one," he repeated to himself, as he locked the door behind him and scampered to the near-by panel to disengage the security alarm. He breathed a sigh of relief that he had got the number right. Last time he didn't, much to the ire of the owner, Johnnie's uncle, Marcello.

"You fucking get me out of bed in this weather. It could keel me.... you understand?" He repeated in his Italian English.

"Johnnie gave me the wrong number," Mickey lied.

"Little Johnnie fuck-up, then Johnnie pay...understand Meekee?"

"Yes. It won't happen again."

"What are you waiting for, boy? Get on with the work. I want it to be...every table and cube...spotless. You understand me?"

Mickey nodded quickly, before immediately getting his cleaning equipment. He'd learnt early not to argue with Marcello. He had a quick-fire temper and although his English was not great, he never forgot anything. As expected, Marcello was true to his word, making Johnnie pay for him being inconvenienced. However, while Marcello was Mickey's day-time boss, Johnnie had become his cubeball manager.

The extra money Marcello charged Johnnie was soon passed on to Mickey, with interest.

But despite the occasional altercations, Mickey had happily left school behind. Cubeball was his life. He hated the cleaning jobs, but he did get to play on the old cubeball tables for free. He also had occasional access to a brand new cubeball cube. It was championship level too, connected to high-powered computers.

If Mickey worked fast enough, he managed to spend an hour practicing on the cube, before the pool hall opened. He'd set the computer at championship level and practice on the highest possible setting. He learnt a lot about strategy there, building more skills. He also joined a local team that Johnnie formed. Johnnie managed the team. Sam, his little brother, doubled as the strategist and the programmer. Every weekend they competed with the best of the local talent in their district. Mickey excelled and soon developed a reputation as the player to beat.

For the most part, he owed his opportunities to work and compete in the sport he loved to his buddy, Johnnie. Of course Mickey had to pay his dues for that favour, which was Johnnie's way. On the night of the local final was such an occasion. They had outplayed all of the competition that season and deservedly received the status as favourites to win. However, they learnt that the rules required that a full team of three was required as the match was to be played on a championship level cube. It was left to Johnnie to select the third team member. This he dutifully did and announced at the one practice session they were allowed at the venue where they were competing that night.

"Guys, meet your programmer for the final." Riley stood beside Johnnie ready to take her place at the computer console. She smiled appreciatively at Johnnie, before casting a glance toward her fellow team members.

"Thanks, Johnnie. I won't let you guys down tonight." Her nerves quickly faded as she hugged Johnnie for giving her an opportunity. Riley looked more like Johnnie's assistant manager than a programmer, as she was dressed in a navy blue jacket and matching slacks that made her look more in her twenties than a 16-year-old. She walked past Mickey who was staring at Johnnie and sat beside Sam at the console.

"Well done Riley, you deserved this," said Sam.

"Take her through the game plans, Sam," said Johnnie, before he took Mickey aside to an adjoining completion room. He closed the door and pointed to an old style pool table, set up and ready to play on.

"Let's play. I'd rather you take out your frustrations on me than your kid sister. Because she's playing tonight and there's nothing you'll say to change that." Johnnie picked up a cue. "I'll break with a power play," he said, smashing the balls with a strike that spread the balls to all corners of the table, before one red ball fortuitously fell into a corner pocket.

"No fucking way, Johnnie! I've always supported you. But this? No way."

Johnnie as usual ignored Mickey's protests, as they circled the cubeball table.

"Quadrant?" asked Johnnie wanting to know which rectangle on the table was excluded for his next pot of the ball.

"Quadrant one," said Mickey, making it a difficult play. Johnnie circled the table a few times looking for the best play.

"Your sister is a smart girl. Why do you make it difficult for her?"

"She's smart alright. But she's young and too impressionable."

Johnnie firmly stroked the cue-ball across two cushions toward the blue ball that he nominated. It struck the ball with sufficient speed but the wrong angle. He shrugged in disappointment. "A smart girl like Riley needs a good mentor. I could be that mentor!" Mickey gave no response, preferring to point at the table for Johnnie's selection.

"Quadrant three," said Johnnie sitting on the stool, resigned to being an observer as Mickey cleaned up. Johnnie maintained his silence until Mickey's third shot.

"You know she's really interested in the cubeball business. Sam thinks..."

"Sam fucking shmam! Your brother is only interested in laying Riley, which is another reason to keep her away from our team." Mickey was about to break into one of his tirades now, which Johnnie stopped short.

"I play to win Mickey, and Riley is the perfect backup for Sam. You didn't moan when I got you the perfect job here, did you? And you didn't bitch when I organised tournaments that won you enough money to buy a car." Mickey held back his words, choosing to continue his break, effortlessly sinking more balls.

"Okay. Riley plays tonight. But if I get any bullshit from her – and I mean it, Johnnie, any bullshit at all - you back me and send her back to school where she belongs. Deal?"

"That's my man, Mickey. You won't regret this. I know your sister is young but she is gifted with a computer brain. With you, Sam and Riley as a team, we can't be beaten."

That night, Johnnie was proven to be right. They swept the competition aside to record the easiest of victories. Mickey waited for his kid sister to step out of line, but Johnnie surprisingly proved to be a diligent role model. Riley was engrossed in her work and appeared to be enjoying the challenge of developing into a professional cubeball programmer.

More surprises came that year too. Not because Riley was exceptionally bright and gifted with cubeball computer technology, although she was all those things and more. And it wasn't because brother and sister had a new found respect for each other. No, they didn't speak much beyond game play strategies. It was all together something different.

Riley had a new friend, Julie or 'Jules' as she was known.

Jules was older than Riley by a year. In fact Riley always had friends older than her, which made perfect sense to Mickey. She was too serious to befriend girls her own age. Riley was a smart girl, bordering on smart-arse really. Mickey disliked all her previous friends. Most were stuck up like her, talking smugly and never doing normal things that girls do. He expected Jules to be the same, but he was in for a surprise.

"Riley's invited her new friend to practice. They're on their way. So be on your best behaviour tonight," said Johnnie.

Mickey shrugged his shoulders instead of responding, preferring to practice his drills while he waited for the rest of his team to arrive. Johnnie's uncle let the team practice on his pool hall's championship cube every Monday night.

"She's a good looker," probed Johnnie, looking for a reaction from Mickey.

"Like her last friend, Daphne?"

Johnnie laughed. Daphne was tall and gangly with a pimply complexion to match her awkward, adolescent frame. She seldom spoke to Mickey and never dared conversation with Johnnie. Both men clearly terrified her. She managed strained conversation with Sam, given her interest was solely in computers. She studied the team's strategies with apparent interest, although Mickey could never understand her conversations with Riley.

"The mathematician. Save me," replied Mickey, as he focused even more intently on his drills.

"I think Daphne fancied you."

"Fuck off!" Mickey threatened to throw his cue at Johnnie, before being interrupted.

"Are you two fighting again?" said Riley, entering the pool hall with Sam and her new friend.

"Riley! My favourite team member," said Johnnie, as he hugged her. Mickey sniggered.

"And who is this angel?"

"This is my friend, Jules. Jules, this is our manager, Johnnie," said Riley, looking awkward and slightly embarrassed.

"A pleasure to meet you Jules," said Johnnie. He kissed her on both cheeks in his best Italian style.

"Have you come to join our team? We could do with another beauty, couldn't we Mickey?" he jokingly asked. Mickey continued practicing his drills, but he glanced Jules way more than once as Johnnie continued flirting with the newcomer. Riley finally interjected. She took Jules' arm and walked with her towards Mickey.

"And this is the man you wanted to meet. Jules this is Mickey."

Mickey awkwardly held out his hand to offer her a courteous handshake. His hand had the slightest of tremors, before Jules held it warmly.

"Hi Mickey, I've heard a lot about you."

"My sister can say cruel things about me at times, don't believe her." Mickey glanced toward Riley. She held her hand to her lips as if she were holding her breath. Johnnie and Sam looked on in expectation. Jules broke the silence.

"I'm really looking forward to watching you play. If you don't mind, that is?"

Mickey held Jules hand longer than he realised.

"Sure," he replied nervously, before turning to Riley in a business like fashion.

"Take Jules to the computer console and show her how things work. Guys, let's get started. We only have an hour, so let's make the most of it."

Mickey played more trick shots than he should have and he was more talkative than usual too.

"Jules, pick a pocket for the blue ball." Jules nervously giggled.

"The top pocket."

"No, that's too easy. Riley, help your friend out," said Mickey. Riley whispered in to her ear.

"The top pocket, but off four walls." Mickey seemed to revel in the challenge.

"Riley, program that shot, but take it to five walls."

Riley enthusiastically responded to the challenge. The cube filled with the five lines the cue-ball would have to take to sink the blue ball. The first computer generated line was curved. It would require extreme spin and velocity to recreate the first of the five pathways to the blue ball. The degree of difficulty for this shot was extreme. Mickey studied his challenge confidently.

"This shot has been achieved in competition only once. It was during the 2038 European Championship, wasn't it, Riley?" Riley checked her computer console.

"Correct. Sid Hall played it in a semi-final. He went on to win the final."

Mickey nodded agreement. He remembered the game well. It was one of the most famous comebacks in European cubeball history. It was often replayed on fan's cubebits worldwide. He'd only occasionally pulled the shot off in practice. But Mickey was confident that night. He lined up the angles, glancing across to his team. Riley and Sam were focused on the monitors, whereas Jules piercing blue eyes stared excitedly at him. She nervously twisted her long blonde hair, seemingly willing him to succeed.

Jules' gaze emboldened Mickey to reveal his special gift to her. He strode confidently to the cue-ball and lined up one of the most difficult shots in cubeball. Then with little thought, he cracked the cue-ball with a force that matched the passion he was feeling. The curve on the first line was more pronounced than the programmed line set by the computer. The force was greater than that played in 2038. The second and third ricochet lines also curved slightly, before the fourth and fifth lines of the shot straightened to strike the blue with considerable force into the top pocket.

Mickey had struck the perfect shot. Sam and Riley sat staring at the console, mesmerised by what they had just seen and eager to re-capture its perfection on replay. Only champions could play this way and it was clear to all that Mickey was developing into one.

"Fucking incredible," said Johnnie. His eyes were wide. Filled with awe for Mickey's skills and expectation with how much he could earn from it.

Mickey didn't hear his appreciative manager. He didn't see the small tear that had formed in his kid sister's admiring eye. His gaze remained on Jules. She brushed her hair back on to her shoulders before resting her slender hands on her hips. Her mouth was wide open, breathing in her excitement for what she had just seen. Then her eyes revealed that there was more to her feelings than that of an adoring fan. Her gaze began to fill with a stirring hunger. Fate was beginning to move into Mickey's life like an evening moon tide.

6

CUBE MUSIC

MICKEY WOKE EARLY TO a silent, sleeping ward. He was starting his second week at CHERCH and he hadn't slept well the night before. A vivid dream interrupted his slumber. Strange he dreamt about 'that match' for the first time in many years. He stepped from his bed on to the cold tiled floor. He gazed at Ludwig's drawing, wondering whether it had been the catalyst. He walked from his bedside to the common washroom to shower. The luke-warm shower woke him fully from his slumber. Maybe his sister was the catalyst for the dream? He was meeting her this morning in the doctor's office to sign his release papers. He had spoken with her on the phone briefly. It was a terse call to arrange the day's meeting, so in truth he didn't want to see her, but he knew he had to.

Despite their falling out, she had remained generous toward him, financially speaking. After all, his little sister was a wealthy, successful, independent woman. Her years of diligently working with Johnnie and Sam had paid off handsomely. She was a much sought after technology consultant to the global cubeball industry. She travelled overseas regularly earning outrageous fees, at times suspiciously exorbitant.

Mickey didn't begrudge Riley though. She had earned her success. He was her big brother but in reality, he was penniless, constantly in trouble and anything but a role model. He didn't want to ask her for handouts. But he needed accommodation. He had lived well on Mars, but only because Riley had arranged subsidised boarding through her business associates. That had now ended. Mainly because he had acted in an appalling manner, trashing the home she had acquired for him. The last of his money had been gambled at the Skydome. So now he had no money, home or friends.

Mickey woke with a headache too, which didn't improve his mood. So he sought the fresh air and calm of the outdoor reserve, hoping it would clear his head. His meeting with Riley was in an hour which made him apprehensive. He was considering what to say to her, when to his great surprise, he saw Ludwig sitting at the same bench in the middle of the reserve. He had gone missing the last few days. He was drawing in his usual deliberate manner as his body rocked to and fro. Mickey sat opposite him and quietly watched him draw. Then when Ludwig finished, Mickey had to speak.

"Fucking unbelievable!" he exclaimed. To his surprise, Ludwig stopped drawing and looked directly at him.

"I heard you might be leaving today?" Mickey ignored Ludwig's question. His mind was on the drawing.

"So why haven't you drawn the last lines?"

Ludwig's gaze was fixed on him now. He never looked directly at a person on the rare occasion he spoke. His body stilled like his gaze.

"Because the music stopped...didn't it, Mickey?"

Mickey's mind returned to that fateful evening. The night he had just dreamt about. *What was happening? How could Ludwig know what he felt that night?*

"Who the fuck are you, Ludwig?"

"I love music. I know when it's perfect. It's what I draw." Ludwig started to rock back and forth nervously again.

"I used to remember the music. But now I only draw."

Mickey believed him, but he wondered what else he knew.

"Draw the last lines. I know you can." Mickey challenged.

But Ludwig refused to draw. *Would not or could not*? Mickey wondered, before he snatched the drawing and pencil from him and drew the last three lines.

"There...fucking easy, wasn't it!' Mickey screamed. But it wasn't easy; it was the hardest thing Mickey had ever done in his life. The memories stung him like an attempted winning pot just failed to fall into the pocket. Mickey had to walk away from Ludwig. He threw Ludwig's drawing back at him. *Breathe slowly*, he thought, as champion cubeball players were supposed to do. He started to walk away not ever wanting to return. But then he heard Dr. Vance call out from behind.

"Mr. Allen, wait a moment."

Mickey didn't turn immediately. His mind raced back to a darker time in his life. He wanted to run but didn't. Instead Mickey turned to the doctor who was now sitting opposite Ludwig.

"Join me," invited the doctor. Mickey defied his feelings and sat down with them.

"I thought we were meeting in your office?" said Mickey in a calm tone that belied his feelings. The doctor sipped on a coffee, before replying.

"Your sister's running late. Traffic's bad. So I thought I'd come and join you." He took another sip. "It's been a busy morning. I needed this." The brew visibly relaxed him as he sat opposite Ludwig and took in the peaceful surrounds. Ludwig had picked out a new page from his box and started a new drawing, oblivious to the drawing Mickey had thrown toward him moments earlier. He worked feverishly on his new drawing.

"You two have struck up a friendship," said Dr. Vance. *Friendship was an overstatement*, Mickey thought, before responding.

"I'm intrigued by his skill, but I don't think anyone in this hospital has recognised it."

"No one except us. Ludwig and I go back quite a way, Mickey," said Dr. Vance. He leaned back in his bench and stared into his coffee cup, seemingly settling in for a long conversation.

"Tell me about him, Harry. His drawings...how does he know so much about my cubeball playing days?" Dr. Vance put his cup down and stared up to the trees, seemingly considering how to answer Mickey's question.

"Where do you start with a life like Ludwig's? He was not like other boys. His name wasn't even Ludwig. That summed him up to a tee. When Ludwig imagined something to be true, from that day on it was true. Nothing or no one else mattered. It didn't surprise his parents, either. Their son had always been a loner, preferring his own company to his parents or friends. They tried hard to change his introverted nature, but to no avail. You see, Ludwig had one other powerful character trait - determination. Once he determined his goals, he pursued them doggedly. So at the age of thirteen he woke up and announced that his real name was Ludwig, end of story."

"So is he sick, Harry?" Dr. Vance shook his head.

"No. He's what we call in the medical profession, a savant. He lacks the normal social skills that you and I take for granted. Savants are highly intelligent, but their brain is wired to a particular part of their brain's activities. This focused hard-wiring of the brain leads to an obsessive behaviour pattern. Ludwig's obsessive behaviour patterns steadily worsened till he was ultimately institutionalised. He was introduced to me when I was a young doctor, around 26-years-old if memory serves me right. I had commenced duties at CHERCH and was finalising my PhD in 'Savant Behavioural Patterns'. You see, this centre is renowned for its work in the area. I was the first to identify Ludwig's condition."

"So, Ludwig is obsessed with my cubeball matches?" Mickey asked. Dr. Vance looked over to Ludwig who remained busy drawing.

"Not exactly. What do you love the most in the world, Ludwig?

"I love music, Dr. Vance."

"You see Mickey, Ludwig's desire for a name change was based on more than a whim. As a young boy, Ludwig regularly listened to music on his parents vid cube. It calmed him, they told me. But one day, he viewed a recording of Beethoven's Ninth Symphony on their vid cube. He was so mesmerised by the performance he didn't sleep that night. Ludwig told me that he was so excited by it that he replayed the symphony in his head. But not in the way that normal people remember music. Ludwig remembered every note, pitch perfect and in the right order. He replayed the full symphony in his head, ten times that night alone, with not a single note out of place."

"The music is perfect," interrupted Ludwig.

"Yes it's perfect Ludwig," replied Dr. Vance. He held Ludwig's arm reassuring him, before continuing his recollection of Ludwig's life.

"By eighteen, he was able to write every musical score ever written by Beethoven. By twenty three he had committed every score to memory. Unlike most other musically inclined savants, Ludwig could not play a single note on a musical instrument. But he didn't seem to care. He happily lived his life playing perfect scores in his mind. Ludwig's life was filled with the beauty and creativity of Beethoven's exquisite music.

And his happiness would have continued for the rest of his life, but for one thing. What do you think that was Mickey?"

Mickey could not think what that might be. He equated Ludwig's love for the 'perfect' music with his love for the perfection of the cubeball game. Whilst Mickey had stopped competing on the world stage, he'd never lost his love for the game.

"I don't know. Usually, when you find something that feels perfect, you don't let it go."

Dr. Vance nodded agreement. "Yes that's true, Mickey. But Ludwig's problem was he had no more of Beethoven's music left to learn. This frustrated Ludwig, for he firmly believed Beethoven was still alive. He searched for the grand musician for a while, not believing anyone so perfect could die. But he finally, begrudgingly accepted Beethoven had died. Ludwig fell into a fitful depression. That sparked a rage in him that increasingly became unmanageable and dangerous. Other great composers were introduced, but none mesmerised him like Beethoven. Mozart, Hayden, Bach, Chopin....one by one he rejected them all. Their genius seemed meaningless to his obsessive fascinations."

"It must have frustrated him. I'd feel the same if I ran out of different game strategies to play."

"Yes, it frustrated and angered him. Ludwig retreated deeper into his mind, refusing to write music or talk, sometimes for weeks on end. His dark mood turned dangerous when he refused to eat. At that point, medication had to be introduced. This had two effects. He started to communicate with the world again, but frustratingly his clear recall of music began to fail him. This terrified Ludwig. All that he could do was write and re-write Beethoven's works so that he would not forget." Mickey listened, enthralled by Ludwig's life story. It touched him on many levels.

"Maybe it was the drugs, Harry. I've seen too many people I care for destroyed by it."

"Yes and no. Ludwig was satisfied with his life, recreating sublime work on paper. To those closest to him, he appeared to have reached a happy compromise in his life, somewhere between normality and complete isolation. He conversed in a disjointed fashion but he at least made some effort. It seemed that he was satisfied with his compromised, drug-assisted life style. But that changed, too and you played your part in that."

"My cubeball final," Mickey responded knowingly, given Ludwig had drawn it a number of times since his arrival at CHERCH.

"Yes. Everything changed, on the night he watched you play in the Illinois state cubeball final. He enjoyed listening to the music on a vid cube, but he rarely watched it. There was something in the random, chaotic patterns that disturbed him. He discovered Beethoven there and was satisfied with that. But mostly he found it to contain a myriad of words, images and sounds that bombarded rather than soothed his senses. Ludwig kept clear of the 'fire box', as he called it. To him it was more threatening than an open fire. If you got too close to a fire you felt the pain of the hot flames, whereas the fire box tortured all his senses."

"Fire box, Ludwig repeated. The words alone agitated him as he rocked his body back and forth."

"It's okay, Ludwig. We aren't going to look at the vid cube." Dr. Vance again paused to reassure Ludwig that all was fine, before he continued.

"Ironically, for all the pain it inflicted, Ludwig remained intrigued by it. How could something so painful bring him such beauty as Beethoven's Ninth? For that reason he listened to his parents for any clues that something exciting may be telecast on it.

That day, they were excited. They talked of nothing else. The state final of cubeball consumed them and Ludwig took notice. A record national viewing audience was anticipated, as you were young and gifted but very much an underdog. It seemed the whole nation was caught up in it."

"Tell me about it. I was hounded by the press day and night," said Mickey.

"Well, Ludwig surprised his parents that night, when he chose to view the championship battle. At first, little excited him as the words, images and sounds bombarded and disturbed his senses. Ludwig was about to leave the room when something changed. For the first time since Beethoven's music, the 'fire box' calmed him. A number of coloured spheres were floating in a cube. It relaxed him. But his calm was shattered as a player with a stick disturbed the peace by spread-eagling the balls across the cube. It created chaos in the calm and seemed a pointless exercise to Ludwig. He disapproved at first, but unexpectedly out of the chaos came a music he had not heard before. What was that, Ludwig?"

"I saw Mickey play perfect music."

"Yeah, I played well for most of that night," said Mickey.

"I remember it too, Mickey. You played cubeball with a wisdom that belied your youth. Ball after ball was guided into the eight pockets that cornered the cube."

"I was in the zone, once I settled my nerves. I could have potted anything at that point."

"But it wasn't your ability to pot balls that awed Ludwig. It was the role of the ball and the precise pace that you placed on each and every shot. To Ludwig, you weren't playing merely to sink balls and win. You were orchestrating motion on the table that transcended the game. You created music on a canvas that night - like an artist."

"So did he just start drawing my shots from memory?"

"Not quite. He had to understand the game first. It unsettled him, but he had to listen to the background noise provided by the commentary. By the second game he had learnt the rules sufficiently to put context to his drawings. Ludwig tolerated the commentator's annoying voice, so that he could understand the rules of the game."

"Terrible noise Dr. Vance," interrupted Ludwig.

"But then the commentator's voice faded in your mind, didn't it?"

"Yes, I heard the beautiful music."

"There was something in the role and pace of the balls as they bounced off the walls. At some point during one of your mesmerising breaks, Ludwig began to match your play with a series of Beethoven symphonies. He synchronised the composer's music with the match play. The two were in harmony. He wondered if you appreciated Beethoven too. Or was it mere coincidence? But in every frame of every game, your play was mostly musical and perfect, whether winning or losing."

"Yeah, there was plenty of both. It was the best of thirteen games and after two hours we were tied 'six a piece," recalled Mickey.

"Ludwig sat enraptured by the contest. Not because it was close and hard fought. He found a new Beethoven symphony hidden in the way you play. Each break in every game blended excerpts of symphonies and concertos. He'd all but given up his search, but now he had chanced upon a new forum to appreciate his maestro, committing twelve new musical scores to his memory. He drew each game from memory as you took the half hour break before the commencement of the final frame. This provided enough time for Ludwig to sketch all previous twelve games. He drew every shot played with the precision of a conductor. He finished drawing the twelfth game just before the commencement of the final and deciding frame and neatly stacked the twelve pages in order. Then he set the thirteenth blank sheet for the final match. He hadn't been this excited since he discovered Beethoven's music. It was a musical score he would never forget."

"Nor have I Harry, for very different reasons," said Mickey. He looked to want to say more, but held his words back. So Dr. Vance continued.

"So you see Mickey, I've been Ludwig's doctor for a long time." said Dr. Vance.

"Did he remember any of my other matches?" asked Mickey, curious now as to the extent of Ludwig's fascination.

"Every match you ever played."

Mickey wanted to talk to Ludwig but he was frantically drawing another game, seemingly oblivious to their conversation.

"I bet you've never had a fan quite like Ludwig?"

"Not even close."

Mickey laughed at the thought of his game-play being the equivalent of classical masterpieces. For one, he hated classical music. In fact he hated most music. It was more a distraction than a calming influence. Cubeball was all Mickey needed to calm his mind.

"Harry, I'm tone deaf, the idea of my match play being musical is preposterous." Dr. Vance shrugged his shoulders. He was unable to offer an explanation. Then, Mickey sat forward on his chair in excitement.

"I sure as hell could do with a team strategist with his memory. Is he certified? I mean will he be stuck here for the rest of his life?"

"Ludwig can leave any time he likes. He chooses to live here now," said Dr. Vance.

Mickey laughed at the irony. Deep down he identified with this strange man. Ludwig was filled with pure genius, yet he had no constructive way of showing it.

"So you're telling me that he could walk out of this nut house today if he wanted to?"

"I would almost encourage it. Both of his parents died a decade ago, leaving their estate to him, including property which is currently rented. He's a relatively wealthy man who can do as he chooses. But he has simple needs and for the last decade he's been happy to live here," said Dr. Vance.

Mickey interjected, "But why here?"

"It's pretty simple, I'm his only friend. As you have no doubt worked out, he doesn't make friends easily."

That made sense. It was clear to Mickey that Ludwig didn't need friends. So what was so strange about that? He was no different. He'd only had two real friends in his life, Johnnie and Jules.

"Pity he can't talk much, or I'd have him in my next cubeball team," said Mickey. That sparked Dr. Vance's interest.

"He could meet you regularly on day release. Who knows, you both might be able to make it work." Mickey was unconvinced.

"How? He doesn't talk? The strategist has to direct the team, particularly in pressure situations."

"Ludwig could be more normal. Controlled medication could lift his cognitive capabilities."

"Then do it," said Mickey enthusiastically.

"There's a price. Ludwig's ability to remember music would diminish. At times Ludwig rejected the drugs preferring the beauty of his life with music. Since viewing your first cubeball game he's been torn. He saw firsthand how real life activities could be filled with beauty too. Often as he watched your matches he wished he could be there in the auditorium with you. It may not be obvious to you, but Ludwig has been excited that you have been at our centre for the last four weeks. So much so, he has returned to medication. He wanted to get to know you Mickey. He wants to understand where your perfect music comes from."

"I don't know myself. How can I help?"

"Just play the way you were born to. Let Ludwig work out the rest."

Mickey was beginning to hatch a new plan in his mind. He thought to share his ideas but Ludwig interrupted him.

"I've finished the music, Mickey." He passed his drawing to Mickey. Every shot played at the State Final was now on the paper. Mickey studied it. "You've got a hell of a memory my friend." It was a game imprinted on Mickey's memory too, but for reasons very different from Ludwig. That game would resonate through his life, like a cue-ball smashing the triangle of red balls to all corners of the cube. One single event would create a chain of events that could not be controlled, once unleashed.

State Final

MICKEY'S EIGHTEENTH YEAR STARTED brightly. He had become a rising star of cubeball and he was earning good money. He bought the car of his dreams and had rented his own apartment near Jefferson Park, close to where his team practice, Chris's Billiards. Most important of all, he was in love with Jules. Mickey was living the life he'd always dreamed of. Jules had given him the faith to be his best. Mickey always wanted to play well, but now he had someone he wanted to be proud of him.

Mickey wanted to live with Jules too, but she did not. For all her self-assuredness and the many happy times they had shared, she harboured mixed emotions. There was sadness in her that could not be shaken. Ironically, her sadness mainly came to the fore, soon after their happiest moments.

They spent most of their time together at Velvet Underground. Jules was a committed gamer, so she spent a lot of her own time there. Mickey usually joined her for a recreational game they could both enjoy, before spending a night and Mickey's apartment. It was late afternoon and Mickey was sharing a 'search and destroy' mission with Jules in Velvet Underground. As usual, Jules led Mickey through the maze of castles and forests that surrounded them. Mickey enjoyed the games, but he mostly enjoyed watching Jules as she easily navigated the many challenges they faced, as part of the game. She lived for the thrills that the gamer life provided.

"Take this," she said, handing Mickey a supp to swallow. "We'll soon be tackling the hardest section and I want us ready."

"We already took one," replied Mickey.

"This is a really difficult challenge. The supp will give you an edge."

"How about we skip the game for a while?"

"Are you tired, Mickey?"

"No. It's not that. It's just that we've been apart for over a week. I missed you."

Jules smiled knowingly. She could melt Mickey's heart with her sweet smile. She kissed his lips softly. "Only for you, babe. I know a cool bar hidden in this game. Only the true gamers know this place. Like to see it?"

"You know I do," Mickey replied, holding her close to him.

Riley felt Mickey's desire for her, as they embraced. "You have missed me," she said with a cheeky giggle.

These were the times Mickey loved. Riley forgot about her gamer life, as he forgot his cubeball life. They could just be together. They became lovers soon after they met. Passion took over early, perhaps too early. For despite their strong sexual attraction, neither really knew each other that well. Mickey accepted all too easily that they meet irregularly, so that they could both continue their 'other life', without each other.

Their physical closeness strained under the weight of many unresolved problems, the main being, Riley's obsession with gaming. Mickey, more than most, understood obsession. Cubeball was his life. But he always encouraged Jules to watch him play, whereas Jules rarely invited him to her gaming nights. She would go missing for days, sometimes weeks without contacting him. After nearly a year together, their relationship was straining from their irregular time together. They were slowly drifting apart.

Their special night out a month before he was to compete in the state championships was a pivotal turning point.

"You're late," said Mickey, clearly annoyed. Jules kissed his cheek warmly.

"Sorry, the game ran over."

"We'd planned this for some time, Jules. Just once...."

"I know, Mickey. I did think of you. I nearly forfeited the game, but it was my chance to reach the top one thousand list. I thought you'd understand."

"We planned this. You promised me. After waiting an hour and not hearing from you, I nearly gave up and headed to practice."

"Mickey, I'm sorry."

Mickey hugged Jules. He knew there would be no benefit from arguing further. He held her tight, wanting to say more about her behaviour, but not.

"And I did win. I'm officially rated 993rd in the world!"

"Then we will celebrate in style. Where would you most like to be on such a special occasion?" Jules' crystal, blue eyes lit up with expectation.

"The Galaxia?"

"Yes, the very one. I've booked a table. If we walk fast, we'll make it on time."

"Oh that's so sweet! You know I've always wanted to go there," said Jules, before kissing him warmly. Mickey held her close, forgetting his earlier irritation. He loved to surprise Jules and see her pretty face fill with joy.

"I have another surprise too."

"Tell me now," insisted Jules.

"No, I'll tell you during the meal," replied Mickey. Jules playfully slapped him on the chest, before taking his arm. They were just a short stroll to the Galaxia, one of the most expensive restaurants in the city.

They entered the tree-lined courtyard that shaped the natural entry into the restaurant. Natural silver-birch trees and lush grass made for a naturally, calming enclosure. It was a world away from the high-tech wizardry that made the Galaxia the place to be seen. Mickey and Jules were younger than the typical clientele that dined there, but he was relatively wealthy now, from his many cubeball victories.

Mickey guided Jules to one of the benches under a large tree and took out a rette.

"Something to make the night more memorable," said Mickey. He lit the rette and shared it with Jules. She looked at Mickey questioningly, before inhaling the rette.

"This is new?"

"It's an epicure rette. You will not forget dinner," he said, taking the rette and inhaling it deeply. He then kissed Jules lips. His taste buds were already enhanced by the rette. Erotic desires filled him as he felt the warm sensation of Jules soft lips on his. Jules responded with feeling.

"Kiss me again just like that," she said. Mickey kissed her cheek softly, before holding her close to him.

"We should always be like this my darling. Let's make a pact on our special night. No more arguments," said Mickey. Jules brushed her lips on Mickey's cheek, before squeezing tight against his body. "Let's eat, Mickey."

The restaurant was filled with the scent of spice. Rette vapour swirled through the air creating candescent swirls around the cubebit lit tables. Most of the diners consisted of couples, but they were much older than Mickey and Jules.

"Johnny raved about this place," said Mickey, before they both sat down. An overly attentive waiter handed them their menus.

"Thanks, give us a few minutes," said Mickey, with a false smile.

"The prices are crazy. You can't afford this," said Jules, but Mickey waved his hand.

"If I win the state final, we'll be able to dine here every night."

"And if you don't?"

"Let me worry about that." Jules shook her head and studied the menu.

"I've never heard of any of these dishes. It's written in French," she said.

"Yeah, it's kind of weird. But it's okay. Johnnie told me their best dishes, so you just relax and let me handle everything." He pulled out another rette. This one was a relaxant. He lit it, took two deep draws and then handed it to Jules. Mickey could tell that she was still hyped from her gaming. Her cheeks had a violet flush, a sure sign of narcs. He thought about asking but held back. Jules looked out of place in her street jacket, tee-shirt and jeans, which accentuated her discomfort. She drew heavily on the rette as she gazed out at their surroundings.

"I feel like I'm at Cinderella's ball."

Thirty other couples were enjoying various stages of their meals. The tables were lit up by their 'story-meals'. Specially developed cubebits framed each plate with holographic images that lit up their meals. Images floated around the plated cuisine. Some were log fire images that appeared to warm the meals. Others were elaborate deserts that appeared to float in light snow fall.

"It's beautiful, Mickey."

"Nothing but the best for our anniversary," said Mickey, taking Jules hand and gently kissing her slender fingers. She smiled at him, before looking out again to the sea of cubebits. The images had a calming effect on her as she drew again on her rette.

The waiter returned. "Would you care to order now, Mr. Allen?"

"Yes. I've been told your French inspired dish is the specialty of the house?"

"Yes. It is a traditional French cuisine from Lyon and our most popular dining experience."

"Two please and a bottle of your Chateau Lafite-Rothchild," said Mickey, pointing to the wine on the menu.

"An excellent choice, sir," said the waiter, politely collecting the menus before leaving.

"This is too much, you..." Jules stopped mid-sentence. Small tears formed. "Mickey, you deserve a better girlfriend than me. You're going to be a champion."

"You think I'll win?"

"Yes I do. But if you don't win this tournament, it will be one soon. You're blessed with a special gift." Mickey reached out and held Jules hand.

"Why are you crying?"

"I'm happy for you. Your dream is coming true."

"What about our dream? Is it coming true?" Mickey asked.

Jules withdrew her hand to reach for a tissue in her coat pocket. Mickey recognised the top of a narc container as she reached for her tissue.

"You've helped me so much with my gaming, but I'll never be the best in my sport, like you."

"You could be. I can't match you. You've got quick reflexes and concentration..." Jules cut Mickey short.

"Don't do that, Mickey." Jules glared at Mickey now, making him regret his words.

"It's easy for you. You can pick up a cue and play like a master. You forget that most people have to work harder than you to win. If gamers like me devote all our young lives to practice, we might get lucky and break into an 'A-list' and earn enough money to survive. Then we have to compete with narc-enhanced competitors. What then?"

"You don't have to..."

"Don't say it, Mickey. Don't start that lecture again. Just because you can beat anybody without narcs, doesn't mean us mere mortals can. Gaming is saturated with narcs."

Two waiters interrupted them. One carried the wine and the other the meals. The Chateau was placed on a small cubebit on the side of the table. The opened champagne bottle was enclosed by a holograph. Snow lit by evening moonlight gently fell around it, creating a romantic setting. Both meals sat on holographic generated embers that crackled beneath the sumptuous quenelles. The soft light radiated from the two dishes casting a warm hue on Jules face. Her eyes shone from the moonbeam she gazed longingly toward.

"I wish it was always like this, Mickey." She held out her slender hand for his. Mickey caressed her hand affectionately with his.

"It could be, baby. I cherish you. You know that don't you?"

Jules smiled warmly at him as she briefly gazed into his eyes. Then she turned her attention to her meal.

"I don't know whether to eat it or gift-wrap it." They both laughed, before she gave a puzzled look at her assortment of silver cutlery.

"Use the largest knife and fork," he said, before picking up the correct cutlery. "The ones on the outside."

"Johnnie told you how to use the cutlery, too?"

"Yes he may be an asshole most of the time, but having him as my manager has its benefits."

"You're too hard on him, Mickey. He works hard for the team's success."

Mickey scoffed. "You don't know Johnnie half as well as me."

They devoured their quenelle and watched the embers slowly fade as their delicious feast disappeared from the plates. The waiter poured the last of the Chateau into their glasses and the holograph changed from the moonlit snow into a candle, as he removed the bottle from the table.

"You said there was another surprise?" said Jules.

"I've booked a room for us. We stay here tonight."

"No, Mickey. The meal was expensive. To stay here is too much."

"Nothing's too much for you, my love. I booked the chalet room."

Jules had heard of the chalet room. It was the most expensive in the hotel. The room was surrounded by a purpose built cubebit that could recreate the most famous chalets in the French Alps.

"It's a beautiful thought, Mickey, but I can't do this. I don't want you to waste any more credits tonight."

"It's my credits to spend as I wish. It's our anniversary, Jules. I wanted to do something special."

"Mickey, I didn't come here to celebrate." Tears formed in her eyes, which she brushed away with a tissue.

"You make this so hard," she said, drawing deep breaths.

"What's so hard about spending a night in a beautiful French chalet? I would have thought..." Jules cut Mickey short.

"Enough, Mickey. I'm not staying with you tonight. I'm not staying with you any more nights. I'm leaving. This relationship is not good for me or you."

"Jules, you're just emotional tonight. It's probably the mix of supps and ..." Mickey stopped mid-sentence.

"Go on, say it. The narcs. Say it."

"I can help you."

Jules stood up. She threw the serviette on the table and stared at Mickey for a time, before speaking.

"You can't help me, Mickey. You never could. But I've found someone who can. This is my one chance and I have to take it now."

Mickey sat back in his chair, too stunned to speak. Sadness swelled in his eyes.

"I'm doing this for both of us, Mickey. This relationship will only bring pain. Jules looked away from Mickey, out to the restaurant. "Look how happy these couples are."

"Just like us, babe."

"Do you think so?" Jules said. She picked up her napkin to brush tears from her cheeks. She stared at the table, seemingly summoning the courage to say more. "I'm not happy, Mickey. I have enjoyed our times together, but I don't want to continue with this. I think it's better we part."

Mickey wanted to say something, but the words wouldn't come. An uneasy, sad silence engulfed the table. Jules touched Mickey's hand softly, more in sorrow than affection, before she uttered the words she had to say that night.

Goodbye Mickey." Jules turned and walked determinedly to the door, not looking back. Mickey wanted to run after her, but he held back. She had done this many times before and had always returned. However on what was meant to be their most special night, she did not.

Young Mickey sat in the dressing room of 'The Cauldron'. He was about to play the game of his life, one he'd imagined a thousand times over as he practiced. He'd spent long years perfecting his skills and dreaming about this moment. He was ready to show the world. But there was one problem - Johnnie.

"By all means, play the game of your life. Just lose!"

Johnnie's words rang in his mind, demands uttered just days before the biggest game of his life, angering but not surprising him. All Johnnie cared for was money and power. The beauty of the craft had long vanished in Johnnie's mind. Johnnie was only happy when he controlled people.

Mickey too felt his suffocating control. At first he justified Johnnie's demands as 'one off', but in truth his friend never gave without expecting a lot in return. Every favour was counted by Johnnie and stored for later repayment and usually when there were high stakes and maximum impact. At first Mickey held strong against Johnnie's outrageous demands.

"I'll play my game tonight, no matter what amount of money you lose!"

Mickey was unaffected by Johnnie's threats. He wanted to win, not only for himself, but for Jules. He'd accepted she needed to leave him, but he hoped that she may again support him as a friend. This was the biggest match of his life and he held out that Jules may still come to see him compete. He checked his cubebit again.

Where are you, Jules? He thought, as he tried one more time to call her. He'd heard Jules' erratic behaviour had snowballed into chaos over the last month. A deadly blend of drugs and alcohol had left her dangerously exposed. They had not met since their dinner at the restaurant.

Can't you at least tell me you're watching the final? Mickey sent a text. He waited until the last minute for a reply but his cubebit remained silent. For one moment Mickey felt like leaving the Cauldron and abandoning the game, but he was a cubeball player and professionals controlled their emotions. He breathed deeply and calmed himself before he made his fateful journey toward the playing arena, ready for the match of his life. Win and he'd be guaranteed a CWC contract.

The Cubeball World Circuit was run by a powerful and wealthy organisation. It managed the top players in the world and screened live worldwide, guaranteeing a viewing audience of over a billion people for their final. The best players won lucrative contracts to tour the world circuit, which was incentive enough for the 'up and comers' such as Mickey. The top one hundred ranked players joined the international pro circuit and instantly became global 'house-hold names' competing for vast prize monies all around the world.

This was Mickey's first game in The Cauldron, although he wasn't new to its gladiatorial atmosphere. He'd watched every championship either live or on vid-cube since he was a young boy. The stadium held ten thousand fans, which was not a lot by football standards. But there was something unique about its design, combining intimacy, acoustics and state of the art technology to create a feeling like no other. As challenger, Mickey was the first player to walk into the arena.

"Ladies and gentleman, boys and girls...introducing...the rising star of cubeball, Mickey...Allen," said the announcer as the spot lights poured down from high to the young challenger. Mickey stood alone in the bright light's rays. He was caught off guard by the noise generated from his introduction.

He had sat in the Cauldron as a fan and heard the power of ten thousand screaming fans, but never directed at him. The roar rushed from the seats high in the arena down toward him like the approach of a giant wave in the distance. His senses rippled when he felt the energy of the fans' cheers crash around him.

Mickey's first reaction was to duck, which embarrassed him. He half smiled at the silliness of his reaction. So he quickly feigned a boxer's duck and weave before smiling cheekily at his fans. Then another wave of energy engulfed him. The light of a thousand cubebits flashed before his eyes. Initial shock turned to exhilaration as he absorbed the energy. The powerful wave of light and sound almost lifted him as he walked to the playing arena.

Of course, the inner sanctum wasn't some simple pool table, set in a well lit rectangular playing area, like the old days of Snooker. The modern cubeball arena was more an elaborate television set. A busy hive of activity surrounded the inner sanctum, taking up the equivalent of three tennis courts. The playing arena was divided into three distinct areas.

Mickey approached the first, the Gaming Area, where the punters could place bets in between games. Gambling was an elaborate system in its own right where a bet could be placed on anything from the biggest break to the match result. The floor space accommodated the willing punters who gambled in between games. Many punters placed bets directly on their cubebits, but ritual still played its part with 'face to face' betting just as popular. Many queues had formed but most fans had lined the barricades that bordered the red carpet walk way Mickey headed down.

"Go Mickey...take him out in seven games, laddie," came one cry from a punter holding a hand full of betting receipts and waving them as if they were already worth a thousand credits.

Mickey looked beyond the playing arena to the far side of the inner sanctum, the third area. Everything looked different from the floor of the arena, particularly the vast array of screens that made up the technological viewing platform for the fans. From the stands, the giant vidcubes were impressive but from the floor they dwarfed him, seemingly floating more than eight stories above the ground. The two largest vid-cubes were twenty metre cubes and provided the fans an alternate view of the live action. They were equipped with 3D technology that provided real time digital information to assist the 'gaming' and 'game play' audience. Beneath the two large cubes were four smaller ones that added game odds for the gambling audience.

At the centre of the 'inner sanctum' was the playing arena. The three-metre playing cube was imposing. At opposing sides sat the player's teams, the *strategist*, *technologist* and team manager, surrounded by equipment befitting a Skydome flight launch pad. Sam and Riley were so busy with preparations they only briefly noted Mickey's arrival into the playing arena.

Mickey stood with the announcer on a platform bathed in strobed and coloured lights that created a tic-a-tape feel. *Breathe deeply* he told himself, controlling emotions that could threaten his ability to play well. It was *show time* now as the announcer built further excitement for the full house and the one billion viewers.

"Played in the state league for just one year...twenty-four games...twenty-four wins...undefeated...national rising star winner...Mickey Allen," said the announcer, baritone like.

And then the loudest roar hit him, like a train had just torn through the steel structure of The Caldron toward him. Mickey could only wave and smile at a crowd he could not see, except for the explosion of the camera flash firestorm.

To his relief, the announcer directed him to join his team as the excited crowd waited for the state and national champion to enter. Unexpectedly, Mickey was comforted by the sight of Riley sitting with Sam and Johnnie. Normally he would hide such affection, but he needed something to level him and bring him back from the euphoria of the moment. Nothing less was required to play well.

He could tell Riley felt his affection too, smiling briefly before her stony-faced look of determination returned. Her eyes focused back on the job at hand as she readied the technology for Sam. Sam was equally focused as he reviewed potential power plays.

"All set?" asked Johnnie, getting an affirmative nod from Sam. He then shook Mickey's hand, no doubt seeking equal share of Mickey's limelight. This match was an opportunity for his team, but Johnnie had other involvements in the industry, most of which Mickey did not know or care for.

"Make it a great game Mickey, just get the result I asked for...okay?" said Johnnie smiling broadly and slapping his champion on the back, belying his true feelings. Mickey returned an equally forced smile.

"Glad you're in the front seat to see the result," said Mickey belligerently. Johnnie maintained the smile, but only until the lights turned from them to the champion who was about to enter the auditorium.

"Fuck this up and we're finished...understand?" Mickey believed him for he was sure Johnnie would have his own mother killed if she crossed him. There was something in him, a determination to get his way no matter the cost. It was a kind of madness, or a gamblers instinct that drove him to risk all to win.

Mickey defiantly turned his back on Johnnie and walked to the playing cube to pick up his cue. It looked more like a sword in his hands as he glared at Johnnie. *Never bet against me*, he thought, his determined gaze not wavering. He would defy Johnnie's command to lose this match. Mickey was back in the zone now. He was focused on winning and ready to show the world that an artist had come to play.

Johnnie seemed unaffected, almost cocky. Then the lights exploded around the inner sanctum for a second time. But Mickey's gaze was not diverted from his manager. Johnnie drew his cubebit from his pocket to make a call all the while holding his gaze on Mickey. He talked with someone, but gazed at Mickey with a mocking scorn on his face. Who was he calling? For an instant Mickey wanted to know but he would not be bribed. *I win tonight* he thought. Then he turned toward the playing cube, resigned that he would not look Johnnie's way again until his victory.

The first six frames were a blur, for try as he might, the atmosphere-induced euphoria drowned Mickey. The more seasoned champion Ricky Calen, recognised Mickey's 'big game' nerves and took full advantage, offering him no chances. Even the fans had little sympathy, cheering loudly for a quick kill from the champion who held a convincing six-nil advantage. Mickey was staring at an embarrassing seven to nil loss. Worse still, he remained unsettled as he was about to open the seventh game. Knowing this, he delayed his opening shot, trying to settle his big game nerves.

It was at least quieter now as many disgruntled gamblers had left their seats, no doubt trying to cut their losses from earlier bets placed on the young challenger. Mickey glanced across to Johnnie for the first time since the match started. At least he was happy, as he readied to win a small fortune on his loss. He saw Johnnie's smug smile as he joked with one of his punter friends. Then miraculously, the thought of thwarting his manager's money driven strategy made him angry enough to overcome his nerves.

Mickey strode toward the cube as if he was playing on the old family table at home. He visualised its worn felt and trade mark tears before making his perfect opening. The cue-ball purred toward the back left-hand side red ball, disturbing just two reds. Then it floated back to the front wall behind the undisturbed yellow ball.

This he repeated six times, making no attempt to play attacking shots. Mickey was more concerned with finesse and finding his touch. Jammed against the cushion, the champ played repeated quality replies, demonstrating his considerable guile, spin and touch to play without penalty. But then on his sixth stroke, he disturbed four of the reds. At that, Mickey made his move. It was a break full of bravado, given one error would end his tournament. But he'd found his natural game again.

"Power Play," said Mickey without consulting Sam. It seemed a desperate call as the odds of a strong break were low. If he made an error, his opponent would have the next break as a double point play, too.

Sam reacted, fearful that Mickey had made the wrong choice. But Mickey ignored him. The crowd had hushed, too. Not because they thought Mickey would win. More that they believed the young star's run of twenty four straight victories would come to an end. Of course, Mickey had other plans. From this point on he'd play 'his game', win, lose or draw.

In a display of skill and confidence that belied his years, Mickey potted every ball – ten reds and six colours, with a double point power play bonus, totalling a perfect score of two hundred and fourteen points. The break stunned the audience. He had achieved a maximum possible score, but the speed in which he scored it was a lightning five minutes and twenty three seconds. Whether he won the match or not, Mickey's break would be replayed around the world as the quickest ever.

Mickey had also shown versatility – a slow, defensive, patient opening game full of finesse, followed by an attacking 'hurricane' like style to clear the table. The next five games went much the same way as Mickey continued to astound. Slow cautious shots until his opponent made one error. He immediately followed with another power-play and large breaks which were sufficient to claim the game without further play.

The spell-bound crowd were caught up in the emotion of the greatest comeback in the history of the championship tournament. The crowd noise reached fever pitch by the end of the twelfth game. The challenger and champ were tied at six games each. And the screaming would have continued unabated except Johnnie called for an unexpected twenty minute time out.

They were alone in the change room. The doors were locked. Sam and Riley remained in The Cauldron, fine tuning their equipment for the deciding game.

"You've showed the world what you're capable of. They've noticed. You'll win contracts no matter what happens in this game. So it doesn't matter whether you win, lose or draw!" pleaded Johnnie.

"So if I'm such a star, why the fuck would you bet your house against me? Don't hold me accountable for your fucked up life!" said Mickey defiantly.

"It doesn't work that way in my world. You think this game is all about skill? The best player wins? But it can't always be that way. How do you think you got into this tournament at all? Do you remember all those fucking small tournaments? Do you remember the 'wild card' entries?"

"Yeah I won'em, that's what happened!"

"I paid big money to influential people! That's how you fucking got into those tournaments. I used my money, not yours, you ungrateful fuck!" Mickey looked away. So Johnnie stood over him.

"I already bet my house on you to just get you here. But do you care? No you have better ideas! Mr Righteous has come here to win on his skill! You didn't spend any of your money on that, did you? Johnnie will cover me! Johnnie will spend a small fortune on the technology to make this team. And what do you contribute? You spend your money on some pathetic junkie bitch and let your one and only friend take up the tab for everything else!"

Mickey could ignore Johnnie's tirade about his selfishness. He'd heard that before. But he couldn't ignore his taunts about Jules.

"Don't bring her into this. She has nothing to do with our team."

"I've got every right to bring her into this. You always claim how special she is to you. But if she's that special, where the fuck is she?" Johnnie turned his gaze to the four corners of the empty change room. "Where is she Mickey?"

"What's that got to do with anything? She's not on our team."

"Well for one, you've won large cash prizes. Where's your money?"

Mickey said nothing. What could he say? It was true he had spent most of his winnings on Jules, to fuel her addiction.

"You've given most of it to your so called girlfriend. And where is she now? She's never been to any of your matches. She doesn't care about what we have built. So now you have a chance to make one sacrifice to get us financial and what do you do? You say no because your skill is more important than the very people who have supported you!"

Mickey knew a lot of what Johnnie said was true. Johnnie had risked a fortune to build the team. But playing cubeball was the only thing Mickey knew how to do. He lived for the game and he played better than anyone on the planet.

"It's all I know, Johnnie."

"Well unlearn...and fast. You win this game and we lose everything we have worked for as a team. And with no money how do you think your little girlfriend will survive? Just think about that!"

"Stop bringing her into this," said Mickey, but Johnnie talked over him.

"I'll bring her into this...she's fundamental to our problem. Besides, if you really love her think about this. Why hasn't she at least called you on the biggest night of your life?"

Mickey's concerns turned to fear. Johnnie knew where Jules was. "I can tell you why she hasn't called. While you've been walking around on the stage showing your 'god given' skills to the world, your so called girlfriend is ringing every dealer in town looking for a tear."

Mickey couldn't ignore Johnnie anymore. Jules had rung Johnnie that night, but not him. "Where is she?"

Johnnie smiled smugly. "Lose this game Mickey and I'll tell you." Then he left the room. Mickey immediately picked up his cubebit to call Jules again, but there was no answer. Mickey had never felt so alone.

8

Homecoming

Dr. Vance pointed Mickey to the chair beside his sister as he sat down opposite them behind his paper-filled desk. Riley forced a strained smile to both men as if they were passing acquaintances. Riley was dressed immaculately in conservative blue skirt, matching jacket, white business blouse and complemented by Italian leather shoes. Dr. Vance was about to speak when Riley's cubebit rang loudly, interrupting their meeting.

"I'm terribly sorry. I do have to take this call." Then she stepped outside.

Mickey smiled knowingly at Dr. Vance. Sure she had to take the call. It fitted her corporate persona. He thought w*hy couldn't she just turn her cubebit off once in a while?* But that was Riley. She was successful, in demand and too busy for anything else but her business associates.

"I have two papers for you both to sign. One for your release and one for Ludwig's day release," said Dr. Vance, not waiting for Riley's return.

Mickey quickly signed both papers as if it were a formality, still unsure whether Riley would cooperate with his plan. He wanted to walk out of that office and never talk to either Dr. Vance or Riley again. But Mickey sensed his meeting with Ludwig had been more than coincidence. The guy was crazy. That he knew. But there was something about his fanaticism for the game. He possessed a familiarity that intrigued him enough to want to see if teaming with him could work. Winning his sister's confidence was something else though. He distrusted her and despised the way she flaunted her wealth and power. It was as if she had become a clone of Johnnie Draxma. *Just a few months*, he thought to himself, he could handle her for a few months.

"Okay...well I'll step out for a while and let you talk to your sister. Let the nurse outside know when you're done and she'll call me," said Dr. Vance, leaving to attend patients.

"Yep, won't be long," said Mickey confidently, but feeling the opposite.

Even if he won Riley's support, could he really compete again? He hadn't played cubeball matches in a long time. He wasn't rated. Worse still, new players were entering the game with new technologies that lifted their capabilities. 'Tech-glasses' were developed that gave a player a better read of game strategies. Better eye implants were used giving them better scanning capabilities. Every game Mickey had ever played was recorded and analysed in detail, providing strategies to beat him. Combine that with tailored supps and the illegal planck and they were almost super human players. It was the new drugs that changed everything, for the worse.

Mickey had played his best cubeball because he had the ability to see the table in detail. But his was a natural ability rather than a skill driven by drugs. He still believed he had that 'sixth sense', but he wondered if he now needed more. The planck he used on the Skydome had a potency that tempted him to use more. And why not? He was penniless, homeless with one chance left. There was nothing left but to calm himself for Riley's rage and disappointment – *breathe deeply*, he said to himself as all good cubeball players do.

Riley walked into the office, stress in her voice and her eyes glued on her cubebit. She looked momentarily relieved though when she saw the Doctor had left his office. Mickey waited, knowing Riley would speak her mind.

"That was Stuart," she said, shooting him a glare.

"He sent me the cleaning and repair bill for your apartment," she said, waiting for Mickey's usual belligerent response.

Mickey wanted to respond to his kid sister like he didn't care. Yeah the rich kid, who made good, but also the sister who deserted her friends when they needed her. He wanted to tell her too, but he was in a corner that he needed to get out of. He had to eat humble pie and they both knew it.

"Thanks Riley," he muttered, just audibly.

Riley looked to be momentarily taken aback before she responded. "What were you thinking, Mickey? That was a friend of mine. He did me and you a special favour."

Geez, when did she ever give a fuck about friends? Mickey thought.

"I wasn't thinking, I was wrong...I'm uhh...you know...I'm sorry." Then he quickly changed the subject.

"But I want to make it up to you, Riley. I've had time to think things through in here. Let me make it up to you?"

Riley sat quietly, appearing to consider her response. "Okay, Mickey. Tell me how you think you could possibly make it up to me after all the fuckups you've made in your life."

Mickey too, considered his words. Riley was justifiably mad, but he saw a familiar look in her expression, a kind of hope in her eyes, that told him she wanted to believe him. This he knew was driven more by guilt than any notion of love, and Mickey always played to it.

"I want to compete again. But this time I'll do it differently. Business won't come first and definitely no manager like Johnnie."

"That's your plan? How do you expect to compete? Do you realise that small local competitions have high entry fees to play in, let alone the larger competitions."

"I can still compete, Riley. With the right team, we could beat the best."

"It's been ten years, Mickey."

"I know. But I've kept up with all the major match-plays. I know all the top hundred competitors' game-plans and I know I can beat them."

"I've heard this before." Riley looked unimpressed. She cast a dismissive glance at him, before turning her attention to her cubebit.

"Look, I know I've let you down many times before. Hell, I initially returned here to borrow more credits from you. So, you're right to be suspicious. But something happened in this hospital. I'm not sure exactly what, but I do know that I met a guy who understands my skills." Riley shook her head in doubt.

"Go on."

"Fuck, you should meet this guy. He has perfect recall of every championship match I ever played."

"So what? Com can do that."

"It's more than that. He sees what I see when I play. No one else has been able to do that. Not even you." Riley lifted her gaze from her cubebit.

"That's because you never let anyone close enough to fully get you. Not even...." Riley stopped mid-sentence. She turned her cubebit off and gave her full attention to Mickey.

"Spell out what you want."

"I need a month, maybe two. Let me practice with him. Then I'll know for sure."

"Where did you have in mind?"

"I hear you have a table at your place?" Mickey sat back. He dared not risk saying any more. Riley's demeanour was stern as she deliberated her decision.

"One month and that's only because I'll be away for most of it. Not a day more. When I return, I expect you and your new wonder strategist to impress me, or you're out. Clear?" Mickey raised his hands defensively. He was in no position to argue.

Mickey walked through the expansive entry to his sister's home and beamed a smile toward her.

"This place is huge," said Mickey, surprisingly hugging his sister.

Mickey wasn't exaggerating. His sister lived in opulence. The two storeys home was shiny new, with impressive two door marble entrance and a grand wrap around staircase to the second floor. Mickey gazed at the opulence. He was about to follow his sister, when he realised Ludwig had not joined them. His attention was taken by something outside in the front manicured garden.

"Ludwig, this way," said Mickey impatiently.

But Ludwig's attention was drawn to some minor detail, doubtless an irrelevance to any normal person but important to him.

"Looks like he's counting something...the plants maybe," said Riley.

Mickey laughed. "Yeah, in the car he kept studying the number plates on all the cars. He kept count of everyone that passed us and then he claimed to cross reference them to their first letter. He thought there was some kind of hidden code that could help him find his way around town. This is the guy that's going to develop my game plan!"

"You told him that the arrangement was temporary?"

"I told him, don't worry. I'll have a new place by then." Undeterred, Mickey shrugged off her concerns. He was more excited by the prospects of practicing with Ludwig, who finally joined them.

"So where's the cubeball room?"

Riley had bragged about it without exaggeration as she proudly led Mickey through a number of grand rooms, to her 'billiard room' as she liked it called. It was aptly named as it was tastefully decorated in the old style, free of technology and surrounded by memorabilia of all the old billiard and snooker champions. Dozens of framed photos of the stars from yesteryear adorned the oak panelled walls. Hurricane Higgins and Rocket Ronnie were just a few of the stars from the last century displayed. Mickey had adored watching their old games as a boy.

In the centre of the room stood a restored antique billiard table, masterfully crafted to mint condition. The table alone would have cost a small fortune. Money was seemingly not an issue for her these days. Mickey examined the table for some time, sliding his hand gently across its imported felt top. *Perfectly balanced*, he thought, not needing to play a single stroke to know its roll was pure and straight. It was the type of table both Riley and Mickey dreamed of having in their family sunroom at home. Mickey held back his tears, but only just.

"I didn't realise you loved the game this much." He studied the magnificent table before finally rolling a ball across its surface. The cueball rolled true and stopped a centimetre short of the far cushion.

"It's....wonderful, Riley." Then he rolled a second ball. This time it came to rest within half a centimetre of the far cushion.

"Keep it that way. This room and this home are special to me."

Mickey firmly crashed a third ball into the other two balls, lifting his gaze from the table. "When do you fly out?"

"In exactly a week, but I already told you that." Looking mildly annoyed, she led Mickey to the adjoining room, complete with bedroom and ensuite. This would be Mickey's sleeping quarters for the month. Ludwig was to start with three 'day visits' for the first week to see how he'd cope. Mickey was eager to settle Ludwig in quickly. Even though time was limited, Mickey was confident he'd know if they could work as a team by month's end. He knew it was a long shot, but something in Ludwig's game sense sparked a familiar feeling he once had for the great game. And what better way to test it then on an old style table where skill was what counted not technology.

Mickey and Ludwig quickly settled into a training routine, much to Riley's consternation. Fortunately, she was too busy with travel preparations to make her feelings known. In fact, Riley arrived home late most nights after a number of long preparatory meetings with clients. But not so late that she didn't find Mickey still practicing in the billiard room.

"Don't you ever stop, brother dear?"

"I could say the same about you," retaliated Mickey, before hanging up the cue for the night.

"I need a tea, before I get some sleep. Like to join me?" Riley asked.

"Yeah, I can't sleep anyway." He followed her to the expansive kitchen. Riley looked tired and why wouldn't she be? He didn't recall her taking a break from her consultancy in many years. She was always driven by her work. Even as a little girl she had ambition. Mickey regretted that he hadn't helped his kid sister enough. As her elder brother he'd allowed her to be overly influenced by Johnnie during her early formative years.

He knew Johnnie would drive his kid sister hard. He'd reward her, but there would always be a price to pay. Of course, Riley lapped it up, working diligently on developing game technology. But Johnnie soon enticed Riley to develop gamer technology and then accounts technology for his growing business. She did a deal with the devil alright. Mickey had made similar mistakes early on, but he never strayed into Johnnie's murky business dealings. He'd warned her many times too. But that fell on deaf ears. Riley had a latent talent for business and an eagerness to learn, no matter the consequences.

"How'd loony Ludwig go today?" Riley asked as she passed a hot tea to Mickey.

"I've got my work cut out. But you wouldn't believe his memory for games."

Riley sat opposite Mickey with her tea and sandwiches.

"Like some?" She offered.

"Nah, won't sleep."

"So from the little you told me, your plan is to get a 'wild card' and compete in the national championships?" Mickey felt an argument brewing, but he was in no mood to give her the satisfaction.

"Yep, that's the plan. It's two months away and by then I should have a good idea whether Ludwig is up to it."

"Shit, you never listened to Sam. What does it matter if you have a good strategist?"

"Yeah, I learned that lesson the hard way. They sure found a way to beat me in the end."

"So how does a good memory beat today's superior technology?"

Mickey thought to avoid her jibes by going to bed. But for the first time in a long time, he felt confident his plans could work. Sure it was the smallest of opportunities, but something about Ludwig changed his outlook.

"You gotta see this guy. It's more than memory. I can't place it, but there's a familiarity between us. It's like he understands me when I play. He knows the shot I'll take before I have even thought about it. It's spooky."

"Well, I won't see him for a month, Dubai is calling. Just remember what I already told you. Entry fees into championship competitions are exorbitant. I won't waste good money on you, if you can't show me how good you are on my return," said Riley.

There was a strained pause between them, which happened more often than not. Although Mickey felt she wanted to say more. He could always read her face when she had a secret. She would pause and look away, as if she were debating whether to reveal her honest or contrived thoughts.

"Johnnie's over there you know. In Dubai," she blurted, seemingly regretting her words immediately.

Mickey sniggered knowingly. Riley hadn't uttered his name for years, yet he'd always suspected their alliance remained. Her wealth reinforced it. Riley's lifestyle meant she had serious connections. And the top of the tree in cubeball was Johnnie Draxma. Mickey wanted to say more, plenty more, but it would have to wait. He sat there expressionless, quietly studying his tea cup. He gently pushed the tea cup toward Riley, before getting out of the chair.

"Give him my very best regards," said Mickey, sarcastically. He retired for the night claiming tiredness. But he didn't sleep much that night. His dark past had roared back into his life.

Mickey woke from his fitful sleep late morning, to the sound of knocking at the front door. What began as taps progressively turned louder and insistent. Mickey knew it was Ludwig.

"Okay...okay I hear you," screamed Mickey in the hope he'd stop. But Ludwig continued on undeterred, louder if that was possible. Ludwig wasn't one for social niceties. He would have tapped for another hour and cared little about annoying anyone within earshot. Mercifully, Mickey opened the door before he knocked it down.

"This better be an emergency!" said Mickey.

Ludwig looked blankly at Mickey not understanding his inference.

"It's eleven o'clock, the time we arranged."

"So it is," said Mickey, surprised he had slept in so late.

"I'm just about to eat. Care to join me?"

"No thank you, I had breakfast at the hospital. Dr. Vance organised a taxi for three o'clock this afternoon," said Ludwig, making sure he made Mickey aware. Ludwig had a disturbed look on his face. No doubt, leaving the CHERCH was a challenge for his new cubeball team member.

"That sounds like a plan. Well let's get you to the cubeball room." Mickey felt unsure how he should respond to Ludwig's disjointed thinking. He quickly guided him to the room to show Ludwig where he would work.

"I shifted this small desk in here for you. There are plenty of blank drawing papers and pencils, too."

Ludwig calmed somewhat at the site of the desk and placed his 'drawing box' on it. Doctor Vance had told Mickey that above all else, Ludwig valued familiarity, both with his surroundings and in his routines.

"I won't be long. I just have to shower and eat. Will you be okay?" said Mickey, nervously surveying the room for items that may agitate Ludwig.

Ludwig didn't answer, preferring to arrange his papers and pencils in an orderly fashion so that he could commence drawing his game patterns. Mickey watched him for a time. Ludwig never seemed to worry about being watched. Once he withdrew into his world of music, nothing else seemed to matter.

His desk organised, Ludwig turned his attention to the grand billiard table. The coloured balls fascinated him. It was as if he had never seen a billiard table. Perhaps he hadn't? Mickey thought. Maybe he'd only watched cubeball on the vidcube? Mickey didn't bother asking. He wouldn't answer anyway. So he left Ludwig to his thoughts, to shower and eat breakfast. Could he partner a savant in the forthcoming national championships? Mickey laughed as he headed upstairs. In truth it was unlikely. Maybe the drugs had affected his judgement more than he'd care to admit? Or perhaps Riley was right. This was an act of desperation by a player who had peaked many years ago.

Ludwig was so taken by the sight of the championship table he never heard Mickey leave the room. In fact he only ever took notice when people asked him a direct question. Their conversational remarks never registered that they were talking to him.

Ludwig had watched every televised championship game Mickey had ever played. He'd seen his exhibition games on these antique tables. But nothing had prepared him for experiencing the actual feel of an antique billiard table. Vid-cube streams were realistic but it could not reveal the texture and feel of a real table.

He cautiously walked around the table, his open palm gliding over the playing surface felt. New sensations overwhelmed him. The texture of the surface was not smooth as he anticipated. It had a bristly unevenness that made him uncomfortable. Unlike normal people, Ludwig interpreted the world through symbols, both mathematical and musical. He found irregular images or patterns disturbing.

That's why cubeball fascinated Ludwig. The order and routine calmed and shielded him from the usual chaotic activities that filled the world.

From an early age he learned to block out the disorder of life, often sitting in the corner of a room with his eyes closed, gently rocking back and forth humming to himself. The swaying motion provided a natural relaxation. Predictability was Ludwig's coping mechanism. Cubeball's set rules played to a standard scoring mechanism that was predictable. What he did not realise until now, was that old style cubeball was not played on a perfect surface.

He always imagined the balls glided over a perfect surface. But this was not true. The surface was a myriad of fine felt fibres that rippled across his fingers and palm. It scratched his skin like the 'fire box' twisted his mind. He felt only pain. He stepped away and sat at his desk, refusing to look at the table again. He retreated into his mind and started to draw Mickey's state final championship. He closed his eyes and visualised that perfect game. Then he drew steadily, seeking comfort from the music those lines made in his mind.

That was Ludwig's life. He walked a tightrope every day of his life as he kept the chaos and disorder of life from his perfect world. But now an overwhelming feeling came over him. The wolf was at the door.

"That's better," said Mickey, shaved, showered and fed. He scanned the room, relieved that nothing had been dislodged or damaged by his unpredictable guest.

"What do you think of the table, Ludwig?" Mickey asked, not getting a reply.

Geez, he's in one of his meditative moods, thought Mickey. Ludwig was slowly drawing on a blank sheet of paper, in between long stints of closing his eyes, humming quietly to himself and rhythmically rocking back and forth on his chair. He glanced at Ludwig's drawing, which was immediately familiar to him. He was drawing the state final again. Mickey resigned himself to a quiet afternoon of match practice, with little input from Ludwig. So he turned his attention to the table and surveyed the balls that had been set up ready to start a game. He decided to re-enact that same final game, shot by shot. He, like Ludwig had a total recall of the match. Maybe in re-enacting the match, he might spark some interest from Ludwig. So he struck the exact shot he played in the final deciding game of the championship match. Ludwig didn't look up. Mickey looked at the table. The balls were exactly aligned as they were over a decade ago.

"How's that for an opening? Mickey looked to Ludwig for a response. No reply." "I said..." said Mickey raising his voice, but he stopped mid-sentence as Ludwig appeared to become more agitated as his rocking motion was more accentuated.

Mickey shook his head in frustration and turned his attention back to the playing table. He lightly brushed the side cushions as he walked right around the table, studying the balls. Standing behind the cue-ball, he looked to be contemplating his next shot, but his mind was firmly in the past. Instead of playing a shot, he threw his cue firmly at the scattered balls and walked out of the room, directly to Riley's bar, where he helped himself to a bottle of Scotch.

"Here's to Johnnie, my trusted and loyal manager and to Riley, my equally trustworthy kid sister." he said, before he downed the glass and filled another.

9

DOWNFALL

"*WELCOME BACK VIEWERS, WHERE we are screening live from the Chicago Cauldron. The stage is set for a gripping final game that has see-sawed all night. Rick Calen took a commanding lead early and then the young challenger, Mickey Allen, fought back. He seems to be on a role now, Vince?*" said Floyd, one of two cube-side commentators.

"*I think you're right, Floyd. He's played some fantastic cubeball, stunning the capacity crowd here tonight. More importantly, he's surprised Rick Calen. If Mickey maintains his form, we'll have a new Illinois champion and he'll be the youngest ever.*"

"*Thanks, Vince. Well, let's settle in folks for what should be an enthralling finish.*"

Young Mickey Allen had the national champion beaten. He could tell by the way he looked, or rather how he didn't look. A defeated player always removed their gaze from the cube and in particular their opponent. Mickey was in full flight, a deflating experience, even for a world class player like Calen. His only chance would be if Mickey lost his rhythm in the break between games.

But despite Johnnie's antagonism and his veiled threats, Mickey still felt unbeatable. Sure, he feared for Jules safety, but even Johnnie was not capable of threatening her life. Mickey commenced the final game much the same way as his previous six winning games. He played defensive but highly skilled shots that left the champ with no opening.

Six sublime shots turned to eight, ten, twelve, up to sixteen shots and counter shots which left the crowd hushed. Someone had to make an error and no one wanted to miss who would succumb to the mounting pressure.

Mickey revelled in the challenge but the longer the game went the more he worried about Jules. He readied himself for a seventeenth defensive play when he saw something in the pattern of the balls that made him consider a different riskier strategy. He could feign a shot that would appear a mistake, offering the champ an easy red but difficult colour. Calen would have a potential pink and opening to split the reds, but it would be a difficult high risk strategy. Mickey believed it a chance to make Johnnie believe he tried to lose the game.

The strategy grew large in his mind, a small gamble that he may lose, but he still played 'his game'. Mickey slowed the game. Then he looked Johnnie's way. They both shared a knowing glance. At that, Mickey made his fateful play, providing the smallest of openings to Calen. The game result would be determined by lady luck that night. The reigning champ would have to earn the championship using a high risk strategy. Mickey would miss a shot like this nine times out of ten. *Good odds*, he thought to himself as he sat down to observe his opponents counter play. The dice had been rolled.

Young Mickey's challenge was accepted. Calen attempted the high risk shot. The atmosphere around the cube engulfed it like the old days at the crucible. Everyone knew this was a gambler's play and the champ was not usually one to take such high risks. But Mickey had offered him one chance to end his 'hot run'.

"Power Play," said Calen confidently, copying Mickey's strategy. Doubling the points would most assuredly win the game for the player who didn't make a mistake. So there they both stood, striding the global stage, leaving the whole world breathless for one frame. A champion was about to make a bold statement, or a brash young challenger was about to take his place.

Mickey felt the weight of the circumstance but his mind turned to Johnnie's words. Was he bluffing as he so often did or was Jules in desperate trouble? In a way, Mickey didn't care if the champ succeeded or not. He just wanted the deciding frame over.

The champ cleaned up the first red ball and positioned on to the pink as well as anyone could. The all important shot on pink was as demanding as they get. The ball would have to be sunk into the top right hand pocket. The angle was difficult and allowed no room for error. Getting that done was half the story. The cue-ball had to be struck with exacting power and spin to strike three walls before dislodging the red balls sufficiently to open up the frame. Pin point accuracy, or lose. He also had to hit the triangle reds on the back right side so that the cue-ball spun away from the triangle rather than lodge into the pack of reds.

Mickey admired the champ's coolness under pressure. He took time to sight and prepare, but once he determined the shot, he struck confidently. His cue-ball hit the pink perfectly, squeezing it in to the narrow opening of the right side top hole. No error. The cue-ball ripped sideways with extreme spin across the table like a heat-seeking missile. First wall, second, third were struck at the right speed and angle. The cue-ball headed for the triangle of red balls at a diminished but sufficient pace. At first Mickey thought the cue-ball was too straight on the triangle, but the spin had sufficient power to hit the back right side of the triangle, dislodging four balls before the momentum of the spin continued it safely away from the red balls. The frame was open.

All Mickey could do was wonder what could have been as he watched the perfect shot played by his world class opponent. Could he have made that shot under pressure? He would never know. The remainder of the game was a formality as Calen developed a large enough break to win. Mickey didn't like losing, but the skill of Calen's shot on pink was sublime. He had issued a daunting challenge. Calen had gambled his skill against the possibility of losing with an inspirational break that he would never forget.

"Congratulations, stunning break," said Mickey graciously, shaking the winners hand. He wasn't sure whether the champ heard him as there was a thunderous noise of applause that surrounded them. But Mickey did hear the champ's words.

"Thanks Mickey, not half as good as the last six games you played. I expect we'll meet again," said the equally gracious champ.

The final celebrations wrapped up in a blur of supporters' cries, flashing lights and media obligations. Mickey met his commitments, but his mind remained on Jules. Fortunately, he was soon swept aside by the media as they moved to the champ. Mickey then confronted Johnnie, who was surrounded by his industry friends.

"That was a great game. So close," said Johnnie, consoling his man in front of the fans and his friends, keeping up false appearances. Mickey would have none of it, pressing him.

"Where is she?"

Johnnie knew his player well and replied quickly, knowing Mickey would not remain with his team that night.

"I know the place. Good luck finding her," he replied.

Mickey stood closer, threatening to cause a scene.

"She's in V.U."

"Velvet Underground? I might've known you'd try to pull that one, you prick!"

"I'm sorry to disappoint you, but it wasn't me this time. I wouldn't spend that kind of credit on anyone, least of all your girlfriend."

"Who then?"

"No idea. I tried to find out. But whoever it is, he has some serious connections. No one will tip me. She's disappeared into a black hole in V.U. Not even the law could find her. So good luck with your quest, but don't blame me if you can't find her."

Then Johnnie turned his back on Mickey, returning to his business associates.

Mickey knew exactly where to go. Velvet Underground was the place to where all serious gamers found their way, sooner or later. It hosted the 'search and destroy' class game Jules passionately competed in - Exoplanets. You could also obtain the most potent supps and rettes there. It had become the preferred location for all kinds of drugs, particularly the new crop of illegals. The best gamers teared on illegal narcs most of the time. How else could they be the best? But many who were not highly ranked played alongside them. Jules was one of them. Unlike the professional gamers, she was hooked on planck, not the game. Extreme focus was required to advance through the hundreds of Exoplanet grades. Mickey had played it with her and failed even at the elementary levels. Winning was beyond him, unless he plancked.

Jules plancked regularly. She spent most of her time lost in and around Exoplanets. And like most committed gamers, she got hooked on planck. A gamer's life was a constant challenge of handling the highs so that they could play like no other, but then counterbalancing the lows through rehabbing on supps and rettes. Velvet Underground was where the Exoplanet gamers played, rested and recovered from the demands of their game. V.U. felt like a whole other exoplanet designed to entice gamers to play long and hard. You could come into this place, play till on the verge of death and be fully fit in a day. The best treatments the world could offer were there – but at a price.

Mickey drove his car out of the stadium at speed through the heavy exiting traffic, ironically cursing those he tried to delight at the match. To make it worse, Jules still had not returned any of his calls.

He was convinced something had to be wrong...very wrong. He at least knew her general whereabouts. Of course it was one thing for him to know this, but it was another to actually locate her in the maze of underground tunnels that made up V.U. For the real subterranean world that hosted the holographic digital site couldn't be more different. V.U. hosted the best retrieval hospital in the solar system. Ironically, those who sought it had to endure the harsh 'real environment' that few would tolerate. But this is where the gamers came to get their hands on every supp, rette or technology implant that was unobtainable in the legal gaming world. It was Las Vegas in a cave.

"Welcome to Velvet Underground, sir. How can I help?"

"Thanks, I'll take a suit, tech glasses and a hover."

Mickey knew he'd be below for longer than he cared. All 'long termers' needed insulated suits to survive the cold dampness of this underworld. Few however had the funds to waste on expensive hovers.

"We'll need ID checks," said the assistant.

Hovers usually meant one of two things. The hirers were either police, or loved ones looking for someone. Mickey handed his ID to the surprised assistant. V.U. was not a place frequented by identities. A global identity like Mickey would only draw bad press if he were photographed here.

In no time, Mickey was suited and positioned in the launch cubicle, ready for his descent into the subterranean worlds of V.U. The one kilometre descent would take three minutes, just enough time for Mickey to get used to his new 'skin'. The suit automatically acclimatised his body temperature. It also had a defence shield that automatically protected any part of his body that was threatened through fall or attack. V.U was a cavernous city at the end of a maze of long tunnels that connected to over a thousand other caves. These caves were the homes of the thousand 'digital worlds', digitally re-created planets and moons that had been fully mapped in the last hundred years. It housed the gaming world's craziest, brightest and most desperate.

Mickey's supps were taking effect as he readied his tech glasses to help him 'tear' through worlds. But in which would he find Jules? Johnnie had said V.U. but he didn't believe him. He was sure she was on one of the planets.

"Olympus Mons." Mickey instructed Com. He hoped Jules would choose the most popular destination. It was also popular with gamers who competed with her. The cubicle hit ground. Mickey adjusted his hovers. They had to be tight around his feet and ankles as hovers maintained a three centimetre distance between the surface and his feet. He remembered the hours he had spent with Jules learning to hover walk. Once skilled, you could vertically float/fly through your digital world.

He released from his cubicle and quickly built hover speed. The momentum was sufficient for him to float for minutes without any more need for exertion. He floated toward the Mars entry and used the time to deliberate his strategy. Mickey was naturally good at hovering, but it wouldn't be enough. He had to cover a lot of ground and quickly. So his first stop would be to 'planck'. He could have bought some at the entry, but he'd learnt off Jules that the illegal planck could be bought at any planet and at half the credits. You just had to know where.

"Com, station 223b." He'd learnt the illegal command off Jules. And within ten minutes Mickey was walking through the biggest candy store for gamer addicts. Supps and rettes of every variety were displayed in the largest *pharm* on the planet. Packets of herbal rettes filled the first aisle – a twenty-metre long, two-metre high display containing a billion credits worth of stock. The second row contained a similar stash of supps. These two rows alone were bigger than any legal pharm. But there was a third aisle, containing every known variety of narc. Jules had told him about this V.U pharm, but he never really believed her. The narcs on show would have been worth atleast a trillion credits.

He picked up a cylinder of Saturn Planck, a packet of rettes and an e-rette. Small security cameras followed his every move as well as high powered holo-scanners. Such high powered security was usually reserved for large banks, but the sum total of their displays and reserve stock would amount to more than the largest of banks.

"That will be one hundred and eighty thousand credits, sir," said the sales assistant.

"I haven't got time to merge it. Can you do that for me?"

"Certainly, sir. That will be another twelve thousand credits."

Mickey pointed his cubebit sensor at the register and the transaction was automatically recorded.

"I'm in a hurry. Will that take long?"

"About five minutes for the e-rette. Would you like us to merge the rettes too?"

"No, just the e-rette."

Mickey had the capability to merge the planck with his own cubebit, but it would take time he did not care to waste. The process itself was simple. Holographic technology could synthesise the planck and load it to the e-rette. The challenge was to do it without being detected by the authorities. Jules had shown him the process, but it would take a few hours. This pharm had specialists who could quickly and securely hack the process without detection.

"Your e-rette, sir. Happy gaming."

"Thanks," said Mickey and he quickly left.

He tried to call Jules on his cubebit. No answer. So he texted her. *I've just left V.U. and heading to Olympus Mons. Pick up Jules and talk to me.* The text was received and read, but no response. At least he knew Jules was on line. But he didn't wait for a reply. Mickey set hover to full capacity and ran hard so that he could fly in the digital world. He flew past the tangerine rocky outcrops of Mars toward Mons City.

Unlike the real Mars settlement, Mons City was surrounded by a vertical city. Skyscrapers impossible to build on Earth or Mars dwarfed the largest mountain in the solar system. Mons City consisted of two cities, the Left Bank and Right Bank. Each city was built at the base of Olympus Mons, forming the largest boulevard ever digitally designed. Two parallel lines of skyscrapers extended thirty kilometres out from the Martian mountain and five kilometres apart. There was only one way in to Mons City and that was through the boulevard. Hover lines crisscrossed between the two cities making a Tokyo train station look like a country town. Twenty two million gamers (most online from their home) competed in this game. Around fifty thousand actually entered the game from V.U. Most of them were there to hide from the real world or rest and recover from the demands of the game. About another thousand were like Mickey, looking for someone. It was a melting pot of technology, human energy, drugs and dreams. So much had been won, lost or wasted in this boulevard of broken dreams. Mickey slowed as he entered Mons City.

"Safe mode," he instructed, as the hover took control of his speed.

"Com, link favourites."

Mickey sited his favourite destinations. "Hawkeye," he said and the hover automatically re-directed to the appropriate hover line. Hawkeye was a mid-size skyscraper on the Right Bank. It stretched twelve kilometres into the Martian sky and had a 'floater', a two kilometre high building that floated above it. Between the two buildings lay a European waterscape. Mickey and Jules met there often. V.U. was where they became lovers. The hover line to Hawkeye was five kilometres and a five minute journey.

"Europan scape," he said, and he was quickly moved to the Hawkeye entry and a lift to the thirteen hundredth floor. He exited to a waterscape marvel. The warm waters of Europa that lay twenty kilometres beneath its icy surface had been recreated between the Hawkeye's base building and the floater. He moved seamlessly from the Martian air into the Europan waters. The invisible force fields that contained the waters afforded Mickey a sweeping view of Olympus Mons. He took in the view and text Jules again. *Jules pick up, I'm at Hawkeye.*

Again the text had been received and read. Mickey could do no more but wait. He marvelled at the view of Olympus Mons for a time, before he turned from the force field and glided into the ocean depths of the Europan waters. The kilometre deep waters were home to a thousand digitally re-created life forms that had been discovered in the real Europan waters. He hadn't descended more than a hundred metres when Jules' text finally arrived. *Meet me at Paris in Tango.* Mickey was relieved. He would be talking to her soon. He could have been searching Exoplanets for a year and not find her, if she wanted that. There was hope. Mickey floated to the surface, walked through the auto driers and returned to the boulevard.

"Com, Kinetic Quarters," he instructed and traversed back to the Left Bank. He arrived at the expansive icy smooth floor of Paris in Tango. The ice methane floor was a favourite haunt for gamers to relax and unwind. 'Tango Retreat' was on the eleven hundredth floor of Kinetic Quarters. Like Hawkeye, it had a fifty floor floater. At its base was one of the best computer systems in the digital solar system. Com-controlled light and sound streamed mood visuals on to the frozen methane expanse and the hundred plus gamers who were dancing to the rhythms.

Mickey floated across the building top's open expanse in search of Jules. It was another two hours before he spotted another familiar face. But it wasn't Jules.

"How the fuck did you find me?" Mickey said.

"Do I need to state the obvious?" replied Riley.

"You organised this?"

"I'm helping Jules. She called me because you wouldn't leave her alone. She was my friend too."

"Where is she?"

"She won't tell me. Jules doesn't want to see you. That's why she asked me to come here and talk to you."

"You put her up to this." Mickey stood over Riley in a threatening manner.

"Of course not. Think, Mickey. I could have just as easily called you. I'm here for her and for you. You're going to have to accept that she doesn't want to see you anymore."

"What would you know? She loves me."

"She did love you very much. But she wants something else more. She wants success like you. But she can't without help."

"You mean narcs. That's the very thing she doesn't need."

"You're right. But you can't help her make that choice. That's a decision she has to make without you. She has to take that step by herself."

"She'll die in this narc-ridden sewer."

"She could. But Jules could also recover here if she chose."

"Some friend you are. Riley. God help you if I find out that you knew where she was. So, for the last time, where is she?"

"She wouldn't tell me. I swear Mickey. I don't know."

"Fuck you, Riley and your friend, Johnnie. Fuck you all!"

Mickey brushed her aside as he left her. He spent a week searching V.U. before giving up. Jules had gone.

Mickey disappeared from the cubeball world for an extended period. He holed up in Velvet Underground, spending drug-laden days hoping Jules would join him. Mickey had purposefully stepped away from the sport he loved. His life had become a chaotic, blurred, montage of his former self. He'd suffered two losses - Jules and his commitment to cubeball.

He'd spent three weeks in one of V.U.'s best apartments. The miracle was that the hotel allowed him to stay that long. Just one week in, the spacious room was awash with rettes, narcs and alcohol. But hotel management lost their patience on the fourth week. Mickey would have moved hotels if he'd heard from Jules. But she had disappeared and refused to answer his calls. Mickey had to accept that Jules had left him. So he returned to his cubeball hall to a tumultuous welcome for the local hero who had almost won the state championships – the youngest finalist ever.

Mickey felt anything but a hero, having spent the last month trying to kill himself with drugs. But everyone he met wanted his time. Even Johnnie seemed to have forgotten the low ebb of their friendship as he shared and encouraged the adulation.

"I got next season's fixtures organised, you'll be a national champ next year," said Johnnie enthusiastically as he sought to sign Mickey to the next year's contract.

"Show me the clause where I only play to win!"

"Hell Mickey, put it behind you. Look at what that game brought our team. We have new equipment and training facilities and a contract for the season! We've made it to the big time. But if it'll make you happy, I promise I'll never ask you to throw another game."

Mickey wasn't about to put everything behind him. No amount of money would return Jules.

"Our team is missing one person in case you didn't notice. Where is she, Johnnie?"

Johnnie shrugged his shoulders. "Mickey, if I knew that I'd tell you. She's gone in deep, too deep for any of my connections to find her. Face facts, she doesn't want to be found."

"Ever since our school days, you've told me how well connected you are. Now, you tell me you can't find the one person I care for?"

Johnnie held Mickey's shoulders tightly as he spoke, as if trying to physically shake sense into him. "Mickey, you're like a brother to me. If I could find her I would. You've got to accept she left you and doesn't want to see you again."

Mickey had pressed everyone he knew about Jules' whereabouts. No one pointed the finger at the man he trusted least, Johnnie. He looked Johnnie in the eyes, hoping he could see through Johnnie's explanations, before he sat down behind his desk and picked up some papers to peruse them.

"By the way, you're behind in your rent. It seems you've drained your account. What do you want me to say to your landlords?" Mickey knew he had spent all of his winnings in Velvet Underground.

"What do you suggest?"

"Sign this contract and I'll fix things for you," said Johnnie, as he passed the contract to Mickey to sign.

He wanted to believe the team he played for cared about Jules. But all of them had moved on too quickly for his liking. Reluctantly, Mickey signed another year long contract, a lucrative offer, but as generous at it appeared Mickey felt it a contract with the devil. He should have been happy about the sizeable contract. But he felt only disappointment, spurned by doubts that would linger in him for a long time to come.

10

New Beginnings

MICKEY RETURNED TO RILEY'S billiard table, slightly intoxicated, but determined to recreate every shot of the final game of the state championship. He successfully played every shot, except the champ's winning break. He had made countless attempts, too. For Calen to make that shot in a final was remarkable. He glanced Ludwig's way, thinking he may agree. But he said nothing as he continued to draw. He looked increasingly perturbed as he drew ever furiously. Mickey considered ringing Dr. Vance as his condition appeared to deteriorate.

"You okay, buddy?" Mickey said, sitting beside him in the hope it may be of comfort.

For the first time Ludwig listened to him, which was a start.

"Your game is not perfect. This is perfect," he said, rocking back and forth and pointing at his drawing.

"Yeah, I couldn't replay the champs shot, pretty fucking pathetic really," Mickey joked, believing Ludwig had watched him practice.

"No. Your match was not perfect. I don't understand."

"You mean my shot, before he won the match?" Mickey approached the table and gestured him to watch.

"I'll play the game and you tell me which part of the match was not perfect. Okay?"

"No! Not perfect. This is perfect," Ludwig closed his eyes now and put his hands to his ears.

"Okay, settle down. I won't play." Mickey was losing control of the situation and he feared that Ludwig may do himself harm. There was little he could do but call Dr. Vance.

Dr. Vance arrived and immediately moved Ludwig to the lounge room which seemed to calm him. Mickey watched cautiously, fearful he was the reason for Ludwig's agitation. To his surprise Dr. Vance settled Ludwig quickly.

"Like a coffee, Harry," said Mickey as Dr. Vance sat down.

"No. I had my fill today,"

Mickey waited for Dr. Vance to explain Ludwig's condition. He thought the worst.

"Looks like my plans of involving Ludwig were too ambitious?"

"Quite the opposite. I've learnt a lot about Ludwig's condition today. Well done, Mickey."

"His face turned red and he nearly passed out, Harry! What do you mean, well done?"

"Look, I know Ludwig can look crazy at times, but the one thing he has never done and will never do, is harm himself."

"So what's wrong?"

"Imagine that you were completely deaf and you played cubeball all those years only seeing the balls, never feeling them or the table. Ludwig experienced the game only on what he saw. The game would be a very different experience would it not?"

Mickey nodded agreement. "Are you saying he can't hear or feel?"

"No his senses are very strong. Too strong. What you have to remember is that he has only watched you play cubeball on the vidcube. He has never experienced a live game either on an antique table or on a cube. So he had no sense of how that felt. For all intents and purposes, he believed the game was played on a perfect surface, unaffected by earthly sensations such as felt and gravity."

"Why would that freak him out so much?"

Dr. Vance turned to Ludwig. "Why is the game here wrong?" He pointed to the billiard room.

"It is not perfect. No music." Ludwig held his ears again, as if he were discomforted by the memory.

"It's okay, Ludwig. We won't play again." Dr. Vance turned to Mickey.

"Ludwig has played every televised game you ever played over and over in his mind. Today, for the first time in his life, he experienced what an antique pool table actually felt like. And what does he find? Well for one, you weren't playing the perfect game he imagined."

"So?" said Mickey.

"The games he imagined are his idea of a perfect place. Your televised matches were the equivalent of a serene place further calmed by music. He finds peace there, but that tranquillity was taken from him today. The harsh reality of 'real' cubeball was forced into his imaginary world, with all its new sensations. Ludwig simply couldn't cope with it. He had what's best described as an acute anxiety attack."

Mickey didn't fully understand Dr. Vance's explanation, but he was sure of one thing.

"Well, we're pretty well fucked then. l suppose it was a bit of a long bow, turning a loony into a competition class cubeball strategist," he said, accepting the inevitability of failure.

Dr. Vance sat quietly, seemingly unconvinced.

"Look, I can tell you this much. Ludwig may be in shock at the moment because his imagined perfect world has been distorted. But his dream has always been to play beautiful music. That won't change. Today has just made him aware of what he is confronting. He may retreat further into his imaginary perfect world or he may choose to face the dangers of the real world."

"Harry, I've got a few months to put some sort of team together for the national championships. Do you think he has any chance of playing?"

"Well, he's done it before. I mean with appropriate medication and commitment, Ludwig has the ability to lead a more normal life. Just to get here and meet you for practice sessions was a big step. This set back is manageable, but it will be up to Ludwig. If he wants to join your team, he will do what's required."

Mickey was uncertain, but he had no other plan.

"Well, now what?"

"Ludwig needs a lot of time to internalise his experience. For the time being, he returns to the hospital with me. He has lifted his intake of drugs in the last month and l will be suggesting that he further increase the dosage. This is a big step for him as the drugs reduce his ability to remember his music. When that happens, panic sets in and he seeks consolation through his drawings. I'm hoping that with the extra dosage, he'll turn to helping you directly, as you play cubeball, rather than drawing. It's a gamble, but it's worth it if we can draw Ludwig more into the real world." Dr. Vance then looked directly at Mickey before continuing to speak.

"You'll have to be very patient. Deadline or no deadline, you can't force the issue. You have to accept the circumstances and work only within Ludwig's timeframes. Do you think you can make it work?"

Mickey wondered what he was getting himself into. The idea seemed good at the time. But nothing was clear now. He gazed at Ludwig sitting alone, rocking back and forth humming a tune. Ludwig gazed at his drawings, seemingly too frightened to look at the billiard table in the centre of the room. How different it looked when not engaged. It was just another piece of furniture. Yet when the play began, it had an imposing presence like an egotistical old uncle demanding attention. This game was Mickey's life. And he knew it was a life he'd turned his back on for too long.

Cubeball offered him a way to succeed. It was the only place where he could show the world his skill and love for the game. But there was also a darkness too, that could wrap around him and suffocate the light of the game he loved. In that painful place, Mickey sought refuge through a deadly cocktail of drugs. In that regard, Mickey felt he wasn't too different from Ludwig.

Dr. Vance and Ludwig headed home, leaving Mickey alone in Riley's fortress. Nothing could be done except wait for Ludwig to unscramble his mind. Mickey's mouth was dry and his mind raced. *Don't fuck up*, Riley had told him just before she left for the airport. And Mickey agreed reassuring her. But alone in the house he quickly forgot his promise as he headed for Riley's well stocked bar. Instead, he chose only to remember when she fucked up 'big time'.

"Eye for an eye," said Mickey, as he made a lone toast to his successful sister and scoffed another scotch. It wouldn't be his last.

The shrill of the cubebit woke Mickey from his drugged slumber. His neck was sore from lying awkwardly on the sofa that he had made his bed for most of the week. His headache was another story.

"I'm coming!" he shouted, while searching for his cubebit on all fours. He kept his head bowed as it throbbed every time he raised it. He pushed aside empty bottles, rette butts and empty supp packs as he searched for his cubebit. To his anger, he'd left it high up on the bar bench, forcing him to stand.

Mickey hit answer on his cubebit, mercifully silencing the call tone.

"Hi Mickey. It's Dr. Vance. How are you?"

"I've had better days," he said as he rested his aching head against the bar, eyes closed.

"Good news. Ludwig wants to return to practice. He's been through a lot but he wants to face this challenge." Mickey responded in a disinterested tone. He knew he should have reacted positively, but he couldn't think straight. His eyesight was still blurred from the mix of drugs and alcohol. But he managed a small response.

"What's the plan Doc?"

"Are you okay, Mickey?"

He considered telling Dr. Vance the truth. He'd been on a bender all week, trashed Riley's house, felt like shit and didn't care about his plans. But he thought better of it.

"I'll live."

"Ludwig has been on an intensive ration of medication this week. He's even accepted an increased dosage level which surprised me. He's only done that once before. Mickey, this means he really wants to play cubeball with you. He'll lose a lot of his memory capacity, so he'll increasingly need to record games he's forgetting. Somehow I'm hoping he'll make the switch from recording games to helping you create new ones."

Mickey wanted to be excited but his condition wouldn't allow the connection. His drug-fuelled week had scrambled his senses.

"So...the plan?"

"We can start next week. I want to work with you to see if he can make the transformation, but you have to understand that this is a big undertaking for us all. Is it what you really want Mickey?'

"Name the day, Harry," he replied, more interested in getting his body under a soothing shower.

"Next Monday morning, okay?"

"Sure."

"By the way, a guy by the name of Manny Reeno called in. He heard you had been sent here."

"What did he want?"

"He was disappointed at missing you. Then he asked for your address."

"Tell me you didn't do that, Harry."

"Of course not. Your private details are confidential."

"That's good, Harry."

"Is there a problem?"

"No. I just get a lot of fans trying to find me. They're just nuisances, mainly."

"He did enquire about Ludwig. Did you mention Ludwig to anyone?"

"No. Say, when did you say we will meet?"

"Next Monday morning. Will that be okay?"

"Yes, that's fine. I've gotta go now." Mickey hung up probably too quickly. Then he threw up. Many hours passed before his drug-filled body began to recover, but only after many coffees. As his thoughts began to clear, Mickey wondered whether he'd be capable of playing at all, let alone inspire his strange new partner. He also wondered about Manny. Meeting him was not a coincidence. The question was: why had he taken an interest in Mickey? Or more to the point, who was paying him to take an interest? By lunch time Mickey's fears were overpowering him. He wanted another drink, but the only saving grace was Riley's well stocked bar had been emptied from his weeks indiscretions.

Like Ludwig, Mickey suffered from anxiety attacks. Unlike Ludwig, Mickey turned to alcohol for relief. This was his dark side of cubeball. For all the pleasure the game gave him, he knew there was a price to pay. Business and gambling was a deadly cocktail that led to unpredictable consequences. As hard as Mickey tried to be unaffected by its seedy tentacles, his life seemed to be draw in by it, usually for the worst.

TRAINING

MICKEY EMPTIED THE LAST of the bottles into the brimming bin, whilst mentally calculating the cost of his lost week. He had drunk seven bottles of spirits, and two dozen bottles of wine. *About five hundred credits would cover it*, he thought, as he tallied what he owed Riley, rent excluded. But he'd also used the last of his supp and rette supply. That would be harder to cover.

But the debt aside, Mickey was pleased with his clean up job. He'd worked all morning on the bar/lounge. It looked almost new again, barring the two carpet stains. Even the tell tale odours of alcohol and rettes had all but vanished. He was about to practice cubeball drills, when the quiet was broken by the tapping noise that was unmistakably Ludwig at the front door.

"You're early," said Mickey as he invited Ludwig and Dr. Vance in.

"We tried to call you," said Dr. Vance.

Mickey laughed before pointing at the vacuum cleaner and cleaning chemicals still sitting on the bar.

"Sorry, I couldn't hear a thing with the vacuum cleaner on. Anyone for a coffee?"

Dr. Vance declined, whereas Ludwig ignored his offer, preferring to sit at the small desk beside the cubeball table to set up his drawing material. Mickey noted his eagerness.

"You're keen," he said, drawing no response from Ludwig. Mickey shrugged his shoulders and the Doc smiled knowingly.

"What you've got to understand about Ludwig is that he only responds to questions clearly directed to him. Watch and learn."

"Ludwig, would you like me to make you a hot cup of coffee before we begin practicing cubeball?" He said, gaining an immediate response.

"Thank you, yes l would like a cup of coffee. Black, no sugar," replied Ludwig, to Mickey's surprise.

"You see, Ludwig is incapable of discerning implied conversations. That's your first lesson about savants. Look directly at him, whether he's looking at you or not. You'll find that he generally looks down to the floor and rarely makes eye contact as that unsettles him. But don't take that as if he isn't listening. If you look directly at him and ask him a clear question, most of the time he'll answer."

Mickey gestured he understood before he disappeared to the kitchen. On his return, he placed the tea on Ludwig's desk. Then he practiced some cubeball in front of Dr. Vance and Ludwig.

"So where to from here, Harry?" said Mickey.

"Why not show Ludwig how you won that game with a perfect high score and record time at the State championships?"

"Sounds a plan," said Mickey as he set up the table with the red and coloured balls. Mickey was pleasantly surprised to see Ludwig had stopped drawing so that he could watch him play.

"One thing you must understand is that my practice play is never as good as match play. I make more errors and repeat shots until l get it right. And of course, I have no opponent."

At that Mickey put on a demonstration that had Ludwig and Dr. Vance enthralled. It was as if he had the ball on a string, stroking and caressing the twenty one balls to wherever he willed them. Mickey was like that, if there was an audience, he'd put on a show. He played twelve perfect shots effortlessly.

"Yep I can still play alright," said Mickey with a satisfied look on his face. Then he turned to Ludwig to get his thoughts, but he was busy recording the perfect break in one of his drawings. He had an enraptured look as he drew the music that was Mickey's perfect break. For a brief moment Mickey sensed his beautiful symphony by the way in which he joyfully drew the lines. *How perfect must it feel for him?* Maybe it was good for him, but it would be of no value to the team.

"How can we prise him from his drawings, Harry? This won't win us a championship."

"Ludwig, can you stop drawing and stand with Mickey at the table?" said Dr. Vance, but Ludwig kept drawing.

"It's perfect. I must finish it," said Ludwig as he precisely re-created Mickey's perfect break.

"There, for you Mickey, it's perfect." Ludwig proudly handed the drawing to him.

"Thanks, I don't know how you do that, but you remember every shot. But this time I want you to play with me. Will you stand at the table and direct me on what shots I should make?" said Mickey, looking toward the Doc, who offered him a reassuring nod of agreement.

"It's too noisy," said Ludwig shifting uncomfortably. Mickey gazed the Doc's way for advice.

"You've got to understand that Ludwig's senses are very different to ours. They're finely tuned and allow him to remember all your shots. But on the down side he's overly sensitive. Unexpected noises make him uncomfortable, certain textures also. To us this billiard table has a smooth surface, whereas Ludwig believes it course and jarring."

"Well that's the ball game, then," said Mickey resigned to failure, but Dr. Vance had other ideas.

"Ludwig sit back at your desk, I want you to help me with an experiment. Will you do that?"

Ludwig had worked on many experiments with Dr. Vance over the years. Most he enjoyed, so he sat down and waited for his instruction. At that, Dr. Vance orchestrated an experiment.

"Mickey, make a bold break, not defensive."

Mickey set up the table and made a shot he played in a national championship trial, where he split the red balls so that all but two remained behind pink. The reds were in a slightly different position and the black ball lay perilously close to the top right side pocket. He was about to point out the best response shot when Dr. Vance interjected.

"Okay, from this point, no talking Mickey. Ludwig, you draw the most appropriate shot selection for Mickey's next shot without showing him. Then Mickey you play your shot without seeing Ludwig's notes.

I want you to continue that process for every shot till the end of the game. Mickey must play the shot you drew. If he doesn't, tell Mickey he did not play the right shot and stop the game. Got it both of you?" Both indicated that they understood and set the game in motion.

Amazingly, they got to the fifth shot before Ludwig called Mickey to stop.

"Not perfect. Green off three cushions into top left side pocket is not your game," said Ludwig. He drew an alternative play that recommended a two cushion shot into the middle left pocket, drawing a wry smile from Mickey.

"Ludwig has remembered the game I played when the challenger called a power play. But I didn't call it this time."

And so the day continued as all enthusiastically got involved in their role play and re-created match conditions. After a while, the three looked like a team of bridge players enjoying the discussions about tactical choices and power play calls more than the game itself. Mickey usually hated the tactical side of the game but involving Ludwig endeared him toward it. Ludwig became a different man, laughing and conversing, seemingly free from the constraints of his condition at times. But after a half day's practice, Ludwig's enthusiasm waned as he tired. So he retreated back to his drawings. The noise appeared to overwhelm him as he increasingly put his hands to his ears and his body rocked to and fro. Dr. Vance noticed it first.

"It's time for us to finish. Ludwig's tired and in need of medication. But he'll be ready tomorrow." Mickey agreed quickly, out of concern for him.

"Let's go my friend," said Dr. Vance, as he took Ludwig by the arm and helped him pack his box of drawings. Mickey escorted the two of them to the waiting cab before he turned directly to Ludwig.

"Great work today, Ludwig!" Mickey was surprised by Ludwig's response. He hugged him for a long period.

"You play his music," said Ludwig.

Mickey looked to Dr. Vance with a puzzled expression, too surprised to respond. Ludwig did not show affection and yet he held Mickey close like a brother.

"Looks like you've got yourself a team," said Dr. Vance, before guiding Ludwig to the cab. "See you tomorrow," said Dr. Vance. Mickey was still too overcome to speak. He smiled and waved as the cab sped away. Only then did he allow the tears to well in his eyes.

The following day of training moved forward predictably as Ludwig was guided to develop his skill at predicting Mickey's shots rather than recording them.

"That's ten shots in a row...that's the best you've done so far," said Dr. Vance.

Ludwig was more alert too, as a result of increased medication. He still rocked back and forth, at times lost in his own imagination, but he was talking more. At times he stood beside Mickey studying the 'state of play' up close. The uncomfortable coarseness of the felt table top still unsettled him, but he relished the chance to play perfect music with Mickey. On one play, Mickey slotted the ball perfectly, impressing Ludwig so much he insisted Mickey explain how he felt when he played so flawlessly.

"When I'm in the zone, it's as if the whole game slows down. I can see everything in detail. Even the varied role of a ball as it hits small impediments on the table surface. My last shot was affected by a small piece of lint just in front of the pocket, but not enough to miss sinking it. I hit a little harder to compensate for it."

"I feel those shots. They're filled with music. I feel happy," said Ludwig.

Mickey sensed Ludwig's mood too. Every time he had been in the zone and faced the most challenging of shots, Ludwig's expression changed. Firstly he expressed excitement, knowing the depth of the challenge and finally a joyous reaction to its success. It fascinated Mickey that Ludwig could identify the great plays from the average.

"When I'm really focused on my game, I see the playing surface with great clarity. Even the humidity and smoke in the air can change the speed of a shot."

"And then there was the national championship," said Ludwig knowingly.

"Yes, you're right. On that special night, my senses were finetuned, like time had slowed. I could see every bend and turn of the balls. How did you see that match?" Mickey asked, trying to better understand Ludwig.

"I felt a new symphony that night. You stepped out of Beethoven's world into another. You played your own music."

Both stood saying nothing more, experiencing the joy of the memory. All the while Dr. Vance sat back in his chair with a satisfied smile.

And so the days and weeks continued, all three helping refine the new cubeball team. Dr. Vance spent less time with his patient as he'd gained confidence. Mickey learned that routine and familiarity were important to Ludwig. Although his odd behaviour still concerned him. Ludwig often disappeared to the bathroom for over an hour, mystifying and worrying Mickey in equal measure. But Dr. Vance was always available, in person or by cubebit, to explain Ludwig's oddness.

"He doesn't brush his teeth like you or I. Sometimes, when Ludwig's stressed, he brushes each tooth individually and rinses with water after each tooth."

Mickey also learned of Ludwig's fascination for prime numbers, particularly the first prime number – two. It dominated Ludwig's day in so many ways. When he used the bathroom, he always required two towels, two soaps and two tooth brushes. At first, Mickey refused to help his colleague with what he considered trifling behavioural oddities, but he succumbed to Ludwig's endless demands for the sake of calm. In the end, Mickey became as obsessive about organising Ludwig's working day as Ludwig himself.

The effort was worth it as Ludwig increasingly drew less, preferring to discuss strategies as Mickey played. By the third week Dr. Vance left Mickey and Ludwig to work together unassisted. By the fourth week, Mickey was confident they could compete in the upcoming national championships. The two had become friends of sorts; born from their shared love for the game. But despite their success, Mickey worried he was blinded by his will to succeed. He needed an outside opinion from a professional who didn't mince words.

Riley was arriving home next Monday. She would pass judgement on them both. Importantly, Ludwig's strategist skills were growing. Riley would see that. But she would also pass judgement on her brother's drug problems. He couldn't dispute that drugs had played its part in his rise and fall in the world of cubeball, but something in their growing bond made Mickey want to rise above his problems. He was determined to show Riley that he could take her criticisms, rather than run from them.

Riley was arriving home earlier than expected. Mickey wanted to clean the bar room carpet one more time but her imminent arrival put pay to that. Ludwig too held Mickey up. He had stayed with Mickey the last two nights as Dr. Vance thought it a good idea. However, this day his morning routine felt to be taking an especially long time.

"Ludwig, I can't have you still in this shower when Riley arrives!" He said for the third time, but failing to motivate him.

That was all Mickey needed, Ludwig throwing a 'dummy spit' in front of Riley. The empty bar and stained floor would be hard enough to explain. But having Ludwig freak out in her bathroom would be the last straw. Mercifully Ludwig emerged from his cleansing routine before Riley arrived.

"I've set up your table. Sit there while l make us a coffee."

"I forgot the towels, Mickey. I have to fix the towels."

"Okay, but do it quick."

"I can't do it quick, l must do it right. Two towels," said Ludwig, unsettled by Mickey's demands.

Mickey had learnt a lot about Ludwig over the last four weeks and one thing he was sure of was never to over-stress him.

"You go to the bathroom and fix the bathroom towels just the way you want them." Mickey kept the facade of his outer calm going only until Ludwig disappeared into the bathroom.

"*He'll be the freakin death of me!*" He thought, just before the door bell rang.

Mickey opened the door to his sister who was surrounded by two large suitcases, a shopping bag and travel bag. The only thing she held was her handbag which she had opened.

"I can't find my house keys," said Riley, not thinking to greet her brother. So Mickey made amends for her oversight offering a greeting that belied their frosty relationship. The extent of his embrace unsettled Riley for a moment before her suspicions took over. She said little choosing to study each of the rooms as she walked with Mickey up the stairs to her bedroom to off load the cases.

"I could sleep for a week," said Riley as she dropped her cases on her bed. Mickey dropped the large case he carried beside the other bags, before making further gestures of gratitude.

"I could make a coffee for you if you want to rest."

This built Riley's suspicions to straining point. Her brother hadn't offered to do anything for her since she was five-years-old.

"There's a noise in the house, do you have someone with you?" Riley said heading for the bedroom door to go downstairs.

"It's Ludwig. You remember him?"

"How could I forget?"

Riley headed straight for the billiard room to investigate the noise. Ludwig sat at his table drawing, swaying in his normal back and forth motion and humming an indecipherable tune. Riley studied Ludwig for a moment before she turned to Mickey and gave him one of her pained looks.

"Let's have that coffee."

Mickey felt one of her moods coming on and remained as agreeable as he could be. Normally he'd respond by walking out of the house never to return. But Mickey was genuinely grateful for the month he had been given. He also had to explain the state of her bar room which would not go well if her mood remained.

"Sure, let me make it."

"Mickey let's cut this shit, what are you after?"

"I'm just grateful that you gave me this month, I had a chance to sort things out in my head."

Riley's face remained deadpan as she waited for Mickey inevitable punch line.

"So, what have you sorted?"

Mickey didn't answer straight away, for he wasn't exactly sure what he had sorted. But more importantly he wanted to hand Riley a hot brew of coffee before he filled her in on the accidents.

"For starters, Ludwig could be a bloody brilliant team member. You should see him Riley; he understands cubeball strategies like they're second nature. It took a little while to get him out of his shell but I think he could make it."

"Why don't you just work with Sam again? He's available you know."

"He's that asshole's little brother, that's why," he said, a little more angrily than he wanted.

"Besides, Ludwig will be better, despite his deficiencies." He then turned to the more delicate matter.

"And we all have deficiencies, Riley."

"What have you done Mickey?"

Mickey faced his moment of truth.

"I can't lie; l let you down in the first week here in your home. I started drinking again, well...more than started."

Riley needed no more hints as she walked directly to her 'gutted' bar and 'soiled' lounge room.

"Fuck Mickey, you promised!" She opened all the bare cupboards that had contained her stock of liquor. Her mood didn't improve when she saw the state of her imported carpet.

"Did you have a party here? Because I swear if you have, you're out of my life for good!"

Mickey quickly reassured her. "I'm not proud to say this, but it was just me. I never had anyone over here except Ludwig and his doctor. I swear, Riley."

"Why should I believe you, after all the bullshit stories you've told me over the years? You can't even own up to the fact that you're a drug addict."

Riley was visibly upset now. She looked on the verge of ridding him forever from her life. Yet the promise of success felt so close for Mickey. He was a gifted cubeball player, talented enough to be the world's best. He also knew there was another neglected corner of her mind that pained her. Despite his despicable behaviour toward her for most of her life, he believed she felt some responsibility for his situation. Tears welled in her eyes as she contemplated what to do. She stood still for quite some time, seemingly torn, unable to make a decision.

"I don't want to help you again. I'm tiring of helping a lost cause Mickey. But for my own reasons, I'm prepared to give you a last chance. But only if you reform yourself, not on your terms but mine."

Mickey could read Riley well and always knew when there was no arguing with her. He knew she didn't trust him. He trusted her even less. But these past resentments could be faced another day. He couldn't deny he broke his promise to her and on that alone he needed to repay her for the damage. But there was more at stake now. He'd been lucky enough to meet Ludwig and even luckier to play cubeball with him over the last month, all thanks to Riley. It was time he stopped pretending to be her big brother and let her take charge. It was time he co-operated.

"Riley, I know I've denied my problems with drugs and that was wrong of me. I want to repay you for all the times you've helped me. I really do."

Riley was momentarily touched, before she named her demands.

"One: you return to the hospital and attend the drug clinic sessions. You leave that hospital when Dr. Vance clears you. Two: you and your wonder partner play a challenge match against the team of my choosing. If you're half as good a team as you say you are, I will join your team for the upcoming championships. If you're not, I choose the team."

Old tensions surfaced in Mickey's mind as Riley took control of the agenda. Why should he yield to her demands? Had she earned the right to run his life? But Mickey's old hunger for the game was returning to him, a hunger that had driven most of his earlier life. He owed it to that younger Mickey he once was, the wide-eyed cubeball player who competed not for money or fame, but for the pure love of the sport.

"Okay, but if I meet those demands, will you promise to do something for me, something I've wanted for a very long time?"

Riley looked in no mood to make promises, but she surprised Mickey. "No. I won't make any promises until you earn it. If you make it past the challenge match I organise, then ask me."

At that, Mickey and Ludwig left Riley's home to return to the hospital. Mickey was happy to come under the guidance of Dr. Vance. In the two months he had spent getting to know Ludwig and Harry, he had learned to trust them. Mickey had experienced many things in his life, but trust was a currency he knew little of.

"C'mon Ludwig, let's go home!" He joked to his stunned new playing partner. Ludwig offered only a confused look before speaking.

"Where is your new home?" Mickey laughed as he opened the door of the cab Riley had ordered for them.

As Ludwig got into the cab, Mickey turned back to his sister. "Oh I nearly forgot. I had an enquiry from an old friend, Manny Reeno. I think you know him, don't you?" Mickey held a poker face as he studied his sister's reaction.

"Never heard of him. Should I have?" Her expression was dead-pan, but her right hand moved nervously to her cheek as she stroked it in a calming fashion.

No, I guess not. I'll see you on the other side of therapy. I'll be ready for you then," said Mickey, before getting into the cab with Ludwig.

12

Renaissance Man

THE NEXT MONTH WAS filled with many surprises for Mickey and his sister. Riley was surprised that Mickey got through the rehab so quickly. Dr. Vance had provided a compelling report to her. Whilst Mickey was not an alcoholic, he was made aware that he was perilously close to becoming one. Even more surprising, was her brother's new found determination to kick his habit, in the main due to his unlikely friendship with Ludwig. Mickey was surprised by the transformation of Riley's billiard room into a cubeball competition gaming room. The antique billiard table had been removed and replaced with a championship cubeball cube.

Riley had been true to her word. Once Mickey was given a clean bill of health, she organised the most challenging of matches. Mickey had to play a one-off match against a rising star of the game. There would be no audience or media. The team Mickey and Ludwig faced was none other than the infamous Carrie Heller, a brash star of cubeball, who was considered by many to be a future world champion. Her strategist was a face from the past, Johnnie's brother, Sam.

"I've been following your career with interest. You have a big future it seems," said Mickey as he was introduced by Riley.

"Big future? I'm already a star. What planet have you been living on?" said Carrie, providing Mickey no more than a limp hand to shake and little more interest.

"So shall we get on with it, Janie?" she said to his sister. "I can only spend an hour here, which should be enough," said Carrie, contemptuously.

Who the fuck's Janie? Mickey thought to himself, realising they were clearly more than acquaintances. They carried on like two socialites. Mickey felt like he was eighteen again, Carrie's age. He could feel the passion burning in him again too, not for any desire he had for her, more a passion to deflate her substantial ego. Ludwig didn't fare much better with his fellow strategist.

"Pleased to meet you. Been in the game long?" said Sam to a hapless Ludwig.

"I'm not in the game, I watch the game."

"Whatever," mocked Sam as he sat business-like at his computer station ready to compete.

Yes, they were quite a pair alright. Carrie looked more like a punk rock singer than a cubeball player. Small wonder she had reached goddess status among her fans. Her black hair was adorned with silver ringlets and complimentary silver pins and clamps that pierced her ghost white skin. Jet black top and pants matched her hair, nails, lips and heavy eye shadow. Her gothic appearance was colourless, bar two green jade rings to match her flashing jade eyes and her equally colourful language, which she used often, in between chain-smoking rettes.

Toss the coin, darling. It's time for me to teach Pop how we play cubeball now."

Riley responded by tossing the coin. "You call, Carrie."

"No, age before beauty," she replied.

Mickey tried hard to ignore her taunts, as he self-consciously removed his well worn jacket. He flung it onto a chair beside Ludwig. He didn't call immediately, preferring to make them wait for him.

"It's a sports coin. You call heads or tails, or maybe you've forgotten, Pop?" Carrie took another heavy drag on her rette, before signalling to Sam to turn on some background music. Loud music drowned the room, causing Ludwig to clutch his ears.

Mickey turned his gaze to Riley and shook his head.

"I won't call until you can hear me." Riley nodded and instructed Sam to turn the music off.

Mickey continued to delay his call in the hope it would anger his opponent. Not that he could see her eyes. She wore PE glasses, offering an enhanced view of the 3D holograph streamed above the playing area. But Carrie's stiff stance showed her growing anger. She held her cue firmly, like a weapon. It was in a way. She was using the latest CC (computer carbon) cue, very expensive technology that automatically balanced when making a shot.

He knew he was in a battle. His young opponent looked as if she were going to war. Carrie was so hyped she had to be awash with narcs. She no doubt had plancked too, so that she could interpret the massive data supplied by the PE glasses. A heavy user usually suffered puffy eyes and a dilation of the pupils. Carrie was hyperactive but her heavy makeup and PE glasses hid the tell tale sign. Under match conditions a player would be required to undergo checks, but Riley ruled out such conditions. Mickey was sure Carrie was dosed to the maximum so that she could play at her optimum level.

"Heads," said Mickey finally, winning the toss.

He elected to break, opting for a defensive opening to test her skill level.

"Thought you'd make it harder," said Carrie, before she turned to Sam for advice.

"2053 Luxembourg play," said Sam in his usual monotone voice. Mickey believed Sam had no emotions, given the inordinate amount of time he spent studying strategies. He sounded more like Com than a human being.

"What's the level of difficulty, Sam?"

"Five cushion strike with a 98 percent level of difficulty."

Carrie twirled her cue like a gun-slinger, before she turned her gaze to Mickey.

"Power-play," she said pompously, inhaling again on her rette. The room was already filled with the smokey fragrance of her rettes. It seemed to swirl around her as she strutted around the cube, theatrically providing commentary to her own play. Her shot selection was lightening fast, but deadly accurate. Carrie walked around the cube as if she owned it. She played at a level Mickey would not compete with, that night or any night.

She had won the first game of the best of five in under five minutes, making good her threat to leave within the hour. When Mickey thought it couldn't get worse, it did. Carrie cleaned up the table again with a maximum score. She belligerently risked losing with a firmly hit opening that split a number of reds but fortuitously landed behind green in a snooker position. Mickey played a good defensive stroke but Carrie sunk another high risk shot and from there won the second game.

Mickey looked to his partner Ludwig and did the only thing that could help them. He called time out. One more loss and Mickey's dream was over. So he took Ludwig to another room to speak privately.

"She's the best player I've ever played against; I can't beat someone that good. You're the strategist. Give me a plan."

"You're better than her," said Ludwig in a matter of fact manner.

"In case you haven't noticed, I have had two shots. They were both excellent defensive shots. Yet she still cleaned up the remaining balls and won in one break! That means she wins and we lose!"

"You're too busy watching her. She plays by numbers. There is no music in her game, therefore she is predictable. She hides behind her facade of invincibility. Ignore her act and play your game. She can't beat your music."

Mickey agreed that he had been mesmerised by her gothic floor show. He had to focus on how he should beat her. Ludwig's advice made sense.

"There's an old adage my friend. Fight fire with fire!"

Mickey strode back into Riley's cubeball room with new purpose. He re-imaged Carrie from the larger than life rock chic performer she pretended to be, into the young inexperienced eighteen year old that she really was. Without the fancy dress show she was little more than a child, albeit a talented one. But she relied too much on her expensive technology. This time he relaxed so that he could play his own game – and Ludwig's.

"What do you suggest?" Mickey said quietly to Ludwig.

"She plays the front of red triangle to perfection. It's very calculated and practiced. Test the back."

Mickey gestured his agreement, walking to the table and striking the cue-ball at perfect pace. He played a two corner shot that just kissed the back of the red balls, hardly dislodging a single ball. It was a perfect defensive shot that failed to impress his challenger.

"Pretty crude, Pop," said Carrie as she struck a powerful spin shot to the left side back red ball. It fizzed sideways as it struck the first of three walls to come to rest on the front wall behind yellow. She left Mickey a 'high risk' option on the one and only dislodged red. Mickey ignored her smirk. His faith in Ludwig's game plan was growing.

"Power-play." His matter-of-fact call amused Carrie. She lit a rette in an attempt to unsettle Mickey.

Mickey's decision seemed odd, almost desperate. The odds of knocking red in the pocket was tough, but to lose a nominated quadrant through a power play made the attempt near impossible. Carrie sucked on her rette a few times before nominating. She had pole position and wanted Mickey to know it.

"Quad two," she said before arrogantly stubbing her rette out, seemingly ready to play the next shot.

"How generous," he said, deadpan.

Then he proceeded to slam the red ball into the quadrant three top pocket with an unnerving ease. He followed up with six blistering shots that left him one shot from victory, but Mickey defiantly waved that chance and played a defensive stroke to allow his opponent a chance at a stunning victory. She had one power play where she could win the game by potting all remaining reds and colours.

Mickey opted to play his defensive stroke into the top right corner. He jammed the cue-ball in close to the loose black ball. The one and only potable red lay at the bottom end forcing Carrie to play another 'down cube' shot. It required the correct amount of spin and touch rather than the accuracy of her computer assisted lines.

Mickey was testing her. Computer assisted shots were flawless on direction but less reliable on spin analysis. Carrie would have to put the correct amount of spin on the ball or miss her chance at victory. Sam confirmed that it was her only shot. Sink it and she'd win. Miss and Mickey would have identified her 'Achilles heel'. For the first time since the match started, she concentrated. No show could save her now, only talent.

Carrie attacked the extremely difficult shot with her usual confidence. There was a one in one hundred chance of success. She struck the ball with strong spin, but it was too severe. She left the table open for Mickey, who quickly made a match-winning break. She conceded the game and quickly lost the match, three games to two once her game flaw had been exposed. True to character, even her defeat was ungracious.

"I was in a hurry tonight, Pop. Next time we play, will be different. I'll actually study up on your history," said Carrie, before turning to Riley.

"I'll have my payment now, if you don't mind?"

"Wait at the car, I'll bring it down," said Riley, clearly annoyed with Carrie before disappearing up the staircase.

Carrie stormed toward the car, Sam in tow while Mickey stood at the doorway watching his vanquished foe.

"Please call again. It was such fun having you over."

"Up yours," said Carrie, middle finger raised and eyes glaring, as she stormed to the car. Mickey then had to make way for his sister who presented her with a large package. Mickey's feelings of victory turned to suspicion as he considered its contents. Riley returned inside passing by him without raising her eyes.

"She didn't come cheap?"

"It was worth it. Like a celebratory wine?"

"Sure. Let's toast to our new team."

Mickey and Ludwig sat at the dining table as Riley poured the wine. Ludwig was finishing his drawing of the five games. Mickey sat quietly and watched Ludwig as he swiftly drew all five games with pin point accuracy. He was about to point out his favourite shot of the night, but Riley handed him his wine.

"Looks like you haven't lost your form after all these years in the wilderness."

"Secret weapon," said Mickey, turning and nodding in Ludwig's direction.

Riley almost laughed as she looked at Ludwig, who seemed incapable of talking, let alone directing strategies.

"So what's the big secret?"

"I could ask you the same thing," said Mickey, still wondering about the contents of the envelope. She changed the subject instead.

"Well, I'll keep my part of the bargain. I'll do what I can to get you in the upcoming world championship. It will mean you play one more match, so I've arranged another surprise for you."

Mickey looked at Riley suspiciously. "You know I don't like your surprises."

"You'll like this one. I've arranged a training session with an old sparring partner of yours. You're going to have a half-day session with Rick Calen. If you impress him enough, he'll agree to give you a direct entry into the world championship under his rating-allocation."

Mickey was genuinely surprised. Allocations were only afforded to the top five teams in the world rankings. That allowed them to select one other team of their choosing for the chance of a wild-card entry into the national championships. Teams would pay large sums to the top five teams for such a privilege. Riley either had a lot of influence or a lot of credits to splash at Calen.

"Win, lose or draw, whatever prize money I earn is yours, Riley. I'll repay all my debts."

"Well I'm glad you have faith in the prodigal son here. But have you considered how he would react to the lights and the noise of The Cauldron? He seems to freak out whenever a car blows its horn let alone the sounds of ten thousand cheering fans."

Mickey didn't show it but he hadn't given that scenario much thought. With the competition just a few weeks away he had no idea how Ludwig would react.

"We'll be there and we'll win. I've done it before and I'll do it again." It was true, he had done it before. Mickey had immense talent. It was only his desire that let him down. When he chose to try, he could do anything. But Riley was right. He didn't know if Ludwig could handle large crowds.

Mickey soon found out. He took him to an exhibition match. Ludwig sat with his hands over his ears, rocking back and forth in distress throughout the match.

"He's a savant. He'll be okay," said Mickey to the nearby concerned onlookers.

But Mickey wasn't sure if he'd be fine. Once the cheering started, Ludwig retreated within himself, as if a mountainous wave was about to crash over him. Even worse, this was only an exhibition. There were no more than a thousand people. How would he cope with a CWC sell out match?

By the third game, the crowds really roared with excitement. Ludwig was in agony. Mickey tried to calm him by walking to the back food stalls but once there Ludwig refused to return to his seat.

"It hurts, Mickey. Take me home," Ludwig pleaded, before sitting in the corner of a cafe, refusing to move till Mickey agreed.

There was nothing to do but leave. So he took Ludwig back to Riley's place.

"How did it go?" Riley said politely, on their return from the match.

"I called Dr. Vance and he suggested he rest here. If he gets worse we may have to take him to the hospital," said Mickey, helping Ludwig to a spare bed room.

"You like a coffee? Riley said.

"I could do with something stronger!"

"Was that one sugar or two?"

Mickey slumped back on her sofa as if someone had died. "It's over, Riley. You should have seen him there. It looked like someone was pressing hot steel through his head!"

"You weren't to know."

Mickey sipped on the strong coffee, recalling the evening. "I nearly got taken away by the cops. Some people thought I was harassing him."

"That reminds me of the night you got Johnnie and Sam taken away by the cops for a fight you started. Johnnie was so pissed. He was going to end the team that night and Sam didn't speak to me for a week!"

"Yeah I remember it well. It was one of the few times I didn't end up in the shit!"

"You were so drunk that night you started two or three fights. Johnnie and Sam got you into the car then returned to get me. That's when their fight started."

Mickey didn't recall a lot about that evening, but he remembered the arguments that followed the next day. He'd never seen Johnnie so angry.

"Did he ever find those guys?"

"Sure did." Riley nodded her head. "You don't want to know what happened."

"Well that's just it isn't it? I never knew. Whereas you did."

"You always think that you're the one hard done by," said Riley, leaning forward in her chair, seemingly wanting to say more, but not.

Instead, an uncomfortable silence ensued, a regular almost expected ritual between two siblings that long ago chose to leave things unsaid. But then Riley broke the standoff.

"We could try technology."

"What? Sit him a hundred miles away from the stadium and wire him to your computer," said Mickey, unimpressed.

"No, we could head-set him so he would only hear your voice or the sounds from the cube."

Mickey liked the thought although he wasn't sure what the CWC would make of it. But it would be obvious to the regulators that Ludwig suffered from a serious autism. It seemed a fair request.

"You're not just a pretty face are you?"

"The latest ear inserts can provide complete block out of external noise. Ludwig could be standing next to a jet airplane and he wouldn't know. He likes music too doesn't he?"

"Beethoven, his namesake."

"Any particular concertos?"

"He remembers every concerto and every symphony Beethoven has ever written."

"I'll have it downloaded by week's end. Let's see if that cheers him up." said Riley.

Mickey's confidence grew. He dared to dream again. "If we get Ludwig game ready, the three of us can't be beaten," he said, Riley half agreeing.

"Keep your deal and play well and I'll be there as I promised. But don't forget there are international players wanting to sign me up for their teams."

"You can have all the winnings. I've come to play, not to make money."

"I made a deal with you Mickey. I keep my promises, too. I've cleared my schedule for the first month. I just hope you can make it a month to remember, for all the right reasons."

Mickey could be determined when he chose to be. He was as driven by cubeball as Riley was driven by the business of the sport. Either way, they were both stubborn individuals who'd never retreat from a challenge. Mickey believed his dream to be unfolding, almost two decades after his first young, fancy-free tilt at fame.

A week later, Mickey took Ludwig to a club match to test his new 'ear plants'. A crowd of over a thousand had assembled, which made Ludwig very apprehensive.

"Can't we leave, Mickey? Crowds, don't like crowds," he said, as he nervously fidgeted with his plants.

Mickey responded by turning the music volume up, which he operated from his cubebit.

"There, how's that?

"Beethoven. I like Beethoven."

The 'ear plants' had the right effect. Ludwig could hear no external noise. He took to wearing them everywhere. He attended more club matches with Mickey, unfazed by the noisy crowds as their jarring cheers were replaced with Beethoven's soothing music. Nothing could spoil his day now as he spent hours reliving the music that he had memorised. Ludwig had found an effective way to move through the world, free from the debilitating noise of general life. He could also better focus on the job at hand.

Riley too had gotten fully involved in the team's aims. She prepared players' dossiers for the upcoming world championships. Flaveau and Carrie were considered the favourites to win the tournament. But this would amount to nothing, if Mickey couldn't gain entry into the tournament. Riley had proved true to her word. Mickey was about to meet with Rick Calen at the famous historic cubeball centre - Chris's Billiards in Jefferson Park, Chicago - for a half-day practice session. The last time Mickey played Calen was ten years ago at the national championships. There was no championship cup on the line today, but the stakes were still high. Calen would decide Mickey's fate for the up-coming world championship.

"You haven't changed," said Rick, shaking Mickey's hand warmly. Mickey wanted to say the same, but Calen had aged. It was no secret that his health had deteriorated the last year, so much so, that he announced his forthcoming retirement from cubeball after the world championship. Even then, he was listed as the reserve player in his team.

"It's great to see you again. It doesn't feel like ten years," said Mickey.

Rick slapped Mickey's shoulder and laughed broadly as he responded. "No. For me it feels like twenty years!"

His pale face reddened from the laughter, bringing life back to his drawn, tired face.

"So, you want to return to this crazy life, Mickey?"

"If you'd asked me a year ago, I would have said you're crazy. But, I feel like I've got something left in me, Rick. Do you really think I'm stupid to return?" Mickey asked, genuinely.

"It's a different world now. Strategies on the whole are computer driven, with most players learning their craft in unison with computer programs. Whereas we learnt on an old table, practicing endless combinations of spin, curve, straight line and pace. The new generation mainly play straight shots, with differing amounts of topspin backspin."

"So it's the same trends overseas?" Mickey asked.

"Probably more so, European teams spend huge sums of money on new technology. We'll be playing robots in another ten years. There's prototypes playing now, I mean they wouldn't win at club level at the moment, but it's only a matter of time."

Mickey was encouraged by Rick's take on the current state of the CWC and its players. To compete they had to know their competitor's skills and Riley was the best in the business.

"Pity you're not competing this year in England," said Mickey.

"Yeah, odds are we would have met again, but I'm happy to be the reserve for this tournament. But jokes aside, it's great you're having a go again," said Rick.

"We'll see how great my decision was. I might not win another match."

"You're too good not to win. You might go a fair way into the tournament, too. That's if I give you a wild-card." said Rick, honestly.

"I've got Riley on the technology so we should be okay there. I'm just so far behind the trends and my strategist is a bit of a risk, to put it mildly." Rick laughed.

"Yeah, word gets out. l hear you got someone who has never been on the circuit. A quiet sought of guy."

"That's right, not just the circuit. He's never worked in the industry. But he can read the game like no one else I've met."

"Well you've always played the game your own way. You kind of go with your instincts anyway, don't you?" Rick said.

"I don't know any other way."

"Are your instincts strong with this guy?"

"Yeah, he's good. But because of his condition he struggles to verbalise what he knows, which could catch us out in an important game. That's the gamble."

"You know in the past twenty years I've played everyone who is anyone and all the world's best. They were deserved world champions too. They played cubeball at another skill level all together. Blessed with concentration, quick thinking, team leadership...they had it all. But if I think back over all the games I played in my twenty years of competition, our state final was the most memorable. Your comeback from six nil was amazing. I'll never forget the way you played that night. No one has bettered that performance to this day. So if you say this guy has the instinct to compete, don't doubt it."

"I always played because I wanted to share my skills with appreciative fans. They don't fully understand those skills. But Ludwig...it's like he can read my mind. He knows the way I want to play."

"I don't doubt you, Mickey. The way you played those games that night. If you have a strategist that knows where you find that special place, use him," said Rick. Then his expression turned serious.

"I've always wanted to ask you something, Mickey."

"Shoot."

"That night, six all...you were invincible. I had given up...actually no it was more than that. I wanted to keep seeing you play like that all night. I would have gladly lost that game just to see that type of play...yet you seemed to stop. Why? You could have won that game."

"That was quite a night in my life. But I tell you, I didn't expect you to make that play. It was near impossible and yet you pulled it off under immense pressure. That's always been your biggest strength, 'calm under fire'. For some reason, I wanted to test you and it was to my regret!" Mickey said.

"That's a relief. I hope you're not offended, but at the time it crossed my mind that our match may have been fixed. It's rife on the circuit these days."

"You won fair and square," said Mickey, looking at the cube as if remembering, but working hard not to look his old friend in the eye. He had always admired Rick's skill and grace and felt no need to 'muddy the waters' about that special game. For he believed the retiring champ deserved his win that night. He'd issued a big challenge that night and Rick was good enough to take it.

"So, enough of reminiscing. Let's see what you've got," said Rick, as he turned his attention to the cube. "I've set up Com. I want you to play our state final last game – both players. Impress me enough and I'll give you the wild card into the nationals,"

Mickey nodded his approval for Rick's challenge. "Seems fair."

He selected a cue and moved quickly into action. "Com, set out the first shot of Calen versus Allen, last game."

The line of trajectory holograph filled the cube. Com automatically described the shot facing Mickey. "Degree of difficulty..."

"That won't be necessary, Com," interrupted Mickey.

"You don't mind if I light a rette?" Rick asked.

Mickey nodded his approval, before he focused his attention on the job at hand. He knew he could re-create every shot, except one - Rick's famous shot on a power-play that turned the match. He breezed through the many defensive shots he and Rick played. This built his confidence. Rick must have seen it, too, for he spoke after twenty minutes of studying Mickey in silence.

"You see Johnnie lately?" The question unnerved Mickey, but he did not show it, choosing to keep his eyes fixed on the cube and his next shot. It was the fateful shot he made that allowed Rick a chance to get back into the match. He knew Rick was testing his nerve.

"I haven't seen Johnnie in ten years," said Mickey, before perfectly re-creating another defensive shot.

"You do realise Johnnie is the most powerful figure in the CWC now?" Rick was prodding, but Mickey wouldn't bite. He studied the lines of Rick's 'wonder shot' before replying.

"I don't care for that side of the sport. I never have."

Rick lit his second rette, before sitting back in his chair. His gaze was fixed on Mickey now, like he was actually competing with him, not watching.

"Really? The word is that Riley is being groomed as the heir apparent."

Rick's words slammed Mickey's mind like a g-force break into the undisturbed triangle of red balls. Mickey used all his willpower to control his emotions, keeping his gaze firmly on the cube.

"Com, remove trajectory lines. I'll play this shot unassisted," he said confidently, but feeling anything but. The shot he was attempting was famous. It was a near impossible stroke, requiring the exact mix of power, spin and nerve. Rick was no doubt testing the latter.

"I understand Riley is a free agent these days," replied Mickey, as he set himself to play a shot he missed more times than not.

"My friend, there are no free agents in this sport now, especially from Johnnie's business tentacles. His reach has gone beyond our national borders. He has his greedy hands on everything that makes money. He's global now."

"Like I said, I've kept clear of him."

Mickey's mind raced, as he circled the cube, preparing himself for one of the most difficult shots ever played. Perspiration trickled from his brow, but he wouldn't wipe it, while Rick held his steely gaze on him.

"Keep clear of him. Do you really think you can do that, Mickey? He's more than global now. He has people throughout the solar system. That's one of the reasons why I'm retiring from the sport."

Mickey took deep breaths. Rick was messing with his mind. What was he intending? Was he warning Mickey? Or was he merely testing his nerve? If there was anyone he wanted to show his iron nerve to, it was Rick. Mickey strode to the cue-ball and set himself to shoot the near impossible shot. He cracked the ball with full power and the right amount of spin. The ball moved torpedo-like toward the target. Both were quiet now. The cue-ball would have the final say.

Mickey recreated a shot only a champion could make. He watched the ball fall into the pocket and the remaining reds spread perfectly for his follow-up break. Only then did he turn to Rick.

"I'm not retiring, Rick. I've returned to Earth to compete again. Will you back me?"

Rick nodded his head, signalling Mickey didn't have to play anymore shots. "Count on my support, Mickey. I hope you can bring back what our sport has lost this last decade. Just don't lose your soul in the process."

He stood up and shook Mickey's hand before embracing him. "Just be careful who you trust." To Mickey's surprise, a small tear formed around the veteran's eye.

13

COMEBACK

MICKEY'S LIFE DRIFTED AFTER Jules left him. He was affected in so many ways by her disappearance, as was the team. The level of trust had fallen to alarming lows after the tragedy, literally tearing their team apart. Somehow they made it work but Mickey refused to compete in the CWC tournaments. He believed the CWC was awash with illegal betting and 'dirty money', which wasn't far from the truth. More team managers were also involved in the illegal gambling scene, providing further pressures on players to perform to their corporate demands. Skill didn't matter as much as performing to 'business requirements'.

Illegal substance abuse too had spiralled out of control. The difference between winning and losing increasingly came down to technological and chemical enhancements that raised player's capabilities to gain competitive advantage.

With Johnnie as his manager, Mickey knew his game would be compromised, so he wouldn't sign a contract for the CWC, preferring to play in the exhibition circuit, where he could demonstrate his skills relatively free from business demands. Mickey even enjoyed it for a time, getting the chance to play with some of the stars of yesteryear. But inevitably it lost its lustre, feeling more like training sessions for a big game that never eventuated. Fun soon turned to boredom as he played without challenge in his life. Eventually, he turned to drugs for fulfilment. For apart from the two exhibition matches he played weekly, Mickey had a lot of time on his hands.

He regularly visited Velvet Underground now, increasingly indulging its pleasures, rather than search for Jules. Mickey maintained his cubeball practice discipline, but only for four days in the week, rather than his usual six. The bad habits of drug abuse and declining motivation slowly crept over him like an ocean tide. He turned away from his team and spent more time with his new friend, Max.

"Hey, Maxie! Where have you been? I've been waiting here an hour."

"I'm exactly on time. You're just early. What happened to practice?"

"I had a free day for a change," Mickey lied.

"You should have called me."

"No matter. It gave me time to stock up. I picked up Angel Fire and Planck."

"I hope you got plenty. We'll need it," said Max, as he reached for his inside pocket.

"I kept my side of the bargain. I hope you kept yours. What's the big surprise you promised?" Mickey asked.

"We, my friend, have two passes to the Skichute."

"So, what's new? You've been training me at Skichute for the last year."

"This isn't some normal pass." He passed the two tickets to Mickey. "This is our pass to Skichute – Mons. We have a live digital pass to the Mons National."

"You're fucking kidding me, Max? That's been booked out for six months."

"I told you I had influence. We get to compete in real time against the best skichuters in the world."

Skichuting was a potent mix of ski-boarding, hang-gliding and parachuting. Every year, a world championship race was held on Mons. The thirty best racers in the world competed for crucial world ranking points. Thirty digital skichuters' also competed with those racers in real time.

"I'm not good enough for this. It's too hard," said Mickey.

"You are good enough. You've paid me good money to learn this sport and learnt it well, you have. So join me and compete." Mickey looked less than enthusiastic. The course was a monster to race down on your own, let alone against thirty real and thirty digital racers.

"Trust me, Mickey. You can handle it. Those guys will be a hundred metres ahead of us in the first ten minutes anyway. So we'll only skichute along-side the digital racers for most of the race. But we've got a chance to watch the best there is, even if it is for a short time."

"When do we race?"

"In two hours."

"What!" Mickey immediately lit a rette and offered another to Max. "Angel Fire, I think we're going to need it."

Both lit up. Then they headed to the skichute dome for suiting and equipment. It was aptly described. The huge dome-shaped expanse housed five hundred skichuters at a time. They were held in suspension by high-wires. They wore purpose built 'sensor suits' that coordinated real feelings with the holographs generated by their ski-goggles. The equipment included skies, fly-wings and a parachute. Generally, skichuters competed with other digital skichuters. Only occasionally, the lucky few were given a chance to compete in a real race.

Mickey and Max lined up with thirty digital racers in the back row. Three metres in front of them were thirty of the best skichuters in the world. Mickey looked beyond them to the famous Mons slope. He was about to race down the biggest mountain in the solar system. He looked across to Max, who was beside him. Max signalled for him to take deep breaths, before he spoke to Mickey.

"Just remember, follow me. But if I should fall behind you, follow the tracks made by the professionals. If you can, stay in sight of the last placed professional racer, you'll be able to follow their lines." Mickey nodded and breathed in the manufactured mountain air, reproduced by V.U.'s state-of-the-art climate control systems.

"Competitors, the starter countdown will commence in five seconds," said the starter.

Mickey was nervous, but his senses were as high as Mons from the Angel Fire he had inhaled. Every part of his body was in overdrive. His heart pounded out blood like one of his opening power shots in cubeball. Fear limited him, but his heightened senses emboldened him. Mickey was seeing every particle of snow, large.

"5-4-3-2-1-Go!" Mickey felt he heard the starter's voice a second before the sound waves reached his ears. Adrenalin screamed through his body ensuring a perfect start. Mickey even managed to ski alongside the professionals for the first two hundred metres.

"Great, Mickey. Ignore the competitor beside you. Stay focused on the competitor in front of you with the number 8 on his back," said Max, via their com linked helmets.

"I can't see anything. I'm banked in," screamed Mickey.

All the better. You're about to hit a steep descent. Stay with number 8."

Mickey felt the ground fall from beneath him, like he had just skied off a cliff. His skies were almost hovering across the steep slope of snow.

"There's a left bend coming in five seconds. Prepare to turn at full speed."

Competitors had cleared away from Mickey, allowing him clearer vision. Number 8 remained three metres in front of him. He saw the bend and wanted to slow. He was going as fast as a runaway train and feared a bruising end to his race. Max must have sensed his fear.

"Don't slow, Mickey. Focus on 8. Balance your body how I taught you."

The bend was small, but it felt like a right hand quarter at the speed he was skiing.

"Fuck, Max. If I fall on this bend, so help me, I'll spear you on the way through!"

Max laughed. "Stay focused, Mickey. The fun has just begun."

Max wasn't exaggerating. Just as he got through the bend at speed, he felt the slight incline of the slope. He was on the first of four jumps. Mickey had practiced jumps all year and knew how he should navigate it, but never at this speed.

"Keep your skis perfectly straight. Legs slightly bent. Focus on balance and stay with 8," said Max.

Mickey wanted to pull out of the race, but in-between the terror and excitement, his exhilaration won out and willed him on. He flew high into the air, losing sight of the ground and the competitors. His training taught him to hold his position for the inevitable landing. He fell perfectly, but he was now six metres behind number 8.

"Oh fuck! Tell me I can slow now," said Mickey. He was speeding up and heading for a swivel jump. There was a kilometre of steeply declining straight run down to a curved embankment that spun them thirty degrees to the left. His pace was now frightening.

"Hold your pace, Mickey. No brakes. If you slow now you'll have a pack of digital skiers slam into you."

Oh, that's fucking great. Remind me never to ski with you again, if I live to finish this."

Mickey had no other option but to stay with number 8. He could hear the roar of the digital competitors behind him. His only savings grace was that his sight was radar-like, from the Angel's Fire. If he could block his fear and focus on what he needed to do, there was a possibility he'd finish the race. Number 8 was nearly out of sight now, so Mickey focused his gaze on number 8's tracks. He ignored the fear and set his body for the looming g-force turn that would test all his skill. He focused so intently, he began to imagine he was a cue-ball on a cubeball cube, hurtling towards the wall at a thirty degree angle. The lines in the snow looked like Com's holographic trajectory lines drawn in a cubeball. Mickey saw every minute detail of the line imprinted by the skis of number 8. Small pressure points made by the left and right skis were observed down to the individual snowflake. Mickey was in the zone. In that place he could beat any cubeball player. Today he had to ski like a champion.

"Perfect, Mickey. You're on the traverse. Stay on number 8. Hold your speed and no braking. You have to hit the next bend at maximum speed," said Max.

The traverse was long and allowed him time to set his mind for the coming storm. He hit the bend perfectly and maintained his focus on the ski lines of number 8. He was out of sight now, leaving Mickey an uninterrupted view of the second half of the course. He approached what appeared only sky, as he thundered toward the last extreme descent. He literally flew over the hump that signalled the second last ski section – a two kilometre straight run toward a towering ski jump that would make him air-born for some thirty seconds. He could handle that, but it was the landing that was tricky. It headed straight for a five metre wide entrance to an underground tunnel. This was the only way through to the final section of the skiing.

Mickey was travelling close to one hundred and forty kilometres an hour, by the time he hit the jump. He had to avoid the temptation of braking, both before the jump with his skis, or in the air, by opening his fly-wings. The tunnel had to be approached at extreme speed or he would not make the distance for the fourth and final jump. He hoped for an instruction from Max, but he must have been out of his range now. He held his focus on number 8's line, as if they were railway tracks across a one-way bridge. *He was going fast, but number 8 was going faster*, he thought, trying to will himself through the final obstacles. The snow around him was becoming a blur, but the lines in the snow were shimmering with clarity. Mickey held his correct stance as he hurtled into the last jump. He was over it in a flash, again losing all direction as he flew, seemingly toward the Martian sky. The air stung his exposed neck as he rode the wind. The noise of its flow battered his eardrums, until the thud of the landing took its place. Mickey had landed on course, but only just. He entered the three kilometre tunnel that descended deep into the mountain. He grazed the entry with his left shoulder, but maintained his balance, centring his position and hurtling at even faster speeds toward the final jump. He had no time to think as the jump was upon him in what felt like seconds. The ice was hard in the tunnel compared to outside it. Mickey could no longer see the tracks of number 8, not that it mattered anymore. He hit the last enclosed jump at over one hundred and fifty-five kilometres an hour, just fast enough for him to reach the final obstacle between him and the finishing line.

Mickey screamed out of the tunnel into the air. "Engage fly-wings," he said, stiffening his body and pointing it like a bullet to a far off green laser-line etched between two rocky outcrops across the Martian air. Carbon wings filled the gap between Mickey's outstretched arms and his straightened body. He had to hold the wings in place until he cleared the laser line a kilometre from where he exited the tunnel and five kilometres above the ground. Mickey was on an Angel Fire induced high as it was, but the flight through Mons valley had his heart screaming. He held his body and head rock solid, daring only glances at the magnificent canyon that surrounded him. It made the Grand Canyon look like a ditch. The green laser-line grew in intensity as he rocketed toward it and to the final challenge. Relief filled him as he flew twenty metres above the laser line he had to pass. Nothing could stop him from finishing. But he wasn't satisfied with that anymore. Mickey wanted a final adrenalin rush as he disengaged the fly-wings and commenced his plummet to the finishing line.

He could have cruised to the end with his fly-wings engaged if he chose. But Mickey hungered for another rush. The Angel Fire made him crave for more. He pointed his body straight down to the Martian soil.

"Disengage fly wings," he said, and rocketed to the ground without any wind-break.

Mickey wanted to feel real speed. His height was five kilometres, which meant he had no more than sixty seconds before he would need his last piece of equipment – the parachute. He screamed like a comet straight down. The g-force made his sight blur as he began to spin. The land was circling him ever faster now. He lost track of the time. He was in a perilous free-falling dance with death. Mickey left his decision to open the chutes on instinct alone. Light encircled him like a beautiful chorus. He didn't even care if he crashed and died at that moment. He was in that place that he loved about cubeball. However here on Mons, he was the light that danced around the perfect cubeball shot. No thoughts, just at one with the universe.

"Hit your chute, Mickey," said Max, who must have been above him now, watching his deadly spiral to the ground.

Mickey hit the chute, not because he wanted to be safe, but because he wanted to feel that high again – and again.

It was not until late in the evening that Mickey realised what he had just done.

"Fuck Mickey, thanks to your dance of death trick, you actually beat two of the real competitors. That's never been done by a digital before."

"Yeah, I'm that good." Mickey said brashly. The combination of Angel Fire and three hours of drinking had made him agreeable about anything.

"You could sign a contract with them if you wanted."

"I don't care about contracts. I want to do this, a whole lot more. Another drink barman," he demanded. He downed his tenth scotch with a bravado brought on by his drug-induced state. But the room was beginning to swirl around him. For a moment, Mickey thought he was high in the sky again spinning toward Mars. His body rocked as he gazed at his empty glass.

"Why won't anyone serve me," he said angrily, tossing the glass toward the bar, just missing the barman.

"Wooh, steady on, Mickey," said Max, as he cast a concerned look toward the advancing security men.

"I'm not steady...I'm..."

Mickey couldn't finish his words. He looked around him, dazed and confused, before he fell to the floor.

Security soon called medical, as Mickey was unconscious and frothing from the mouth. "Take him to detox," said the medical officer, before Mickey was whisked away to a specialist clinic. "What's he been on?" The medical officer asked.

"He smoked Angel Fire today and lot of scotch tonight."

"How many Angel Fires?"

"He had three. One, before the Skichute and two after."

"He'll have to stay overnight. We'll clear his body of the drugs, before counter-balancing his metabolism with 'resolving supps'. He'll be remedied by the morning," said the medical officer, matter-of-factly. This was not their first job for the day. Velvet Underground had many hundred O.D.'s every day, which was no real surprise. This underground world dealt with the most potent drugs in the solar system and the most extreme addicts. They had built their name as the place for gamers to go, because it was safe. It was important to gamers that they could overdose to levels that allowed them to perform, and equally important that they had easy access to recovery units.

Mickey returned next day to his cubeball world, seemingly unaffected by his adventure at Skichute – Mons. But that was his life now. He played the minimum amount of exhibition matches he could get away with during the week. Then he'd return to his other world at V.U.

No one else seemed to care either. Riley and Sam seemed satisfied, developing their technology skills. Johnnie skimmed the profits so that he could develop areas of the business that Mickey did not care to know about. The cubeball team had become a sham, meeting just before the match and departing just as quickly after. But everyone seemed satisfied enough with the arrangement.

Mickey was drifting and it would have stayed that way, too, if not for the beginning of a new phenomenon. A new cubeball star had been born. His name was Jean Flaveau and he was promoted by the CWC as the best ever. Mickey wouldn't have cared much except that he saw something in Flaveau's game that intrigued him. It wasn't that he played like Mickey, quite the opposite. Every time Mickey predicted his next shot, Flaveau would play the antithesis.

Initially annoyed, Mickey ultimately was beguiled by his different style. How could anyone become so good with the shot selections he played? Mickey practiced against himself, emulating Flaveau's strokes to better understand his style. Flaveau's unique game also renewed Mickey's interest in competing. He shocked his team by informing them he wished to return to CWC tournaments and compete in the upcoming U.S. National Championships.

He raised it at the team meeting. Every week, Johnnie, Riley, Sam and Mickey spent an hour reviewing business strategies and outcomes. Mickey barely tolerated it, saying little, listening less as mostly Johnnie rambled on about sponsorship deals, parallel marketing and other business opportunities. Sam paid them no notice, seemingly more occupied with his cubebit. Mickey tuned out all together, thinking more about his adventures in Violet Underground. Thankfully, Riley engaged Johnnie for most of the meeting. They would speak in their business language, caring little about Sam or Mickey. So Mickey uncharacteristically interjected in one of their commercial conversations.

"I want to compete in the Nationals this year." Johnnie and Riley looked at each other. Both seemed genuinely surprised.

"Maybe you've forgotten something. You chose the exhibition circuit these last five years. If you'd have competed like I told you to, you might have had a chance," replied Johnnie.

"What about a wild card?"

"With your reputation? None of the top five teams want to give you a second chance. They're too busy building their own teams."

Mickey turned to Riley. "You spend every team meeting telling us how smart you are. Here's your chance. What would you do, Riley?"

Riley closed the report she had been presenting to Johnnie, seemingly giving her undivided attention to Mickey's question.

"We could try and get Flaveau to play an exhibition match with Mickey. We would have to pay his team big money, but I hear he is looking for good players to practice with." All eyes turned to Johnnie.

"You think you can still compete at that level? Because Mickey, I don't see much enthusiasm from you these days."

"I've studied him. I can beat him." Johnnie sat forward in his chair and rubbed his hands together, like he was gazing at a case filled with credits. Perhaps he was.

"Get on it, Riley. If we bring Flaveau to an exhibition, you gotta promise me you'll bring your A-game. Deal?"

Mickey showed more enthusiasm than he had in the last five years as he shook Johnnie's hand. "Sure, it's a deal."

It took a week of fierce negotiating, but Riley got the signature of the world's rising star of cubeball. They were to play a one-off exhibition, the best of thirteen games. The media immediately took an interest in it. *Fallen Star Makes Comeback* – themed every headline around the globe.

Johnnie, ever the opportunist, ensured every media obligation was met. Even Flaveau took second place to the interest in Mickey's comeback. By the time the dream exhibition match actually came to fruition, the media frenzy had hyped Mickey and Flaveau's encounter as the 'Match of the Century'.

The night of the exhibition match had arrived and many of the critics were predicting an easy win for Flaveau. But that didn't bother Mickey. He knew he could compete with this gifted new star. He saw a lot of himself in the talented young man, a natural who plays his own game in his own unique style.

It was Mickey's first big match since the state final seven years ago. It didn't feel too different. Reminders adorned the long corridor that led him from the change rooms to the playing arena. Signed framed photos of stars past and present lined the walls. Mickey's photo hung there too, as the national rising star of the CWC. Flaveau's photo adorned the corridor just six years later.

"All set, Mickey," said Johnnie.

"Yeah. How about you? Got your bets in place?"

"I've gone for you, if you must know. Didn't bet the house though, given you're such a fucked up drunk." Johnnie replied matter-of-factly, before leaving Mickey alone in the change room.

Mickey didn't care that he'd upset him. Their friendship had been poisoned a long time ago. So it was natural, almost comfortable that they regularly insulted each other. Like a long, spiteful marriage, there was no talk, just a lot of noise.

"Ready to go, sir?" said a CWC assistant, more insisting than asking.

It was only an exhibition, but interest was so great it received global coverage. Three minute breaks were required between every game to satisfy the sponsors. Johnnie sealed lucrative sponsorship deals for their team, too. Mickey gazed in the mirror, studying his *Budweiser* logo. Well at least they had a true believer, he thought smiling to himself before he entered the corridor that connected to the arena, where he joined Flaveau at the entry.

Both stood at the arch entry waiting to be introduced to the cheering crowd. Mickey was surprised by Flaveau's stature. He looked bigger on television, but he was no more than five and half feet tall and stocky.

"Pleased to meet you Mr. Allen," said Jean. He had a courteous manner and a deep French accent.

Mickey exchanged pleasantries, noting his admiration for Flaveau's unique style of play. "I've enjoyed watching your matches." Jean was refreshingly friendly, not at all affected by his growing fame.

"Likewise Mr Allen, I admired your game for the short period you played the circuit. You have a unique style like me, but different...no?"

"I try," said Mickey, pointing to the high tech cues they both held.

Never a truer word was said as most modern players mastered 'programmed play' first, ahead of instinct and skill. Of course it had to be expected, given the sheer power of modern computing technology.

"May the best man win." Jean shook Mickey's hand, before turning from him to prepare for the show and the forthcoming battle.

Mickey's only advantage of having 'time off' from the circuit, was that opponents only had his strategies from seven years ago. A lot had changed since then. Mickey had developed an entirely new game plan that he thought could beat Flaveau. They walked into the arena to the flash light storm and media circus.

The referee tossed the coin high into the air, "Mickey to call."

"Heads," he replied, winning the toss. "You break, Jean."

Flaveau nodded and quickly played a standard opening break. The cue-ball clipped a back red, bounced off three walls and settled deep behind the yellow ball. Mickey hadn't competed with a quality player in many years, but he felt comfortable with his game and the strategies he and his team had planned.

Conjecture raged around the arena. Commentators and spectators alike had considered this moment over the last week. Could Mickey still play? Mickey glanced Flaveau's way before lining up his shot. Flaveau stood with his hand rested under his chin, seemingly contemplating Mickey's competitive abilities. It was for Mickey to lay the tone of the match. Exhibitions could go one of two ways. It could remain a friendly competition, where both players allowed each other liberties, for the sake of entertaining the fans. Or it could become a dog-fight, where neither competitor would give latitude.

Flaveau was typically a slow starter, preferring to play cautiously in the first few games. Mickey believed he was at his most vulnerable then. Despite that, he was always considered a 'front-runner'. If Flaveau got early wins, he generally cruised to an easy victory. It was crucial that Mickey had early victories, for history showed Flaveau was at his most vulnerable. Only ten competitors had managed to win the first three frames against him and five of them managed to go on and win the match.

Whilst Mickey's shot was to be played from deep on the back wall, he did have the dislodged red open to a potential pot. It would require a two wall high spin hit on red into the back left pocket. Mickey called the shot and Sam plotted it. "High difficulty, ninety-two percent chance of failure," said Sam.

Mickey struck the cue-ball a fearful crack that slotted the red straight into the pocket. He backed it up with an equally confronting strike on the blue ball. It fell equally easily into the top pocket. The follow-through spin was quasar-like, as the cue-ball viscously spun back into the clump of reds, leaving his break wide open. Mickey cleaned up in eleven minutes.

He'd come to play.

The second and third game went much the same way, although it was harder fought. With every victory to Mickey, Flaveau chose to tighten his defence. Where the second game took Mickey forty minutes to win, the third took an hour. The victories built his confidence, but his body wasn't following suit. Mickey appeared the master to everyone who watched, but despite his master-class, Flaveau appeared fresh and not in the least intimidated. Mickey sat and refreshed in between every break, whereas Flaveau stood. His demeanour was upbeat and he appeared to be revelling in the challenge.

By the end of the third game, Mickey called time-out. He confidently strode to the change rooms with Johnnie, before slumping heavily onto a couch. Johnnie stood nearby, excited about what had just happened.

"I just checked the ratings. They are through the roof! Win this and you'll go straight into the Nationals."

Mickey looked unconvinced. "I could beat this guy, fresh."

"Are you okay, Mickey?"

"I don't think I can continue to play like this, if I have another long game like the last one."

Johnnie walked to the fridge and opened the door. "Drink some supps. There's any kind you want in there," he said, pointing to the well stocked fridge.

"Supps won't help. I need something stronger."

"Are you kidding me? You can't Planck during a match! There's testing straight after the match. You know that."

Mickey had never needed Planck to compete before. He even shocked himself that he had confided to Johnnie that he craved it. But his strength was leaving him and that would mean that his concentration would falter, not long after. No one had seen his declining stamina, except Flaveau. And why wouldn't he? Flaveau knew what all top CWC players required – skill, daring and supreme concentration.

Mickey got up and took a supp from the fridge. He downed it quickly and then drank a second, before slumping back into the couch. Johnnie tried to encourage him but Mickey ignored him. Ten minutes passed before he dragged his weary body from the couch.

"Whose break is it?"

Johnnie raised his eyes in surprise to Mickey's question. "It's your break, Mickey."

Mickey was clenching and unclenching his hands in an attempt to revive his playing hands. Then he stretched his shoulders and neck to will himself back into the contest.

"It's make or break. I have to play an attacking style, because I couldn't take another long game," confided Mickey. Johnnie smiled one of his false smiles, before slapping him on the shoulder in an encouraging manner.

"One winning break and I've got him," said Mickey, in a determined manner. They were walking back to the contest together. Johnnie responded positively, but seemingly more for the crowd than for Mickey, as he looked at the adoring fans that surrounded them. Mickey was relieved, for Johnnie didn't notice the almost imperceptible shake that had started on his left hand. This had never happened to him under match conditions before. For the first time in his life, Mickey thought he may lose.

Mickey opened the game with a defensive shot. The cue-ball sat perfectly behind the brown. Flaveau countered with much the same play. Neither gave each other an opening after ten shots apiece. The crowd hushed with expectation of who would falter. Against the flow, Mickey made the first error. Thirty minutes into the game, he left the cue-ball a centimetre wide of safety – cubeball could be a cruel game. Flaveau swooped, unleashing a faultless break to win his first game.

Mickey's will was being tested. He knew Flaveau would make him earn a win from this point on. His energy reserves were emptying at an alarming rate, leaving him more prone to error. Flaveau quickly won the next two games as Mickey's concentration flagged. They were three-all. Flaveau remained fresh and confident whereas Mickey looked defeated. The speed of the defeats did provide some consolation for Mickey. He had enough energy for one last tilt at a match-winning break.

Flaveau opened with his usual solid defensive play. Mickey countered with a defensive play of his own, but he deliberately left the slightest of openings for his competitor. A three wall shot to slot a red into the front left pocket was on offer. Flaveau didn't take the bait, preferring to shoot a similar defensive shot. Mickey had a similar offer.

Flaveau returned to his seat, pressuring Mickey to take the bait. Mickey ignored him and sipped on his glass of water, seemingly contemplating his decision. He turned to Sam, buying more time.

CUBEBALL

"Defence and offence best options and the odds," he said. Mickey had already decided to play offence, but he gained another valuable minute to rest before he took his last shot at victory. He could hardly lift his arm to drink the water, let alone play a match-winning break. His hand tremor remained imperceptible to the general viewing audience, but he feared that would not last much longer. Perhaps he could not play at the professional level anymore? Had he had one too many drug-fuelled weekend indulgences? Doubts filled him.

"Offence only a one percent chance of success. Recommend defence option," said Sam. Mickey nodded, before taking a final sip of his water. He hoped it charged him sufficiently to pull off an unlikely victory. Then he turned to Sam.

"Offence, Sam."

Mickey strode to the cube. The challenging holographic lines filled the cube, accentuating the difficulty of his attempt. He had a one percent chance of sinking the red, then a near impossible task of splitting the remaining reds sufficiently to open up the table for a match-winning break. He lined up the shot. A single drop of sweat fell on to his cue. Mickey could literally see his energy evaporating.

He cracked the cue-ball with power, across the three walls. All in the arena watched, as the red rolled less than perfectly toward the pocket. They hushed as it delicately clipped the corner, its spin edging it perilously close to the edge. The crowds' collective gasp appeared to exert its own energy as the red ball finally slipped into the pocket. Everyone's attention was drawn to the red; so much so, it drew their attention to where the cue-ball ended only as an afterthought. Mickey had succeeded in splitting the reds sufficiently to have a chance at victory.

The tension of that shot unnerved Mickey sufficiently to trigger his hand to shake. He lodged it in his pocket to hide his condition. He hoped his hand would steady sufficiently to have one last shot at victory. He waited for the crowd to settle, before he did the unexpected.

He turned to Sam. "No assist," he said confidently, surprising his team with his bold call. He removed his hand from his pocket and held his cue firmly, to steady his shaking. All the while he studied the cube and decided on his final break. It was near impossible. Even worse, any miss would hand the game to his opponent. Mickey didn't care. He could hardly stand, let alone play. He acted decisively, playing on instinct alone. His first four shots were sublime, earning him sixteen points. Then he followed up with a perfect three wall pot to open up another sixteen points. This left him the hardest shot of all. Sink this pot and he would be open to ten more shots that would earn him a match-winning lead. Normally, he would have taken a little extra time on such a challenging pot, but Mickey had run out of time. He lowered his chin to the cue and hit the cue-ball toward its trajectory – four walls, before hitting red into one wall and on to the far end pocket. The ball was on target all the way. Its line was never in doubt, but its pace was border-line. The crowd again hushed as the red ball captured the world's attention. The ball rolled and rolled toward the finish line, like a marathon runner not sure if he could finish. A collective sigh was released by all, as the red ball snaked to within a hair's breadth of falling. Mickey had misjudged.

Flaveau cleaned up the last of the balls and claimed the match. Normally, Mickey would have been gutted by such a narrow miss. However, he was too exhausted to care. He shook Flaveau's hand, before uncharacteristically hugging him.

"Great match, Jean," he said. Jean spoke to him in their embrace, but Mickey did not hear him. The room began to spin. The next thing he remembered was the throng of officials, team-mates and Flaveau, talking to him, concern in their eyes.

"Are you okay, Mickey?" said an official. It took him a minute to re-gain his bearings. He was sitting in his competitor's seat.

"Water, I need water....mouth is dry," he whispered. He couldn't remember, but he realised he had passed out in the arena. He wanted to say he was fine, but all he could see was his left hand shaking uncontrollably. Mickey didn't know it yet, but he had lost more than he had bargained for that night.

Mickey walked into the team meeting at Johnnie's office, late as usual. For once he felt good about himself, having almost beaten Flaveau. The encounter had drained him however. Mickey was in no mood for lengthy meetings. He wanted to leave the team as soon as he could and head to Velvet Underground. Unfortunately, Johnnie had other ideas.

"How are you feeling, Champ?"

"How do you think I feel? I lost....narrowly."

"Yeah. You could have beaten that guy, if you had prepared properly."

"I nearly beat him. What are you so disappointed for? I got you your precious ratings, didn't I?"

Johnnie didn't respond immediately. He looked firstly across to Riley and Sam. Both had their gaze lowered. Something was wrong. Johnnie turned his cubebit on and lay it on the table.

"Yeah, we got a lot of press attention," he said, before turning on a recorded news item. Two sports commentators were discussing the game as pictures of the last game were streamed.

"It was a shame to see a talent like Mickey Allen in decline," said one of the commentators. Close-ups of his final shots were analysed.

"We saw glimpses of his rare talent last night, but can he re-gain his pre-eminence? Unlikely, is our verdict. He struggled to play seven games, so championship length matches seem to be well beyond him."

The holograph stream showed close-ups of how his hand shook at critical moments in the game. Repeated replays highlighted how nerves were beginning to get the better of him. This meant death in the high pressure world of cubeball. The commentator's damning words continued.

"The question has to be asked. Does this great game have yet another star of the game linked to substance abuse?"

Johnnie turned his cubebit off. "In answer to your question, Mickey: you got us ratings alright, a pile of ratings. More like a pile of horseshit!"

"All rumours. Ignore them," said Mickey, coolly.

"Ignore them? Fuck, do you believe this guy?" Johnnie screamed, as he turned to Riley and Sam. "Let me give you a lesson in business. Media companies don't raise rumours for no reason. They don't allow their commentators to randomly accuse cubeball stars of drug addiction."

"I wasn't on drugs. I played Flaveau clean and almost won."

"Are you sure of that?

"What do you mean?"

"I mean, did you take any drugs in the week before the match?"

"They took my samples after the match. That seems clear enough to me."

"Answer the question, Mickey."

Mickey's anger built. He lit a rette instead of answering Johnnie. He was right, though. He had taken drugs at Velvet Underground. He took them regularly. But he never used illegal drugs for cubeball. What angered him most was Johnnie raised these issues in front of Riley.

"Could you get me a coffee, Riley? Mickey asked.

Riley stood up quickly, seemingly welcoming his request to leave the room. But Johnnie had other ideas.

"Stay there, Riley," said Johnnie, stopping Riley in her tracks. He turned to Mickey. "Do you know Alex Tenko?"

"Sure. Everyone knows him."

"He came to see me a few days ago, asking questions about a little rumble you caused in Velvet Underground."

"I had a few drinks. So?"

"It seems you had a little more than that. He got hold of some medical reports that he wanted to release in the Chicago Tribune."

"Can we talk about this alone?" Mickey asked.

"No, this affects all of us. Tenko didn't just see me. He interviewed all of us. It seems he wanted to do your life story, as sad as it is."

Mickey looked around at his team mates. "Not one of you thought to tell me?" Mickey said, in an accusing tone and his gaze set firmly on Riley. Johnnie interjected.

"Don't blame them. I ordered they tell no one. I also had to pay expensive lawyers to slap a refraining order on his proposed column. The last thing our team needed was you mouthing off publicly about it. You had a big match to focus on, too – remember?"

"I wouldn't have said a word. How about you remember something, Johnnie? I'm the one who actually draws the crowd. They pay good money to see me, not you three."

"Most of them come to see your opponent. To them you're a flash in the pan," said Johnnie. He was moving his arms, expressively, as his anger grew. Finally he eyeballed Mickey, revealing the faintest of grins, before he spoke.

"We think you're washed up too. Bring me the contracts you drew up for me, Riley." Riley walked over to Johnnie, careful not to look Mickey's way. She passed him two contracts.

"This is your contract, Mickey." Johnnie handed it to him. "This contract requires your resignation from our team. Sign it now and you will receive a generous payout in recognition of your efforts. I have included a one-way ticket to Mars, where you will reside, while investigations continue about your drug habits. Don't sign this and I will sue you for slurring the good reputation of my business."

Mickey looked straight to Riley. "You knew about this?" Riley went to reply, but Johnnie cut her short.

"Riley wrote it for me, on legal advice." Johnnie handed Mickey the contract. "Sign it now, or see me in the courts."

Mickey held his gaze on Riley. She refused to look up at him. Guilt was written in her slumped demeanour. He read the contract. It was short and simple. He was to leave Earth with five million credits and not have any business dealings with any of his team.

Upon carefully reading each page, Mickey signed the contract and handed it back to Johnnie. "Good luck with your business. You're going to need it."

Johnnie shook his head and smiled broadly. "We won't need luck. You see, you're talented sister also signed up the biggest cubeball star on the planet. Our new member, Jean Flaveau, will join our team next week."

Mickey pushed his chair over, showing his disgust. He walked toward the door and then turned back to look at the team he was about to leave for good. He lit a rette while he studied them. Johnnie had his usual smirk. He'd got his way again. Sam sat as far away as he could from his team. He would have had no say in the matter of sacking Mickey. He was and remained a disinterested observer. Riley, as ever, stood close to Johnnie. Guilt filled her downcast face.

"Johnnie may have been the ring leader in this little coup d'état, but I know only one of you had the brains to pull this treachery off," said Mickey, his gaze remaining on Riley. He drew deeply on his rette, flicking ash on Johnnie's expensive desk, before he threw his burning rette in Riley's direction.

"I don't know who you are now, or what you've become. But you're not my sister."

He walked out the door, with his copy of the contract under his arm. Mickey didn't look back, vowing he'd never cross their paths again. He was done with being a cubeball player.

14

DESERT TRANSACTIONS

MICKEY WALKED SLOWLY FROM the bus stop, coat firmly wrapped around him, as protection from the morning breeze. Riley's home came into view just as his phone rang. It was Riley.

"Mickey, where are you? Ludwig will be over in an hour for practice. Remember?"

Mickey had to think quickly, his head hurt which didn't help things.

"Yeah sorry, would you believe that I stayed at Rick's home for the night. We got talking about old times, and well, he insisted I stay. I'll be back shortly,"

Mickey tidied his clothes and fixed his hair as best he could, but he knew he would look rough. Fortunately Riley didn't see him as he entered her home and raced to the bathroom to shower and freshen up. Even after the shower he looked like he felt, hung-over and drained. He went to the kitchen and made a strong coffee. He hadn't taken his first sip before Riley joined him.

"So you stayed all night with Rick. It must have been a fun evening?" Mickey knew she was fishing for a response, so he lied.

"No, it was quite early in the end. It was good to catch up, but I think I caught a cold." Riley shot him a suspicious glare, but to his relief she changed the subject.

"Our flights are being organised. I have yours and mine and Dr. Vance is organising two tickets. Apparently Ludwig would not come without him, so he's taking a month's 'R&R'. I wish I had a doctor like him."

"Ludwig's a wealthy man, he can cover it." Mickey sipped his coffee. He wanted to just go to bed but he had to get through the day without suspicions. "Got anything for a headache?" Riley handed him a couple of supps before updating him further.

"This is your ticket. One business class from O'Hare International to Dubai."

"Is this about that backer you were talking about?"

"Yep, he's the client I just worked with. He is sponsoring a local team so they can compete in their next national final. The game is really taking off there. It's up to us to convince him that we could help them. He knows your history, so we need to allay any fears that you won't do well. I think if we can convince him that we'll at least make the quarters, he'd be in. You have to wear his logo of course."

"Sure." Mickey detested wearing logos, but he needed to appease his sister and win her confidence.

"So what will this backer want me to do?"

"He wants us to play a few exhibition matches with his best team. It'll cut short our preparation for the championships but their team isn't half bad and it will keep us out of the limelight in London. They can be hell over there, particularly to a player with your reputation."

"Suits me. How good's their best team?"

"Karim Raman, Youssof's youngest son. If he's as good as he says he is, you've got a challenging game on your hands. But he's never beaten anyone of consequence in his short, young career. So treat it like a master class. Teach him rather than tell. Middle Eastern men are big on saving face. Insult him and you insult your backer." Riley was about to drill Mickey on Middle Eastern culture before she was interrupted by a familiar insistent knock on the front door.

"What'll they make of Ludwig?"

"We simply make them aware of his condition. If anything they'll be intrigued."

Ludwig walked beside Dr. Vance who had joined him for this practice session, no doubt eager to hear of Riley's plans for their impending trip. Ludwig looked different somehow to Mickey as he studied him. He couldn't place it at first but he was noticeably calmer than he had ever seen him. He normally twitched and humped his shoulders when he first walked into a room, no doubt due to his anxiety, but he was steady on his feet and upright.

"How are you, Ludwig?" Mickey said, holding his arm to show his joy at seeing him.

"I'm well Mickey, I want to watch you play now," he said, not acknowledging Riley. Dr. Vance shot a knowing look before speaking.

"You have an eager partner, Mickey. Ludwig's strictly kept to his medication program and he's spoken of little else but to work with you in practice. It seems that he has composed new music to your latest games, or should I say new strategies." Ludwig waved his new drawings at Mickey.

"Okay, we'll disappear to practice if you don't mind." Mickey's migraine was fading from the supp, but he also wanted to move to the darker lights of the billiard room.

At that Mickey and Ludwig left for practice, whilst Dr. Vance and Riley sat down to organise a travel itinerary that would not be too stressful for Ludwig. This would be the first time Ludwig had ever travelled on a plane, let alone headed overseas on a four week tour. There was much to be organised.

The early morning flight from Chicago to Dubai was long, taking up most of the day. The flight tired everyone, particularly Ludwig who was agitated by the time they got through customs to the Luxor Hotel. Mickey always felt sorry for Ludwig. His condition did not allow him to enjoy new experiences such as flying. Ludwig was doubled up in pain and rocked back and forth, convinced the plane was about to crash. Mickey wanted to help his new team mate, who was slowly becoming his friend, but he knew he couldn't. Mercifully, Dr. Vance was at his side.

The special head phones Ludwig wore had worked well for most of the journey, but the plane's descent affected him badly. From that point on Ludwig stayed close to Dr. Vance until they arrived at the hotel. Mickey hoped the familiarity of a hotel room might calm him.

"We meet at the front desk at 11am. Don't forget to change your watches and get your wake up call," said Riley, before turning to Dr. Vance.

"Do you think Ludwig will be okay?"

"He'll be fine...some rest and quiet will do him the world of good," said Dr. Vance, taking the key in one hand, Ludwig's in the other and heading for the lift, eager to settle Ludwig.

Mickey and Riley were left in the quiet foyer to ponder Ludwig's condition. But it was late and both were tired from the long flight. So Riley suggested they discuss their plans to entice Youssof Raman's support in the morning. With luck, they would have their financial backer by week's end.

Youssof Raman sent two chauffeurs in new, four wheel drives to take them to their morning's activities. Both men were dressed in the traditional robe and headdress. Mickey and Riley were directed to the lead car and Dr. Vance and Ludwig to the second. The day was dry, hot and still, like every day in Dubai. Mickey welcomed the cool relief of the air-conditioned vehicle as they drove along the palm-lined streets of the modern, desert city.

Dubai was as spectacular from the ground as it was from the air. The giant luminous buildings of the night before took on a new aspect of ambitious, artful angles. The architecture was daring. Free flowing, sail shaped architecture dotted the water's edge, whereas sharper contemporary lines dominated the inner city.

"We've picked up the guests and will be arriving in thirty minutes," said one of the escorts over his cubebit.

Youssof Raman's paleaceous property lay on the outskirts of the city. Dubai was a city planned and built only in the late twentieth century. Reminders of pre-industrial, tribal history abounded. The city was so planned that the border between it and its natural land was striking. Water from desalination plants offered plentiful supplies to plant and human alike, but where the irrigated green ended, hot sand swept the desert plains. It was also a city of duality - fertile, irrigated, modern, lined with lush green lawns, palms and water features; and the natural land of hot barren desert, sand dunes and camels. And underpinning this mix was the business of oil and the promise of fast riches.

Powerful family elders ran their business like a sheikdom. Whereas their Western educated sons managed it. Youssof Raman was such a man. He was middle aged with a memory of the old ways but Oxford educated and trained in business. The two vehicles came to a slow stop at the end of the palm lined driveway to the entry of his palace. It was hot, but the water features provided a cooling effect.

"Please come this way," said the chauffeur as he led them into an expansive area that was their tea room. The room was as large as a normal western home. The floor was covered with the finest Persian carpet. Equally impressive antique chairs and serving tables bordered the four walls.

"Mr Raman will be with you shortly, after prayer," he said before leaving all four alone in the spacious quiet room.

The four sat quietly for a few minutes before servants came in with refreshments. Two men dressed in white free-flowing robes carried Arabic tea and cake. Gold embossed glass tea cups were placed on the side table by a servant, while another poured the tea. Unlike western tea, it had a sweeter flavour and orange colour. Mickey cautiously sipped it. He found the flavour too sweet, but he finished it all the same. Dr. Vance and Riley enjoyed it more, whereas Ludwig did not drink any. On the other hand, the baklava cake was enjoyed by all. Other seats were arranged in front of them, in preparation for Mr. Raman's arrival. Riley took the time to explain some of the Arabic customs as they waited.

"It's considered impolite to present the soles of your feet to an Arab, so sit upright with both feet on the ground. Also never use your left hand to greet them, always the right hand."

The group of three, Mr. Raman and his two sons soon arrived. They were courteous but formal. Mr. Raman shook the hands of each team member rather than greet them in the customary way of kissing both cheeks. He introduced his sons, Ahmed and Karim. Both were polite, saying little as they followed their father's lead. Introductions complete, Mr. Raman sat down first, before inviting his guests to sit, also. Only then did his sons follow suit.

"So good to see you again, Riley. You must have taken our country into your heart, given it's your second visit within a month," said Mr Raman, before he turned to Mickey.

"This is your first time in Dubai, Mr. Allen?"

"Yes it is."

"Well I hope you enjoy your stay with us. I know our cubeball team is very excited to meet you. Riley has made much of your rare talent for the game."

Mickey was not a great one for conversation in groups, so he smiled offering an agreeing gesture rather than words. After the normal pleasantries, the discussion turned to business. Riley took over, providing a powerful case to Mr Raman of the benefits he could gain from sponsoring their team.

"Thank you Riley, your proposal is very interesting. I know that time is pressing for you and your team, but I'd like to consider it further. As they say in my country, the desert must be crossed slowly, purposefully and never alone. I would like to see your team in a match play situation before making a decision. Would you honour us by playing against my team tomorrow night? We will set up our finest antique table for the occasion. I had heard you enjoy the old game Mr. Allen?"

Riley cast a glance to Mickey who nodded his approval.

"We'd be honoured to play your team. We would appreciate some time to rest and then practice on the table you have prepared. A day would be sufficient."

Mr Raman looked to his eldest son, Ahmed, who appeared happy with the arrangement.

"But of course you all need rest. You have come a long way. My men will return you to your quarters. Please rest, relax and enjoy our fair city. We shall organise the match play for tomorrow night," said Mr. Ramen, courteously shaking hands with all.

"For now, please enjoy the refreshments and then my drivers will return you to your hotel when you are ready. I will leave you with Ahmed, who will arrange the practice times with you. Unfortunately, Karim and I must leave, but we shall enjoy meeting you all again tomorrow evening," said Mr Raman before departing.

An hour later all were returned to the Luxor. Dr. Vance was grateful for the free time as Ludwig had become anxious from the day's events.

"I took Ludwig for a walk, but he cut it short as the heat unsettled him. Although, I think it's more the long flight. It has exhausted us both, to be honest," said Dr. Vance, before excusing himself and Ludwig, for the remainder of the day, leaving Riley and Mickey to dine at the hotel's restaurant alone.

"Raman reminds me a lot of Johnnie. He never spoke about the game once. It was all business," said Mickey.

"Well the game is big business. We could compete in the championship with no support but we wouldn't get past round two using standard equipment. We need the best equipment to win. You know that, don't you?"

Mickey wanted to win alright. Nothing would give him greater pleasure than to beat Johnnie's team, but not at the expense of being beholden to another businessman's agenda.

"Look, I know you're doing a lot here and don't think it's not appreciated, but I'm not signing another one year contract ever again. Just make that clear to him."

"I don't think we'll be under that much pressure. I want him to agree to give us access to his world class equipment. We have to give him sponsorship rights to our team. His son is an 'up and comer' but he will fall at the first round. Raman knows that, so why wouldn't he sponsor us, if we can compete way past the early rounds?" said Riley.

Mickey wanted to believe Riley's confident explanations, but experience told him otherwise.

"These discussions remind me of Johnnie and you know the spell he cast over people with his lies and deceit?"

"Mickey, for once in your life trust me. I've been working in this industry for nearly twenty years, so give me some credit," she said.

A pause of silence enveloped the table as brother and sister read the menu. Rather than risk argument, both ordered their meals, before Mickey broke the deadlock.

"So how is Johnnie, is he still here in Dubai?"

"No. He's back in London. He was here briefly on business, the last time I came here. He asked about you."

"What did you tell him?"

"I told him what I wanted him to know."

"Which was...."

Riley half smiled, keeping him waiting, as she often had done as a young girl back at home. She knew Mickey hated having information kept from him. He glared at her to illicit a response.

"Well I told him the truth. You were making a comeback and that you were keen to compete in the world championships this year."

"And..."

"I told him that I'd back you if you showed you still had the form to compete."

"Come on, Riley. Don't feed me what I already know. What did he say?"

"What could he say? You're not under contract to him. He laughed and reminded me that I was dealing with a washed up drunk who wouldn't get past the first round."

"So that's all he said?"

"Pretty much." Another uneasy pause ensued as they ate their meals.

Mickey wanted to believe her, but Riley and Johnnie went back a long way. Mickey watched their business-like relationship over the years. Then there were his drug-driven missing years, He was sure they worked together for most of those years, too. The truth was it was only a year since Riley split from Johnnie, for reasons he never heard, but wanted to know.

The next morning started the same as the last. Two chauffeurs picked them up and they departed for a 'destination unknown' to practice for the night's game.

"I don't know where the venue is Mickey. It's a surprise apparently," said Riley, settling into the comfortable back seat of a black 4WD.

Mickey didn't like surprises and his dismay turned to shock as the two vehicles passed the city barriers and made their way into the great desert.

"We are about an hour from our destination," said the driver, offering precious little more information for the remainder of their journey. Mickey wondered about the suitability of the venue as they left the safety of the graded gravel road to head directly for a sea of sand dunes. An hour into their journey, the driver broke their building anxiety.

"We are nearly there, but we would like to honour you with a special experience along the way. Most locals come to this place at least once a year," said the driver proudly.

All Mickey could see was layer upon layer of sand dunes, tall as trees. They were deep in the desert. There were no roads or palm trees, just sand. As they approached one particularly large dune, Mickey noticed that the other four wheel drive turned right away from them and quickly disappeared from view. He was about to ask where they were headed, before the site before him took his breath away.

Their vehicle had come to a stop at the top of a huge sand dune that looked down into what looked like a massive crater surrounded by six large dunes. A minute later the other vehicle came into view at the opposite side.

"Wow, nice view," said Mickey.

"Now the fun begins," said the driver pointing straight down.

Mickey held the arm rest tight. The vehicle headed straight over the top of the large dune and down to the bottom of the sand dune. Mickey managed to contain his concern as the vehicle accelerated down the sand dune. They hit the bottom at speed and then continued to snake up to the top of the opposite dune. Just before reaching the top, the second vehicle flashed past them as they headed in the opposite direction.

"Holy shit...too close," cried Mickey, certain they would collide with the other vehicle. Then they did the whole process again. After multiple descents Mickey's fear turned to excitement as he realised they hadn't come to bury their competition in a fiery sandy desert, they had come to play.

"This is our most popular pastime - dune surfing," the driver said proudly.

Mickey's car was stationary on top of a dune now, so he watched the other car. They tore down the steep sandy slope much faster than before. They hit the base of the dune hard, spraying sand high above the bonnet, before drifting hard right in their traverse up to the top of the opposite sand dune. It drifted right than left before reaching the top with enough pace to finish with a three hundred and sixty degree spin. Mickey was now well and truly ready to get into the spirit of the adventure.

"We've got to do that," he said, ready for anything, before Riley interrupted.

"I don't want to spoil the party, but Ludwig is susceptible to anxiety attacks from sudden, unexpected movement. Could you please check with the other vehicle that he's okay?" The driver quickly spoke in Arabic on his walkie talkie, before turning to Riley.

He is rocking backward and forward...is that a bad sign?"

Riley looked at Mickey for a reply, "Could be, is he saying anything?"

Again delay for the discussion in Arabic and a translation.

"Your good doctor friend says that Ludwig is too busy laughing to be able to talk, should we stop and take you to the next venue?"

Mickey and Riley looked at each other and simply laughed.

"Let's see how quick you can drive down that sand dune, I don't think we feel like going to practice just yet," said Mickey.

At that the two drivers gave them an hour of thrills they would not forget. It was an experience that would surprisingly change the nature of their challenge in ways that no one in their team would predict.

By midday they arrived at the 'venue' for their challenge. It was a large marquee erected quite literally in the middle of nowhere. A hot shimmering breeze had gathered offering some relief from the dry desert heat. Neatly rolled up flaps surrounded the colourful marquee, allowing the breeze to flow through and further cool the large shaded shelter. Old style candles lit the inside, creating an exotic feel. Persian style pillows split the shelter into two distinct areas, one a playing area where a cubeball table sat in its centre, brightly lit by a traditional chandelier filled with a hundred candles. The other section had been prepared for dining, where a feast of lamb and salads had been prepared.

"Some of our people will join you for a lunch in a few hours, but for now we have provided refreshments in the playing area while you practice," said the driver, leaving the four to survey their surrounds.

The team soon settled into practice, as the staff provided refreshments of tea and iced juice on request. Riley studied her cubebit's program, detailing the game history of their opponents for the challenge later that night. She reviewed their game strengths and weaknesses and discussed some of them informally as Mickey practiced his shots. Dr. Vance and Ludwig sat together near Riley watching Mickey practice his drills.

"It's a match-play table with almost perfect balance. Key that in," he said to Riley, before turning his attention to the other two.

"So Ludwig had a bit of a laugh today, Harry? That's a first!"

"Something about the spin of the wheels and its effect on the fine sand gave him a feeling of immense joy," replied Dr. Vance, looking toward Ludwig to see if he would respond. Surprisingly he did.

"It was perfect Mickey, perfect spin and finesse, like you in match play," he said, before returning his gaze to a drawing he was completing.

Mickey thought back to the fun they had on the giant sand dunes and the preciseness of the driver's control over their cars. It wasn't too dissimilar to cubeball, spin wise. Of course the surfaces were like 'chalk and cheese'.

"Yes it was a welcome break," Mickey said, as he shot another set of drills. Balls smashed easily into pockets, first directly, than off one cushion, two and three cushions. Mickey looked pleased with the table and his form. Ludwig surprised Mickey by suddenly standing up and directing him, which he didn't do unless asked.

"Repeat that three cushion shot, Mickey. But this time strike it with strong left side spin so that you curve the cue-ball with the same force back in behind the middle brown ball."

"That's a three cushion shot. I'll need to hit the ball too hard. That would make the result too unpredictable."

"You must. It's a perfect shot, Mickey. Counteracting spin and speed will set up the right balance and motion. Shoot it Mickey." Ludwig demanded.

"Okay, settle down maestro!"

Mickey set up the balls so that he could practice the demanding shot. The chances of pulling it off were less than fifty to one and that wasn't under match conditions. But he was happy with his form and had the time to experiment. Mickey cannoned the shot with a power he rarely used in match play. Such explosive power was too hard to control.

Riley also watched enthralled by the shot selection Ludwig had requested. She set her cubebit on 'full scan' to ensure the shot was recorded and compiled in case a unique strategy evolved. Com provided strategies based on plays made in the past. It could not create new plays. Riley had access to every televised game ever played in championship tournaments. Com's shot selection was always based on the shot of least risk. That also usually meant straight shots with no side spin. Angled spin could not yet be accurately calculated by technology given the variations in cue position on the cue-ball let alone the pace in which it was struck. Ludwig's idea seemed fanciful; many had tried and failed, having the occasional winning streak of a few games but ultimately the ball would be left vulnerable and vulnerability meant losing. Mickey was one of a few who could play spin capably.

"I'm putting it on full scan," said Riley.

"Thanks."

Mickey visualised the shot for a moment before he cannoned the cue-ball into the red, exerting whipped spin that curved the cue-ball in a visibly large arch toward the first cushion. The red ball had already fallen into the chosen pocket by the time the cue-ball was spiralling into the second cushion. The violent spin and arch of the ball had disappeared after hitting the third cushion, now floating toward its destination.

Ludwig's rocking ceased. His gaze excitedly devoured the beauty of the shot as if a divine spirit were about to descend to the green felt surface. Mickey stood enraptured also, half believing Ludwig's shot selection may reveal a unique possibility hidden inside a complex but risky shot. All watched the cue-ball, hanging on its vital last turn as if it were the last thread of a rope holding them from a deadly fall. The ball just rolled past the brown leaving it in the wrong position – vulnerable.

But that did not appear to dampen Ludwig and Mickey's enthusiasm for what had just occurred. They both lent on the table for a time, surveying something elusive, as if there were a visible force imprinted on the table. A full minute passed before Mickey spoke, more with resignation.

"Like I said Ludwig, I'd have a one in fifty chance of getting it right. It's an impressive shot when slotted, but in match conditions it's too risky."

"It was beautiful, Mickey. Play your music for the world," he said, before returning to his notes and recording what he had just witnessed.

Mickey practiced the shot a few dozen times to placate Ludwig. Predictably, one shot was perfect but the others left his ball vulnerable.

He couldn't play those odds under match conditions. Mickey shrugged as he looked to Riley.

"Scan it into a few games. Who knows, Ludwig might have something," he said, before returning to normal practice.

Mickey's request was in the best of hands. Riley was good at her craft and dogged. She spent hours running her program over the 'come in spinner' shot she jokingly dubbed it. But she also knew that though Mickey wasn't the best player in the world, he was the most naturally talented. If anyone could change the way the game was played, he could.

Practice had been business like for the remainder of the session. Mickey played well. Riley had her 'tech programs' ready. Even Ludwig had his games drawn and seemed satisfied with himself. All were relaxed and ready for battle as they sat at the western corner of the marquee and enjoyed the desert sunset.

It seemed a magical place to be, as the stifling hot heat gave way to the cooling breezes of the dusk desert. A tribe of locals and their camels appeared high up on the sky line, as they slowly headed south. Mickey sipped on his tea, as he took in the desert view from the comfort of their enclosure.

"Nice way to get a financial backer."

"Well they're a country seeking opportunity. You know, over a hundred years ago, this desert was their world, but then they discovered rich oil reserves and built the modern city we see today," said Riley.

"Hard to believe it all happened so quickly," said Mickey.

"Is that how Raman made his millions?" Dr. Vance asked.

"Initially yes, but his sporting interests are quite large now," said Riley.

Ludwig was oblivious to the conversation as always, but he was sufficiently relaxed to leave his drawings and take in the desert twilight. Something in the closest sand dune had captured his attention. He appeared to be captivated by the fine grains of sand. Suddenly he spoke.

"The rhythm of sand is a beautiful sight."

"You liked the way the cars glided over the dunes?" Mickey replied.

"I feel calm, like when you play cubeball," said Ludwig. That sparked interest from Dr. Vance.

"Ludwig has always been comforted by movement, particularly the rhythms of nature. I remember the day he sat mesmerised by the movement, sounds and smells of a nearby waterfall. He studied it for hours, unwilling to leave."

Riley joined in the conversation. "Most people are comforted by nature as it's a relief from our technological world."

"Yes that's true, but it wasn't the flow of the water that comforted him. His interest was for what lay beneath the water's surface. A small school of fish inhabited the stream and Ludwig studied their ability to swim in formation even though the water was turbulent from the waterfall. Small plants, twigs and stones fell from above into their area of water and yet they maintained formation," said Dr. Vance.

"Nature's way," said Mickey.

"Yes precisely. Interestingly he felt the same calm from our 'dune surfing' venture. The roar of the vehicle's engines disturbed him, but when Ludwig saw the way in which your vehicle gracefully snaked up the dunes, his mood changed. It fascinated him that a mechanical device could float effortlessly up that large dune in a beautiful, musical manner. Even in the harshest of environments the driver created beauty. He searches for grace in a mechanical world he finds unsettling," said Dr. Vance.

"So why the music?" Riley asked.

"His love of Beethoven is not so much about the rhythm. To Ludwig most of the symphonies, fugues and so forth are regular, not unlike mechanical rhythm, but soaring above it, independent patterns form sometimes transcending or even contradicting the beat. It's in that hidden place where he finds grace and natural peace. It doesn't have to be analysed, it just is." Dr. Vance was about to continue but Ludwig interrupted.

"I see the rhythms just as you do, Mickey."

Mickey couldn't deny he felt something when he played well. Sometimes he did feel a hidden force when he was 'in the zone'. In that place, he could play any shot, for he saw the table 'large'. His senses went into overdrive and that allowed him to play perfect cubeball without really concentrating. It just naturally happened as if an outside force channelled through him.

"We both share a unique view of the game. You with your drawings and me with the way I play the game. If you could play, you would play exactly like me. I sometimes think you can read my mind." Ludwig smiled and gave a drawing to Dr. Vance, prompting him to speak.

"You know up until today I would have considered that a plausible observation. But Ludwig did something today that he's never done before. He drew a cubeball game with his usual attention to detail. I thought nothing of it until I asked him which game he had drawn from your past match plays. For the first time he told me he had drawn a game he wanted you to play."

The cold desert night enfolded around the marquee as lights burned bright for the specially fitted cubeball playing area. Guests of the Raman family started to fill the makeshift arena. Mickey smiled and greeted them as he waited for Riley's final game plan check. Their competitors arrived and eagerly went about their warm-up drills, as they prepared for the match. Mickey watched Karim Raman practice his drills. He was young, but did have some talent and potential. He would not be an easy victory for Mickey. He turned to Riley.

"Ludwig's strategy locked in?" he said.

"Locked and loaded, ready to apply at your call," said Riley.

The agreed tactic was to commence play with the usual strategies before experimenting with Ludwig's new game plan. Mickey won the toss, deciding to break first in a 'best of seven' set. His form was good from practice and he proceeded to play near perfect cubeball easily winning the first two games. On the third game he considered using Ludwig's strategy.

"How does his game stack up?" Mickey said, as Riley ran the program based on the previous two games.

"Ludwig's game has a low probability of giving them difficulty… around sixteen to one," said Riley.

Not bad odds, Mickey thought to himself as he approached the table to experiment with Ludwig's unique game play. He signalled his intention to play it, exciting Ludwig. Mickey knew it to be an unnecessary risk but the idea that a 'non-player' such as Ludwig could even visualise match-play fascinated him. More importantly, he wanted to understand his new friend better. Perhaps through playing his game, he may feel his music, too.

Mickey had played himself in and was seeing the game 'large' as he caressed his opening shot, a defensive stroke that left his opponent wedged on the front cushion. Predictably, Karim played his shot awkwardly breaking up the red triangle to allow Mickey some easy pots.

He could see an easy win by potting the next ten balls with little difficulty, but instead opted to play a ripping spin shot based on Ludwig's game plan. He struck the cue-ball with a force that looked impressive but provided no points. Even worse, it provided the young challenger some hope of winning. Karim played a two cushion shot to sink a red, much to the delight of the parochial crowd. He confidently struck a fifty eight point break, just short of a victory.

There was sixty points left on the table if Mickey called a power play. But there was no easy shot available to him. Ludwig's strategy of extreme spin provided a slim opportunity of victory, but a higher degree of difficulty. Everything was reversed, ball placement, pocket selection, angles. Mickey liked the challenge but he struggled to visualise more than one shot ahead - and it showed. He failed to sink the red and left his ball in a vulnerable position, allowing the young challenger to win the game, much to the delight of the partisan followers. Riley called a break as Mickey joined her and Ludwig to plan the next game strategy.

"Did that game feel as bad as it looked?" she said, making her displeasure clear to them both.

"I know it looked bad but there's something different about that style that holds promise," said Mickey, looking toward Ludwig.

"You played music tonight, Mickey," said Ludwig, leaving Mickey smiling and Riley not.

"That music made you look like an amateur trying to show off. In case you didn't notice we lost. But you're the strategist. What exactly do you recommend for the next game, maestro?" Riley asked.

"Play more music, you must play the right symphony," said Ludwig repeatedly, before he left them to sit at the table to draw.

"You didn't have to do that, Riley. He means well," said Mickey.

"Mickey, the guy's half mad and you want to bring him to a championship. I could get you an experienced strategist in London that would at least help our team. This guy has no idea!"

"I don't need a strategist. You're twice as good as anyone you'd find in London anyway. Just stay with me on this one."

They weren't close but they were family. Riley was running out of patience. Mickey knew she had spent a small fortune to arrange this venture and rightly expected Mickey to deliver. As a business woman, risks were not in her vocabulary, yet she had taken one with him.

"Do what you want. You always have. For what it's worth, here's my read out on the game plan," said Riley.

She passed him the best game play odds and said no more, turning her gaze to the computer screen. Mickey knew she wouldn't say anymore till after the game. He'd reignited old wounds. Mickey looked at Riley's game strategy sheet. They were good odds. They made sense. Then he turned to Ludwig. He was furiously scribbling his new game plan. No solution there. So he headed back to the table unsure of his next move. Mickey surveyed the crowd of Arabs dressed in traditional robes. Most drank tea as they waited excitedly for the game to recommence. Then his gaze turned to one person, his young opponent. Karim looked more like one of his fans waiting to see his hero play. Mickey nodded appreciatively to the young man. That instant, he decided his strategy.

"Hold your strategy, Riley," Mickey returned to the table and played one risky opening using a combination of extreme spin and power. Ludwig's strategy ensured a red would be pocketed, but there was a possibility that another ball could fall, leaving a winning opening for his opponent. Luck was with him that night. The table was filled with red and coloured balls scattered to all corners.

"Key in your strategy now, Riley," said Mickey. He followed Riley's strategy to the letter, playing a winning break with safe, sound cubeball play. He promptly won the match in five minutes, providing his new fans a wonderful exhibition of cubeball that they would not forget.

The following morning, Mickey and his team sat together enjoying the victory breakfast. This was their final meeting in Dubai before they would re-unite in London. Riley was flying out of the country a day ahead of the other three to make preparations for the team. Mickey was happy with his game play, but he wondered whether he won too easily.

"So, do you think we have his backing?"

"It's difficult to judge. I'm meeting with Raman and his son, so that's a good sign," said Riley, fixing the bill and preparing to leave.

"They've organised a practice session for you at their local cubeball complex. It's quite a sight apparently and after your performance last night, you can expect a crowd." Riley left for her taxi, leaving Mickey with Ludwig and Dr. Vance.

"Seems we've got a following," said Mickey.

Ludwig nodded agreement before he handed Mickey his new drawings.

"I keep seeing new games for you to play." Mickey studied the games. They were unlike any of his previous drawings. Then Dr. Vance interrupted his thoughts.

"What Ludwig really meant was he wants you to practice more. These drawings are practice drills to help you play his type of game."

Mickey dropped the drawings on the table, genuine surprise written on his face.

"Ludwig, I half expect you to pick up a cue and start playing next week. Let's go practice!" he said, hailing a taxi. Ludwig hesitated, shooting Dr Vance a worried look.

"I can't play cubeball. I just like to hear the music."

"Yes, Mickey and I both know that," said Dr. Vance, as he shook his head in annoyance at Mickey's humour.

The main Emirates cubeball stadium was still being built although the many smaller surrounding venues were complete. Mickey, Ludwig and Dr. Vance were led into one of them. Even their small venues were spectacular. The stadium was intimate, but state of the art technologies were evident. Their driver accompanied them and doubled as their tour guide. He proudly described its many features.

"We hope our country will host next year's championships. Here is your practice cube. Do you require the equipment to be turned on?" He pointed to the 'com tech' area.

"Just the cube," said Mickey.

A minute later the cube was lit up. It was one of the finest cubes he'd seen. Little wonder players now opted to play straight line shots most of the time. Between tech glasses, eye implants and this high resolution holograph, shot selection was becoming increasingly the choice of the com tech strategist.

'Straight line' shooters were so well drilled they rarely made mistakes, making games quicker and closer which suited those bestowed with running the cubeball industry. In fact the games structure bore little resemblance to the one Mickey last played. Even championships were 'best of seven games' up to the quarter finals and then thirteen for the final series. Each game usually lasted no longer than ten minutes. Even a game was divided by compulsory five minute intervals to satisfy media and gambling requirements. The two optional time outs were also lengthened to half an hour, making it a sponsor's dream.

"Well, we better start practicing your game plan, because even if we do manage to somehow win using your strategies, we won't the following year," said Mickey, sure that Ludwig's formula would be eliminated through CWC rule changes.

"Won't you play next year?" said Ludwig mystified.

Mickey didn't try to explain himself. He simply laughed at Ludwig's naivety and proceeded into his usual practice drills. He started with straight pots, then one cushion, two cushion and three cushion pots, firstly without holograph assistance and then with it. Mickey was enjoying the new cube as were the growing crowd of onlookers.

"Superb graphics, let's get to your drills," said Mickey, wanting to put on a show.

The appreciative small crowd were educated in the subtleties of the game, so he slotted in a few trick shots between Ludwig's strategy drills. Ludwig's set plays were challenging and required full concentration. He felt like a jazz pianist faced with the task of playing Beethoven's symphonies. The skill and touch required to slot the ball in the correct spot were too demanding. At best he slotted thirty percent and that was not sufficient for match play.

"I don't know how you dream up these difficult plays. It's just too hard," said Mickey, frustrated by its demands.

"You can do it, Mickey. You've played this music before."

"Okay maestro, I'll have one more go and then we call it a day."

This time Mickey did not play any trick shots for the young crowd. As frustrated as he felt, he did feel a certain beauty with Ludwig drills, but he had to play at his best. Mickey concentrated his mind on the light as he visualised the shots. He shut out the sounds around him so that by the middle of the game he saw the balls large. The light in the modern indoor arena was state of the art 'shine' technology. It lit up the playing area, eliminating all shadow, providing a view of ball spin, second to none. He adjusted to it and then felt the beauty of Ludwig's game play for the first time.

The young crowd sensed the new level of his play. An appreciative stillness engulfed the playing area. To the enraptured fans it appeared Mickey was playing a different game, new and enticing. Mickey's eye was in 'the zone' as he observed the game in glorious detail. The balls were gliding to places they ought not to run and yet they did, as if new natural laws had been invented just for this play to unfold. In this place Mickey forgot about Ludwig's drawings, choosing to play on instinct. Stunned silence surrounded him, eager eyes absorbing the sight and motion unfolding. Spin and curve replaced straight lines, as if a new force were moving the balls other than gravity. The final ball of the final game rolled perfectly into place before Mickey again became aware of his audience. The crowd broke the silence and applauded as if the king of Persia had walked into the room. But Mickey ignored the adulation and placed his first gaze to his brilliant, strange and unforgettable team mate. Both had tears in their eyes and both knew they experienced a special symmetry. Mickey wondered if he would ever play so perfectly again. Would it only be a special moment lost in time?

"I have it all here," said Ludwig, pointing to his head.

Mickey smiled a relaxed sigh, as he knew that this special man would remember every shot he played that day to a pin point accuracy that not even the world's most powerful computer could ever hope to recall. They were ready for London.

15

LONDON CALLING

MICKEY, LUDWIG AND DR. Vance arrived at Heathrow International mid morning and re-united with Riley at the custom's exit.

"Get ready for an English welcome," she warned.

Riley had not exaggerated. It seemed half the press filled the large terminal. Mickey was surprised by the interest he drew, given it was a decade since he competed. To his relief Riley had organised a limousine for Dr. Vance and Ludwig, saving them the stress of dealing with the press throng. Mickey however, was in for a long morning.

"Welcome to England Mickey, how's it feel to be competing again?" fired a reporter, followed by another twenty quick-fire questions.

Mickey amicably handled the media pack, until a reporter asked about his personal life.

"How's your battle with drugs? Some say it's ongoing? Do you think that may have an impact?"

Riley interjected before he could respond. "That will be all now, thank you for your interest," she said, before scurrying Mickey into a second limousine.

"Central hotel," she said, almost drowned out by the surrounding reporters' scrum.

"Who the fuck do they think they are!" said Mickey, now safely out of earshot.

"They are the same old reporters seeking the same old headlines. Get used to it Mickey or leave the industry," said Riley.

Riley's experience showed, having travelled with many successful teams over the last decade. Every detail had been organised, ensuring the transit between the airport and the hotel was streamlined and incident free.

"Want to hear the good news?" she said.

"That would be a change," said Mickey.

"Raman accepted the sponsorship deal and you won't believe what clinched it."

"Try me."

"Raman's son decided the deal," said Riley.

"Ahmed?"

"No not Raman's eldest son, his youngest, Karim. Apparently he was in the crowd that watched you practice yesterday. He said it was the most wonderful exhibition he had ever seen. He was so impressed he swore to his father he would practice diligently to become as good as you. Mr. Raman confided to me that Karim would never practice. In fact he was very lazy. But now he can think of nothing else."

"Good thing I practiced Ludwig's strategy. It went over well with the locals."

Riley looked genuinely surprised by Mickey's response. Before she left Dubai, Ludwig's strategies were on the verge of being dumped.

"What happened out there?"

"I saw the light," said Mickey, not explaining his meaning.

The London traffic was running freely for a work day morning, providing a speedy ride to their hotel. The day was overcast, making him happy, as he wanted to remain indoors, free from gazing eyes. The media pack unnerved him and he felt like a drink.

"Now for the bad news," said Riley, interrupting his thoughts.

"Must we?"

"Yes we must. Sponsorship doesn't come without a price."

Mickey resigned himself to hearing the demands. A sponsor would want his pound of flesh.

"Let's get it over with," he said, resigned to making his day worse. The London cab pulled into The Strand, just a short ride to their hotel.

"You'll have to attend two one hour interviews with Phil Reid from the BBC. He will ask you a range of questions, some about your life," she said before Mickey interjected.

"No fucking way!" he said, but Riley ignored him.

"Two one hour interviews that will be cut down into a half hour profile that they are running on all the fancied or interesting players. The good news is that we have input on the final format. If you don't like what they say, it gets edited."

"I get the choice of what gets edited?"

"Most of it, but you have to answer questions on any topic," she said.

"Sounds suspicious?"

"Mickey, no one has got that big a concession except you. If you can't deal with it we may as well go home now.

Mickey stared out to the tourists making their way around The Strand. They looked to be going about their business, free to do as they wish. Mickey imagined he was one of them, walking the streets of London free from the spotlight of the global media. But life as a CWC cubeball player could never be like that.

"What else," he said, sensing Riley held back further bad news.

"You must of course wear our sponsor's logo when dealing with the media. All the shirts are in your room, for every occasion, shirts for playing, practicing, dining out and so forth."

"Shirts for fucking?" he said sarcastically. Riley ignored him and continued.

"You'll also play three exhibition matches for charity. That's it."

Mickey accepted the conditions. What else could he do?

The limousine pulled into the elegant courtyard of their hotel. The Rosewood Hotel was one of London's finest. The traditional Edwardian architecture gave it a feeling of luxurious history. Mickey could imagine horse-drawn carriages delivering their guests to the hotel entry. He would have enjoyed strolling through the hotel's grand gardens and rooms, but he suspected the press were not far behind them.

After checking in he disappeared straight to his room. He felt like a drink, but the fridge was bare. No doubt Riley had requested an alcohol ban be enforced by the hotel management. Mickey opted for a hot bath. He set his cubebit for an island scene and smoked a rette. His comeback was about to commence and already he was questioning his ability to handle life as a cubeball star. The press had unnerved him too easily. How would he handle the finals if his team managed to get that far? He drew heavily on his rette and allowed the calm of the lapping waves to rest his mind. He hoped that rettes would be all he needed to handle the rigours of the championships. But he couldn't be sure.

Evening's dinner was organised downstairs for the team and Mickey honoured it, although he planned to exit early and find a quiet bar somewhere in the small lanes of London. But to his surprise, Riley had arranged wine for the table and a quiet corner away from the busy restaurant's clientele of worldly travellers.

"I've arranged practice to be held at a cubeball venue not far from here. It's a small pub actually, but they have a serviceable cubeball room that fits our needs, good facilities and private."

"Near a pub, I'm surprised you risked it," said Mickey jokingly, referring to his alcohol-free room.

"Glass of wine?" retaliated Riley, before continuing.

"Our equipment arrives there tomorrow, so we should be able to commence practice by tomorrow evening...about 7pm," said Riley. Dr. Vance was the first to respond.

"Ludwig and I will be there at seven. I've never seen him so keen. That last practice session is all he talks about."

Mickey poured his glass of wine and took a large first sip. He was about to take his second and finish the glass but something about Ludwig's enthusiasm stopped him. His look was similar to that of Raman's young son after he beat him in the match play. The eyes expressed an admiration that bewildered Mickey. He knew he played the game well, better than most and that of course invited admiration. But he always felt the admiration was undeserved. Most of his adult life he had spent hating the very industry that seemed hell bent on rewarding him. Now on a night where he could only think about drinking, Ludwig looked at him as if he were a saint. Usually people's expectations brought out the worst in Mickey, but that evening Mickey sipped quietly on the wine provided for the remainder of the night before retiring to his room as good as sober.

In the lead up to the championships, Mickey's and the team's practice routine was relatively uneventful. Practice sessions allowed him to build his form as well as experiment with Ludwig's practice drills. Mickey also had the first of his two interviews, which he handled surprisingly well. His confidence was riding high and he let his team know it.

"We could win this championship on this form. It's all going to plan, Riley."

"You're not the only one thinking that. The press have listed you as the dark horse."

"Finally, the press are talking about the tournament. It's about time."

"Someone else has noticed your form, too," said Riley.

"Who?"

"Johnnie arrived from Manchester a few weeks ago and he's eager to catch up with you," said Riley, who had just returned from a press meeting. The mere mention of his name made Mickey suspicious and defensive.

"What'd you tell him?"

"Shit, here we go again. l told him nothing. l told him that I'd pass the message on to you," said Riley, head shaking.

"Where'd you meet him?" Mickey questioned.

"Fuck off, Mickey! I'm not going to be interrogated every time Johnnie talks to me. You ring him and tell him if you want to see him or not. I couldn't give a shit if you ever saw each other again."

Mickey's suspicions remained, particularly when Johnnie Draxma came into the conversation. Johnnie never had a meeting with him without an ulterior motive and that motive never strayed too far from money. He thought at first to refuse the meeting point blank, but intrigue got the better of him. Mickey calmed himself before speaking to Riley.

"I'm sorry, Riley. You're right to let me know. As a matter of fact I do want to talk to Johnnie," he said, leaving his sister surprised.

Johnnie's office was a swank affair. His taste for all things expensive hadn't changed. It was an old office block near Holborn station, heritage listed and lovingly restored. Inside it was ultra-modern. It had an open structure with high roofs and steel exposed beams, creating unorthodox angles. At its entry sat an efficient young lady, dressed in fine tweed and long, brown straight hair neatly tied back. Her red brimmed glasses belied her corporate appearance as did her cockney accent.

"Mr. Allen for Mr. Draxma," she said before asking Mickey to take a seat.

No more than a minute had passed and one of his assistants was in the foyer greeting him.

"Johnnie won't be long. He's just finishing up a department meeting. He asked me to show you around our offices," said the assistant who introduced herself as Danielle.

Mickey was taken around a maze of offices cordoned only by low removable partitions. He lost track of the myriad of departments Danielle reeled off – marketing, international gaming, domestic gaming, technology were all he remembered. Yes, Johnnie had done well for himself. Not that Mickey was surprised. He was a household name in the industry and his number one player, Flaveau, happened to be the world champion.

Mickey was flattered by the warm greeting. But the tour of his business was too cordial for his liking. It felt like he was an old friend being welcomed back to the fold. Still, he thanked Danielle for her guide around Draxma Incorporated before being shown into Johnnie's office. It was smaller than his old office but impressive none the less. The large oak desk alone signalled opulence. Mickey was seated on a matching green leather oak chair in wait for the president.

"The prodigal son returns," boomed the voice of his ex-friend and ex-manager, Johnnie.

Mickey stood and turned to be greeted by Johnnie, smiling with his hand extended to shake his hand. Mickey accommodated and surprisingly smiled back. Not that he had any deeply hidden warm feelings for the guy. His first thought was that Johnnie had aged in the last decade; his thick black hair had receded to alarming proportions. He looked much older than his advertising billboards showing him shaking hands with his champion, Flaveau, inviting Londoners to the world championships. The two exchanged pleasantries as best they could before Johnnie got to the point.

"So how does it feel to be the comeback kid? What took you so long? Has it been ten years?"

What a question. Mickey didn't really know all the reasons why he returned to the game. Money was one reason. That's what brought him back from Mars. But now he was on Earth he wanted more. Maybe he wanted to repay Riley. Maybe Ludwig made him see an opportunity. Maybe he just got bored with the way things were. The truth was Mickey didn't know why, and even if he did, Johnnie would be the last person he would tell.

"It just felt right," said Mickey.

"I hear you're in good form, too. Think you can win?"

Mickey couldn't help but think about whether Johnnie had gambled a large stash of his company's money on him or his champion. Either way he wasn't going to grace him with an answer.

"You're the expert. What odds have you got on me?" Johnnie laughed at the irony.

"Well, I think that Flaveau is unbackable, but I always liked to bet on a dark horse," said Johnnie, as he sat down behind his desk. He had the look of a businessman about to make a deal.

"You've assembled yourself a good team, too. Your sister has become the best in the business. Have you realised that yet?"

"You trained her. She must be the best," countered Mickey. Johnnie made a forced smile but chose not to respond to Mickey's sarcasm.

"I don't know about your strategist though. I have no history on him."

Mickey could not bear any more of his mental jousting.

"Johnnie, get to the point. Why did you want to see me? I sure as hell know it wasn't because you missed me."

"Charming as always. Did you happen to take any notice of what my assistant Danielle had to say to you? I mean, I know you're not a lover of business except the payment part for your services. But if you haven't already realised, you're a big story in this country and a big story means big money. Danielle took you through our gaming department and I'll bet everybody got up to greet you? Want to know why?"

"Yeah they were all pleasant. I don't know why. Maybe you told them what a shit I am and not to upset me," said Mickey.

"I wish! The gaming industry is the biggest segment for gambling in cubeball now. Globally, it's worth billions every year. So every year gamers challenge our electronic stars at tournaments which culminate in a world championship at the same time as the real deal. My techo's represent the CWC top ten of the gaming world. So when a player makes the top ten it's important that we sign them to a contract so that we can use their name and image. We also sign up any popular talent that becomes a cult hero to the gamers. Do you want to know the latest cult hero?"

"You're telling me that gamers worldwide think I'm a cult hero?" said Mickey half laughing.

"Yeah, what a laugh, a two bit drunk who's wasted his life is idolised by millions of fans. Maybe it's the rock star thing, you know 'rebel without a cause', fuck the world kind of thing. But you're it and I'll pay you well for the use of your 'brand', even bigger if you actually do well in the tournament, which I greatly doubt," said Johnnie.

"What's the catch?'

"Man, I've met some dumb asses in my time. The only catch is that your name will last as long as you're in the headlines. I'll pay you good money now, but when you drug out again as I'm sure you will, the comeback kid will be forgotten. Then the brand will be worthless and I'll end the contract."

Mickey stood up, he'd heard enough. Nothing had changed. Money still ruled Johnnie's world. But that in itself didn't upset him. It was the way he contaminated anyone who came into his life. At least Mickey knew what Johnnie wanted.

"I'll talk to Riley, she manages my affairs and we'll get back to you."

"Fine, the deadline is this week. I want your name on our books throughout the tournament," said Johnnie, a little too confidently.

No handshakes this time as Mickey showed himself out. At that moment he had no intention of ever talking to Johnnie again but he had to ask one last question.

"You never told me who you intended to back for world champion?"

Johnnie sat back in his high leather chair. He looked up to the ceiling, almost as if for divine intervention, before he responded.

"The last time I did that it didn't exactly end in bouquets all round, did it? I'll send our contract to Riley. Sign it by Friday."

By the time Mickey had sufficiently collected his thoughts, dinner had arrived. The team were meeting in the hotel restaurant to review the week ahead. Mickey was famished. He hadn't eaten since the morning. He hoped that he had outgrown the old hostilities between them. But his memories of Jules disappearance and the betrayals of that year had resurfaced. Mickey arrived late at the restaurant and was surprised to be greeted by Riley who was with a friend.

"Mickey, I'd like you to meet Lisa, an old school buddy of mine. She went to our elementary school for a few years before her family transferred to London. I caught up with Lisa at last year's tournament."

Mickey tried to place the face but he did not recall her. She had an unassuming attractiveness that lit up when she smiled. Mickey wished he were in a better mood but his meeting with Johnnie still occupied his thoughts.

"You'll be dining alone for a while. Lisa and I can't stay for dinner tonight and Dr. Vance and Ludwig are running late. But I wanted to talk to you before we left. Like a drink?" Mickey gratefully accepted her offer, leaving him to chat with Lisa.

"So I finally meet Riley's famous brother," said Lisa in a warm and friendly manner.

"Famous for all the wrong reasons I'm afraid."

"What do you do for a living?" he said feebly, too stressed to concoct good conversation.

"I'm a journalist," said Lisa, waiting for a reaction and getting one. "Don't worry; I'm not trying to get a scoop. I do travel writing mainly and now and then I get to play 'ghost writer'," she said.

"You write fiction," said Mickey unsure of what she meant.

"No, a ghost writer for famous or infamous people, mainly biographies," she said.

"Oh I see...do you find it interesting?"

"It depends on who I'm writing about I guess. The travel writing can be fun, particularly when my editor needs a story about the south of France."

Mickey could tell she was not exaggerating. Her face glowed when she mentioned travel. He guessed she was good at her craft too, not because of her eloquent language but from the quality of her clothes. She was in casual attire but even her jeans looked 'designer label', with overcoat, scarf and woollen hat perfectly matching her Italian leather boots. Mickey realised how unfashionable he must have appeared to her as he tried to cover his cheap clothes with his equally cheap overcoat.

"Wine for my brother and tonic for you, Lisa,' said Riley, as she returned with drinks.

"We have to head off to a show tonight, Mickey. Lisa insisted," she said, glancing at her friend and smiling. "Did the meeting go well?"

Mickey was unsure whether he should share his thoughts with Riley and her friend from the press. But he liked Lisa and didn't want to appear too stiff and defensive.

"He wants to sign a contract for the gaming rights to our team. I told him I'd talk to you first. We have a week apparently. It sounded lucrative but you know my thoughts about Johnnie and contracts."

"He had mentioned it to me on the phone a few days ago. I told him that it wasn't my decision and that he should talk to you. Do you want me to look at his proposal?"

Mickey wondered why Riley hadn't mentioned her conversation to him prior to the meeting but he didn't want to raise sibling grievances in front of her friend. He wanted to say an outright no in defiance, but sipped on his wine and thought about his words before speaking.

"Sure, have a look and let me know what we would be letting ourselves in for."

Mickey would let his sister negotiate with Johnnie. It would be interesting to find out how important that alliance would be to her. Riley quickly drank her drink as she checked the time.

"Okay then, I should receive his contract in the morning, first thing. You know Johnnie where money is concerned," said Riley before guiding Lisa to stand up and leave for their engagement.

"I'll see you in the morning then," said Riley and they were gone.

"Yeah, I look forward to it," he said to himself, downing the glass of wine and ordering another.

Some ten minutes later Dr. Vance and Ludwig arrived for dinner. Mickey was about to order another wine but one of the guests appeared to be paying him a lot of attention. Was it the ever watchful press? He couldn't be sure, so he ordered mineral waters all round to accompany their meal. Dr. Vance updated Mickey on Ludwig's condition as he did regularly.

"I've never seen him this happy. He drew another ten games today."

"That's good, but I won't be able to practice every game you create, we have precious time as it is to practice," said Mickey, prompting Ludwig to respond.

"Why not Mickey, don't you want to play music?"

"I do, but we have a competition to win first," said Mickey looking to the Doc to help him explain.

"Doesn't my music help?" Ludwig began to get stressed.

"What Mickey means is that he has to approach his games in many ways, depending on his opponent. Your strategies will have an important role, just not in every game," said Dr. Vance.

"I need to draw more Mickey, I keep hearing the new music and I don't want to stop drawing it in case I forget it," said Ludwig. Mickey didn't look to Dr. Vance for guidance this time.

"Keep drawing my friend. It is important. I promise to study each game tonight," he said, relaxing Ludwig.

"I always feel calm and happy when the music plays in my head. The outside world is too noisy. How do you find the world, Mickey?"

Mickey was pleasantly surprised by Ludwig's question. He spoke like a good friend. Ludwig was increasingly trusting and confiding in him.

"We're birds of a feather," said Mickey. Ludwig's face went blank, making Mickey and Doctor Vance laugh.

"He means you and he are very much like each other," said Dr. Vance, putting light on his puzzlement. Ludwig felt the need to hug Mickey.

Mickey held him close, accepting their developing bond. In a world he found distrustful, Ludwig offered him a naive almost childlike friendship that he accepted openly.

"I feel less stress when I'm on medication but my memory blurs. l lose the beautiful music. I must write the new music," Ludwig confided.

"I know. But we'll make plenty of music together, I promise you that," said Mickey.

"He keeps re-organising his drawings. There were so many, we had to buy him a new bag to hold them all. His life's work is in that bag. It's his treasure," said Dr. Vance.

Mickey felt a brotherly responsibility for Ludwig. Money and contracts were looming and the tide of a global industry's force was casting a shadow over all of them. He had never been one for 'caring and sharing', but this strange man with a unique take on the world was influencing Mickey in subtle ways that he didn't understand. He enjoyed the meal with his team that evening and resisted the urge to end it with a 'night cap'.

Mickey had a busy morning ahead. The BBC interview was scheduled for mid-morning followed by a number of practice sessions. He was in the restaurant earlier than normal to enjoy a quiet breakfast before Riley joined him, no doubt ready to provide news of Johnnie's offer. Mickey wanted to believe Riley had his best interest at heart, but he suspected she and Johnnie still had an alliance that he could not break. Both of them were filthy rich. How did Riley obtain such wealth at her age? Questions about his sister's loyalty pervaded his mind. She was good at her trade. Too good.

"Have you ordered?" said Riley as she approached Mickey's table from behind him.

"Just coffee. How was your night?" said Mickey.

"Sore head, but self inflicted so I can't complain."

"She seems a good sort."

"Yeah, she's a good friend. She's coming to watch us compete next week."

"Does she like cubeball?"

"No, it seems a sudden interest," said Riley half smiling.

"What's that supposed to mean?"

"Nothing."

Mickey wasn't buying into her taunts as he changed the subject. "Any word from Johnnie?"

"I got the contract. It runs for the length of the tournament with an option for you to extend to the year should you make the quarter final. It looks solid to me," she said.

"What's it worth?"

"You'd earn fifty thousand credits for the tournament and an option of a quarter million for the year. You would have to make appearances though, as long as they don't conflict with Raman's obligations." she said.

Mickey didn't show it but the price floored him. He would earn a quarter of a million credits just to have his name on Johnnie's game ware. It seemed too good to believe.

"There must be a catch?"

"Well, you have to make the quarters for starters. But other than that, you only have to make two appearances in London over the next calendar year. It looks water tight. Pretty standard these days, Flaveau would be earning a million a year on game ware."

Mickey still thought it too good to believe. Johnnie always got his pound of flesh for money.

"Tell him I'm not interested."

Riley didn't show it but Mickey knew she was pissed. He couldn't blame her though, she had forked out a small fortune getting the team to London, but Mickey figured the bills were being payed by Raman now anyway.

"The sponsorship is enough and you can decide the cuts between us. Take it all if you want." said Mickey.

"A hundred percent then," she joked.

"If you want. But I do need some cash for new clothes. I can't keep walking around in these rags," said Mickey dead pan. Riley smiled again, which annoyed the hell out of him.

"Rather sudden isn't it?" she said continuing her taunts.

But Mickey would have no more of it, picking up the morning paper and pretending to read the headlines. The truth was his mind was a mile away, wondering whether his life was about to take a more pleasurable turn.

The press interview was held at the site of the finals, 'The New Crucible' as it was fondly named. The New Crucible was the 'Lords' of world cubeball. It was built in and around the old London Olympic stadium, a hub of sport, dining, theatre and leisure activities.

The complex was fitted out with one multi-purpose indoor stadium that seated thirty-five thousand and another six smaller stadiums holding around ten thousand. The CWC's offices were close by and a myriad of other related industries, making it the true home of cubeball.

Mickey had a familiarity for the stadiums from viewing the live telecasts of the annual world titles on television but he had never experienced them first hand. The interview was set up in the 'Ronnie Anderson' stadium where the semi-finals would be played. It was considered the finest of all the stadiums, holding ten thousand but maintaining an intimacy that recreated the same feel of the old crucible.

The room was filled with technology that could get you to Mars and back, but clever design ensured the cube was the main feature. Subtle colours also softened the garishness that affected most of the championship stadiums around the world. Mickey felt the calming effect of the stadium as he slowly walked down the stairs to the inner sanctum. Holographic images lined the walls, creating a rainforest feel. The lighting and acoustic equipment were hidden behind the intricate holographs, so that the stadium's heart, the most famous cube in the world stood out like a beacon. The cube's balance between high technology and craftsmanship left Mickey spell bound. He sat in the stands reminiscing on past battles and speculating on his future battles in this arena.

"Mr. Allen, welcome," said Richard Carrington, the BBC reporter. He invited Mickey to the interview area. Two chairs were strategically placed in front of the cube. Further afield, service and media people busied themselves with final preparations for the opening of the world's biggest tournament. Within minutes, they were ready to start the interview. Mickey was comfortably warm in his bulky overcoat, but on Riley's insistence, he begrudgingly removed it to display his sponsor's logo for the cameras.

"Good to see you again, Mickey. All going well?" said Richard.

"Yes the hotel and practice facilities are excellent."

Richard spent time briefing Mickey on the scope of his planned questions before commencing the interview. He opened with standard questions about his preparations for the tournament, before more revealing enquiries were made.

"There's been much written about your past and your disappearance from the cubeball world for nearly a decade. You were a national champion, managed by one of the best, Johnnie Draxma, and yet you dropped out at your peak. Why?"

Mickey wanted to tell the cameras exactly what he thought of Johnnie Draxma, but given the telecast's global reach, he tempered his response.

"Yes, he's the world's most successful manager now. He got there through hard work and he also demanded a lot from his team. I think at that time in my life I wasn't ready for that level of commitment. I tired of the rigours of professional match play and wanted to enjoy my game more. So I preferred exhibition matches to competing."

"Yes you opted out of the circuit all together at the time when many thought you would be the next world champion. Any regrets?"

"No regrets."

"Then of course there were the much publicised stories of your battle with alcohol, some say that's ongoing?"

"I've never seen it that way. But it is true that I liked to work hard and play hard, sometimes to my detriment."

Richard continued to press the alcohol and drugs scandals, as Mickey continued to deflect them. Unable to pry too much from Mickey, he turned back to his relationship with Johnnie.

Ultimately you left the Johnnie Draxma fold, some say in less than harmonious circumstances?"

"What can I say? I was difficult and he was demanding. We had also known each other since young teenagers and we kind of drifted apart."

"His corporation has been a subject of an enquiry this year as a result of his gambling and financial interests. Did that ever play a part in your decision to split?"

"Large sums of money have always flowed into gambling, so of course it impacts. But I've never got involved in that side of the business."

"So you've never felt pressured to play by anybody else's rules?"

On the whole, Mickey had played the game he loved free from outside influence, except for the state championship. His mind returned to his state final loss as an eighteen-year-old and he wondered whether he would be asked directly about that game. Was he a pawn in the middle of some larger enquiry investigating the integrity of the sport?

"I think all CWC players feel some pressure, given the huge sums gambled on them. I've tried to shut that out and play my natural game, no matter the circumstances."

Mickey hoped his answers sufficient and to his relief Richard left it there.

"So you have a new team and you've been showing good form. How do you think you will do in this tournament?"

"The game's very different from the one I left a decade ago. There are better players, new technology and as you said, vast sums of money gambled. I really don't know how I'll go. But I'll do what I've always done, prepare well and take it one game at a time."

"Mickey Allen, we wish you well."

At that, Richard signalled for the taping to finish, before inviting Mickey for a coffee and 'off the record' chat. Mickey was cold from sitting through the interview coatless and welcomed the chance to warm up with a brew. Coat back on and hot coffee in hand, Mickey relaxed until Richard broke the silence.

"Mickey, I want to reveal some information that I'd advise you keep confidential," he warned. Mickey nodded his agreement before Richard continued.

"Our paper has been investigating Johnnie Draxma's operations for over a month now. Over the last decade, his company grew exponentially. Some of that growth has been as a result of questionable practices. We believe we've uncovered some explosive findings and we expect to go public with those findings soon," said Richard.

Mickey's mind was drawn to the time frame of the investigation – the last decade. Would it include Mickey's dealings with him?

"Richard, I appreciate that you're confiding in me, but why tell me this? I left him a long time ago."

"You know him well, probably better than any other cubeball player and there must have been reasons beyond 'growing apart', that led to your bust-up?"

Richard's implication unsettled Mickey. He wanted to say as little as possible.

"I've come here to play cubeball, that's it."

"And yet, you visited his office for discussions about a possible contract deal," said Richard.

Mickey's fear rose now. Was he being blindly drawn into one of Johnnie's ambushes?

"Riley arranged that meeting. I heard what he had to offer and refused it."

"Have you?"

He was about to press Mickey further before Richard's mobile rang, drawing him into other discussions, and allowing Mickey to collect his thoughts. *Had he refused Johnnie's offer?* Richard's question resonated in his mind as he wondered whether Riley had acted on his request. Carrington finished his call.

"What did you mean by that, Richard?"

"Our contact in Draxma Corporation tells us that preparation for the Mickey Allen gamer' campaign has commenced," replied Richard. Mickey shook his head.

"I met Johnnie. He made me an offer and I refused it."

"Really?" Richard looked unconvinced. He sat forward in his chair and touched Mickey's arm, reassuringly. "Mickey, I promise this is not an inquisition into your past. But you have to realise that we will be soon printing highly explosive information about your previous manager. You, more than anyone, would know how he'll respond. We have to be sure of our facts. We have to leave no stone unturned. Any error would be considered defamatory and costly to us."

"I get all of that Richard. But what possible difference would my signing a small contract with Johnnie make? Not that I have. But if I did, how could that be so important to your investigation?"

Richard offered Mickey a rette and lit it, before lighting his own. He then sat back in his chair and inhaled his rette several times, seemingly considering his answer. He looked around the stadium a few times. He clearly did not want to be heard.

"I'll be honest with you, Mickey. I'm not sure that it would. But we've also learnt through our sources that a mystery punter has taken an interest in your comeback."

"So?"

"His interest is to the tune of fifty million credits on you to win this tournament."

Richard drew deeply on his rette as he gazed at Mickey, seemingly waiting for a reaction." Mickey did likewise. He didn't know what to think. The business side of cubeball always unnerved him. So many people invest their fortunes on CWC games. Players had a huge responsibility to play to the best of their 'natural ability' or questions would be asked. The worst of it was that whether you played fair or foul, considerations of implication hung around all players.

"You think it's Johnnie?"

"Let's look at the facts, Mickey. The punter has money to throw around and a lot of confidence in your abilities. There'd only be a few people in the cubeball industry that fits that description. There's of course another side of this to consider. The odds at the time were 25 to one for you winning the championship. If you happen to pull this off, you'll make this investor an overnight billionaire."

Mickey shook his head at the scale of the bet. He had faith in his ability to compete. But deep down, he'd be happy if he got as far as the quarter-finals.

"The punter's crazy."

"Perhaps. Or he or she knows something others don't. Needless to say, your odds have narrowed somewhat."

"I don't like what you're implying. I've come to play fairly and do everything I can to win. To me, that bet is pure madness."

"We'll take that on board, Mickey. But you have to understand that amount of credit has made a lot of authorities sit up and take notice - drug enforcement for one. You were getting enough attention as it was, but now, the whole cubeball world will be talking about you."

Mickey didn't like where Richard was leading with their 'off the record' conversation. He would say no more to the reporter this day. Instead, he looked at his watch.

"I'm late for my next appointment," he lied.

"Thanks for your time, Mickey. Here's my card. If you would like to speak more about anything I've raised, call me."

Mickey took the reporters card and thanked him before leaving, immediately calling Riley and arranging a luncheon meeting. Old fears surfaced in Mickey's mind as the London cab returned him to the hotel. A decade had passed and Mickey still felt he played with a team that he knew little about. Riley had worked most of that decade with Johnnie. Had she really left his employ? He'd lost count of the number of times she'd said that before and lied. Could she leave the employ of one of the world's most powerful business figures in the cubeball industry? Perhaps no one ever could? All Mickey knew was that events were occurring that he could not control. What he didn't know, was that many more were about to be unleashed on his unsuspecting team.

16

Business

Ludwig's day started like any other.

Order was everything. He rose from the left side of the bed to where he would place his feet into two slippers he had carefully laid out the night before. His 'woolly slippers' were one of his great comforts. Most floor surfaces aggravated him, particularly the sharp fibres of carpet or the chalk board feel of tile. Ludwig would simply refuse to get out of bed.

"Must help Mickey, must help Mickey," he repeatedly murmured to himself, before he peered down to the carpet beside the bed as if it were a sea of sharks.

He always had two pairs of the same slippers in the same condition as he rotated their use until the wool wore to the sole. Then two new pairs took their place.

"Two, must be two," said Ludwig as he cautiously lowered his feet into the slippers, until they were safely secured. He then drank the two glasses of water he had left on the bedside table, the night before.

"Oh, it's all different, very different," mumbled Ludwig, not sure how he should walk to the bathroom.

"Dr. Vance," he repeated. But Dr. Vance did not reply.

"Too many steps. Too many numbers.....but must help Mickey," said Ludwig, considering how he should move himself forward.

"Do it by twos. Must be twos," he repeated, as he slowly advanced to the bathroom, in sets of two steps.

Five minutes passed, before he stood in the bathroom. He and Dr. Vance had carefully prepared it the night before. There were two identical electric gel shavers, again rotated like his slippers. Ludwig disliked shaving, but he learned long ago that he should shave twice a day, morning and evening so that his facial hair did not grow too long. He once shaved a three day growth and never forgot the intense pain of the experience. He experimented with all forms of shavers and ultimately found the combination electric and gel shavers were the least aggravating.

Two face washers finished the job before he showered. Now showering was an all together different sensation for him. The key to a soothing wash was temperature and flow. The hotel's showers happened to be their best feature. They offered precision taps that easily adjusted the force and heat he required. Ludwig luxuriated under body temperature showers and medium flow force. It calmed him, like music. He would sometimes spend an hour under its soothing stream, lost in a rapturous Beethoven fugue. He exited the shower to stand on one of two carefully placed bath mats used on alternate days, as were two towels for drying. Dried, he selected his clothing for the day. Two pairs of various ensembles filled his wardrobe, which he selected depending on the weather. Then Ludwig went about the most important routine of his day. He went to get his drawings.

Some days he would skim the large stack of drawings and relive small excerpts of his favourite music. On more difficult days he would play whole symphonies to soothe his troubled mind. Ludwig spent hours with his notes before he felt ready to face the chaotic sounds of the normal world.

Ludwig looked in the cupboard, ready to study his precious drawings, only to find it empty. Anyone else would simply scan the room for the missing drawings, but Ludwig wasn't anyone else. The disappearance had to have been due to his error. He had not followed his routine correctly that day. He closed the cupboard door and re-organised the whole room as if it were night and he were going to bed. Slippers ready, bathroom ready, bed made, lights out. He then imagined his favourite music before he lay in the bed, pretending to sleep for another night.

When he was ready, he repeated his routine – slippers, two glasses of water, shave, shower and dry before approaching the cupboard a second time. No change.

"Doing something wrong...all wrong," he repeated, as he lay back on his bed, refusing to move any more.

The thought his work was gone overwhelmed him. He couldn't accept his situation, choosing this time to wait for his life's work to re-appear. But with every passing minute, his patience gave way to panic. He rocked back and forth, his mind recreating his morning preparations hoping to remember what he had done wrong. Then a dreadful thought overtook him. What if he never found his drawings? How could he remember his music? All too soon Ludwig could not remember anything. His mind raced. He was lost in fear.

By the time Dr. Vance got to him, Ludwig's mind was lost deeply in his music, desperately recreating symphonies. By the time Dr. Vance had checked and re-checked Ludwig's room and informed the hotel, the whole team were aware of what appeared to be a theft.

Breakfast was a sombre affair. Ludwig wouldn't leave his room. He refused to communicate and more concerning, he refused his medication.

"In this state, he won't take part in the tournament. He'll spend the next few weeks re-writing his drawings. Nothing else will matter," said Dr. Vance.

Mickey could think only of the theft and who would want his notes, whereas Riley's mind appeared to be elsewhere.

"Do you want me to make some approaches to other strategists?"

Mickey snapped his reply. "We do it with Ludwig or not at all!"

His mind returned to the theft. There could only be one person responsible for this. It had to be Johnnie. He thought Johnnie was the mystery punter too. Audacious million credit bets weren't new to Johnnie. He'd bet sizeable fortunes before on Mickey's games, both winning and losing. Mickey considered calling the police, but knowing Johnnie they would never see Ludwig's notes again.

"This smells like Johnnie's involved," Mickey said, casting a suspicious glare, Riley's way.

"How would I know," she replied.

"If you don't know who the thief is, maybe you know who the mystery punter is, he said, opening the morning paper's sports headlines.

"Here we go again. The minute something's suspicious, blame me," said Riley, as she read the article.

"Well help me out. We're minus our strategist and the only solution you offer the team is to replace him. What do you expect?"

"Okay, okay, settle down. If you think Johnnie is behind all of this, I'll call him now," Riley replied, picking up her cubebit, ready to dial. Mickey raised his hands and shook his head.

"No. I want to see him in person."

Mickey cursed himself for not thinking through their situation. He knew better than anybody that Johnnie would stop at nothing to get his way. Ludwig's notes should have been better protected. Now he had to negotiate with his former manager. And negotiations with Johnnie guaranteed that there would be a high price to pay.

"Arrange a meeting with him today," said Mickey.

"You're not seeing him alone again. I'm your manager and backer. We go together." Riley insisted.

Mickey didn't disagree. If anything, he'd be able to gauge how close the two really were. "Okay, do it," he replied, before turning to Dr. Vance.

"Don't worry Harry, I'll get those drawings returned to us and Ludwig will be on our team come Monday morning," said Mickey, more in hope than with conviction.

Mickey and Riley entered the offices of Johnnie Draxma just one day after Mickey vowed never to lay eyes on him again. But Johnnie always got his way. Once you started business with a man like him you never really stopped. They both walked past the reception and straight into Johnnie's office. Johnnie was on the phone and didn't look surprised by their impassioned entry. He courteously ended his phone call, before giving Mickey one of his smug looks.

"What brings you here? I didn't think I'd see you in my office again." Mickey didn't buy it.

"You don't have to bullshit to me. I want it back."

"Want what back?"

"Ludwig's game plan drawings were stolen from our hotel. I want them back."

"London's a big town, Mickey. Anyone could have broken into your hotel rooms."

Mickey shook his head and turned to Riley, inviting her to join the conversation. Riley accommodated.

"You or someone you know stole important papers and we need them back. Let's just cut to the chase. What's your price?" Mickey showed displeasure that Riley wanted to pay him, but Riley cut him short. "Leave this to me, Mickey," she said, returning her gaze toward Johnnie and waiting for his reply.

"Well if some thief pinched your papers I could hire people to find them for you, but that is costly you understand?" said Johnnie.

"Enlighten me," Riley replied.

"At least half the fee I was offering you yesterday. But if you could find a way to sign our contract now, I'd be happy to do it gratis, given we go way back and all."

"Well, your partially right, Johnnie. I'm prepared to reduce the price by half of what Mickey's actually worth to you. My conservative valuation, given Mickey's recent, dramatic rise in odds to win the tournament, is ten million credits. Have you read the news? Mickey's rated equal favourite with Flaveau."

"Ten million? You must be fucking joking, Riley. In case you forgot, he's a substance addict."

"You'll have to stop living in the past, Johnnie. I have his latest medical records. He has an all clear from a reputable doctor. But as you said, given we go way back, I'm prepared to sign a contract for five million credits, subject to my star player agreeing and you finding the misplaced papers."

Johnnie sat forward in his chair and rested his chin on his two prayer shaped hands. He briefly looked pissed, before he willed himself to smile and reply.

"Riley, Riley. How I've missed you."

"I'll get you your man's papers by tonight, together with our new contract." promised Johnnie.

"Thank you, Johnnie. Mickey and I will discuss the contract and send you our reply in the morning. It's always a pleasure doing business with you." Riley said. She stood up, straightened her Versace suit and politely shook Johnnie's hand. Mickey trailed behind her, shaking Johnnie's hand unconvincingly. Johnnie nodded, holding his forced smile. For the first time that Mickey remembered, Johnnie was lost for words. Mickey wasn't sure whether to be happy or annoyed. Had Riley out-witted their old manager or were they about to sign a deal with the devil?

The team was re-united that night as they enjoyed good conversation and good food. Ludwig looked a different man. His drawings had been returned. He was back on medication and was almost back on track.

"Johnnie delivered Ludwig's strategies, a counter signed contract and the cheque," said Riley.

Mickey was surprised that there was no 'sting in the tail' and that Johnnie followed through to the letter. He still wondered what future compromise would have to be made. But he had read and re-read the contract and it had no hidden clauses. So now, he just wanted to share in Ludwig's happiness. His new friend had made difficult changes to his life, to help him play the game he loved. Mickey admired his courage.

"We've already put that money to good use. Ludwig agreed to have his work put into a safe deposit box," said Mickey.

"Why would they want Ludwig's notes?" said Dr. Vance. Mickey and Riley cast a knowing glance at each other.

"Remember that we are competing in the world championships. Teams will do just about anything to gain an advantage," said Mickey before Riley continued.

"There is widespread theft of 'game plans' but usually of 'tech programs' not hard copy. The game is so much bigger than just this tournament. New game programs are highly sought. Teams will pay millions for quality programs that offer them a competitive advantage. So there is a great temptation to obtain these drawings illegally."

"So Ludwig's drawings are seen that way?" said Dr. Vance.

"It's possible that word got out about Mickey's new style of game. Many watched him practice in the Emirates. It was an oversight by me to be honest. The 'tech' recordings of Mickey's games have always been secured. I just never thought that they would look at Ludwig's drawings in the same way," said Riley.

"So this Johnnie character was responsible. Why don't you just report him to the police?" said Dr. Vance.

"I don't know for sure that he was responsible. I'll never know. But I'm sure he could find Ludwig's notes for us and that's what matters right now," said Mickey.

"Well I'm glad I went into the medical profession!" Dr. Vance joked before continuing.

"The one good thing out of all of this is that Ludwig designed a new game. He was so elated by their return he drew a special game for you, Mickey," he said, turning to Ludwig.

"This is my gift, Mickey. Thank you for finding my work," said Ludwig, proudly handing his new game plan to him.

Mickey felt inspired by the way Ludwig pressed on. He battled every day of his life just to 'fit in' to the world. Walking into a busy street would feel like walking a mine field and yet he continued on, even to the point of walking into a world championship tournament.

"Ludwig, if there's a way of winning this championship, I will find it," said Mickey, in an emotional tone.

He hugged Ludwig tight to show his admiration and then he did something he hadn't done in a long time. He turned to Riley and hugged her.

"I'll never forget what you've done for me. You really have become an accomplished and polished manager. I'll do my best to win your faith in me, Riley."

Riley wasn't usually emotional, but Mickey's unexpected display of affection surprised her enough to raise a few small tears. Mickey gazed at her sister and knew a mixture of emotions drew her tears that evening. It was likely she had unleashed a cocktail of potential reprisals merely by being on Mickey's team. He wasn't sure why she had taken the risk, but he wanted to repay her. He just hoped there was no hidden agenda this time. Riley soon collected her composure again.

"Lisa asked about you. She has an upcoming work function and no date. Interested?"

"It'd be fun, but the tournament starts Monday," said Mickey, unconvincingly.

"You don't play until next Friday and I figured you'd be in need of a break by then. If we get through to the quarters you won't have your next match until the following Monday."

Mickey wanted to agree but something stopped him.

"She's a great girl. No drugs, no problems. You'd have fun," said Riley, reassuringly.

Mickey wondered about the soundness of her idea. He had been no angel over the past years. He'd got used to dating for pleasure on Mars, whereas Lisa was a genuine person. The thought both scared and excited him at the same time.

"I don't know, Riley."

"Look, let me tell her you like the idea and that if you have no media commitments you'd come. That way you have an escape clause. Fair?"

Mickey smiled to himself. His little sister was ever the negotiator. He agreed to her plan before returning to the team's job at hand.

"Practice tomorrow at 10 a.m. We have some real challenges ahead. It's a world championship and there are no easy matches, so we need to do our homework to have any chance of competing. How's the 'tech' plans?" said Mickey.

"All potential games for the first three rounds are in. Your competitors are young Brits. They're not rated, so they are all very beatable," said Riley, confidently.

"I need to slot one of Ludwig's games in each round. We won't refine it without testing it in match play. Are you happy with that?" said Mickey.

Riley looked anything but happy, but she accepted Ludwig's unusual game plans.

"Let's enact them when you have a good lead or else in an opening game. That could confuse them tactically."

"Agreed, although I want to look at Ludwig's latest drawing, too," said Mickey.

"My new game is unique. The music is new," said Ludwig.

"Unique is definitely your strong suit! Any thoughts, Harry?" said Mickey.

"I'm sure of one thing; you are drawing out his latent talent. For the first time, Ludwig is seeing the application of his work and that's got to be beneficial. It's like bringing back Beethoven's deafness," said Dr. Vance.

Mickey agreed. Some of Ludwig's game plans were unusual to say the least. But, game changing or not, Ludwig was contributing more unique game plans regularly for the team. Mickey wasn't sure whether any of his ideas would come to anything, but he did know that he would not progress to the final week without creative new approaches. He just hoped they would find that unique formula in time.

The grey morning was cold and fog had settled on to the quiet London streets. There was a sole light on in the bar as Mickey walked through the door and greeted the owner.

"I think I'll be putting my money on you next week," said Bob, impressed by Mickey's early arrival.

"I expect free drinks then, Bob!" Mickey joked, before walking into the cubeball room. The room was cold but its scent comforted him. The cube was an old model that had been upgraded. The timber wall's aromas reminded him of his parent's sunroom back home. It comforted him as he remembered his early playing days, learning his stock and trade.

Mickey arrived early, not through any desire to practice his myriad of drills. This was the less glamorous side of cubeball, not unlike a lone swimmer 'swimming the lines'. But it was a pre-requisite that the best players had to do. No one would ever play the game if they knew the lengths a player had to go to play consistent quality cubeball. That was Mickey's hidden strength. He had the concentration to practice his craft.

The first hour went quickly as he honed his straight pots, then one cushion, two cushion and three cushion shots. His form was good, as he achieved a ninety percent success rate. Riley would give him exact data when she wired his game plays into the comtech. The second hour he practiced spin drills where he would attempt to land his cue-ball on a pre-determined marker. This was a less exact science. He gained a success rate of fifty percent - an unacceptable risk.

Yet Ludwig's game plans were built on angular rather than straight shots. The risks of his strategy were high, but the rewards for practicing it could make the difference. Mickey was further motivated to practice spin as there were only two players in the world who could master such a demanding strategy, he and Flaveau. For that reason, Mickey persevered with Ludwig's radical ideas. There was another reason. It gave him pleasure. Ludwig was right. There was a musicality about spin that reminded him why he loved the game.

Mickey was so focused by his practice he barely noticed the others arrive. Riley busied herself, looking her usual efficient self as she set up her comtech programs. Her years of experience in the industry showed, particularly her uncanny ability to sift through hundreds of potential game plays to identify the right one for every situation. Mickey wouldn't get past the first round without her instinct. Not long after, Ludwig and Dr. Vance arrived. Ludwig was unable to contain his excitement. His eyes were glued on Mickey as he practiced, fearing he may miss seeing a 'perfect game'.

Mickey practiced diligently for another hour. Then he looked to Riley to set the game play programs on the 3D holograph so that he could re-enact her strategies. He had played himself in, having already drilled for two hours so he did something different. He turned to Ludwig for advice.

"What do you make of Riley's game plan? Does she play music?"

Riley looked surprised by Mickey's question, as Ludwig offered a reply.

"Riley plays numbers. I always see numbers and colours. Complex colours yes, but no music."

"How about you Riley, what do you make of Ludwig's game plans, do they provide you any sense of music? Mickey asked.

"The truth?" she said looking to Mickey for support.

"Absolutely."

"Ludwig has a remarkable memory for game plays but I haven't seen any ability in him, to create unique game plays that would beat quality players."

Mickey then turned to Dr. Vance.

"Harry, you've spent a lot of time studying our progress. What do you make of how the team is going?"

Dr. Vance sat contemplating, half smiling as if he had been anticipating the question.

"Each of you has a single mindedness to achieve your best, but I don't see any connections that would mould you into a successful team. You're a team of individuals."

Mickey nodded in agreement before revealing what was on his mind.

"That's the truth of it. I know Riley alone could progress us through the first few rounds, but the better teams will find a way to beat our uncoordinated structures," he said, before turning to Riley.

"You and I have played together for years and yet I have little idea how you do what you do well and I expect you'd say the same of me... right?"

Riley nodded an agreement she had known for years.

"Sam, to his credit bridged that gap. But we don't have a world class strategist this time, we have Ludwig," said Mickey.

"I offered to get you a good strategist," said Riley defensively.

"I know what you have done for me, Riley. But I want to give us the best chance to win this competition and to do that I need new strategies. Ludwig offers one and I vote we use them, sparingly, but use them none the less." Riley resigned herself to supporting Mickey.

"Okay, so I enter his programs and work the odds which will be high. I can't see how that improves our chances of winning."

Mickey knew the idea was bordering on desperate and yet his instincts told him it was their best chance of winning. He turned to Dr. Vance.

"Any ideas, Harry?"

Dr. Vance studied the drawings for a while before he offered his thoughts.

"Well it seems to me that we have three distinct approaches in our team. Riley analyses by the numbers, Ludwig by music and you based on skill. You and Riley undoubtedly have special skills for this sport whereas Ludwig is an unproven quantity. If you are to use his latent talents you'll have to find a way to better understand it."

Mickey pondered how they could do that. Time was short, although Ludwig's game plans could be used sparingly in the early stages of the competition. He turned to Ludwig.

"Okay, let's focus on your new game. Describe the music you heard when you wrote it?"

Ludwig appeared overjoyed to be asked to describe the beauty that was in his head and he immediately rattled off Beethoven symphonies that best described his latest game.

"Riley can you download these?" said Mickey.

Riley nodded as she went about retrieving his selection from her files.

And so for the remainder of the morning, practice had turned into a classical music master-class much to the surprise of the pub staff who supplied their refreshments. It wasn't until early afternoon that Mickey played Ludwig's full game plan, using a selection of Beethoven's music playing in the background to recreate how Ludwig imagined it should be. Mickey could see the excitement in Ludwig's eyes as he commenced recreating the elaborate game to a range of different symphonies selected by Ludwig. Mickey didn't normally enjoy classical music but he felt the music helped him play the difficult shots with more accuracy.

The game itself was Ludwig's most difficult. Mickey may not have fully appreciated the complexity of Ludwig's music compilation, but he felt it through the demanding angles his strategy required. By the fourth attempt at the game, Riley was feeling as frustrated as Mickey.

"We have got a final to play tomorrow."

Mickey wanted to disagree but could not. He felt no closer to the magical feelings that Ludwig claimed to experience from his game plays. The music playing in the background actually started to grate on Mickey's mind rather than calm him. Finally, he had to turn the music off.

"Agreed, let's have a break and finish with some standard drills before we call it a day," said Mickey, disappointed that the practice had not advanced any new strategy.

The team ended a long practice session tired and no closer to discovering unique game plays that would help propel their team into the final rounds. Dr. Vance took Ludwig back to his room directly after dining, whereas Mickey and Riley lingered in the restaurant longer. Mickey sipped his glass of wine, while Riley studied her cubebit.

"Your odds have slipped behind Flaveau," she said.

"Don't you ever rest, Riley?"

Riley looked up from her cubebit briefly, to respond. "Only when I'm sure I can afford to." Riley's devotion to her cubebit annoyed Mickey.

"Can't you drag yourself away from your cubebit just this once and talk to me?"

Riley turned her cubebit off and placed it in her handbag. "There. Satisfied?"

"I've been thinking about that deal you pulled off with Johnnie."

"Yes."

"It seemed a coincidence that your price was five million credits."

Riley stared back at Mickey, in no hurry to respond.

"What are you asking, Mickey?"

"I'm asking what I didn't want to raise in front of Ludwig or Dr. Vance. This deal seemed way too easy. Johnnie doesn't lie down like that, especially for five million credits."

"Do you think that Johnnie is the only person in this industry with power and influence? Haven't you once taken the time to find out anything about my career?"

"Well, you're successful of course, but..."

Riley cut him short. "...but not as successful as Johnnie?" Riley shook her head in disgust. "You've been away for ten years, Mickey. Things have changed. I've got the top ten teams in the world knocking on my door, wanting me to help them. They'd pay me a small fortune to become their manager or consultant, whereas you treat me as if I'm still your kid sister. Johnnie may be the wealthiest cubeball manager, but I'm the best. So how about you show some appreciation for what I'm doing for you? And while you're at it, some trust and respect wouldn't go astray either."

"I do admire you, Riley. The trouble is I've never handled the business side of cubeball well. Someone's wagered five million credits on me to win the tournament. Now, suddenly I'm one of the favourites."

"You keep telling me how good you are. What do you expect?"

"I can play better than anyone on my day. It's just this fucking industry is suspicious about how we compete. If we have a good match, they suspect narcs. If we have a bad match, there's the possibility of match fixing."

"Get used to it, Mickey. You knew what you were getting yourself into."

"I can handle the media and industry officials. I can't handle corruption from those in my own team. Johnnie was corrupt. You know that."

"So again, what are you asking me, Mickey?"

"Are we trying to win this legitimately?"

"Spell it out. What do you think I've done?"

"Did you wager that five million credits, knowing you could get that sort of money from Johnnie, once you influenced the odds?"

Riley held her best poker face, as she seemingly considered her answer.

"I'll answer this once, so long as you promise not to question my business methods again. Do we have a deal?" Mickey nodded his agreement immediately.

"I'm your manager, but I'm also a strategist on the team. It's illegal for any player to gamble on a tournament they compete in. Is that clear?" Mickey nodded agreement again.

"As your manager, I want you to focus solely on what you do best and not waste any more energy on what happened in the past. Promise me that, Mickey."

Mickey didn't answer back immediately. It was true. Riley was a successful industry leader now, not unlike Johnnie. But that was what worried him. He wanted to keep questioning her, but he had to acknowledge that Riley had supported him when she didn't have to.

"I promise, Riley. I shall keep my head in the here and now. No more questions about what has gone before."

"Good. Then it's time I retired for the night. I want a clear head for the match tomorrow. I suggest you do the same." Riley said, before getting up to leave.

"I'll wake up in a more positive frame," he said, as she walked toward the exit.

Mickey prepared to leave himself, but he remained restless about the events that had unfolded. *His first match was scheduled for the mid afternoon, more than enough time to recover from a few late 'nightcaps'* he thought. An hour later Mickey had disappeared to a small pub in a nearby lane to relieve his anxiety. It was the start of a long night.

17

The Qualifiers

The shrill of his cubebit woke Mickey.

"Are you coming down for breakfast?" said Riley.

Mickey had slept through breakfast, hung-over from his previous night's antics. He thought for a moment to quickly shower and join them but his aching forehead changed his mind.

"Let's catch up later for lunch; I feel a bit under the weather, probably something I ate," he lied.

"Do you want Dr. Vance to check you out?" Riley asked.

"I'll be fine. I'll just rest up here for a while and catch up with you at one and then a practice session at three," he said.

Mickey wanted to go back to sleep but he forced himself to shower. He spent the next half hour willing his headache away and trying to justify his behaviour. *I should easily win tonight, even if I am off my game*, he thought, knowing he must not prepare this badly again.

Why had he gone drinking the night before such an important match? He promised Riley he would trust her and focus on the here and now. But his self-doubts and fears were re-surfacing. Maybe everyone was right? He was drug-dependant. If that were the case, he was an undeserving contestant in the world's preeminent cubeball competition. For himself, he wouldn't have cared, but Ludwig and Riley had given their support. They believed in him.

Mickey threw down a few supps before calling room service. He was at least hungry, which was a good sign. His heavier binges usually left him with no appetite except for more alcohol. Mickey worked room service hard that morning as he detoxed on a combination of eggs and bacon, showers and a gallon of coffee. By the time he entered the arena with his team for the first of potentially eight matches to reach the finals, Mickey hoped he would be ready to play.

The game was set in one of the smaller arenas, given it was the wild-card qualification round. This suited him in a way as playing to small crowds eased his nerves. It felt more like practice sessions than a major tournament. The stadium held a meagre crowd of a thousand fans, which belied the intense interest shown in this match. It drew a record viewing audience and record betting for a first round. Mickey had started an overwhelming favourite given the large sums of money being directed his way to win the tournament.

Mickey recognised many in the crowd. Most were professional gamblers representing their various syndicates. There was no doubt his entry into the competition had drawn a lot of interest. They would pour over his 'form' and make financial decisions in the many millions of credits on how far he would progress. Mickey didn't like playing to those fans. His skill wasn't appreciated. He was an investment. But one face in the crowd stood out to Mickey - Riley's friend Lisa sat in the front row. Mickey smiled when he saw her and found himself glancing to see if she sat alone.

Mickey then cast his eye to Riley and Ludwig who were positioned at their comtech pod. Ludwig looked remarkably calm, no doubt because of the piped symphonies streaming through his earphones blocking the unsettling noise of the fans. Riley was her usual businesslike self as she readied the game play programs.

"Ludwig's game slotted in?" said Mickey.

"Slotted for the middle games," she said, about to say more, before the announcer called to Mickey and his opponent to commence proceedings.

Mickey's opponent was the youngest player in the tournament. He was the same age that Mickey had been when he won a national championship cup; eighteen. But his opponent looked older than his years, no doubt from the many years of practice he had put in just to get a wild-card entry. Mickey felt undeserving as he stood beside the young up and comer, who would have sacrificed most of his tender growing years practicing endless drills to play what would be the biggest match of his life. Mickey on the other hand had recently returned from an extended lay off and had spent the night before the match drowning his body with alcohol. Deep down, he felt he didn't deserve a victory. And the way he played in the opening three games, his instinct was right. Three games down, the young lad looked to be cruising to a convincing victory.

"Have you come to this tournament to win or make up the numbers?" said Riley, angered by her brothers seeming capitulation.

Mickey knew the true reason for his poor form but he wouldn't admit it to her, choosing to change strategies.

"Slot in Ludwig's game and let's see what happens. Think it'll work?" he asked, looking to Ludwig.

"You're the only player in the world who can make it work. Play so they hear your song."

As Mickey stood watching his young opponent break, he hoped he would get the chance. The young man's confidence was high. When a player reached that level of confidence, it was difficult to salvage a comeback, no matter how Mickey played from that point on.

As Mickey feared, the young player opened with four cracking shots. His game lifted to another level as he strutted the table like a seasoned veteran. His demeanour took Mickey back many years to when he first started competition play. In that place Mickey never lost. He had all but capitulated now, resigned to his fate, until the young challenger did something Mickey never did. He turned to the cheering fans and raised his cue, conductor like, and egged on his growing legion of adoring fans.

In that instant, he withdrew his focus from the field of battle. It was a short moment, but Mickey sensed it could be enough. Cubeball was a cruel game that could turn on you like a serpent. Mickey had already paid the price for his alcohol fuelled indiscretions from the night before; it could now be his challengers turn.

Not surprisingly, the young man's next shot fell just short of its mark giving Mickey a small opening to counter attack. The door was left slightly ajar. Mickey called a power-play. It was a difficult shot to call for 'double points' and it surprised his opponent. Brashly, he chose not to sit down, no doubt believing Mickey couldn't make the shot.

In a way he was right, Mickey didn't make the next shot, not the one everybody expected any way.

Mickey played a sublime spinning shot that cracked the red ball across four corners into the top pocket. The cue-ball then spun violently backwards and with curve to set up his next seven shots. The set up was supreme. No other player could have finished the game as Mickey did, not even Flaveau. The crowd was mesmerised by the artistry of the unfolding break. More so his opponent, who never recovered from the exhibition that Mickey handed out over the next seven games. He won decisively.

Mickey shook the hand of his young opponent relieved by his victory, for it was a match lost by his opponent. He turned to his team and saw the joy on Riley's face. He had not seen that for a long time. It lasted just a moment before she turned to her computer screen and went about her job of recording the programs with her usual efficiency. Mickey smiled to himself as he approached her.

"There were a few interesting new manoeuvres in that set of games. I think that'll make our opponents take notice."

Riley did not look up from her screen as she spoke. "I think your odds will re-firm again to equal favourite."

Even Ludwig interrupted, due to his excitement. "Thank you for playing my music."

Mickey hugged Ludwig, expressing his delight about Ludwig's contribution. He had used it on the vital fourth game and played the first four shots to perfection, before reverting back to his normal strategies.

"We'll use your plays more Ludwig, but always at the right time in the game. I want to play more of your strategies, but I have to practise."

Mickey knew he had a weapon that would unsettle any player in the world if he could master it. Just four shots were enough to throw his young challenger that night, but more experienced players would not capitulate so easily.

Mickey waited outside on Holborn Road for a time to watch the passersby on the busy London thoroughfare. Large crowds swept by him, many disappearing into the underground's bowels, just as many heading for end of work drinks. Mickey was one of them. But he was an hour early and nervous about the evening. Lisa had invited him to a work function, so the restaurant would be full of journalists. He re-checked the map to locate his whereabouts.

The restaurant was situated in a small laneway well away from the busy Holborn Road. Mickey immediately relaxed as he walked through the narrower, less crowded streets. He located the 'Little Opera' restaurant where they were meeting. Then he walked on further, in the mood for exploration. He spotted an old England pub and was tempted to enjoy a few pints but thought better of it. Being drunk at a journalist dinner would not be wise. He opted for a little cafe on the corner of a 'five way' intersection. He chose to sit in a quiet corner near a window that took in its expansive views. He sipped on his coffee for a while when a familiar voice interrupted his thoughts.

"Mickey Allen, how are you?" Mickey turned to greet his cubeball friend from the space station.

"What a surprise. How are you, Manny?"

"I couldn't be better. But I'm not surprised to see you. I've been watching your matches on the cubebit. You look different?"

Mickey had shaved his stubble and shortened his hair for the night's date. He felt a little self conscious about his transformation. He was dressed in fine clothes as well. His sister had already given him a hard time and now Manny was also reminding him of his new appearance.

"Great games last week! You beat some of the best English talent. I had tipped some money on one of them too, so you cost me money! I'll back you from now on. I hope you make it to the finals and beat Flaveau. I've never liked him."

Mickey smiled and said he would do his best. They chatted briefly before Mickey went to excuse himself to meet Lisa. Manny changed the conversation to business.

"If you need an extra weapon in your armoury, call me okay?" Then Manny slipped him his business card.

Mickey accepted it. "The last time I did that, things didn't exactly turn out well did they?"

"I'm sorry about that, Mickey. I couldn't afford to get caught by the law, given my record, if you know what I mean."

"Manny, you could help me."

"Anything, Mickey."

"Never speak to me or come near me again, okay? If you do, I'll report you to the police. So just fuck off and never bother me again."

Manny raised his hands, defensively and nodded agreement, before disappearing into one of the small lanes. Mickey was relieved to see the back of him. He was getting enough press interest. He didn't need his own drug scandal as well.

Mickey finished his coffee. Then he walked back to the Little Opera restaurant. It was richly adorned with flowing royal red curtains and theatre memorabilia. Small stages were built on two opposite walls of the restaurant, where operatic singers entertained intermittently. Mickey admired its finery and attention to detail. He was also glad he was dressed appropriately. An immaculately dressed waiter escorted him to his table, where Lisa was already seated and studying the menu. She was dressed in a delicate blue dress that took Mickey's breath away. He approached her nervously, unsure how he should greet her. Lisa sensed his uncertainty and warmly kissed the side of his cheek.

"Well, what do you think?" She turned to look at the decor of the restaurant.

Mickey's gaze said it all. Lisa was a beautiful woman who was way too attractive for the likes of a man like him.

"You're quite a sight."

"I have some bad news. We've been dumped by my work colleagues, so you'll just have to dine with me tonight."

Mickey was pleased and relieved he could dine in a more congenial atmosphere. He soon relaxed too. Her charm was infectious as were her beautiful green eyes. Conversation flowed and soon Mickey felt he could speak openly.

"I was relieved when you told me the function had been cancelled. Journalists get me a little nervous."

"Thanks!" joked Lisa playing on Mickey's unintended slight. Both laughed, further breaking down their barriers. By the time entertainment commenced, both felt comfortable in each other's company.

"So, how are you enjoying London?" Lisa asked.

"All I'm seeing is the hotel and where we practice. I want to see more, but it's difficult."

"I'd hate to be a celebrity. I like my privacy too much," said Lisa.

"Yes, you learn how important your privacy is when you lose it. I tried to get my privacy back, when I went to Mars, but there'd always be someone who remembered me." Mickey started to feel more relaxed with Lisa.

A waiter interrupted them. "Would you care to order drinks, Mr Allen?"

"A glass of Merlot," said Mickey, as he nodded to Lisa to order. "The same," she replied. Mickey watched the waiter return to the small bar at the front of the restaurant. The tables were beginning to fill with the evening's bookings.

"It's funny when I recall my younger years. I thought of nothing else but achieving fame. I'd practice on my family's old billiard table for hours. Riley would pester me all day to play her, but I'd tell her she had to practice a lot more before she would be good enough to challenge me. I'd be lost in my own world, pretending I was in a championship tournament, competing with all the stars. Poor Riley would get so mad with me. She'd have to practice in the morning, because I had the table the rest of the day."

"Weren't you the nasty older brother," said Lisa, cheekily.

Mickey grinned as he nodded agreement. "I could have been better. How about you? Are you from a large family?"

Lisa reacted to Mickey's question. She paused while the waiter handed them their wines. She then sipped slowly on it, seemingly thinking of her past.

"No, I was an only child."

"Lucky you," said Mickey.

"My father wouldn't say that. My mother died a year after my birth.... in an accident."

"Oh, I'm sorry. I shouldn't have been flippant."

Lisa touched Mickey's arm. "No harm done. She died nearly thirty years ago."

"It must have been hard."

"At times. Harder for my father, though. He had to be both a father and mother to me."

"He sounds an amazing man."

"The most amazing man in my life, right now."

"So there's no other man in your life?" Mickey asked, looking embarrassed by his boldness.

Lisa smiled and touched his arm a second time. "It's okay to ask. I divorced five years ago. He wasn't so amazing."

Conversation paused as the entertainment drew their attention. A tenor took his place on the small balcony stage, beside a musician who was tuning his violin. Lisa sipped her wine and watched in expectation for the music to start. Then the tenor announced he would commence soon. Lisa turned to Mickey.

"Enough about me. Is there a special person in your life, Mickey?"

Mickey was emboldened by Lisa's forthright demeanour. He decided to talk candidly with her.

"Not for a very long time. It seems I don't handle relationships very well."

"I hope you don't mind me asking so many questions. It's the journalist in me," she joked.

"It's okay; I'm complimented that a beautiful young lady should choose to dine with me. I couldn't think of a better way to get away from the demands of this tournament."

Both smiled before a photographer snapped a photo from afar, unsettling Mickey for a moment.

"You see what I mean. It's hard to get away," said Mickey.

"Well at least you're not a married man or you would be front page headlines in the morning," said Lisa, following her humour with a serious question.

"Riley told me about the disappearance of your girlfriend when you were young. It must have been hard for you?"

Mickey enjoyed Lisa's company, but balked at revealing too many details about his intimate past. After all, she was a journalist. But Mickey had held on to uncomfortable feelings for too long. He felt he could respond to her.

"We were young and very much in love for a time. I was thinking of parting from her. But then she disappeared to Velvet Underground to fuel her drug habit. Even now, I still feel responsible for that. I used my prize money from cubeball to fuel her developing drug habit." Lisa gazed at Mickey now, concern filling her eyes.

"You can't be sure of that. It's likely she would have found a way to pay for her drugs with or without you. An addict will find a way."

Mickey smiled and took a sip of wine to steady his emotions. He was about to speak when the tenor and another singer returned.

"We wish to sing a beautiful operatic piece, written by Giusseppe Verdi in 1872. It is a song of tragic love from the opera, Aida – O terra addio. Enjoy!" At that the lights were lowered and the entertainer sang for the many couples enjoying their candlelit dinners.

Mickey sat quietly listening to the romantic serenade wash over the attentive crowd of diners. Small candles shimmered on rich red table tops, casting delicate patterns that danced across elegant walls of rich red velvet, gold and silver awnings. Their passionate tones and violin accompaniment affected the mood of all, taking Mickey's mind to other places. He thought of Jules and the brief joy they shared. Then he thought of Ludwig and Riley. Hope was beginning to return to him. He had a chance to start anew. Something in the light danced in his mind, as it did when he played cubeball. For the first time, Mickey felt that special place outside the confines of the four corners of his competition table.

Lisa saw the joy in Mickey's eyes and touched his hand. "It's beautiful music, isn't it?" Her deep green eyes conveyed their own sweet music. Mickey felt her beauty dance with Verdi's serenade. He didn't speak, choosing to gently caress her slender hand instead.

18

Semi Finals

MICKEY WOKE WITH A spring in his step, having qualified for the semi-final the night before. He'd been winning matches over the past week with a foreboding ease that had set up an encounter with the tournament favourite, Flaveau. The reigning champion was expected to win his fifth world title in a row, but the odds were narrowing.

Mickey arrived for breakfast early, greeting his team with an uncustomary enthusiasm. Riley managed the barest of nods, returning her gaze to the morning paper. Dr. Vance was equally cheerful as he spoke glowingly of the morning's breakfast. Whereas Ludwig ignored all, fine tuning his latest game play for the coming final.

Mickey tapped Ludwig's shoulder to get his attention, but he was lost in his drawings and the music streaming from his firmly clasped earphones. Mickey attempted a greeting which as always was ignored. At that, Mickey headed for the well stocked breakfast buffet and returned with an overloaded plate and sat beside Riley.

"Do you realise that when we play Flaveau tomorrow night, it will be almost ten years since we last played him?" said Mickey.

Riley dragged her gaze from the paper and looked to Mickey.

"Do you know eating that much for breakfast could give you very high cholesterol?" Mickey ignored her taunts, so she continued. "If I recall, you lost the match, because you weren't fit," she said, looking accusingly at his breakfast.

"Let's be prepared this time," said Mickey, as he placed two of his sausages on Riley's plate.

"I've set up the game plays for tomorrow night. I'm waiting on Ludwig's drawings, which we'll have by the morning's practice," she said, looking to Dr. Vance for confirmation.

"He told me it's all but completed, but he wanted another day to go over it again," said Dr. Vance. Mickey sensed Riley's annoyance at being made to wait, so he changed the subject.

"To think we'll be playing Flaveau again and at the New Crucible. It couldn't be more perfect," said Mickey.

Riley sipped on the last of her coffee before she picked up her paper again, this time passing it to Mickey.

"Well there'll be a lot of people watching with interest, particularly the media," she said, laying the second page story on the table for Mickey to read. The headline read *Champions –Fair or Foul?*

The article, written by Richard Carrington, alluded to the cubeball industry being awash with illegal gambling, game fixing and drugs. The article also alluded to an upcoming interview with Mickey. The interview promised to lift the lid on the ugly side of the world's most popular game, in particular Johnnie Draxma, the controversial manager of the world's largest cubeball company. Carrington went on to note Draxma's questionable dealings and management style, including a drug scandal involving a close friend of Mickey's.

Mickey was enraged. Someone had betrayed his trust and passed on information about his personal life. *Could it be Lisa?* He thought. The coincidence seemed too strong. He tells Lisa, a journalist, about the loss of his girlfriend and the next day it's headlines.

"You told me you reviewed the tapes of the interview and that there was little that could damage us. This could end in the courts! I want to see the interview tape".

"All the explosive comments are from Carrington. He uses insinuation and other reports to make those accusations. There is nothing from your interview," she said.

"Well. Where did the drug scandal come from? Your good mate Lisa?"

"That could have come from anyone Mickey. I know Lisa and she doesn't work that way. She always protects her sources."

"So who the fuck do you blame for this disaster?"

Riley was on the receiving end of Mickey's vindictiveness, drawing attention from everyone in the restaurant, except Ludwig. Riley answered in a low tone.

"Screaming in a public place won't help. It will just get you another headline you don't want." said Riley, succeeding in calming her brother.

"Look, think about it. Anyone could have provided Carrington with the drug scandal. Carrington's doing a piece that threatens to expose Johnnie's company. What do you think Johnnie would do about it when he hears you have made indirect accusations? He rakes some muck himself and tries to discredit your name."

"So Johnnie released information about Jules?" said Mickey.

"I don't know that for sure. But it makes a hell of a lot more sense than blaming Lisa."

"You may be right, but I want to see the tape of Carrington's interview today and I don't want any journalist, Lisa included, within a hundred miles of our team's preparations. Is that clear?"

Riley agreed and left quickly to retrieve the tape for his viewing.

"I've got to go, Harry. Tell Ludwig practice is cancelled until tomorrow morning," said Mickey, also leaving immediately.

The media demands of professional cubeball were weighing down on Mickey again. Ironically, the game he loved could be also damaging. Even worse, his personal life was laid bare to the public. He wanted to believe his sister's explanation that Johnnie was behind it. But he had been betrayed by her many times before. Of one thing he was sure, Johnnie Draxma was returning into his life and Johnnie was never one to do anything by half measures. This time Mickey had to be ready.

Mickey had practiced for two hours by the time Riley and Ludwig joined him. His good mood from the previous day had evaporated. Friendly greetings were replaced with suspicious glares.

"Well?" he said.

"Any reference to friends of yours consuming drugs will be removed from the tape," said Riley, happy with her mornings work. Lawyers had been lined up at great cost to ensure that outcome.

"And?"

"Johnnie's lawyers have threatened to sue the paper if accusations are made or insinuated. I've seen to it that your interview has been edited so that those accusations can't be deemed as coming from you."

"Okay. I want to see that interview today," said Mickey, before he turned his mind to practice.

As it was, time was precious and they had just one session to fine tune Ludwig's game. Mickey was satisfied with his morning's drills and believed he could beat Flaveau. He couldn't rely entirely on his normal game. He needed something new.

"Is Ludwig's game downloaded?"

"Last night," said Riley.

At that, the next two hours were used practicing Ludwig's game plan. Much to Riley's consternation, Ludwig's game plan proved too challenging.

"Are you sure you got this game right?" said Mickey.

Ludwig nodded his head enthusiastically, affirming his confidence that this game could unnerve the four times champion of the world. Doubts remained with everyone except Ludwig.

"This can only be played after twelve close fought matches. Then you will see the music," said Ludwig, no doubt in his voice and conviction in his eyes.

Mickey could only shrug his shoulders at his sister and resign to his fate that night.

"Well that's it then. I'll see you all downstairs in the lobby at six for the cab. We've got a match to win!"

The New Crucible had the energy of electric expectation. Flaveau, considered invincible just two weeks ago, was in the battle of his life against a foe he'd only met once before and just won. The smart money was with Flaveau, although his one and only victory over Mickey was ten years ago. Mickey's decade in the sporting wilderness had been analysed by the media for two weeks, whipping up a hysteria that gripped the cubeball world.

Intoxicating as Mickey's story was, his team was an unproven grouping that was hastily put together. Their victory still seemed improbable. Mickey led his team down the famous red carpet stairway into the 'hallowed arena'. He was followed by his strategist, a curious music loving savant who said little and provided strategies on paper. His much guarded game plays were the subject of much analysis and stoked the flames of cover ups for an industry that was tainted by match fixing. The team's comtech followed, one of the world's most successful, Jane Allen.

The speculation would end tonight. The world had gambled a record seven billion credits on its outcome and a record viewing audience of three billion were watching.

Mickey walked slowly down the stairs and took in the atmosphere this time. He remembered being overawed as a young man by the storm of light from the flashes and roar of the fans. He was no less nervous but his determination had never been stronger. He'd waited ten years to meet Flaveau. The current world champion was the only other player in the world he believed had the complete game that could beat him. This was the match Mickey imagined as a young boy and worked for all his life on Earth.

The team settled into place. Riley checked her programs. Ludwig sat beside her. Mickey hadn't noticed until now but Ludwig had walked down into the stadium with his earphones resting around his neck.

"Are you okay? Are the earphones working?" he said.

"I wanted to hear your game tonight Mickey, I want to experience what you feel," said Ludwig, unsettled by the noise and chaos, but determined to feel his entire match that night.

Mickey held Ludwig's shoulder for a moment to show his respect for Ludwig's courage. He looked to the front row, catching Dr. Vance's knowing glance and reassuring nod that Ludwig would be fine. The moment's pause was broken by the introduction of the world champion. The stadium roared alive again with noise and light, as the world's best player and his team descended to the playing arena.

Introductions done, the two faced each other for the first time in a decade. Flaveau was small in stature but his presence loomed large. He wore traditional black pants and matching vest with red velvet bow tie. He was immaculately groomed with an almost regal presence and an unassuming confidence. Flaveau looked every inch the professional he was and this time he looked prepared.

"So, we meet again Mr. Allen. I have looked forward to this day," said Flaveau with a politeness belying his ruthless determination. Mickey merely smiled and nodded his head.

Flaveau would remember his narrow victory well and would have left no stone unturned to make sure he would win convincingly, this time. The referee joined them to explain the rules and asked Flaveau to call for the coin toss, which he won.

"Well, I believe I shall break this time, Mr Allen," he said, his confidence soaring.

The game was a tight affair. Two naturally gifted players put on a master-class of perfect cubeball. Defence dominated early in each game, whereas both players opted for ruthless offence if they were given an opportunity. A see-saw match continued for the first twelve games. The crowd were enthralled by the close fought match, all wishing it not to end. Time out was called at six games apiece. Mickey was all but spent from the effort to maintain a six all game sheet. He sat quietly in the corner of the change room not sure how he should play the deciding game. With ten minutes left until game time, he called for Ludwig to sit with him.

"Well my friend, I kept my end of the bargain. We've played twelve games and we are still in with a chance. But I'll be honest with you. I'm too tired to play my normal game, let alone the one you want me to play," said Mickey, studying the game plan Ludwig had drawn.

"Play your unique rhythms, Mickey. Don't play numbers."

Ludwig had sat through the whole twelve dramatic games without his earphones and looked every bit as exhausted as Mickey. His nervous rocking had returned. The noise from the stadium had unsettled him.

"Why don't you wear the headphones for the final match and listen to your music," said Mickey.

Ludwig's rocking slowed as he used all his energy to appear normal to Mickey. He had something to say to Mickey, but he would not respond until he controlled his shaking.

"I have watched him closely, Mickey. He doesn't play music. He plays by numbers," said Ludwig, pausing for a moment as the rocking in his body overtook him.

"Yes, you told me that the last time we played."

"But there's something you need to know," he couldn't get the next words out as the rocking worsened. Ludwig was struggling to control his feelings now but he willed one last sentence from his deteriorating body.

"He will play great songs. But you have to show him your perfect music tonight," said Ludwig, unable to say any more.

Mickey held Ludwig close. He called for Dr. Vance's assistance, waiting until Ludwig was in his good care. Then he faced the final frame of an epic semi-final. He was emotionally exhausted but Mickey wanted to play this game not for the victory or the chance to compete for the world championship final. He wanted to play this game for Ludwig.

"I don't think he should come out, Harry," Mickey said, concern written on his face.

Dr. Vance sat with Ludwig and comforted him. "Count your numbers for me and breathe. That's it, breathe deeply. One, breathe in. Two, breathe out. And again," he repeated.

"Two minutes left, Mickey," came the call from the attendant.

"Thanks," responded Mickey. He stood up and stretched his tired arms, shoulders and neck. "What do you think, Harry?"

"He's okay. Another ten minutes and I'll bring him back to the arena."

"Tell him I'll play his game, when the first opening arises." Mickey prepared to head back to the arena, but Ludwig reacted, by increasing his rocking motion.

"No, no, no..." Ludwig repeated.

"Dr. Vance comforted Ludwig again, repeating his breathing drills. Then he turned to Mickey.

"I'll give him a booster injection. It will calm him, but not immediately."

"Final call, Mr. Allen," said the attendant, more demanding now.

Mickey looked at Ludwig. He was torn between leaving and staying. Dr. Vance saw Mickey's reluctance.

"Go, Mickey. Think about Ludwig's words and play your best for him. That's all he wants. We will return to the stadium soon. I promise."

Mickey's life had been filled with uncertainty and doubt. But he did not doubt Dr. Vance or Ludwig. They both had become important friends to him, friends he could trust to stand beside him, no matter the situation. He nodded to Dr. Vance.

"I promise, Harry. I'll do my best." Then he walked back into the stadium, knowing this may be his last game in the championship. He sat with Riley.

"Where's Ludwig?" said Riley.

"He's with Harry at the moment. Have you programmed his game play?" Riley confirmed but offered him an alternative program game play to consider.

"We play Ludwig's plan no matter what," said Mickey with a steely determination that convinced Riley not to argue with him.

And so it began. The champion started the game with a superb defensive shot that left little opening for Mickey, except one that would require precision - Ludwig's play. Mickey knew that one error would be the end of the championships for him. He set up his shot with due care. He needed to be in the zone, that place where he had no doubts, but that special feel eluded him.

Mickey would have to play 'tough'. He focused his eye past the cue-ball, imagining the spin, curve and trajectory his unique shot would draw. With no further thought he glided the cue-ball on its predestined journey and watched it roll to its intended destination. Mickey had struck his response and stated his strategy – Ludwig's game plan.

Flaveau was suitably surprised by the raw power and high risk of what Mickey had unleashed but true to his championship qualities, he remained unflustered.

Flaveau appeared to relish the opportunity to test Mickey's new strategy. Although defensive, his response was equally sublime. It struck two cushions with extreme spin and curve, before edging between a red ball and the front wall, offering Mickey no openings to attack. Two shots became four, than eight and twelve as the final game became a contest of wills. After twelve high pressure shots, Mickey felt the nagging claw of self doubt scrape his sweaty tired body. He called his last remaining 'time out', hoping he may break Flaveau's cast iron concentration and will.

The mesmerised fans exalted a collective sigh, showing they too had expended much of their energy. Players and fans alike sat on a jagged knife-edge of emotions, too engrossed to move for fear of missing the final chapter of an event to be talked about for years to come. The only movement came from fans that had been locked out from the session.

They scurried back to their vacant seats. Two amongst that small group were Ludwig accompanied by Dr. Vance who assisted him to his team's podium. Ludwig had re-gained some composure and sat next to Mickey.

"I'm sorry, Mickey. I should have been with you," said Ludwig, upset that he had not been by his side. Mickey refuted his sense of failure, instead reinforcing that he admired Ludwig's courage. He confided his fears.

"Flaveau's come prepared for this match. I can't bring your match-play on to the table. He's strangled the play with brilliant defence,' said Mickey.

"I watched his play on the monitor. He still plays by numbers, no matter the situation. That is where he draws his strength, power and belief. He believes he rightfully deserves to hold that power and you must take it from him. You must believe you can take it from him," said Ludwig.

Mickey knew it to be true. He'd held a defensive line until Flaveau left an opening for him, but Flaveau had closed the game with brilliant defence. He had studied Mickey's new game play and read it well. His defensive shots showed he knew what he was protecting his game from, believing he could hold his nerve longer than Mickey. But it was more than that. He was also betting that Mickey would not gamble everything on a single decisive shot.

Flaveau would not allow him to play with the beauty of Ludwig's art, not without taking a risk. Mickey had to play a shot that no computer would map for him. He had to make a shot that no one would predict. Not Flaveau. Not the technology. Not even Ludwig. He had to arrest the game from the world champion with a shot never imagined. Nothing less would do.

He came to the table and viewed the holograph and its projected 'best shots'. They were all demanding, but all similar to what had gone before. Mickey took his time to contemplate his shot, but more importantly, he wanted to see his opponent. Flaveau was respectfully sitting at the far end, but his face told the story. His eyes were wide and excited like a puma ready to engulf its prey. At that moment Mickey knew he had to play his way and make a shot that would not be forgotten. He called "power-play."

He imagined the perfect shot in his mind's eye as he circled the table twice, deliberating his fateful shot. The balls loomed large, but strangely different. The table appeared more circular than a cube as he lowered his chin to his carbon steel cue. The whole shot played in his mind as he drew back the cue to strike the cue-ball with a force that engulfed the whole stadium.

The crack of the cue-ball as it struck its target echoed sharply its warning of an imminent tidal wave of spin and curve that would capture the imagination of every fan in the stadium, or at home in front of their cubebit. In one game changing savage strike, the red ball fell into the pocket as the cue-ball savagely spun into the red triangle, spreading the reds in all directions from the centrifugal force of the cue-ball. Mickey slotted twelve red and black combinations in four minutes, gaining an unassailable lead. He followed that with a perfect defensive stroke, leaving the cue-ball safely jammed behind yellow. Flaveau conceded the game and the match, shell-shocked by the unique high-spin attack Mickey had unleashed. The break was soon nicknamed 'the pulsar' and it had secured Mickey the first semi-final win and a shot at the world title.

19

Final Storm

MICKEY'S BARN STORMING TEAM sat together to watch the second semi-final. Preceding the match was Carrington's telecast of his second interview with Mickey. A vid-cube had been set up for their viewing. Mickey was nervous about the interview. Would it be sufficiently edited? Riley had repeatedly assured Mickey with little success that it would be. Mickey's suspicions lingered, for Riley seemed unusually nervous all day.

"Lisa tried to call you again this morning," said Riley, mockingly.

"I told you..." he started to say before being interrupted.

"Don't be an asshole. She had nothing to do with the leak. Call her!"

"When our job's done," said Mickey, irritated now.

Both sat stony silent throughout the interview. Apart from the occasional rattle of the beer glasses all sat and digested the ramifications of the findings. Ludwig had little to say preferring the sound of his earphone piped music. Dr. Vance remained silent, managing only the slightest of sideway glances to the 'twins' as he sometimes called them. Riley lay back against the sofa, feigning composure while Mickey nervously drank his beer, focused on every word, particularly Carrington's final summation of the state of the cubeball industry.

"Where the fuck did that come from?" he said, referring to 'inside' information about Johnnie's dealings.

"Who knows? It's not our worry."

"Not for now. Johnnie will be on the streets, mopping up those who dared to expose him," said Mickey.

Riley checked her cubebit and got up to leave.

"You're leaving? The match is about to begin," said Mickey, now concerned.

"That was Lisa. Someone's got to do the right thing by her. Talk to her," said Riley holding her cubebit out to Mickey, but he refused.

At that, Riley cast him a glare before leaving the room. She then made her displeasure unequivocal by slamming the door behind her.

Mickey tightened his lips. He cast his gaze toward his team. Ludwig hadn't noticed. He was lost in his own world studying Mickey's last game as if it were a lost symphony. Dr. Vance didn't take his sight from the vid-cube. He'd learnt to not get between their disagreements. Mickey's mind raced back to earlier years. How many times had Riley let him down? He opened another beer, the first of many, as he watched the second semi-final.

The morning practice session commenced noticeably without Riley. Mickey played his drills while Ludwig and Dr. Vance watched previous circuit matches of the other finalist, Carrie Heller. She had won the second semi-final the night before. She made it clear in her victory speech that she expected to be the next world champion. Mickey was in two minds about his contestant. He hated her smugness, but he knew he could beat her. They had only played informally at Riley's home, but he learnt a lot from that night. He only had to block out her theatrics and concentrate on his game to win.

After an hour of drills, Mickey began to get frustrated. Not with his plays, but with Riley. She was never late. Another hour and his frustration turned to concern. But before he could get to a cubebit she arrived, loaded with computer programs and plenty of attitude.

"You heard the result. Carrie...."

"Heller, yes I know," said Riley eager to download her software.

"I brought all of her recorded game plays and will have them online in an hour," she said, returning to her usual efficient, business-like manner.

"Is there anything else you need?" Riley said almost as an afterthought.

"I'll be okay. Ludwig will have his game play ready for tomorrow morning's practice."

Riley half nodded and busied herself with her programs. She seemed to work at a speed that bordered on haste. It was very unlike her.

"I've been thinking about what you said last night. About Lisa, I mean."

"That'd be a change," said Riley, not looking up from her work.

"I'm sorry Riley, you're right. I'm going to ring her after practice and settle things," said Mickey hoping for a positive reaction. But Riley showed only indifference, before he spotted the slightest of smiles.

Mickey walked along the Strand looking for the local pizzeria, where Lisa had reluctantly agreed to meet him. "Yes I think we should meet," was her controlled, business-like response, when they spoke briefly by cubebit. Mickey wondered what to say. He had overreacted to the article and too hastily judged Lisa. He was early, but he sat at their reserved table to wait for her. Whilst waiting, he pretended to study the menu, before a waiter greeted him.

"I'm just waiting for a friend. I'll have water for now," he said to the waiter.

He deliberated over the menu items for what seemed an eternity. Lisa was now twenty minutes late, Mickey wondered if she would come at all. He was about to order his first drink when he saw her approaching from across the street. Her hair fell freely across her scarf and coat. A small woollen cap protected her head from the chill. Mickey tried to collect his thoughts as she entered, but his mind went blank. He stood up and nervously greeted her. Lisa brushed her cheek to his. Her cheek was cold as was her mood.

"Have you been here long?" said Lisa.

"No, I just got here," he lied.

Mickey ordered drinks and attempted to apologise to Lisa, but his words had an accusing air to them, prompting Lisa to get to the heart of their difficulties.

"As you rightly pointed out to me on many occasions, I'm a journalist. But do you know what good journalists do?"

Mickey wasn't about to trust his words again and opted for a neutral shrug of his shoulders.

"Two things. Firstly, they check their sources. Riley told me that you didn't want to see me until after the final, she didn't say why. I guessed that you believed I had something to do with Carrington's article in the paper. Right?"

Mickey wanted to colour his answer in a softer light but instinct told him otherwise.

"Yes, I said that. It seemed a coincidence that the night I tell you about Jules' disappearance, I find it in the next day's paper. I'm sorry, but it crossed my mind."

"Secondly, a good journalist protects their sources. If I were seeing you to gain information for a story, which I wasn't, I'd never reveal the source of my information. So if you wish to continue our relationship, professional or otherwise, we require trust."

Lisa's eyes ignited with conviction. Everything about her manner told him to trust her. But trust was a hard emotion for him to hold. He wanted to believe his friends, but he always sabotaged that feeling.

"I'll try. I promise you that I'll try."

Lisa looked anything but convinced as she sat back and studied Mickey. "Convince me."

"I've spent my life in a small world, chasing little red balls on a cube. That I do well. Then I try to understand the real world, but it's a whole lot harder out there. I can't control people's lives like I control the game in a cube. More often than not, my trust has been burned. I'm sorry that I can't trust as readily as you, but it doesn't mean that I don't want to."

Lisa offered her first warm smile and held out her hand to him. She didn't say anything, she didn't have to. Her soul was opened bare for Mickey. She showed warm emotions of what might be and a hint of an adventure he could be part of.

"I promise next time I have doubts, I'll check the source," he said, holding her hand.

Both enjoyed their meal as they re-visited their fledgling friendship and explored the potential for more.

"So, when are you flying back home?" Lisa asked.

"We have another week in London." Mickey replied. Both gazed at each other intently, saying nothing, feeling much in their silence. Mickey sipped his wine, as he sought the courage to say what he felt.

"I've been thinking of delaying the flight. I'd like to see more of London."

"You have no commitments? I'd imagine a finalist would be in demand around the globe." Lisa said, in her journalist manner, fishing for the story behind the story.

"I actually have commitments here. I have to make two appearances on behalf of Johnnie Draxma's organisation. So I think Riley will schedule a month here, before I play the CWC circuit again."

"A month," Lisa said, moving her hand to her chin, seemingly digesting his words.

"Lisa, it's hard for me to think beyond this match. But when it's finished, tomorrow night, will you join me for lunch the next day. I do want to enjoy more of London and I'm hoping you'll show me your city. Not because it's convenient, but because I want to get to know you."

Lisa smiled warmly, wresting her journalist persona to reveal her feelings. "It would be my pleasure, Mickey," she said, kissing his cheek lightly, but with warmth.

By lunch's end Lisa had to excuse herself for a business commitment.

"Good luck tomorrow and call me when you win! Also, tell your sister to call me. She hasn't been answering my calls," said Lisa.

"I thought she spoke to you last night?"

"No, I've been getting engaged for the last three days. Is something wrong?"

Mickey was disturbed by what she said. "No....no it's fine." He replied. Mickey lightly touched her arm and smiled.

"There's absolutely nothing wrong," he said, tenderly holding and caressing both her arms. No words were needed as they stood close to each other. Mickey gently kissed Lisa's warm lips, before reluctantly withdrawing, but Lisa's passion drew him back. They kissed again, warmly, revealing the desires that were building between them.

"Ring me after the match," said Lisa.

"You'll be the first I call, win or lose."

They hugged, sealing their growing bond. Mickey watched Lisa as she walked away, to her next meeting. He couldn't take his gaze from her. He felt an overwhelming desire to want to love Lisa and trust her every word.

Trust, he thought. Every time Mickey resolved to show trust in people, a dark emotion crept back into his mind; the clawing feel of doubt.

Lisa walked down Rowbury Lane toward her next meeting, unaware that a car pulled out from the kerb, seemingly following her. Mickey wouldn't have noticed, except he recognised the driver. It was Manny. *Could it just be coincidence?* He thought. But he seemed to be driving deliberately a few hundred metres behind her. When she approached a pedestrian crossing, he sped past her. Something was wrong. Mickey left credits on the table and then ran to Lisa. She turned to him, as he called, surprised but also delighted.

"Is everything okay?" She said. Mickey must have looked flustered. Lisa affectionately held his hand as she spoke. "What is it, Mickey?"

"I saw someone I know. I thought he may have been following you." He peered down the street. There was no sign of his car.

"Should I be concerned?"

Mickey wasn't sure how to reply. Manny had never threatened him. But he was turning up too often for him to ignore. "He's a cubeball fan. I've only met him a few times, so I'm not sure. Unfortunately, some fans can act strangely. Would you mind if I walked you to where you're going?"

Lisa smiled warmly. "How sweet." She kissed his cheek lightly, in appreciation. "My chaperone." Then she kissed his lips and whispered in his ear. "A chaperone with benefits," she said, giggling cheekily.

Mickey loved the way Lisa's face lit up when she laughed. He kissed her passionately. "You are so pretty, Lisa. I want to dine with you tonight and show you how beautiful I think you are."

Lisa cupped one hand on Mickey's cheek and studied him as she seemingly contemplated her reply. "I think I'd like that."

Mickey arrived punctually, at the foyer of Lisa's home for their evening date. Lisa was in the newest hotel/apartment complex in London - Clouds. This was not a place for people who struggled financially. Rentals were exorbitant, yet occupancy was always sought by the most fashionable and famous. The hotel maintained the right mix of short-term and long-term tenants. The waiting list was infamously long and growing.

"I didn't know journalism payed so well," said Mickey, as he scanned the luxurious marble-lined foyer.

"It doesn't, but writing biographies for the rich and famous does."

Lisa took Mickey's hand and led him on a tour of her home in London. She commenced with a cocktail at the Grand bar. It was equally fashioned with marble and had attracted a lot of well dressed and boisterous clientele. Lisa must have noticed Mickey's discomfort with the noise. She manoeuvred through the crowd to a quiet corner of the spacious bar. Efficient waiters abounded, dressed in Italian influenced uniforms. Two cocktails were quickly delivered on 'holo-trays'. Two perfectly shaped cocktail glasses sparkled as small stars popped in and out of existence. Mickey lit a rette and offered Lisa one.

"Sense-rettes," he said, signalling his intentions. Lisa accepted.

She drew heavily on her rette and sipped the cocktail. Their night together was transforming into a heady cocktail of sweetness and lust. Mickey's excitement grew. Lisa was a beautiful woman, but the cocktail enhanced his desires for her to breaking point. Lisa must have sensed his feelings as she lightly caressed Mickey's arm. She was about to withdraw her wandering hand, but Mickey stopped her, holding her hand, before gently kissing it. They kissed passionately and then toasted their growing bond. Mickey tapped Lisa's glass, but all he could see was her vibrant eyes. He could feel the erotic foreplay as they conversed. She was wearing an elegant tangerine dress that accentuated her slender body. Her hair fell tantalisingly over her bare shoulders, taunting his growing desire. Mickey gently caressed her hand, before trailing his fingertips on her arm to her exposed shoulder. He brushed Lisa's hair back, exposing her neck. He kissed her neck gently. Lisa shivered in excitement.

"You look so beautiful tonight."

Lisa smiled. "How many women have you said that to, I wonder?"

"Less than you think. But when I said it, I meant it." He kissed her lips, softly.

Lisa drew his lips closer, revealing her feelings. "I do believe you mean it."

They kissed deeply. The chemistry between them was already heightened, but their senses were exploding with lust, from the chemical elixir. Their drinks consumed, Lisa dispensed with the hotel tour as she led Mickey to her home in the sky. The new vertical hotels were a testament to 22nd century technology. Frames were stronger but more flexible, meaning ever higher buildings. They climbed to the eighty-fifth floor and then Mickey followed Lisa into her home. It was surrounded by high-tech window-walls, affording them real-life commanding views of London. The specially designed windows could also re-create high definition views of any city in the solar system. Mickey held Lisa close to him as he took in the expansive views.

"I can see the Crucible," said Mickey, pointing in that direction.

Lisa snuggled her back into Mickey's willing arms. "Show me."

Mickey drew her closer to him as he lined his outstretched arm closer to her line of sight.

"Do you think you can win the tournament?"

Mickey kissed Lisa's neck. "That's not on my mind at the moment," he whispered.

Lisa turned and kissed Mickey passionately. She gazed at him. There was a hunger in her eyes. She brushed past him, extending her hand behind her as she cast an erotic trail across his hips and firming erection. Lisa walked alluringly to her bedroom, sliding her dress off midway, revealing her naked body. Mickey wanted to take her before she reached the bedroom, but something held him back.

Mickey had spent much of his time on Mars engaging in contractual or simulated sex. He hadn't risked engaging his true feelings with another woman since Jules. He wanted to share more than sexual stimulation with her. But he stood fixed to his place by the window as Lisa disappeared into the bedroom. Mickey knew Lisa desired him as much as he wanted her. The air was thick with the chemistry of their growing bond. He stood and deliberated longer than he should have. His face was flushed, his cock hard and his breath heavy as his mind turned back to a previous love. Mickey was filled with a myriad of feelings – passion, lust, fear, abandonment. He stood closer to the window, looking out at London by night. Was Jules still out there somewhere, alone? Was she still thinking of him, as he thought of her? He had asked for a sign that she was still alive, since her disappearance, but she remained silent. "Goodbye my love," he whispered, before turning toward Lisa's bedroom.

Lisa lay on her bed, face down. Her naked body was slender, but the dim light accentuated her curvaceous lines. He gazed at her arched back, firm ass and long slender legs. He stripped off, taking in her beauty. He could see the side of her belly move from her excited breath. He sat beside her and slowly caressed her willing body. Mickey started by massaging her feet lovingly and in a reassuringly tender manner. He slowly slid his hands up Lisa's legs. She sighed with delight. He gently parted her legs revealing her hairless pussy. He caressed slowly around her, making her moist. She began to groan with pleasure as he softly touched her parting lips and sensitive clit.

"I so want you my darling. It's been a long time since I wanted someone this much."

"Really," she replied, doubt in her voice.

"What I meant was, it's been a long time since I made love to someone I cared for this much."

"Ooh," Lisa sighed. She rolled over and looked at Mickey, exposing her pale breasts. "I care for you, too."

Lisa gazed at Mickey, lovingly, inviting him to embrace her. They kissed, gently at first and then their desires took them over as they made love deep into the night.

20

LET THE GAMES BEGIN

THE ARENA WAS HUSHED waiting for the imminent arrival of the two combatants. Two storey state of the art cubes were suspended from high, casting fast moving images, angles, split screens and betting odds. The single cubeball cube sat in the middle of the vast arena like a crown jewel in an exhibition. The gamers in the crowd provided an eerie line of faces, lit up by their shimmering cubebits as they readied to compete online. The global media were there in force, to compliment the biggest show in the solar system. And hovering above all of this was the thick air of expectation. Two players remained, vying to become the best there was. One was a young brazen vamp with enormous skill and an even larger ego. The other was a master of the art of cubeball, but an enigma to his fans. Both prepared deep in the bowels of the colosseum, hidden away from their adoring fans.

Mickey sat with Riley, Ludwig and Dr. Vance saying little. He was keen to begin. Riley sensed Mickey's need for space.

"Whatever happens, you're the greatest player to walk this planet," said Riley as she hugged her brother, tears welling. Mickey held his sister tight. He wanted to say more but the occasion did not suit. She had made their journey possible - a life changing journey, but one he feared had consequences. Riley left to check her programs and await Mickey's entry. She did not look back. Mickey sat pondering his sister's true intent. She had helped him to get this far, yet doubts still lingered.

"Your strategies are slotted in the middle games. How do you read her style?" he said turning to Ludwig.

"She's the most accurate shooter - pin point. Leave an opening for her and she never misses," said Ludwig.

"Any weaknesses?" said Mickey.

"She enjoys putting on a show. Play your own show or become her audience."

Mickey may have trouble with trust, but his faith in Ludwig's analysis had become unswerving.

"I'm just glad you can't play this game. I'd be dead meat!" he said, slapping Ludwig on his shoulder and winking at Dr. Vance.

Dr. Vance laughed before taking Ludwig's arm to head down to the playing area. Ludwig was confused as usual.

"Why would Mickey consider I wish him harm?"

"Put your earphones on and enjoy the game," said Dr. Vance, laughing with Mickey, at Ludwig's expense.

Mickey heard his name introduced as the doorman walked him to the entry. A deafening roar cocooned Mickey in that familiar place. The energy of fifty thousand fans lifted and carried him to the playing area.

A light storm exploded around Mickey as he made the short but eventful entry. Young fans screamed for their new idol as computer driven lights leapt in and around The Cauldron. Phosphorous starlight, fluorescent violet and sun-like gold flooded the arena with electric tension. Mickey opted for no accompaniment music and lauded his choice as he soaked in the rapturous vibrations of fifty thousand fans willing him to win.

His introduction complete, Mickey got back to business, checking preparations with Riley. She was about to speak when a supernova unleashed its fury on the stadium – Carrie Heller danced into the stadium with the irreverence of a rock star.

Heller was aptly named. She unleashed a dark 'heavy metal' show to the melting pot of fans and detractors, leaving no one in any doubts about her. She was loved and hated in equal proportions. Mickey thought her outrageous when first they met. But that was a mere caricature of what he witnessed now. She spared nothing to put on an outrageous demonstration of dark theatrics to offend and entice in equal measure.

She strutted past him with suitable indignation. Mickey felt a war had been declared on him. This would be no match based on the 'old school' of etiquette and decorum. Carrie dispelled any pretence to that notion as she used the cubeball cube as a prop for her theatrics. Her silver cue looked more like a baton of war than an instrument of guile and finesse as she spun it in unison to the throbbing metallic music and light show. Media and sponsor commitments were mocked but subtlety promoted, until eventually the referee took control to begin the contest.

Mickey felt bland and inadequate, as if he had been drawn out of the crowd against his will and thrown on to the stage with a punk rock band. *Focus on your show*, he repeated to himself. But how could he not be drawn into her dark, shocking yet strangely glamorous world. Anything mildly traditional was mocked, the coin toss included.

"I don't care. I'll beat him either way," she said ignoring the coin throw all together. Mickey offered to break to the bewildered referee who gratefully accepted. There was a brief respite for the pre-match photo. Carrie was clothed in a traditional vest but any other hint of convention ended there. Her black slashed jeans, black high heel boots and blood red shirt had holographic 'imprints' that flickered her sponsors logos and anti-establishment graffiti in equal measure, until the referee insisted the technology be turned off. Mickey was dwarfed by her physical aura and even larger ego. He tried to block his feelings of intimidation but failed.

Carrie Heller was more than just a showpiece, too. She was bursting with the finest technological equipment money could buy. Blood red eye implants heightened her gothic appearance. She also had the latest innovation in PE Glasses. They would allow her a microscopic view of the cube's comtech holographs. The cue was fitted with power sensors, which would enhance her straight line shooting. Carrie was armed and ready for battle. She looked a dangerous cocktail of revolution and evolution.

She demanded the game start quickly, which further unsettled Mickey. So he opted for a cautious, defensive opening break to settle his nerves and challenge his opponent. What followed shocked him to the core.

Carrie unleashed the fastest play he had ever seen. Her opening shot was bold, potting a red from a three cushion approach – sublime. The second shot potted the yellow off four cushions and cannoned into the reds to open the table. She cleaned up the table in a world record time – four minutes two seconds and the score was one-nil. The crowd went crazy, stoked further by the brash outpourings of Mickey's opponent. Her show was on the road.

Mickey knew he had to put her game out of his mind. But it was the best game he had ever seen played. His outrageous young opponent had everything on her side, looks, youth, technology and talent.

Just when he thought it couldn't get worse, it did. She had luck on her side, too.

Her opening shot of the second game was that of a club player, hitting the balls with force but no guile. Carrie cracked the red triangle with a high risk power break. Incredibly, it potted a single red ball into a pocket. What followed ended in two-nil on the game card and another world record for the shortest game – three minutes and fifty seconds. Mickey knew what he had to do next. He called his first time-out.

"Fuck, I'm dying out there. She'll have the twelve games to win in the next hour at this rate! Riley, you studied her games. Do you have any ideas?"

"She's playing at another level. It's got to be the implants."

"That and she must be plastered with undetectable narcs. She's literally running around the table," he said.

Neither had answers so Mickey turned to Ludwig, hoping he saw something that could make a difference.

"She's playing perfect numbers, but not music," said Ludwig.

"So I have to play the music. That's how I beat her?"

"No, she is playing numbers at such speed. They are perfect numbers. She will win."

Mickey sat back hard against his seat. He had five minutes left in time-out and no ideas on how to win.

"I'll just keep calling time-outs shall I?"

"Yes. Time-out," said Ludwig.

Mickey rolled his eyes and all but capitulated, before he sensed Ludwig's meaning.

"Time's the key isn't it?"

"Yes, she cannot play this way too much longer. She will slow."

"Riley, set the program for defence. I sure as hell can't beat her but I must slow her game and give her no openings. Let's assume she's plastered with narcs. How long will it take before the effects start to wane?"

"She'll be at her peak for an hour," said Riley.

"An hour it is. Let's get out there and hope the window opens."

Mickey walked out to the playing arena with one strategy – survival. The only positive sign was that Carrie wasn't hurrying to start play. She was smugly providing a mid-match interview to a national broadcaster, predicting her imminent victory. Mickey offered no cameo interviews for the throng of international reporters clambering for some comments. I'll leave that to her, he thought, hoping her narc-induced heightened state would begin to wear. At least she could gain no further advantage. Narcs took twenty four hours to take effect.

The third game commenced late, courtesy of Carrie's interview which suited Mickey. He did all he could to slow the games to a crawl. He took long pauses to circle the table and consider his shot. His go-slow tactics frustrated Carrie and even the fans after a time. But Mickey focused as never before on playing highly defensive shots that could not be quickly turned into a match winning break.

An hour passed before the flood gates began to open. Mickey had dropped two more games and then a third in very quick time as Carrie adjusted to his strategy and drew to a commanding lead of five-nil. She started shooting four and five cushion pots and looked an unstoppable force, drawing Mickey's second of a maximum three time-outs.

The change room was a forlorn site as Mickey considered any options to reverse his fortunes. He had slowed the game as best he could, but Carrie's form had not declined. If anything it had improved. Riley had no solutions, so the last hope remained with Ludwig who had scribbled a game plan in the last hour. It was rough and there was no time for Riley to program it, so Mickey had to play it on instinct. Riley shrugged her shoulders in dismay that Mickey would consider his hastily scribbled thoughts, but Mickey was adamant.

"I could keep playing defensively but she would eventually pick me off. I have to attack now with something different," he said. Ludwig handed him his drawing before explaining the strategy.

"No, you must continue to play defensively. Her speed is declining but she still has the awareness to defeat you. Play defensively as you just did, but for half an hour and then show her your sublime melodies," said Ludwig.

"In half an hour it could be all over," said Mickey but Ludwig paid him no attention.

"When you change to your natural play, show her the finest of music. Show her a game she cannot emulate. Do that and she will not recover her fast-paced game."

Mickey returned to the arena and played much as he did in the previous session. By the half hour Carrie had extended her lead to seven-nil and Mickey was left with a tenuous chance to launch his comeback. Betting odds had bottomed for him to be victorious. Mickey couldn't afford to lose any more games. He had to attack. At least he felt strangely liberated to explore and play his natural game again. He was free from the grind of accurate defensive shot selection. Mickey imagined Ludwig's game play on the holograph. There were a range of shots, all potentially match winning. Ludwig had told him to surprise his opponent with a unique play and in that instant his instincts told him exactly which shot he should use.

Mickey saw the shot. It was a hair's breadth from a typical low risk opening shot but a galaxy of difference in the outcome. It was in the spin. He cracked the cue-ball hard, glancing an open red ball, creating severe side spin that swerved the red ball's line sufficiently to sink a second red into the top right hand pocket.

All, in the stadium, groaned as if Mickey had been extraordinarily lucky. Carrie shook her head at its implausibility too. Even Mickey wondered whether he had been fortuitous. But his instinct had told him otherwise. His confidence soared, changing the momentum. He had forgotten his opponent and his perilous position. He thought only of recreating a perfect game based on his instincts alone. Then he made a call rarely risked in a tournament, let alone the final of a world championship.

"Terminate Holographs."

Mickey was going to play unassisted, on the cube. He imagined Ludwig's last drawing and then played on instinct only. He turned the game into an exhibition of the finest touch play provided in many a year.

The crowd was stunned by his audacious move. More importantly, his opponent was shocked to her core. The strategy had worked. Mickey had played the game of his life at the right time. Carrie's advantage from narcs seemed to be subsiding. Mickey confidently rode a natural high, forcing Carrie on the defence. The match had turned around. Mickey had made a stunning comeback, wining the next eleven straight games to lead Carrie eleven-seven. Unsurprisingly, Carrie called her first time-out.

Mickey stayed on the playing arena with his team, having played eleven games of the highest level, all without holograph assistance. Instead, he relied on using extreme spin and subtle pace. But the strain of playing to that level had all but exhausted him. He opted to return to Riley's set plays for the next game given Carrie's confidence had disintegrated.

"I'll play by the holograph for the next few. Lock the games in," said Mickey, as Riley readied his next set of strategies.

By the time Carrie returned to the arena, Mickey felt in charge of proceedings and ready to finish his brash young opponent. Carrie was noticeably quiet and focused now. She gave no interviews and had no gimmicks. Mickey led by four games and his body language showed it, as he eagerly strode to the table, convinced he would claim the world title.

His opening shot was perfectly played, leaving his cue-ball pin point on the holograph image map. But Mickey's confidence surprisingly tumbled. He had shot the lines to perfection, yet Carrie won the game effortlessly. Mickey attributed it to his overconfidence and poor shot selection, allowing his opponent back into the game, but his suspicions a new element had been added to the contest lingered.

The next game went much the same way. An ominous game pattern emerged, one that surprised him. This felt more a capitulation, but not of his doing. By the third game Mickey was certain as to the cause, but he did not act. His emotions trapped him. His will for the contest waned as a third game and then a fourth was lost. A complete turnaround was played out in front of a stunned audience. At eleven games all, a surprising time-out was called, not by Mickey but Riley.

Mickey accepted her time-out call and walked slowly to the rest room looking a defeated man. Something disturbed his confidence but it was neither the skill of his opponent or his lack of it to win. A new deadly equation had come into this match, one he had feared for a long time.

Mickey asked Ludwig and Dr. Vance to remain behind. He wanted only Riley to join him for their last timeout.

"Well seeing as you're running the show, enlighten me as to what the fuck you're doing?" he exclaimed.

Riley looked anything but 'business as usual'. Her face was stripped bare as she struggled for her reply. It was a reply a lifetime in the coming.

"I think you already know. It's a position you'll be familiar with. Johnnie has bet a substantial amount of money on your opponent tonight. And you know Johnnie. What he wants he gets."

Mickey suspected that Riley had changed the strategies to favour his opponent.

"So you go to all this trouble. You organise me to get to the world's, at great expense to you, so that I lose?"

Riley closed her eyes momentarily. She took a deep breath as she gathered her strength to tell him the truth. And Mickey only wanted the truth now. She owed him that much.

"A long time ago a young girl got the break of a life-time, to work with a successful entrepreneur in an industry she loved. I was like you remember, from the poor end of town, no money for clothes, no likelihood of success. But then Johnnie came along and showed some faith, putting me on your team – against your wishes – remember that? He saw my hunger to succeed and fed that desire. Soon I progressed way beyond being your comtech and branched out into all of the areas of the business Johnnie wanted developed. That business developed into a growing drug trade, legal and illegal. I watched it grow. No, more than that, I eagerly participated in its development, much to my regret."

Mickey watched his sister tell her story, at first with scorn but ultimately sympathy. For he too had worked with Johnnie knowing full well there was always a cost involved. Her betrayal was not a surprise.

"Have you ever been there for me, or are you just happy to build one giant hoax around my skill? Is money all you care about as far as we're concerned? Because if it is, I'll forfeit this game now rather than walk out with you," said Mickey.

"My regret isn't for the illicit dealings of Johnnie's business. It's for the consequences," she said, tears breaking any semblance of self control.

"What do you mean?"

"You know. You've always suspected it. But I never meant her harm from my actions."

"Jules?"

"I never meant her harm. She begged me for the money. She had run out of options. You wouldn't give her any more cash for her addiction. Johnnie had thrown her out. I was her only friend. I introduced her to our world. I was responsible. I...," said Riley, consumed with sorrow and unable to continue her explanation.

Mickey felt her sorrow. He'd felt the same way every day of his life. He felt equally responsible for her addiction. He largely blamed Johnnie for her disappearance, but he finally learnt the truth. They were all responsible in their own way. Both sat for some time consumed by their own memories of the tragedy before Mickey spoke again.

Mickey thought to console his sister, until a powerful thought overtook him.

"Is she alive?" Mickey dared to ask.

Riley's grief consumed her. She walked away from Mickey, unable to face him. She stood by the window and looked out to the street below.

"Tell me, Riley. Is Jules alive?"

Riley moved her hand lightly across the window sill, maintaining her gaze out to the passing traffic. Her hand began to shake, so she clasped the sill to steady it. But then her body shook. Mickey waited in silence, prepared to wait well beyond his time-out, if it meant he'd hear the truth that had been kept from him for ten years.

Riley composed herself, before she turned to her brother. Her eyes were lowered, before she forced her gaze toward Mickey.

"I don't know. I've never known. But there is one person who does. He's always known."

21

FULL CIRCLE

JOHNNIE SAT HIGH ABOVE the arena, enjoying the function he had put on for his associates. This, like his occasional large wager on cubeball matches, was part of his marketing campaign. It was his way of showing his competitors his business domination of the cubeball industry. He could even tolerate a loss from time to time. But he couldn't tolerate disloyalty in his team or among his allies. Tonight's match was close. Too close for his liking.

"So Johnnie, the Bellman deal?" asked Howard Gould.

Howard, Johnnie's newest business associate, tucked into the culinary spread as if it were his last. Johnnie looked on gleefully. He valued allies with a greedy streak. Howard's considerable girth ably demonstrated his predilection for over-indulgence.

"The deal doesn't look promising. I thought you convinced them?" Johnnie replied.

"The Director all but signed the contract. What went wrong?" Howard said, seemingly surprised.

"You went wrong. That's what happened. Nothing happens without that little piece of paper with their signature at the bottom."

"Bellman's a piece of shit. I'll call him now, Johnnie. He's backed down on his word."

"Word's mean nothing, Howard. What good's another call? You're just voicing more meaningless words."

Johnnie looked to the back of his corporate box and signalled to one of his security officers to join him. Then he turned back to Howard.

"So Howard, I want you to do this. Enjoy the food and wine I have generously provided for you and my guests. Mingle with my friends and associates here. You're good at that. Watch the match. In particular, watch Mickey Allen. He's like Bellman's crew, belligerent and filled with some fantasy about cubeball meaning more than money. But you and I both know cubeball is about big business. Can you go and spread the word to our friends here, Howard?"

"Sure, Johnnie."

"Then fuck off and mingle with my guests."

Johnnie then turned to his security officer and invited him to sit beside him in the seat Howard had promptly vacated.

"Manny, my go-to-man. How's my boy?"

"Good, Mr. Draxma," he said with the right blend of confidence and undeniable loyalty.

"Relax, have something to eat."

Manny nodded and picked out an assortment of food.

"Here's your access badge to the playing arena for the next time-out," said Johnnie, as he handed him the badge. "You know what to do?"

"Create a disturbance," said Manny, dutifully.

"You're good at that aren't you," said Johnnie, nodding his delight with Manny's work. "Just remember, wait on my call. Then act, okay?"

"Consider it done, Mr Draxma."

That's what I like to hear. Someone who knows how to get results," he said loudly, his gaze firmly on Howard Gould.

Mickey fought a kaleidoscope of emotions. Sympathy, confusion, shock and anger swirled within him like a jolting cubeball break.

"Did you hate me that much?" Mickey asked.

Riley could not look up, let alone answer him.

"I loved her, Riley."

"I wanted to tell you, more than anything. But if I breathed a word, Jules wouldn't have survived another week."

"She is alive then," said Mickey. He stood up, resolved to act. "I'll kill that fucker!"

"No, Mickey! Don't let him pull your strings. Not on this night. This is your night to shine. You deserve it."

"How can I play, after what you just told me?"

"I promise you, if you play this game, I'll support you in any way I can to get the truth from him.

"Why? Why now?"

"She was my friend, too. You don't think I've wondered. But he always threatened to end my career and Jule's life, if I opened up these wounds."

Mickey didn't respond. He couldn't. He was confused, but he also remained suspicious. He held his gaze on Riley, unconvinced.

"Mickey, look at this." Riley handed him a ticket. It was a one-way ticket to South America. Mickey shook his head and threw it back at Riley, in disgust, before looking away.

"Look at me," she implored. He turned to her. Riley tore up her ticket.

"I was going to leave the stadium once I told you what I knew. If you play this game for me, I'll return to the stadium with you and support you no matter what Johnnie threatens."

Mickey wanted to confront Johnnie this very instant. But something in Riley's eyes, hinted at a determined resolve he had not seen in her for a long time. He had no doubt she was putting herself at risk. Johnnie did not take kindly to disloyalty.

"So why put us both through this. There's no point. I don't care about this game now. I want to find out the truth."

"No point? You're the greatest cubeball player on the planet. I won't sit here anymore and watch you fuck up your life with drugs. You're better than that. After all that has happened…it wasn't your fault Mickey."

Mickey understood most of Riley's emotions bar one.

"Why were you still helping Johnnie up until this night? You seem to still be part of his team?"

"No. I quit over a year ago and have worked as a consultant since then. I helped you because I wanted to make a difference, not because of Johnnie."

"Well what went wrong? It looks to me like you're in thicker than ever?"

Riley wiped the tears from her cheeks and attempted to re-gain her composure.

"The press investigation has closed in on Johnnie's operations as a result of my help. Johnnie knows that. He's already assigned his best lawyers to discredit me. I've been exposed as the whistle blower on his operations. So he will aim at shifting a lot of the blame to me. He has ample evidence of drugs and money laundering. I have aided and abetted him in those dealings for over a decade now."

"Well that's it. I'm not going out there to compete with the smell of illegal operations smeared all over our team."

"You're not implicit in any of this. I am. I want you to go out and compete and win. You deserve that. Johnnie has bet a huge sum of money on Carrie. Beat her and you'll hurt him. As it is, the investigation will put him in courts for years to come. Beat the bastard for ruining your life and your friends."

"You've changed the programs back haven't you?"

"You have the very best game plans now. Beat Carrie. Get what you have always deserved. You are the best player in the world. Show them tonight."

Mickey and Riley joined Ludwig for the final game.

"Time to win a match," Mickey said to Ludwig, as he readied to commence the opening of the twenty-third and deciding game, locked at eleven games all.

"Yes, show her what only you can do, Mickey," replied Ludwig.

Mickey stonewalled into a cautious defensive pattern for the opening shots. Then buoyed by the right programs, Mickey gained the ascendancy. Carrie's confidence was deflated, seemingly knowing that her preceding victories had been hollow. The final game would be played on equal terms. Defence was maintained by both players. The red triangle was hardly disturbed as Mickey and Carrie consistently left the cue-ball safe behind yellow or brown.

The final game was on a knife edge. Then, Carrie made the first error, leaving a slight opening. The crowd was hushed with expectation, before a single call broke the tense silence.

"Time-out," came the call, not by Carrie, but her manager, Johnnie.

Mickey was not surprised, choosing to return to his rest room alone. He knew Johnnie would be waiting for him.

"Why isn't she here? Too scared to face me?"

"She's with Ludwig. We have a game to win."

"I'll fucking ruin her. You know that don't you," said Johnnie, trying but failing to intimidate.

"You know Johnnie, sooner or later someone was going to show you that the industry was bigger than you. It's time you faced that fact."

"Well that may be so wise guy, but a lot of people will fall should you win tonight."

"I'd win just to wipe the smirk off your face."

"She won't get away with this, you know that. Your sister will fall a long, long way - money laundering, drug dealing and embezzlement, for starters. She'll do a twenty year stretch and ten years for anyone who assisted her."

Mickey feared the worst. Johnnie was ruthless when crossed, but he wouldn't let Johnnie see he was intimidated. He desperately wanted to question him about Jules, but Riley was right. It would make no difference to tonight. Johnnie would only use her as a bargaining chip. Mickey would be asked to sacrifice not only this match, but many more matches to come. He trusted Riley's promise. Together, they would find out the truth.

"I wish you could see yourself as I see you. You're no more than a common criminal and no amount of money you steal will change that. You spend your wealth destroying lives, all in the name of building your own empire. Well, you can't buy everybody, Johnnie. I was given a chance to be the best in the world tonight, because Riley helped me. So I'm going to do my damnedest to win," said Mickey, standing up, ready to leave. Johnnie was looking at his cubebit, as he replied.

"You know, Mickey, we aren't that different, you and I. We both have dreams and we both work hard to make sure we live them. It's what all humans do. We survive and grow. You might think you're special, hitting those coloured balls around a cube. You walk around it and pot balls like no other, so that you get noticed and prosper. Welcome to the world, Mickey. Every living thing around you wants to grow and prosper. It's called evolution. So, like you, I make deals with people so that both they and I grow and prosper. I also happen to be the very best at what I do. There are no moral issues here. You, least of all, have no right to tell me what is right or wrong."

"Okay, if it makes you happy, I'll stop calling you a criminal. There are more than enough willing people who want to do that anyway, and they're good at what they do. So let me do what I do. Let me play my best cubeball for my fans and stop harassing me and my team."

"Sure, go ahead and do what you think is the best. But there's always consequences," said Johnnie as he pointed to the vid-cube that was streaming the coverage of the match. The sound was muted, so he walked over to it and turned the volume on. The scene on the vid-cube stopped Mickey in his tracks. Someone he knew was in the playing arena, taking centre stage.

Manny walked over to Carrie and her team, surprising them with his presence. He showed them his security pass as he spoke.

Mr. Draxma wanted to pass on his regards. He's appreciated the entertaining spectacle you have provided." Carrie and her team looked disinterested and continued with their preparations for the final game.

"He also wanted you to know that he is offering you a special bonus payment, should you win tonight." He passed Carrie an envelope, before walking over to Mickey's team.

"Mr. Draxma wanted you to know that he has enjoyed the wonderful contest you have provided tonight."

He then looked directly at Riley. "He is excited about this final game and will watch with great interest."

"I'm excited too," replied Riley, drawing a wry smile from Manny.

"He's particularly interested in you, Ludwig. He wants you to join his team with Jean Flaveau."

Ludwig looked perplexed. "Mr. Flaveau plays by numbers. Mickey plays music."

"Mickey's a washed-up fucking drunk. He's a failure and he will lose," said Manny in a threatening manner. "He plays like this," Manny scratched his nails across their bench.

Ludwig reacted to the torturous sound made by Manny, by reaching out for his arm to stop the noise.

"Let me go you psycho," said Manny, with sufficient noise to draw attention to him. He grabbed Ludwig's arm and pulled it hard.

"Mickey, Mickey, Mickey," Ludwig repeated as he rocked uncontrollably. Manny only let him go after a sea of cubeball lights flashed in his direction, igniting the incident. Everyone in the stadium was shocked by the altercation, except one.

Mickey stared at the vid-cube and watched the altercation, while Johnnie looked on, seemingly delighted with the events.

"It appears there has been an altercation between a security guard and Mickey Allen's team. This is a tragedy. The viewing audience have been treated to a memorable encounter. Can you tell us any more about what has happened, Vince?" said the cube-side commentator.

"Well I can see that the intruder is wearing a security outfit that has the Draxma organisation's emblem. So we have to assume he works for Johnnie Draxma. He did have an official pass, so he was given official clearance. Our play-backs show that he had a brief conversation with Carrie, before he went over to Mickey Allen's team. Something he said appeared to irritate their strategist and the altercation started."

"Thanks Vince. Well we've seen it all tonight. What will unfold next? This has certainly been a final full of surprises. This is Alan Twomey, coming to you live from The Cauldron. Let's take a short sponsors' break."

Mickey's rage overflowed at the sight of Ludwig's fear. He held Johnnie by the throat as he pushed him hard against the wall.

"You fucking prick. All you care about is money. You've fucked up so many lives. You don't deserve to live, you piece of shit." Mickey held Johnnie's throat tight. His rage nearly overtook him. Then he let Johnnie go. He had to help his friend, Ludwig. Mickey turned to head back to the playing arena. Johnnie screamed out to him.

"This is all your doing. Your maniacal will to be the best has done nothing but bring harm to your friends. You already killed one. Do you want more blood?"

Mickey stopped momentarily as he digested what Johnnie had just said. He knew then, the fate of Jules. He finally knew the truth that Johnnie had kept from him for a decade. He started walking again and didn't turn back.

Mickey knew he had to be there for his friends. Ludwig had faced his greatest fears, so that he could support Mickey. Riley had more than likely exchanged her freedom to help him live his dream. Even Dr. Vance had put his career on hold for the team. He walked out full of resolve to pay them all back. Mickey had compromised his dreams once too often for Johnnie Draxma. Johnnie had accumulated a vast fortune on the back of many people's grief and suffering, caring little for them. It was time he played for himself and those who supported him.

"Mickey, Mickey," repeated Ludwig, seemingly in an attempt to block out his threatening surrounds. Dr. Vance was by his side, comforting him. Riley was the first to see Mickey as he returned to the stadium. Her tear-stained eyes were filled with concern as they darted from Mickey to Ludwig. Mickey walked straight to her.

"She's dead, Riley. We have a debt to repay. Set your best game-plans for me," said Mickey, as he lightly caressed her arms.

Riley nodded. Tears streamed down her cheeks from the news. But her sadness did not lessen her resolve. "Debts to pay," she agreed.

Mickey then walked over to Ludwig and Dr. Vance. "Will he be okay, Harry?"

Dr. Vance shrugged his shoulders. "Talk to him, Mickey."

"Mickey, Mickey, you're here," Ludwig said. His eyes were firmly closed. He reached out for Mickey.

"Yes, I'm here. I've come to play your music, my friend."

"Some people don't like your music."

"That's right. Some people never appreciated our music, like we do."

"I want to help you. But I can't think. Forgive me, Mickey."

"You have helped me more than you can imagine. I want you to sit with Dr. Vance now. I want you to enjoy this game and listen to the rhythms I will dedicate to you."

Ludwig opened his eyes to reveal his joy at what Mickey had just said. He held out his hand to Dr. Vance who joined him.

"For both of you," said Mickey, as he shook Dr. Vance's hand.

Mickey took a deep breath and cast a determined gaze out to the sea of fans who sat, transfixed by the drama unfolding. A chorus of sound reverberated around the stadium in appreciation for Mickey.

"Mick – ee, Mick – ee," They slowly sang, before unleashing a cubebit-generated light storm to every corner of the large sports hall.

Ten thousand appreciative fans screened their holographic images up into the rette filled air. A collage of video images detailing significant moments in Mickey's career shone bright above the adoring fans. This final piece of drama cemented Mickey's resolve. He turned to Carrie ready to play.

22

End Game

THE CROWD HAD REACHED fever pitch by the time the two 'would be' champions faced off for the final battle. Carrie was quieter now, prepared for a dog fight. Both acknowledged the crowd and shook hands for the re-commencement of the game. No more time-outs could be called. Mickey's game strategies had been set by Riley. They were a mix of proven plays and Ludwig's high risk strategies. His real task was to move from defence to attack at the right time and incorporate Ludwig's plays sparingly, but for maximum effect.

"Let's put on an exhibition they won't forget. I don't care who wins," said Mickey.

"I want the best player to win tonight. No more bullshit programs. Deal?" replied Carrie, showing one of her few moments of candour.

"You know, one day you'll learn this game is not that simple," said Mickey.

"I don't want to play simple. I want to play spin like you," she replied.

"You should. You're that good."

They shook hands, determination writ large in their demeanour. Carrie respectfully nodded her respect, before returning to her competition persona.

"If you think you're going to get me teary-eyed with your charm, forget it, Pop. It won't work. I've come here to win," she said, ready to become cubeball champion of the world.

Game on, thought Mickey

Carrie strode to the cube to open the frame for the deciding game. The stakes couldn't be higher, so both players maintained immaculate defence in the first twenty minutes. It was a test of nerve, under the most challenging of spotlights. Both held their composure as did the ten thousand spectators. Not a sound could be heard, bar the melodic chip and click of cue to ball and ball on ball. One poorly placed shot could hand over the title.

"Defensive play," said Carrie, choosing caution ahead of bravado. She waited while Sam entered the holograph lines on the cube.

Carrie was playing slower, but with more deliberation. Her narcs appeared to have worn off. But she had her considerable armoury of technology to draw upon.

"Defensive play," echoed Mickey, knowing he had to earn an opening.

Cautious play ensued until Carrie's tenth shot. It was solid, but left open a potential offensive shot with odds calculated to be a twenty-three percent chance for success.

Mickey had his first opening. He looked to Riley. "Offence or defence?"

Riley screened the defence play on the cube. "Suggest defence or L2 offence," she responded, keeping her best poker face.

The L2 offence was in fact code for a more difficult defensive shot, using Ludwig's strategies. Their true aim was to convince Carrie L2 would be a failed attacking shot. Unlike the holographic lines displayed on the cube, indicating an attacking shot, Mickey knew he had to just miss the red pot. It would look like the displayed shot, but the cue-ball would finish a centimetre wide of the mark. Also, the subtle difference in spin would move the one red just shy of the pocket. Carrie would be left with a difficult offence play, requiring extreme spin on the cue-ball. Mickey accepted Riley's call.

"Hold L2 holograph," he replied, before lining up his most important shot of the game.

He went to shoot, but his mind turned to a match he played fifteen years earlier. That night, he played a defensive shot that left an opening for Rick Calen. To his regret, Calen took the opening and won the U.S. National title. Would history repeat itself?

He delayed his shot, choosing to study the cube from all angles as he slowly walked around it. He noticed his team mates as he studied the position of the balls. Riley was anxious. He could tell she thought it too early for such a risky play. He walked further around the cube. Ludwig came into his line of sight. He noticed that Ludwig had stopped rocking. He was absorbed in the game, frantically scribbling on his pad. Mickey walked around the cube and toward Ludwig to seek his counsel. But as he got closer, Ludwig's rocking started. He seemingly did not want Mickey to see his drawings. Mickey stopped half-way between the cube and his strategist and turned to face the cube again. He couldn't see Ludwig's drawings, but he could see what Ludwig saw. They had the same line of site to the cube. He rested the base of his cue on the floor and studied the angles of the balls. He closed his eyes momentarily. For the first time, Mickey felt music. The position of the balls began to move in his mind, as he imagined the plays that should follow. Haunting music filled his mind as the balls spun and swerved in unison to the music of Beethoven. In that instant, he visualised his final fateful plan.

Mickey walked directly to the cue-ball, lined it up with his cue and caressed his shot with the right mix of finesse and spin. The cue-ball turned like a ballerina on ice as it lightly touched a red and swivelled back behind the yellow ball. It looked perfect, but the extra spin had left the red slightly open to the top right pocket. Carrie had her opening, but there was a price to be paid. She'd have to play a subtle spin shot to open the game up and claim her victory. The question was, did she see that Mickey deliberately played it there, or did she think he made a mistake? If it was the latter, Carrie would take the risk and go for victory.

If she sensed it a deliberate trap, she would continue her sublime defensive play. Carrie circled the cube for a full minute, before turning to Sam.

"Best defence and offence plays, Sam."

Two alternative plays lit up inside the cube. Defence had a lower degree of difficulty. Carrie had a choice between a safe play, or an opening she had patiently waited for. She studied the cube from all angles, but mostly from the position directly opposite her opponent's team cubicle. Mickey sat motionless, giving no clue to his thoughts, as her gaze seemed to be set on Mickey, rather than the cube. Another minute passed, before she made her fateful decision.

"Offence, Sam."

Her mind made up, Carrie caressed the cue-ball perfectly along the trajectory plotted. Line and speed were perfect. The only unknown was the spin of the ball as it ricocheted off two walls toward the delicately placed red.

Mickey watched the line from the first wall to the second. Success was agonisingly close. Her spin was exactly how Mickey would have liked it to be, if he played it. The cue-ball appeared to have sufficient spin left as it travelled from the second wall to the red. The line speed and trajectory was pin-point. It all came down to the degree of spin as the cue-ball kissed the red.

The fans in the stadium were hushed, as the final click of the two balls reverberated around them, filling the silence like a thunderbolt. The red ball edged painfully close to the lip of the pocket, seemingly an unstoppable force. Mickey was the first to see that the red ball had its own minute spin that was trickling it away from the middle of the pocket to right of centre. Speed played its part now. If it was a fraction too slow, it would come to lie perilously close to the lip of the pocket.

The hushed atmosphere gave way to a collective outpouring of nervous tension. Their gasps were quickly followed by unbridled chatter as all shared their reaction to Carrie's brave attack. The red ball remained teetering on the lip of the pocket as if held by an invisible force.

Mickey had his opening.

Their well laid plan had worked. Mickey cast an appreciative eye to Riley, before turning his gaze to Ludwig. Ludwig was still now, as if he had never suffered the debilitating effects of his condition.

"Play your music to the world Mickey. Show them what you were born to do."

Mickey had a strong opening, with many plays available for him to achieve his victory. Six offensive shots were streamed on the cube – one was Ludwig's play. Mickey studied Ludwig's strategy and the other five potential shots. Mickey took the briefest of moments to choose. His mind had already moved beyond the opening play to the next twenty-one perfect plays. Nothing less would satisfy him. This game was for a prize far greater than cash reward or a world championship cup. Mickey wanted to feel the special light that allowed him to play what others considered the impossible.

His senses were finely tuned, allowing him to see the smallest of spaces. Roll, spin and curve slowed in his mind. He was ready to play the shots he'd imagined. That was the challenge of Ludwig's music. No one could play it without the finest of instruments.

Ludwig felt the opening chord strike like thunder from high; such was the force of Mickey's opening shot. But from that force floated the sweetest of notes. It was so perfect Beethoven himself must have stood with Mickey orchestrating his play. The notes vibrated like a leftover echo of the opening strike, dropping the first ball into the pocket. A wave of vibrato followed with the triangle of reds falling into open space, like a ballerina into the welcoming arms of her partner. No other ball, but the intended red, fell into a pocket. The game was his for the taking.

Like Beethoven's music, this game was not beholden to the people it entertained or the industry it represented. This play had a beauty in its own right. It stood above the game. Mickey's playmaking contained the subtlety and risk-taking of someone who'd experienced great loss and joy.

His opening plays were simple enough, as if he wished to pay tribute to the grand masters of yesteryear. A cracking pot of the black was a carbon copy of the great Ronny Anderson, a world champion of snooker in the twentieth century. His middle game was a tour de force of his own games. He'd selected his very best shots from the past and fused them into a sublime middle game. But his final shots contained new elements not seen before. He orchestrated a feast of power, spin, curve of both the cue-ball and the surrounding red and colours.

He filled the cube with a ménage of colour and movement, like a scene from Swan Lake. Cubeball had been taken to a unique place that rose above the technology that drove this sport. No player could copy the new movements that Mickey had just played. They had to feel it. They had to imagine it. Mickey had unleashed a series of sublime strokes full of spin, guile, curve and pace that his young opponent would never forget. Mickey had black to pot to go down in history as being the first to win a world champion with a perfect score. Dramatically, he chose a near impossible play to take that honour. He chose an eight wall shot to pot the final ball on the table. This had never been done before.

"One hundred and forty," said the referee as he checked the black ball, polished it and returned it to its spot.

The game had been won, yet the tension in the stadium reached fever pitch as everyone willed Mickey slot the black off eight walls. Even Carrie wanted to see the impossible from her opponent.

The ball sizzled from his cue across an almost vacant cube. Mickey needed perfect line and a blend of power and scorching spin. The cue-ball launched from one wall to another, until it hit the eighth wall, seemingly with not enough pace. The remaining spin surprised all as it sprung life back into the rapidly fading missile. The cue-ball tapped the black, sending it on a final journey of thirty centimetres to the designated pocket. Quiet tension broke as the screams of thousands of the fans willed it into the pocket. The ball hovered on the lip until the collective wills of all who watched appeared to provide the final energy to see it drop in.

Mickey won the game and the hearts of all who watched that night. He was world champion and he'd claimed it playing the perfect game.

Mickey had achieved his lifelong ambition. Not to be the world's best, but to play 'his perfect game' on the toughest of stages. He couldn't remember what he'd just said as he accepted the most prized trophy in world cubeball. But he remembered the crowd's response. A full house of fans stood as one, showing they felt his music too. Mickey's gaze scanned the whole auditorium. He knew that he had successfully shown the world why he played the game. His gaze settled on his friend, Ludwig, who sat quietly, no doubt disturbed by the reverberations. But his eyes never left Mickey. No longer looking down to the floor as was his way. In that special moment he looked straight and strong at Mickey, as if he were gazing at Beethoven himself.

His victory officially recognised, Mickey went to lift the coveted gold trophy for his adoring fans, but then he signalled for his team to join him. Riley, Ludwig and Dr. Vance joined him in the winner's circle, as Mickey lifted the gold cup high above him. Mickey made sure he was facing the corporate boxes at that moment. He gazed in Johnnie's direction and saw something in Johnnie's expression he had not seen before – defeat.

"We beat him, Riley," said Mickey, jubilantly.

"For now, she replied. He knew hard times were ahead for Riley. Johnnie did not like to lose. He had felt his wrath many times, but this time, Johnnie's anger would not separate Mickey from those he loved.

"I'll be by your side, no matter what he throws at you," he said with a conviction that touched his sister.

"I know you will, but I have some very wealth allies who will help me fight him and one close ally will be a whole lot richer after tonight," she said, before hugging her brother. "But this is your night. Don't worry about Johnnie. Go and celebrate, you deserve this."

"We'll celebrate together."

"Oh, I nearly forgot. Lisa sent you a text," said Riley.

"Did she like my game?"

"Very much so. She's looking forward to dining with you this week."

"Tell her I will dine with her tomorrow, like I promised."

Riley nodded, then pushed Mickey toward the waiting crowd. Mickey asked the throng of reporters to wait just a little longer, for he wanted to thank his other team members, too. Ludwig looked confused by the sea of flash-lights, but his ear-phones were fastened tight, no doubt soothing him with Beethoven's rhythms.

"You have done so much for Ludwig, Mickey. I hope you remain friends for a long time," said Dr. Vance, as he shook Mickey's hand.

"I count both of you as my good friends, Harry. I'm hoping you'll join our team on a more permanent footing. Ludwig will be seen as the hottest strategist on the planet now. He'll need you more than ever, to cope with the fame. I also asked Riley to draw up some contracts for you and Ludwig. What do you say?"

Dr. Vance held his hand out to Mickey and shook it. "I say you've got yourself a deal."

Only then did Mickey turn to the press and talk to them. He faced them as the new world champion of cubeball. A new purpose was gathering in his life.

23

CHECKMATE

MICKEY WOKE EARLY AFTER a short sleep. He sat on his hotel balcony basking in the sun's morning rays and the glory of his victory. He sipped on a freshly brewed coffee, before turning his cubebit on.

"Sport headlines, Com."

Mickey smiled contentedly as he scanned the day's lead story. *Mickey Allen – new cubeball world champion.* His life had turned around in just a few short months. He'd conquered the world's best players. More importantly, he may have found his new love. Mickey felt an overwhelming urge to share this special day with Lisa. It was too early to call, so he sent her a text. He smiled as he sent his message, before relaxing again and taking in the view of London. He didn't want the moment of contentment to end. But he knew his success would come with a price. Riley had already committed him to a number of interviews whilst he was in London, as well as exhibition commitments for his new financier, Raman. There was one other contract he was signed to, which concerned him the most – Johnnie's.

He knew it was a mistake to sign any contract with him, no matter how small. But as usual, Johnnie had cornered him. Should he ask Riley to use her lawyers to terminate their agreement? It would be a costly choice, but worth it, for the peace of mind, alone. Then, what would be the personal cost, particularly to Riley? Mickey had to find a way to cut the long tentacles of Johnnie's business concerns that encircled him for all of his adult life.

He checked his cubebit to see if Lisa had replied – she had not. He was about to call her, before a knock on his door interrupted him.

"Riley, you're up early," said Mickey, as he let her in.

"I've organised room service - breakfast for two. Do you mind?"

"It depends. Is it a business breakfast?"

Riley smiled. "Won't you allow your sister a small celebration before the world takes your time?"

Mickey nodded and pointed Riley toward the balcony. "Come through, You're my manager now. So I can't argue with you anymore."

"You may not argue, but you won't be happy with all of my decisions. For one, I have a strong media program planned for this week."

Mickey's delighted expression changed to a more sombre tone. "I'm fine with that, as long as I have today clear."

"I did leave today clear. You have the day with Lisa. I probably have the day with Johnnie," said Riley, her look downcast.

"What can we do? There must be a way we can rid ourselves of this tyrant?"

"You should keep clear of him, Mickey. I'll proceed cautiously. I have good lawyers who can minimise the damage. I created this mess, so I will get myself out of it. I want you to move forward," said Riley, as she looked directly at Mickey and held his hand. "I'm so proud of what you achieved, Mickey. Are you seeing Lisa today?"

"I sent her a text, but she hasn't replied yet," replied Mickey, checking his cubebit again.

"That's unlike her."

"It's early."

"Lisa is an early riser. She always starts her day reviewing the newspapers," said Riley. She called Lisa on her cubebit.

"No reply." Riley looked concerned as did Mickey.

"You don't think..."

Riley raised her hands, reassuringly, before she dialled another number.

"Good morning. I'm trying to contact Lisa Manning. She is a tenant at your hotel. Could I ask you to check if she is home? We were to meet this morning....Yes I'm Riley Allen. She would have left instructions for you to do that, should I have called you....Thank you."

"Instructions? What's happening Riley? Mickey asked. His apprehension was building, but Riley ignored him as she waited on her cubebit.

"Yes, thank you for checking. I'll call again in an hour....Yes, I appreciate that." Riley hung up and turned to Mickey.

"She's not answering."

"Would you tell me what's going on? You're worried about something." Mickey asked.

Riley composed herself before answering. "Johnnie threatened me last night."

"Oh fuck!" Mickey stood up, unable to contain his anxiety. "Let's get the cops now."

"We could, but we don't know that anything has happened."

"What were his threats?"

"He wanted an assurance that I wouldn't testify at any criminal investigation against him or his company. Johnnie knows I'm the informer who supplied Richard Carrington the information for his article."

What do we do now?" Mickey asked, helplessly.

Riley shrugged her shoulders. "Whichever way we go, there'll be a price to pay. Knowing Johnnie, it will be a large price. We both know what he is capable of."

"Are you telling me that Lisa is in danger?"

"Lisa, Ludwig, Dr. Vance, any one of them. Mickey, you call Dr. Vance and check they are okay. I'm going to call Johnnie, now. I'm responsible for this mess, so I need to fix it."

"Don't give in to him, Riley."

"He's too powerful, Mickey. There's no way of beating him," she replied, forlornly.

Mickey gently held her arm. "We'll find a way, trust me. Ring him and find out if he has Lisa. But don't negotiate with him. We must do that together. Okay?"

Riley nodded her agreement. "I promised you that we would stand together from now on."

Then they both made their fateful calls.

"Ludwig and Dr. Vance are in their rooms. Harry told me that there has been no suspicious behaviour," said Mickey, relieved. However, Riley was not.

"Johnnie's detained Lisa and wants to negotiate with us this afternoon," said Riley, trying hard to maintain her composure. She stood up and looked out across London, seemingly studying places Lisa might be.

"Negotiate? We should call the cops now. He's committed bribery and has taken a hostage. He'd get ten years." Mickey picked up his cubebit, ready to call.

"Don't, Mickey. This has happened before and it will happen again. Johnnie's desperate and capable of anything. You know that."

"What will be his offer?"

"I think he'll want me to provide a full confession of my wrong doings in writing, in exchange for Lisa."

"Agree to that and you'll do prison time, not Johnnie. Even worse, you'll never be rid of his threats and bribery. There has to be a better way."

"I can't think of one, Mickey. He has Lisa under tight security. She's probably locked away in the depths of Velvet Underground, where no one could reach her. If we don't follow through, Lisa will disappear from the world, just like Jules."

Mickey slammed the table hard with his fist. The dark shadow that Johnnie had cast over his life had returned. His life had come full circle. Every time he achieved success in the game he loved, someone close to him got hurt. He would have gladly killed Johnnie and rid him from his life once and for all, if he had a chance. But Johnnie was more powerful than before. A hired killer wouldn't get close to him, let alone Mickey.

They both sat quietly, in pains to think of what they could do next. They were to meet Johnnie in six hours time and they needed answers. Mickey thought back to the previous night. Even then, on his most successful night, Johnnie managed to spoil it, having his security threaten Ludwig. He pondered the highs and lows he felt that night. It was a reflection of his whole cubeball life. It seemed that it would never change. But then he considered an element of that night, which may provide the answer. He stood up. Purpose was writ large in his eyes.

"I need to make a private call, Riley. You go now and prepare for our meeting. Can you arrange for Richard Carrington to call me in three hours? Tell him I have some breaking news I want to share with him. That should stimulate some interest."

"Yes. He's looking to break the story any day now, so I'm sure he'd want to talk to you. What are you thinking?"

"I'll let you know when we meet back here. Just get him for me. Okay?"

"Consider it done."

Riley left Mickey alone in his room, to ponder his plan. It was a long-shot, but if he pulled it off, he may finally rid Johnnie from his life and those that he loved. Mickey dialled his cubebit.

Mickey and Riley waited patiently in the foyer for Johnnie to meet with them – no dramatic entries this time. They wanted Johnnie to play his power game, before declaring their hand. They needed to negotiate coolly with him. There would be no margin for error, if they were to leave his office victorious. Mickey didn't show it, but he was more nervous than before his title match.

"Carrington is organised?" Riley asked.

"Yes. On our signal, he will join us. You've arranged the funds transfer?"

Riley shook her head in annoyance, as she responded. "Yes your share of the winnings has been placed in the account you requested. But I..."

Mickey cut her off, mid-sentence. "No arguments, Riley. We've come to settle a lot of old scores. Leave it at that."

Riley crossed her arms tight around her, as she begrudgingly nodded her head. Nothing more was said. A full half hour passed before Johnnie's secretary escorted them into Johnnie's office. He sat behind his expansive desk, not bothering to stand. He had an arrogant smirk on his face as he pointed them toward their chairs. No words passed the three's lips for some minutes. Johnnie looked disappointed as he finally broke the silence.

"Well, here we all are, together again. We should do this more often. But it seems at least one of you has lost faith in me."

Mickey ignored Johnnie's smirk. "We haven't come to reminisce. You know why we're here."

"Do I? Enlighten me, Mickey."

"Where is she?"

"She? Don't tell me you're in love again? Who's the lucky lady?"

"Don't play games with us. Name your demands, so we can settle this mess."

"Your overnight success has brought back your paranoia. I have only one demand," said Johnnie, as he pushed some papers across his desk, in Riley's direction.

Riley deliberately read the pages she was handed.

"What's on it?" Mickey asked.

"Johnnie wants me to sign a confession that I worked subversively to build a narc empire, illegally using Johnnie's resources and reputation to do so."

Mickey laughed. "I didn't realise you were such an upstanding corporate citizen."

"You learn something new every day," said Johnnie, before pushing his pen in Riley's direction. "Sign it."

Riley picked up the pen, feigning to sign the incriminating document. Then she put both pen and paper down and sat forward in her chair, seemingly unconvinced by Johnnie's demands.

"That's a tall order. What are you giving us in return?"

"You know what I'm giving you."

"Enlighten us. I won't sign anything until you explain everything to Mickey and I."

"This sudden brotherly love is so touching," said Johnnie, sniggering. Both Riley and Mickey held their gaze. An uneasy silence ensued, before Riley pushed the unsigned documents back in Johnnie's direction. Johnnie ignored her.

"I want you both to know one fact. I didn't spend half of my life building this business, just to have it destroyed, particularly by the people I helped in the first place."

Mickey reacted. "Listen, Johnnie...."

"No. You listen. You two owe me. I got you both your first jobs in the industry you loved. I did. Not your parents, or friends, or each other. I didn't have to. I got you hired, Mickey. My uncle wanted to get rid of you in the first week. But I backed you. I paid my uncle credits to cover your constant fuck-ups on the job. Then I covered the endless fees to get you into the competitions you needed to be in to become a professional cubeball player. I supported your dream. Or have you forgotten?" Johnnie said, pointing his finger at him accusingly.

"I paid you back ten-fold. I...."

"Shut the fuck up, Mickey." Johnnie wiped his flushed, sweaty face, before continuing. "I backed your dream, and how did you repay me? You took up with some two-bit junkie and wasted your talent on her in the name of love. On the rare occasion when I got you to practice, she hassled me for credits to fuel her drug addiction. The money you squandered away on her was a scratch on the surface. I covered her spiralling debts. I covered her ass, when the debtors came to collect. I saved her from herself for longer than I should have."

"You killed her, you fucking...."

"She killed herself. I just granted her wish to lose herself in Velvet Underground."

"You could have helped her. We could have..."

"She was long gone. I'd had enough of her problems. So I cut her loose."

"We all killed her," said Riley.

"Is the guilt too much for you now, Riley?" Johnnie said, as he turned his angry gaze to her. "Were there just one too many indiscretions for my right-hand lady? You seemed happy to invent new ways to make profits for me."

"We've come to negotiate for Lisa," she replied.

"Like you negotiated for Jules? Wasn't it your idea to settle her into a safety haven in V.U.?"

"Yes, but to rehabilitate her. Not to leave her to die among drug dealers."

Johnnie shook his head, first at Mickey, then Riley. "Your sister's hypocrisy knows no bounds. She master-minds an illegal billion dollar industry around planck, killing thousands of users. I don't recall you begging me to rehabilitate those junkies, too? You knew Jules was never going to rehabilitate. That's why you stopped bailing her out. Jules took Mickey's money, then yours. She was draining the life out of our team."

"I asked you to commit Jules into a narc hospital. But you cast her adrift in that nest of vipers."

"I was over wasting money on the pair of you. Someone had to lead and move the team out of the hole you were leading us down. That's what a manager does. He makes hard decisions. But I'm not your manager anymore. I'm only here to see this contract signed." Johnnie pushed the papers back toward Riley.

"I'll sign these papers when you assure me Lisa is safe."

"I don't know what you're talking about, Riley."

"You signed Jules death warrant. You'd do it again. That's why I left you, and that's why I'd pay any price to be rid of a murderer like you."

"You've got the gall to call me a murderer. Sign this and I'll release her."

"Where is Lisa, Johnnie?" Mickey interjected.

"Somewhere you'll never find her." He glared at Riley as he pointed to the contract on the table and stubbornly saying no more.

Riley picked up the contract again, seemingly reading it one more time, before turning to Mickey.

"The decision is yours, Mickey."

Mickey reached for the contract. "Everything's in place," he said to Riley, shooting her a knowing glance. Then he started to slowly read the contract. Johnnie fidgeted at his desk, openly showing his irritation. The silence was disturbed by Johnnie's secretary.

"There are a group of people making their way up to your office."

"Who?" Johnnie asked, his irritation turning to fury.

"Richard Carrington and two other men. He claims Mr. Allen had invited him to join you."

"Johnnie cast Mickey a suspicious look, before speaking. "Send them in and call our legal team to my office as well."

Johnnie sat back in his chair and watched his secretary leave. He said no more as he seemingly pondered the developing situation. All three waited in tense silence as the next stage of negotiations were about to unfold. Carrington was the first to walk into the room, followed by two large gentlemen who flashed their constable badges.

"Welcome, gentleman. What seems to be the problem?"

One of the constables answered officially, reading Johnnie his rights, before explaining the charges. "We were called to a secured room in

Velvet Underground at 11.15am where we located a Ms. Lisa Manning. She was being held, against her will, by two employees of yours, Mr. Andy Holt and a Mr. Philip Glasser. These two gentlemen are being held in custody at our London precinct. Both have verified that they held Ms. Manning against her will and at your request. Mr. Draxma, we require you to accompany us to our London precinct for further questioning in relation to this matter and others that have been brought to our attention by Mr. Carrington. Do you have anything to say to us before we accompany you to our headquarters?"

"I have no comment to make. My lawyers will be here any moment. I'd like to brief them before leaving?"

"That's fine, Mr. Draxma." Both men stood beside Johnnie as they waited for his lawyers to arrive. Carrington took Riley and Mickey out of Johnnie's office, to update them on events, but Mickey spoke first.

"Is Lisa okay, Richard?"

"She's a little shaken by the ordeal, but she's fine, now."

"Where is she?"

"She's still at the police headquarters. I have to go there now. I can take you both with me."

Mickey immediately nodded and then he looked to Riley.

"You go to her. I'll meet with Ludwig and Dr. Vance and let them know what has happened."

"What have you told the police, Richard?" Mickey asked.

"They wanted to know who gave me the tip-off."

Mickey looked concerned, but Richard reassured him.

"Don't worry. Like all good journalists, I told them an anonymous source tipped me, off-the-record. They won't follow-up." Carrington was about to say more, but he had an incoming call. "I've got to head off now. I've got a deadline to meet. My car is parked just at the front of the building. See you down there."

"I'll be down in five minutes. I just need a moment with Riley," said Mickey. Carrington nodded and was away, as he studied his cubebit.

Mickey turned to Riley. She was studying him, knowingly. "You paid off Johnnie's security guard, didn't you?"

Mickey nodded."Manny is a happy man. I don't think any of us will see him again - least of all, Johnnie. Manny loves to travel."

"How much?"

"I transferred him my entire share of the winnings."

"That's a lot, Mickey."

"I'd have paid him ten times more to be rid of Johnnie."

"And Lisa?" Riley asked with a wry smile.

"I would have paid him a hundred times more, if I knew it meant Lisa was safe."

Riley's eyes lit up with pride as she hugged Mickey warmly. "I'm proud of you."

"What about you, Riley? What next?"

"I'll be fine. In fact, my brother, I've never felt better." Riley softly kissed Mickey's cheek. "Go to her now. You'll have a lot to talk about."

Mickey nodded and quickly headed down to Carrington's waiting vehicle. He was about to start his new life – one filled with new hope. For the first time since his return to Earth, Mickey felt he'd truly come home.